# OSMO UNKNOWN
## AND THE
# EIGHTPENNY WOODS

# Osmo Unknown and the Eightpenny Woods

### CATHERYNNE M. VALENTE

Margaret K. McElderry Books

New York   London   Toronto   Sydney   New Delhi

Like everything in the Eightpenny Woods,
this book has many natures,
and a dedication for each one.

For Michael and Cyndi
We'll all dance together in the Woods one day

For Clark Danielson
Who once told me a Very Secret Story

And for Bastian, who so often asked
For a Big Roar and a Big Squeeze

You got it, kiddo.

MARGARET K. McELDERRY BOOKS ★ An imprint of Simon & Schuster Children's Publishing Division ★ 1230 Avenue of the Americas, New York, New York 10020 ★ This book is a work of fiction. Any references to historical events, real people, or real places are used fictitiously. Other names, characters, places, and events are products of the author's imagination, and any resemblance to actual events or places or persons, living or dead, is entirely coincidental. ★ Text © 2022 by Catherynne M. Valente ★ Illustration © 2022 by Lauren Myers ★ Jacket design © 2022 by Simon & Schuster, Inc. ★ All rights reserved, including the right of reproduction in whole or in part in any form. ★ MARGARET K. McELDERRY BOOKS is a trademark of Simon & Schuster, Inc. ★ For information about special discounts for bulk purchases, please contact Simon & Schuster Special Sales at 1-866-506-1949 or business@simonandschuster.com. ★ The Simon & Schuster Speakers Bureau can bring authors to your live event. For more information or to book an event, contact the Simon & Schuster Speakers Bureau at 1-866-248-3049 or visit our website at www.simonspeakers.com. ★ The text for this book was set in Dante MT. ★ The illustrations for this book were rendered digitally. ★ Manufactured in the United States of America ★ 0322 FFG ★ First Edition ★ 10 9 8 7 6 5 4 3 2 1 ★ Library of Congress Cataloging-in-Publication Data ★ Names: Valente, Catherynne M., 1979– author. ★ Title: Osmo Unknown and the Eightpenny Woods / Catherynne M. Valente. ★ Description: First edition. | New York : Margaret K. McElderry Books, [2022] | Audience: Ages 8–12 | Audience: Grades 4–6 | Summary: When his mother accidentally kills a Quidnunk in the woods, Osmo Unknown must embark on a quest to find the Eightpenny Woods—the mysterious kingdom where all wild forest creatures go when they die—and make amends. ★ Identifiers: LCCN 2021044765 (print) | LCCN 2021044766 (ebook) | ISBN 9781481476997 (hardcover) | ISBN 9781481477017 (ebook) ★ Subjects: CYAC: Fantasy. | Magic—Fiction. | Forests and forestry—Fiction. | Mothers and sons—Fiction. | LCGFT: Fantasy fiction. | Novels. ★ Classification: LCC PZ7.V232 Os 2022 (print) | LCC PZ7.V232 (ebook) | DDC [Fic]—dc23 ★ LC record available at https://lccn.loc.gov/2021044765 ★ LC ebook record available at https://lccn.loc.gov/2021044766

*Quidnunc*, noun. Alternate spelling: *Quidnunk*.
>A person who is eager to know the latest news and gossip. A busybody, meddler, troublemaker, or snoop. First recorded in 1710, from the Latin phrase *quid nunc*, meaning *oh, what now?*
>*Quidnunx*, plural.

—Mr. Merriam or Mr. Webster or Mr. Oxford or Mr. Roget Who Can Say Which?

# FIRST THINGS FIRST

I am going to tell you a story.

It's a rather strange, wild, grand story. In fact, it is a fairy tale. Now, now, no groaning. You are absolutely not too grown-up for fairy tales. Nobody is. The kind of people who think fairy tales are frilly or silly or simple are the ones most likely to get eaten by a witch before next weekend.

But I suspect you don't really mind any sort of thing being grand or strange or wild, so long as it is also exciting, since you are so grand and strange and wild yourself. That's why I have chosen this story specially for you, and why I have chosen you specially for this story. When I woke up this morning, I did not even take the time to pour my coffee. I *knew* that you were out there, even if you didn't know it. You were waiting for this exact story to find you at this exact moment. There is no time at all to waste, even for coffee, when a story has found its person.

I am so glad we have found each other! It was a near thing, too. There were *so* many other books in the shop you or your uncle or your mother or Father Christmas might have chosen. The story was very worried you might miss each other. Why, it could've easily ended up in the hands of the wrong sort, who wouldn't take good care of it the way you will.

No one else would understand it like you.

No one else would be brave enough to listen to the scary bits without hiding behind the bed.

No one else would keep it secret.

And it *must* be kept secret.

We have made a bargain, you and I. It started when you opened the front cover of this book and it will never end, not even when you have closed the back cover. No take-backs. We are conspirators now. Once you've heard it all, from top to bottom, down to the last scrap of fur and coppery scale, you will protect the secret at the heart of this story as I have. You must tell it only to others like you, who can be trusted.

Now, I shall have to insist on a promise. If you do not promise, you must not turn the page. You must put this book away and never look at it again. I'm afraid I am quite serious. I simply can't take the risk.

Not on my account, of course. *I'm* in no danger. I already know how everything sorts itself out. But it is only fair to warn you that there is an explosion at the end of this book. A completely staggering, ferocious explosion. *So* staggering and *so* ferocious that, if I have made a mistake and you are a cruel or greedy or small-minded or, worst of all, *indifferent* human person, I am not at all sure you will survive it.

So you see, this is serious business indeed. This book may look sweet and whimsical and a bit funny, but the truth is, it's quite dangerous. That's why I couldn't share it with just anybody.

It wouldn't be safe.

Now, raise your hand and repeat after me.

No, no, that won't do!

You must say it out loud! No matter how silly it makes you feel. I shall wait until I see your hand. Grown-ups, too. No one is excused. If you don't say the words, I must ask you to close this book at once and put it away at the bottom of your closet and go read something nice and breezy with no magic or secrets or monsters or dark, hungry woods in it.

Are you still here? Very good.

Now say:

*I, (say your name), do very sincerely and most vigorously swear that I, being a friend to all things wild and fierce, shall never tell anyone what I know about the Quidnunx, unless I am one hundred percent completely and cross-my-heart certain that they are, like me, the very best sort of person. The kind of person who will stand back to back with me when fearful winds come. Who always looks up at the moon at night and not only straight ahead of them. Who cannot help but let the dog in the back door when it is cold out, even though they were specifically told not to several times. The rare and special type of person who can be trusted to keep the promise also. Yours very truly, (say your name again).*

There. It's done. I knew I chose the right human being for this story, out of all the millions and billions. Now we will be linked forever, just like the little village and the great big woods I am about to introduce to you. That's one of the things that secrets do best. If you share a secret, you share a life.

I am so very glad we met.

Let's begin.

# SECOND THINGS SECOND

O nce upon a time, in the beginning of the world, a certain peculiar Forest fell in love with a deep, craggy Valley.

The Forest was very dashing. For a forest. Full of tall, thick trees and soft meadows and thorny brambles and a number of clever, bushy animals. The Valley was quite the catch as well, full of great big blue stones and clover and fat black hens and orange flowers. The whole wide earth agreed it was a very good match.

And so the Forest and the Valley decided to do as folk have always done and settle down together to see what they might make between the two of them. They put their heads together and tinkered with the stones and the sky and the moon and the autumn and the spring. They pottered about with mushy dirt and rainstorms and exciting new sorts of pumpkins. They went absolutely bonkers over mushrooms. They experimented rashly with a year boasting four hundred and seventy-eight days, rather than the usual three hundred and sixty-five. They dabbled in badgers; hedgehogs; raccoons; bears both giant and pygmy; red-, green-, and blue-tailed deer; jackdaws; owls; parrots; cassowaries; flamingos;

coots; herons; and pangolins. Most of these weren't meant to live anywhere near the Forest or the Valley, but they were young and rebellious then and cared nothing for anyone else's rules.

They were so terribly happy in those days. There are kinds of happiness I cannot begin to describe to you. They're too personal, too wonderful, too far in the past. This is one of those happinesses.

Even if it's very hard to believe now that the Forest and the Valley were ever happy together.

As often happens with married couples who live alone far from anybody else for years and years, they became a bit cantankerous and suspicious of outsiders. In fact, they became so solitary and set in their habits, so stubbornly determined to have things their own way and no one else's, that they began to look and sound not very much at all like other forests and valleys. This was perfectly all right by them. They didn't care one bit for the rest of the world.

The first serious argument the Forest and the Valley ever had was whether or not they ought to allow magic past their borders. The Forest thought it was an excellent idea. Magic was always interesting. It could turn on you on any idle morning before breakfast. They would never be bored. The Valley thought magic was a dreadful thing, for the very same reasons. The Forest pleaded. The Valley shuddered. And in the end they came to a compromise. They could do that, once upon a time.

They would allow ONE magical object to stay in their perfect little world, so long as it was hidden away very well, and neither of them ever told anyone what or where it was.

Even each other.

As time skipped along like a stone over a pond, the Valley began to long for a village to keep and tend. It dreamed of talking creatures who would sow and reap and invent barns and bread and be both cross and kind toward one another.

At the same time, the Forest began to yearn after talking creatures as well. But it wanted no cheerful barn-builders. The Forest wanted wild bandits to sneak in its shadows and pounce joyfully and disdain both roofs and rules. It wanted glorious, untamed, mad leapers and prancers that obeyed no one's law.

And so, the Forest and the Valley went each to their most secret workshops with their best and oldest tools. Each said to the other: *I shall be late to summer, darling, don't wait up for me.*

At midwinter, the Valley unveiled the village of Littlebridge. The tiny village sparkled with fresh roads that crossed neatly in the middle of town. It had solid bluestone wells and walls, tidy hedges, and neat wooden pens for the trapping of wild black chickens. Best of all, there were seventeen huts pleasingly arranged in a pattern like a sunflower around a cozy market square. A little bright creek ran usefully through the middle of it all. With luck, it might grow up to be a river one day. Over the creek stretched a bridge of that special agate that looked like the night sky. Green (very tasty and healthy) puffball mushrooms grew through the cracks like party balloons.

And in the whistling, wildling snow, the Forest coaxed the Quidnunx to come out and play.

The Forest clapped its hands in delight. It crackled its branches against one another like applause.

The Valley sang with excitement. A smile curled up the edges of its meadows.

But for many years, Littlebridge stayed bright and clean and empty. It waited in the Valley like a flytrap flower, ready to snap its pretty, snug jaws around the only food it wanted: people. Human beings.

The Valley tried not to despair. They would come. They would smell the tidy huts with four rooms each. They would hear about the fat black chickens and their fat brown eggs. The deep, cool well set in the crossroads like a diamond in a ring would call to them. Someone, somewhere, would be looking for just this sort of whitewashed mill, whose wheel already turned invitingly through the creek. Some fisherman would come looking for just such a creek. No one had ever fished in it before, so it was so crowded with trout and bluegills and catfish the water sometimes looked like it was boiling for supper already.

People would come. It was only that people were sometimes slow and stubborn and did not like to believe in places very much different from the ones they knew.

Eventually, the Valley began to suspect it was the Quidnunx keeping people away. No matter how well you set a table, no one will come to eat if a pack of lookie-loo monsters have their great fat noses pressed up against the windows. The Forest argued, quite reasonably, that the Quidnunx were already here while people were, at this point, mostly imaginary. Thus, the lookie-loos shouldn't have to budge one little bit. Also, the Forest felt very hurt that the Valley had called its favorite babies monsters. The Forest suggested, a bit nastily, that perhaps the Quidnunx might move into the village and then they wouldn't have to trouble with humans at all!

The Valley made several rude noises about *that* and refused to speak to the Forest all winter long.

You must always beware if someone is giving you the silent treatment. Usually it means they are making a scheme. When a person is not so busy talking, they have ever so much more time to think. The Valley did not give up. It just stopped asking the Forest for its opinion on anything.

Very quietly, the Valley invented a new kind of mushroom. It sent out the mushroom like a clever little dog and told it very sternly to fetch. Now, the secret of mushrooms (and many other things) is that the bit you see sticking up out of the good black mud, the bit you slice up and fry in a pan with thyme and butter, is only the flower. The rest of the mushroom goes on for miles underground, silent and delicate, nosing through the dark like a sleepy worm. The Valley told the Agatha mushroom to stretch out as far as it could, as far as it took to find *people*, which were animals who walked on two legs and had no tails or very much fur and whose favorite things were building and talking and throwing parties for pretty shaky reasons. Only when it found one should this special mushroom start pushing up its thyme-and-butter parts into the air. So off it went, out of the Valley and through the Forest, who never noticed one new fungus among the millions. It grew as fast as a mushroom can, which is not so fast, but not so slow, either. It stopped every so often to listen for the sounds of talking and building and walking around on two legs.

And all the while as the Valley schemed its scheme, the Quidnunx danced with the Forest. They grew bigger. They grew stronger. They grew wilder and louder.

Finally, the mushroom thought it heard something, the right sort of something. It proudly pushed up its fungus-fruits out of the crumbly, cakey earth. Just then a man was walking home carrying a basket full of stonemason's tools, since he was a stonemason, along with two rabbits and some bitter greens for his supper. Now, this happened so long ago that no one in Littlebridge can remember exactly what the man's name was, so when this story gets its telling, everyone calls him Mr. Unknown and gets on with it. I shall do the same, because I do not remember, either. And I *do* promise to get on with it, in just a moment.

Mr. Unknown could not explain what he saw when the mushroom came sprouting up, but he liked it very much. It had button caps shaped like perfect, tiny houses. Their roofs were green, their walls were purple, and their windows were a friendly orangey yellow. They looked as though someone very small was happily living inside. And they popped out of the ground, hundreds and hundreds of them, right in front of Mr. Unknown, glittering and glowing in the soft blue heart of the evening like fairy lanterns. They led off through the woods where Mr. Unknown had been hunting. He had hunted there most of his life, so he knew very well that nothing like this had ever grown there before. Mr. Unknown looked around to see if anyone else had seen this strange thing so that they could shake their heads and stroke their beards together. But he was alone.

Now, some folk would be frightened. Perhaps they would try to stamp out the mushrooms or burn them up. But the mushroom had gotten lucky. Mr. Unknown was quite a peculiar fellow. He didn't feel frightened at all. He laughed. He looked down. He judged his basket to have most of the things he needed to keep being alive. He thought about his empty stone house with no wife or children in it. He thought about the local lord, to whom he owed quite a bit of coin.

And Mr. Unknown started walking. He followed the mushroom-houses into the wild deep dusk.

The button-cap huts with purple walls and green roofs and glowing orangey-yellow windows went on for miles upon miles. As Mr. Unknown walked the long, long way from the place where he had hunted all his life to the Valley and the Forest we have been talking about all this time, he met others. Some traveling toward home, some traveling away from it, some just wandering. People are always doing that, you know. In every place there are those who cannot be satisfied, who think that if they can only find a different place, there, *there*, they will be able to become their truest selves and to be happy. Sometimes this simply means finding the nearest city and diving into the din. And sometimes it means a very much longer journey than that.

All the way to a Valley on the edge of a Forest.

When the hodgepodge band of wandering humans finally cleared the mountain passes and looked down into the Valley, they could hardly believe their luck. It seemed too good to be so empty. The woods practically boomed with game. The huts shone clean and bright. The black chickens stood as high as your knee, their eggs were rich, and there was no one else around to tell these nervous visitors not to eat those eggs or pen those chickens, or even to charge them rent. It was as perfect a people-trap as anyone has ever made. Just like that, the trap sprang and a wandering became a village. They would all be safe here, and happy, and nothing would trouble them forever and ever.

But there were two things the new folk running their hands along the well-made bridge in shock and wonder did not know.

The first was that the Forest never forgave the Valley. It never would. Yes, the Forest made living, thinking beings out of nothing (and some big sticks). That was just the sort of mysterious, creative landmass it was. But the Valley had brought *strangers*. From *outside*. They could be *anyone*. They could ruin *everything*, and probably would. Worst of all, the Valley hadn't even asked before having all these guests over for dinner forever. Once the humans settled in, the Valley was so happy and busy it rarely had a spare word for the Forest at all anymore. So the Forest dug in its roots and decided not to have spare words for the Valley, either, and definitely not to ask permission to do whatever it wanted to do from now until the end of time.

OSMO UNKNOWN AND

Old married folk say they love each other to the ends of the earth—but somewhere, the earth *does* end. And sometimes (not always, but sometimes) those same folk who loved so well grow so far apart they can't even bear to look at one another anymore, because they don't see kind eyes or easy smiles or big blue stones or tall sturdy trees. All they see is hurt.

I don't mean to shock you, but this can happen with people, too. Not just Forests and Valleys.

And what are their children to do then? For the second thing the humans of Littlebridge didn't know was that they were not alone in this beautiful place. Not a one of them had met a Quidnunk yet.

But they very soon would.

A couple of centuries after all this was said and done and forgotten about, history got itself up and moving, and a boy got busy growing up in the village of Littlebridge. He was the great-great-great-great-great-great-grandson of Mr. Unknown. That didn't mean too terribly much in Littlebridge anymore. It was almost a city by then. Most everyone had a fairly interesting grandparent or two.

What it did mean was this: the boy's name was Osmo Unknown, and he is the beating heart of this story.

## Chapter One

# THE WILD AND THE MILD

Osmo Unknown had always lived in Littlebridge, and nothing interesting had ever happened to him there.

He was born, neither rich nor poor, in a little white four-room cottage on the north side of the Catch-a-Crown River, almost at the furthest edge of town. He thought he would most likely die an old man with a white beard, neither rich nor poor, in a little white four-room cottage on the north side of the Catch-a-Crown River.

He was quite, quite wrong about that.

Osmo Unknown was not precisely the sort of person you think of when someone says the word *hero*. He wasn't impressively big or strong. He didn't have a famous sword or a glorious destiny foretold through the ages. He had thick curly black hair and friendly hazel eyes, the color of old pages and old leaves. He was a bit short and thin for his age, with long clever fingers. The boys in school thought him strange and the girls didn't think about him at all.

On the other hand, Littlebridge was precisely the kind of place you think of when someone says the word *village*. The bell tower in the center of town. The painted houses with straw-and-clover roofs and crisscrossed windows. The schoolhouse and the green-and-brown river full of trout and eels and the tavern with golden, welcoming light in the windows even at eight in the morning. The bits of roof gargoyle and marble rose leaves from an age when folk took a bit more care with architecture. All nestled in a pretty valley with good, steady rain and strong, reliable sun, sandwiched between the steep blue mountains on one side and a deep, thorny forest on the other.

And of course, there was no shortage of mysterious legends no one believed in anymore and stern rules everyone broke when they were young and insisted on when they got old.

What sorts of rules? Oh, just the usual kind. Nothing out of the ordinary.

*Don't go out alone after sundown* and *never eat anything that talks* and *stay out of the woods no matter what, this means you.*

In fact, there was only one single, solitary strange and unusual thing in the whole town. Only one thing you wouldn't find in any other town of the same size and age and climate.

Where the crossroads met in the center of town rose a great red granite pillar. On the very tip-top of the pillar, a silver skull had looked down on everyone for a number of centuries now.

The skull was huge.

The skull was not human.

The skull was almost like an elephant's head, and a little like a great stag's, and something unsettlingly like a tyrannosaurus's. But it was not an elephant, either. It was not a deer. And it was most certainly not a *Tyrannosaurus rex*.

No one paid it any more attention than they gave to the bell tower or the shoe shop.

Except Osmo Unknown.

Osmo paid attention to *everything*. He knew every street and side road of his home. Every wishing well, every stony building and sturdy roof. Good old Dapplegrim Square with Soothfaste Church on one side and the Cruste and Cheddar Tavern on the other. The Afyngred Agricultural Hall and Bonefire Park. The Katja Kvass Memorial Fountain bubbling away pleasantly on the long grass, clear water weeping from a pretty young woman's pale stone eyes and spilling from the wound in her marble heart into a great wide pool. The crumbling Brownbread Mill still grinding wheat into wealth just south of the main part of town. St. Whylom's School in its industrial shadow, looking out over the river. The little Kalevala Opera House that hadn't put on a single opera in Osmo's thirteen years of life. All the fine shops with real glass windows lining Yclept Closeway. The big wide half-burnt steps of Bodeworde's Armory, which had gone up in a blaze a hundred and fifty years before. They'd kept the stairs as a reminder never to get careless with gunpowder again.

Osmo knew them all.

The boy with the hazel eyes had never gotten lost, not once, not in his whole life. He couldn't get lost in Littlebridge any more than you can get lost in your own body.

Osmo hated it.

He hated knowing every street and side road. He hated knowing that the sugar maples in front of Mittu Grumm's Toy and Shoe

Shoppe would always go bright scarlet by the third of October. He hated the ravens that stayed and the sparrows that had somewhere better to be—somewhere he could never go. He hated his dumb ancestor who couldn't even be bothered to come up with a good fake name for the family. On days when he felt particularly angry at the shape of everything, he even hated the Whaleskin Mountains for keeping him penned in with their useless, dopey sheer glittering jagged cliffs.

But most of all, deep down in his bones, he hated that he'd never been lost, not one minute in his life, that he never *would* be lost, not in Littlebridge, not in his little white four-room cottage, not anywhere. Of course there were stories of a much more interesting Littlebridge, long ago when magic and monsters and princesses and curses were as common as tea in the afternoon. But they seemed to have run right out of that sort of thing.

Except the silver skull. Except that one single, solitary, fantastic, wonderful strange and unusual thing. Every time he passed it on his way from one dull, familiar place to the next, Osmo swore he could *feel* its huge, empty eye sockets watching him. Its long, curved fangs reaching out for him. It made the hairs on the back of his neck rise up and his stomach flip over. But that was little enough strangeness for a heart to live on.

Everything in Osmo's world was already mapped out to the very edges of the page. The village ran like a perfect brass watch. All he wanted was to wake up one day and find the hands snapped off and the bell ringing out twenty-five o'clock.

The very worst of it all was this: Osmo Unknown absolutely,

*thoroughly* loathed the entire idea of becoming a hunter when he grew up. Everyone assumed he'd do just that, as surely as the moon changed in the sky. Osmo would follow his mother, Tilly, into the family business, make a good marriage, and keep the little house of Unknown industry chugging along neatly. But he wanted nothing to do with it. Osmo didn't want to kill anything. He didn't want to be good at using his mother's big beautiful gun. He didn't want to know how to cut up pelts and gut a deer and portion out the meat so that it could be made into pies and kebabs and stews and roasts.

He didn't want his job to be *hurting* things.

But he couldn't tell anyone how he felt, and Osmo hated that, too. Hunting was a noble profession. Any family would be proud to have a hunter at the holiday table. He knew everyone had to eat to live, and killing a single deer could mean safety and health for a whole winter. But he just didn't see why it had to be *him*.

The *only* good thing about hunters was that they were allowed to go into the Fourpenny Woods whenever they wanted.

Everyone else was forbidden to cross the tree line. When he was little, Osmo's mother let him wait for her every day, just inside the first clusters of maples and junipers. He used to stare into the shadows, and his soul filled up with the rich, new smell of sap.

But it was off-limits.

To everyone. Forever.

And it was all because of *them*. Everyone knew what would happen if you went too deep into the woods. Something lived in the deep trees. Something no one had seen in living memory, but everyone dreamed of on their worst nights, tossing and turning in their beds as though it were possible to escape. Something with terrible teeth that lived in the dark.

Something called the Quidnunx.

The Quidnunx stayed in the woods. Humans stayed in the village. Meddling with that was beyond foolish. It was pure, screaming madness.

No, each to their own was best for all, agreed the old folk from the mansions to the marshes. Monsters and men do not mix. The woods were very wild and the town was very mild. The wild and the mild of this world do not get along so well, and nobody ever born in Littlebridge was the sort of person to go testing the rules.

Except one boy with very bright, very wide hazel eyes and long shaggy dark hair and no friends to speak of.

Every inch of the Forest the law let Osmo explore was as precious as a whole emerald to his heart. He loved the woods like he loved his mother. And he feared the great tangle of trees, as he feared his father. But he didn't love the Forest for the usual reasons. He didn't love it because it was forbidden. Well, not *just* because it was forbidden. He didn't love it because it was dangerous, and therefore exciting. He loved it because it was secret and quiet and lonely, like him. He loved it because it was never the same twice. You couldn't *know* a forest like you could *know* a village. As soon as you thought you did, it would change on you. The trees that went orange before the harvest last year hung on to their green almost till Christmas this year, and the sound you heard might be a hedge-hog or a squirrel, but it might just as easily be something . . . else.

Osmo Unknown lived and breathed and thirsted for the *Else*.

But until he turned thirteen, all he ever found in the shad-ows were hedgehogs and squirrels and the occasional bright red October leaf, swirling down from a grey, cold sky.

## Chapter Two
# A LOT OF RUBBISH

Osmo Unknown raised his hand impatiently.

"Yes?" sighed Headmaster Gudgeon. "What seems to be the problem, young Master Unknown?"

"Well," Osmo said, scratching behind his ear, "it's just that it's *such* a lot of rubbish."

Gasps went up around the classroom. Osmo sat at a big, four-person desk under a trio of tall, thin windows. The heavy, lazy autumn sun slanted in sideways. The big, blocky shape of the old Brownbread Mill down the way sliced the light into thick planks before it hit their desks. Someone long ago had the bright idea to build the school next to the mill so that the fancified, bubble-scrubbed, book-reading children of Littlebridge would have to look out on a decent day's labor and think about where the bread in their lunches came from.

And so the waterwheel turned and turned through the years. Since the founding of the school, every student had fought a brave but unwinnable battle not to fall asleep to that lulling, pleasant sound.

Just then, Osmo Unknown had never felt more awake.

He'd spoken out of turn, which always set his blood to simmering on its own. But more than that—today, Ivy Aptrick sat next to him. This hardly ever happened, because their names did not sit next to one another in the alphabet any more than their parents sat together at church. Ivy's family was *somebody* in Littlebridge. Osmo's was . . . well. Unknown.

But it had happened today. It *was* happening. Ivy wore a grey dress with grey gloves to match her grey eyes. Her red hair fell over her shoulders like water falling from a wheel. She didn't gasp like the others, but she did frown, which was worse, somehow.

It was Translation Tuesday. They were working together on *The Ballad of the Forest and the Valley*, a beloved piece of antique Littlebridge literature. When they could translate it perfectly, they never had to take another Old Bridgish class again. Every child in Littlebridge had to learn rudimentary Old Bridgish, even though they'd never use it at all unless they went into the church for a living. Every child in Littlebridge hated Old Bridgish. They worked very hard for the right to one day forget all about it.

*The Ballad of the Forest and the Valley* was all about the founding of Littlebridge. It began: *Once upon a time, in the beginning of the world, a certain peculiar Forest fell in love with a deep, craggy Valley.* And that was the most normal-sounding bit of the whole thing.

"It's rubbish," Osmo said firmly. "Whoever wrote this was having a laugh on us. A forest can't really fall in love with a valley, you know. It's only a fable. A metaphor. Land hasn't got a heart. Dirt and rocks and trees can't fall in love, not like a boy can fall in love with a girl. This is just a silly old story."

Ivy blushed, and then he blushed. They both looked back at their papers.

"It's old," Ivy snapped back, "but it's not silly or a story."

The Headmaster shut his eyes and took a deep breath. Adults needed to do that a lot when Osmo was around. "Nobody likes a know-it-all, Master Unknown," he sighed eventually.

Osmo didn't think that was true. How could knowing it all ever be a bad thing? Only *not* knowing things could ever hurt anyone. He *didn't* know it all, of course. Not even close. He very much hoped that one day he might. It was his great ambition.

One of the students at another of the huge four-person desks raised their hand to change the subject.

"What's a pangolin?" one of the older boys said nervously. Gregory Grumm, whose father owned the Toy and Shoe Shoppe. He jabbed his meaty finger at a drawing of one, right after the passage that listed them among the many interesting creatures that could be found in the Fourpenny Woods. That passage was downright child cruelty, Osmo thought. What use was it to read about all the amazing things in the woods when they weren't allowed within winking distance?

"See, that's how you *know* it's a fairy tale and not a real history," Osmo answered before Headmaster Gudgeon got the chance. He couldn't help himself. He loved being the one to explain things. It made him feel tall. "We read about them in St. *Whylom's Book of Zoologicals Near and Far*. Er. Rather. We're *going* to read about them next year in *Zoologicals N and F*." They were very much not allowed to read ahead, but Osmo always did anyhow. "Pangolins are like giant anteaters with bronze scales all over them, and when they get frightened, they can roll up into a ball even a sword couldn't pierce. But there have never been any pangolins around here! I read about them last summer. They live in the hottest and furthest jungles of Java. There aren't any marsupials or flamingos in the Fourpenny Woods, either, no matter what it says. My mother always says there's nothing in the woods but woods. And she should know. It's all just poetry and poetry only has to *sound* pretty, it doesn't have to make actual sense."

"But maybe there *are* pangolins in there because the woods are magic. Magic doesn't have to do what you say," the judge's daughter pointed out. "In fact, nobody and nothing has to do what *you* say, Osmo."

"There isn't any such thing as magic." Osmo rolled his eyes. "*Magic* is just how storybooks spell *science*." He sighed deeply. "Nobody wants magic to be real or fables to be true more than me. The world is just . . . disappointing. Better to get used to that now." But to himself he whispered a promise: *Someday I am going to live in a real city instead of stupid bumpkin Littlebridge. A real city full of millions and millions of clever people who know all about modern things and modern inventions and modern life. Paris. Or Rome. Or Helsinki. I don't even care which.*

Ivy glared pointedly at him and started again from the beginning of the passage. "*Once upon a time, in the beginning of the world, a certain peculiar Forest fell in love with a deep, craggy Valley,*" she read aloud through gritted teeth. Ivy felt very defensive of books, since her father published most of the books in Littlebridge. No one ought to disrespect the books in her presence. "*The first quarrel was whether or not they ought to allow magic past their borders.* See, Osmo? Magic *is* real. It says so right there."

When Ivy read, the translation came easily, hardly any effort at all. When Osmo did it, it took hours and bored him to headaches. Old Bridgish was not a very simple language. And he always felt like the writer was smirking at him, peeking out from between the lines. Which, of course, no respectable writer would ever do.

He couldn't help himself. "No, I don't see. Magic either *is* or it *isn't*—"

"Let us skip along to the passage concerning the anatomy of the Quidnunx and the unfortunate death of Katja Kvass, Miss Aptrick," interrupted the Headmaster. He seemed quite pleased with Ivy. Everyone was always pleased with Ivy.

Everyone flipped through their dusty old pages until they came to one of the full-page illustrations Ivy's father had paid extra for so that St. Whylom's would have only the best for his daughter. It showed the dappled, watercolor edge of the Fourpenny Woods in the background, and in the foreground, sharp and dark as could be, stood Treaty Rock. Osmo Unknown knew the words written there so well he didn't bother to read them now. He passed them every time he went into the Forest.

DON'T BOTHER US AND YOU WON'T GET BOTHERED.
TAKE ONE OF OURS AND WE TAKE ONE OF YOURS.
IF YOU WANT TO BORROW SOMETHING, JUST ASK.
THOU SHALT NEVER EAT ANYTHING THAT TALKS.
KEEP OUT.

But Osmo couldn't let it go. He could never let anything go once he had it in his teeth. "But don't you *see*? They're the worst part! Quidnunx. Don't. Exist. They just *don't*! Maybe they existed a long time ago, like dinosaurs or Romans, but probably not."

"Who's that treaty with then, if there's no such thing as Quidnunx?" asked Barnaby Lud smugly. The Mayor's son. He was the worst of the rich boys. And the worst of the cruel boys and the bigger boys and the angry boys and every sort of boy. "The trees?"

"Most likely another group of people." Osmo shrugged. "*Human* people. Maybe a hostile tribe on the other side of the Forest. Doesn't that make more sense to you than giant child-eating cryptids?"

"Wait, what's a cryptid?" one of the younger girls said, crinkling up her freckled forehead.

"An animal that doesn't exist!" Osmo threw up his hands. "It's just a myth. A myth some Old Bridgish geezer made up to keep us out of the Forest. Monsters in the woods. Every culture has them. Big scary beasts in the big scary wilderness. Better stay at home where it's safe, children!"

Ivy went pale. "Don't say that."

"I will, though," Osmo protested. "I will say it! My mother goes into the Fourpenny Woods *all the time*. She's never seen anything but deer and rabbits. Not pangolins or wombats or giant hairy monsters. None of that's in there. They're lovely woods, but they're just the usual sort of thing. Trees, leaves, deer, meadows. She's a hunter, she would know if there were Quidnunx out there. She'd *have* to know."

"No one cares about your mum!" cackled Barnaby Lud. Osmo's

face burned with the effort of not jumping over the desks to pummel Barnaby's fat, handsome face.

"No, I think he's right," the tavern owner's daughter, Silja, piped up. "My dad says there's no such thing and we should start clearing trees for new houses next year. He says it's like never taking a bath because you're afraid of selkies."

Julka Oft, one of the parson's twin sons, nodded and raised a finger to push up his glasses. "It's just science. No one has ever seen one. No one has ever heard one. No one has even drawn a good picture of them. Believing in something without evidence is the business of faith, and faith is reserved for heaven. There's no such thing as magic. There's no such thing as monsters. And there is absolutely no such thing as Quidnunx."

Osmo Unknown's skin tingled with the excitement of people agreeing with him. He'd never felt anything like it before.

"*My* mother says when I grow up I'll think it's funny that I had nightmares about something so ridiculous," the blacksmith's girl, Freja Highberry, added on.

Headmaster Gudgeon was quickly losing control of his classroom.

"It sounds very much like someone *else* is venturing into the Fourpenny Woods," the Headmaster said sternly, peering over his foggy glasses. "You wouldn't do that, would you, Master Unknown? You wouldn't, because you'd know better than most that it is forbidden to all but registered hunters."

Everyone went quiet.

"Of course not," he said quickly.

He sat down. He wasn't technically allowed *yet*. Not until he'd taken his exams and earned his gun. That took *years*. Monks and doctors had to study less than hunters. Osmo didn't mind that part. He liked books. Books never judged you or called you names or bossed you around. And that book would never let you down like a person might. It was only every single other thing about hunting he hated. But everyone assumed he'd pull it off eventually, so what was the harm in skipping ahead a little?

"There's no such thing as a Quidnunk, that's all," he muttered under his breath. "No such thing as a unicorn, either, but no one argues about that."

Ivy glared at him. But she wasn't angry. She was worried. "Don't, Osmo. If you upset them, they'll come. No one likes to be told they're a myth. Especially monsters."

"I'll say it all day long if I like," grumbled Osmo, and crossed his arms over his chest.

"What about Katja Kvass, then, huh?" one of Ivy's friends protested. "If there's no such thing as Quidnunx, what happened to her? And the others? Just because it hasn't happened lately doesn't mean it never happened at all."

Osmo's face burned and his jaw clenched. "I don't *know*," he said finally, and it physically pained him to use those words. He felt all three of them like little wounds in his stomach. "People just disappear sometimes. It doesn't mean . . . *creatures* took them. Anyway, no one's done it for hundreds of years. You might as well be afraid of a butter churn."

"No, they *ate* her," whispered the innkeeper's son, Bjorn.

"Everyone knows that. *Take one of ours and we'll take one of yours.* Just like it says on Treaty Rock."

"It's a *metaphor!*" yelled Osmo. His face had gone red.

"For *what?*" Bjorn screeched back.

"If there's no such thing as Quidnunx, what's that great blow-off skull in the middle of town from, huh?" shouted Barnaby Lud from the back, surrounded by his friends. "Your dad?"

"I said maybe they *used* to exist," Osmo said through clenched teeth, clinging to the feeling of *rightness* he'd had when this all started out. But it was slipping helplessly away. Maybe he *was* wrong. Maybe he should have stayed quiet. Now everyone was looking at him and laughing just because they all believed in immortal monsters and he didn't. "They're just extinct."

"Shut *up*, Unknown, you turnip!" Lud yelled from the back of the classroom. "Let's just get on with it!"

"Turnip!" giggled Ada Sloe, like it was the cleverest thing in the world. She was Ivy's best friend. Her black braids shook as she laughed. "Osmo the Turnip!"

Headmaster Gudgeon cut them all off and began to translate himself. His droning voice buzzed around the sunlit room until nearly everyone had forgotten how much Osmo annoyed them in their own battle to stay awake.

Suddenly, Ivy leaned over to whisper to him.

"You *do* go into the Woods, don't you?"

It wasn't a question. It was an accusation. Her eyes shone large in her round face. Her long red hair looked like a feast in the sun. "I know you do."

Osmo Unknown considered lying to her. If he lied, then he was a good boy who obeyed the rules and someone like her father could rely on him to spend time with his daughter and not worry. If he told the truth, he wasn't very good at all, and didn't care about rules, and shouldn't be allowed around anybody his own age, in case he rubbed off on them. But it was more exciting to do forbidden things than not to do them, that was just obvious. Which one would Ivy like better? The exciting or the good? He wasn't sure how to play this game at all. Osmo was fearfully good at games of every sort, knucklebones, doublechess, backgammon, dice, cards, deepcheckers. He could beat almost anyone in the village and twice on Saturdays. But this one was too new to him.

He decided to bet on exciting.

"Don't tell anyone," he whispered. "My mother showed me the way. It's all right if you're careful."

Ivy was shocked. She wasn't faking it, either, the way people did sometimes when they'd got a thrill they knew they oughtn't. "You shouldn't. You shouldn't ever. It's against the treaty."

Osmo Unknown smiled at her. He didn't know where this courage was coming from. It felt like being on fire and frozen solid at the same time. For the first time in his life, he didn't know what was going to happen next.

"Do you want to go with me? Tonight?" Yesterday or tomorrow, he would never have been able to ask her. Not Ivy, whose rich father looked at him like he was nothing but an annoying fly on his daughter's sleeve. Besides, what if she said no? Everyone knew Barnaby Lud was going to ask her to the Frost Festival. It was inevitable, like winter itself. She would never go anywhere with a boy like Osmo. A hunter's son with nothing in his pockets but an old name. Osmo knew that. But somehow today, it slipped out. Somehow, today he was brave. And nauseous. But still brave. Now it was out there, sitting between them. Something would have to be done with it.

"Yes," Ivy breathed. "No," she corrected herself. "Yes," she said again. "No. No. I can't. I couldn't *possibly*."

This strange boy couldn't be Osmo Unknown, not in a hundred years, not the weird, quiet kid with a doublechess piece always in his pocket and too many thoughts in his head to keep them from spilling out of his mouth. Who was this new person? This boy who just *did* things because *why not*? Who leaned back with a sparkle in his hazel eyes and whispered in the ear of the richest girl in town: "All right, if you won't go to the Forest, come to the Frost Festival with me."

Ivy didn't answer. But she smiled. Just a little. Just the corner of her mouth.

The bell rang. The students shot out of the room like cannon fire. The afternoon broke through the windows and called them all out into itself, full of light and sharp smells and freedom. But not Osmo. He couldn't move. He was shaking like a thin little tree. What had come over him? What had he done? That smile . . . that was a yes. Wasn't it? It was. It had to be.

The Headmaster beckoned Osmo to his desk with one long, crooked finger. It had white hairs on the knuckle. Osmo hung his head and dragged his feet.

"There, there, son," Gudgeon clucked gently. "You're probably right. We are modern people, after all. No need to set a plate for old superstitions, eh?"

Osmo nodded. He was right. He'd known he was, and now there could be no doubt, not when even the teacher agreed. He clung to old Gudgeon's words. He *had* to be right. Because if he wasn't, if there really was such a thing as magic, as a haunted forest, as Quidnunx . . . then he really *shouldn't* be going into the Fourpenny Woods alone all the time. If it was all true, the rules were there for a reason, and he might have to stop breaking them. In fact, he *should* stop. Immediately. He should stop and stay at home until the hunters' exams and grow up and grow old doing what everyone told him to do so that he didn't get eaten by something more ancient than time and winter and the moon.

And Osmo Unknown couldn't bear the idea of stopping. He thought he might really and truly rather die.

So, you see, monsters *couldn't* exist. It would be too cruel.

The Headmaster cleared his throat pointedly. "But there is *being right*, and there is *not being disruptive in my classroom*. Now which of these do you think you ought to embrace, going forward?"

"Not being disruptive in your classroom," Osmo mumbled.

"Right you are. Run along now, Mister Skeptic," the Headmaster barked.

Osmo grabbed his books and bolted out of the classroom, across the hall, and down the great carved staircase of St. Whylom's School for Excellent Young People.

## Chapter Three
# A BLACK-RIBBON BOY

It was autumn then, and red was king.

Even at an hour before midnight in Littlebridge, even with shadows as thick as coat sleeves hanging all round. You could still see the red leaves fluttering on the trees. And the red glass in the fancy windows and the red sheen on the moon reflected in the deep black water. The riverbanks ran over with red leaves, red rose hips, red zinnias, red squashes growing wild for anyone to take.

In an hour or two the river would be swarming with happy festival-goers looking for a sneaky bite. He took a deep breath of all that red autumn goodness, red tinged black by the chill October night. The air smelled like woodsmoke and apples and the honeysuckle water Osmo had borrowed from his sister Lizbel to tame his mane of hair and make it smell nice enough to meet Ivy Aptrick before the First Frost Festival began.

Osmo stood waiting for her at the foot of the little bridge of Littlebridge, which was not actually so little as all that. Torches burned all along its arched walls. Big green round mushrooms swelled up between the stones like party balloons.

Osmo could look upriver one way and see Cammamyld Heights, where Ivy lived. All those beautiful houses so rich they didn't even have gardens, just gates and brass doorbells and narrow stained-glass windows. If Cammamyld people wanted basil for their supper, they *bought* it. Like *city* folk. They didn't grow it outside their kitchen window like Osmo's family did. And he could look downriver, past the old Brownbread Mill with its great always-turning waterwheel, toward the Felefalden Flats, where the Unknowns lived. All those miles of cottages and farms and wooden fences and idiot smelly sheep.

It was quiet. For now. In a moment, Ivy would come and she would be red, too, her long red hair that matched the world this time of year. Everything would be red and perfect. Most everyone else was already in Dapplegrim Square, getting ready for the stroke of midnight and the start of the feast. Osmo clutched five or six flowers in one hand, wild spotted lilies from the edge of the Forest, to remind her that he was a daring, dashing, exciting, wild sort of person. He'd tied them together with one of his sister Oona's precious hair ribbons. She only had two, but she knew what this meant to her brother. She hadn't even thought twice about parting with one. And given the choice, without his even asking, she offered him the black ribbon, her favorite. That's what Oona was like. Osmo often felt he should be that way, too, a black ribbon boy. And he did try. But it never seemed to *work*. He had so few things that he could never give them up, he just held on fiercely until everyone else went away and left him alone and even then, he still couldn't let go.

The moon rode high in the sky. It shivered off its red haze and turned big and silver and flat as a bony kneecap. Its surprised, gap-mouthed face stared down at him as it moved through the stars. He glanced toward the Sampo Bell Tower. It had chimed eleven ten minutes ago. He bit the inside of his cheek nervously.

Osmo pulled a chess piece out of his pocket. He always carried one, for luck. A different one every day. His own, private super-stition. Years ago his father had gone all the way to the city on the other side of the mountains to sell their greens and blood sausages and Unknown's Goodest Stout—the best beer in the Valley. This was how the family kept bone and breath together as the game slowly faded from the woods. Everyone said Unknown's Goodest Stout was the best thing for a hard day's work, or if you were sick, or if you'd had to skip lunch, or especially if you were sad. Osmo wouldn't have known. None of the children were old enough to have any themselves yet, not even to test the batch.

On that special day, Mads had asked each of his babies what he ought to bring back for them. The little ones wanted toys and candy, the middle girls wanted thread and needles. The usual sort of thing. That's where Oona had got her ribbons. And it's where Osmo got his doublechess set. Mads had given him such an odd look that Osmo never forgot it.

*Wouldn't you rather have a good knife or new boots? A man should ask for something useful, not a silly game.*

But Osmo wanted what he wanted. He would not be budged.

Today he'd brought a white queen in his pocket: as white as the bony midnight moon, as noble and important as Ivy. He rolled it over the tops of his fingers, deftly, like a stage magician about to do a trick.

Ivy was taking a long time. It was probably harder to get ready when you had long thick red hair and so many different dresses to choose from and twice as many shoes. Osmo only had one pair of his own, so it was easy to be on time. He told himself to be patient. In another moment or two, he'd see Ivy's little silver lantern come up over the bridge, and the world would never be a lonely place for him again.

He was terrible at being patient.

She'd smiled. She *had* smiled. The smile said she'd come. You wouldn't smile like that if you didn't want to come. You'd frown. That was how faces worked. Wasn't it?

The bell tower bonged out half past eleven. He could hear the voices of everyone he knew gathered in the square. No one moved on the narrow little streets. Everyone was already where they wanted to be. Osmo held on to his flowers very tightly. No, Ivy wouldn't do that to him. She was kind and good. Maybe something was wrong. Maybe he ought to go to her house and see if she needed help somehow. Perhaps she was ill. Perhaps she had fallen down the stairs.

A cold wind wicked away tears from Osmo's eyes. The moon came out from behind a starry cloud. It didn't look surprised anymore. Only sad and knowing.

"Nobody asked you," Osmo grumbled at the moon. "What do you know about anything down here anyway? Shove off, you turnip. Sky turnip."

The moon obediently covered herself up in clouds again. Osmo sighed and spared one last glance toward Ivy's long, empty, lovely street. No one was hurrying down the lane, hoping against hope that her dear friend hadn't thought she wasn't coming and left already. No. It simply wasn't going to happen. Osmo knew that and the moon knew it, too.

He turned away from the rippling river. His nose tingled miserably and he knew in another minute he'd cry, *really* cry, so he sniffed hard and broke into a jog to stop the tears before they could get him. *Come on now, be a man*, he scolded himself. That was what his father always told him. In their house, *Be a Man* was a complete argument. Once Mads said it, the conversation was over, no matter how Osmo positively *boiled* with the unfairness of it. He was the only boy, so the whole weight of those words was his alone to lift. Papa barely seemed to notice his sisters. He kept a whole variety of disapproving stares just for his son. But all that was beside the obvious point that the only actual hunter in the house was his mother, so what did being a man have to do with the price of venison? Why couldn't his father just let him be Osmo?

Osmo decided to outrun those tears. He ran up the familiar old jackknife-angle alleys and byways of Littlebridge toward Dapplegrim Square. Past the dark windows of the Kalevala Opera House, the shuttered-up Afyngred Agricultural Hall, the CLOSED FOR THE DURATION OF THE FESTIVAL sign on the bright blue door of Mittu Grumm's Toy and Shoe Shoppe.

The distant roar of the First Frost Festival grew louder and louder until it swallowed him up. Osmo tumbled into the thick of it, big scarlet banners and garlands of golden flowers hanging from every streetlamp. Violins and drums and pretty glass flutes playing old songs even babies knew by heart. Strands of little square paper lanterns painted with pale winter scenes, strung from weather vane to weather vane over the plaza. The big round table full of party bags stuffed with candies and penny prizes for everyone to take home when they'd exhausted the night. The good, wholesome smell of root vegetables roasting, all slicked down with honey. When Osmo's great-grandmother was little, the roasteries had offered meat, a hundred kinds, rabbit, reindeer, hedgehog, badger, white fox, even seal, shiny with browned blubber. But now? There'd been no wild boar sandwiches or roast pheasant or beaver stew for years. Tilly Unknown hadn't shot a deer since Osmo's tenth birthday. The Fourpenny Woods only gave up rabbits and minks anymore, and those few and far between. He'd asked his mother about it once, but she just stayed quiet for a long time until he changed the subject out of sheer awkwardness.

The hunters knew something, Osmo was sure of it. But you couldn't make a hunter tell you the color of their own eyes unless they already wanted you to know it. These days, you took your turnip or onion or big red beet and you thanked the roaster for it. They smelled rich and nice turning over the glowy coals.

The stars danced in their country squares overhead and the great ancient Quidnunk skull looked down approvingly from its pillar and it would all have been so perfect, except that Osmo was alone. But at least his nose wasn't tingling anymore.

He told himself not to look for Ivy. *Go watch the puppet show.*

*Go chuck something in the bonfire for luck. If she's here, she's here, and if she isn't, she isn't. You won't be happy either way so just go win a jug of red pear cider off Adelard Sloe, you know you can, the game's a piece of old cheese once you know the trick.* Osmo stared glumly through the crowds toward the shadows dancing round the bonfire. Was that one Ivy? Or that one? Or maybe that one . . .

Osmo Unknown tore himself away. He darted down Cacherel Lane, past Izzo Grumm's puppet show and Miss Melanie Coddle's Shooting Gallery and Jack Skriver's Win-a-Hat Wheel. He bolted between the rows of ice sculptures waiting for Mayor Lud to come and judge them. The statues towered over his head, flickering orange and red in the bonfirelight, just barely not melting in the unseasonal warmth. A tree full of glassy ravens sweated cold water down the trunk. A cow with huge frosty horns dripped steadily from its swollen crystal udder. And a great shaggy beast with teeth like Death's own secondhand scythes leered at him as he passed, weeping ghoulishly as its eyes slowly melted in its head. Osmo barely looked at them. It didn't matter. Helka Cutt was going to win. She did every year. It was easy when your family owned the ice pond outside of town.

*That's just how it is,* Osmo thought sourly. Littlebridge wouldn't let you win unless your family had started out winning on the first day of the game.

Adelard Sloe saw him coming. He didn't look happy about it, either. And why would he? Osmo first took a prize off old Ade when he was only four years old: a golden ball the size of a grapefruit. The ball had shone defiantly from a blue velvet cushion on the front counter of Sloe's Stupendous Throwing Game for ten years. The grand prize. No one ever thought it was *real* gold. Carnival games always cheated you. And one of the cheats was usually the prize itself being absolute rubbish that fell apart as soon as you got it home. But Osmo hadn't cared. It could have been made of pure sheep manure and he'd have wanted it just as badly. It was a *prize*. A prize meant you were good.

No, not good. *Special*.

And everyone would cheer and hug you and look at you with big proud shining eyes and you would *stand out* and that was all his four-year-old self needed to know.

He'd watched everyone else try and fail to throw a clay ball into a big painted Quidnunk's hairy, toothy mouth. You got a smallpenny prize for knocking out one of the teeth, a fourpenny prize for sinking it in one of the eye sockets, and an eightpenny prize, the grand prize, for a single straight shot down its peeling, grinning gullet. Osmo had watched the angle of the punters' arms, the path the ball took through the air, the different sounds it made as it thunked uselessly into the wooden board or, occasionally, the tin teeth or, most interestingly, the back of the Quidnunk's mouth before bouncing promptly out again.

Little Osmo had stepped up, all skinny arms and knobby knees and hungry eyes and clever heart. There was no such thing as sadness then. Only one sister. No school. No one but him and his parents and the First Frost and the golden ball and pumpkin wedges roasted in honey for after. His cheeks flushed hot and Adelard Sloe, not quite so fat then as he was about to get, roared out:

"Oooh, don't we have a big boy here! Gather round, everyone! Look at this strapping young beast! Thinks he's got the *guts*, thinks he's got the *stones*, thinks he's got the *sheer brute strength* it takes to beat Sloe's Stupendous Unwinnable Throwing Game? Come on, gather in closer! Oh, ho! We've got a real bruiser on our hands, here, haven't we? Why shoot for your supper, Mrs. Unknown? I bet your boy can crush a deer's skull in his bare hands."

"Come on, Addy, that's laying it on a bit thick." Osmo's father had shushed the old carnival barker. But nothing slowed down a professional like Sloe. A big crowd gathered. Bets already rustled through the men's hands.

"You think I'm joking? I never joke!" Adelard snickered. "Why, not since the first days of the world has Littlebridge seen such size, such force, such power! You've got me, young Master Unknown! I surrender, take all my prizes, just leave me with my wits!"

Osmo had glared up at him, his cheeks thin, his chest narrow, his height nothing much at all. He let the man talk. He'd figured it out. There was a false back in the Quidnunk's throat. You couldn't see it properly on account of all the paint and lights, but it was there. If you hit it straight-on, the ball would never go in, no matter how perfectly you aimed it. Sloe was a *cheater*, that was all. His game was a lie, and lying was *wrong*. People who lied didn't deserve to have a golden ball.

"Come on, darling, let's just go," his mother urged him.

But little Osmo just waited until everyone stopped laughing. He looked Adelard Sloe right in his cheating eye and took one giant step to the left. He grabbed the clay ball, wound up, and threw it as hard as he could. It sailed so satisfyingly through the air and smacked into the inside of the Quidnunk's cheek before tumbling down, missing the false backboard, and plunking into the basket on the ground.

No one made a sound. Adelard's face had gone bright red the second Osmo took his giant step. His parents stood there as still as a pair of Helka Cutt's ice sculptures. Then a cheer went up like a firework and everyone *did* hug him and cheer him and look down at him with big round proud eyes and it was the absolute best moment of his entire life. Sloe had handed over the golden ball in a dreamlike trance, as though his soul had slipped out of his body and made a run for it.

The ball wasn't half heavy enough to be solid gold. His mother explained gently that it was nothing but clay stuffed with horsehair and dunked in paint. But to Osmo it was a world. A golden planet with mysteries in its seas. It meant he'd won, once. It meant it was *possible* to win, even in Littlebridge, even if you were nobody. He still carried it with him everywhere. School, the market with his father, the woods with his mother. Even now, it rode along in his satchel, knocking solidly against his hip as he walked.

Adelard Sloe's Stupendous Throwing Game boasted a massive jar of Osmo's father's own Goodest Stout on the grand-prize blue cushion these days. It was Sloe's daughter, Ada, who sneered at Osmo in class and joined in calling him a turnip. Osmo supposed it wasn't Adelard's fault his daughter was a snot. Or that the prize wasn't the least bit golden anymore, and something he'd made himself besides. That hardly mattered, though. It was still a *prize*.

The old man had changed up his tricks over the years, enough that Osmo still got excited at the first sighting of Sloe's finely painted booth. Enough that he had a painstakingly saved smallpenny in his pocket right now. He'd brought it to win something for Ivy, to show off a little, he admitted to himself.

But that didn't matter now, did it?

The carnival man saw him picking his way through the crowd and frowned. The frown went all the way down to the tips of his beard.

"Just take it," Old Sloe snapped.

"Oh, I couldn't, Mr. Sloe! I'll throw for it, I don't mind."

Osmo gazed into the wooden Quidnunk's maw. In the daytime, it was the most unfrightening drawing you ever saw. Shaggy and googly-eyed, poorly done antlers, a nose that seemed to've been sketched by someone who'd only heard of noses in distant fables, and wobbly lips junked up by dull tin collapsible teeth. A mess of beasts mashed up together: part tufted owl, part woolly mammoth, part kangaroo, part orangutan, part polar bear, part elk, and part coconut. But in the torchlight, it grew shadows and depths, nests of nightsparrows in its hair, killing frost in the depths of its eyes, hunger in its gaping black throat.

Nothing like that could ever *really* have existed. Osmo hadn't wanted to say why he was just so sure of it to Master Gudgeon. It made him feel silly and a bit . . . naked. He had all his clothes on, but somehow his *brain* felt naked. The truth could do that, sometimes. But Osmo knew that nothing like the Quidnunx could have really existed in real life because nothing like that could just be . . .

*gone.* Like a rocking horse in a shop window. Stolen away from the world right under everyone's noses. Humans were still around, and humans were little delicate teacups next to that prehistoric iron cauldron. So it just wasn't possible.

Sloe shoved the jar into Osmo's hands and hauled up a new one for the cushion. Osmo tore his eyes away from the beast in the booth.

"Nothing fair about you, Mr. Unknown," Sloe grumbled. "Not since you were knee-high to a dragonfly. Now get out of here, I can't have people seeing how you do it so they can rob me of my very own ribs until the sun comes up."

Voices bubbled up behind him.

Voices Osmo knew.

"I'll win it for you, Ivy. I'll smash its ugly eye in. Watch."

"I *am* a bit thirsty. Maybe I could have a try . . ."

Osmo had just enough time to wish this weren't happening before it was determinedly happening, all around. Ivy Aptrick and Barnaby Lud and their friends, all glossy and flushed and breathless with the cold. A blur of furs on their collars, soft leather shoes, and glistening eyes. Osmo's guts twisted sourly. She wasn't ill. She hadn't fallen down.

"Hi, Daddy!" Ada Sloe said brightly, but her father shook his head. No fraternizing while the game was on.

Barnaby slid his smallpenny over the boards to Old Sloe. He stood in front of the wooden Quidnunk with the hole cut out of its mouth, hefting the weight of the ball. He ignored Osmo entirely. Not cruelly. It simply wasn't worth Barnaby Lud's time to know he was there.

"Don't be silly, I said I'd win it *for* you. Why do you need to try?" Lud said, eyeing up his shot.

Ivy rolled her eyes. "Because I don't lie in my bed and dream at night about watching you do things, Bee," she laughed.

Ivy placed her own smallpenny on top of Barnaby's and took the ball off him. She lined herself up directly in front of the false Quidnunk gawking mutely at her, its mouth gone misshapen and formless in the evening.

"There's a trick to it, isn't there? I've heard there's a trick," she said. "Do you know?"

Osmo startled, suddenly noticed. Suddenly watched by Ivy and Barnaby and their throng of friends. He met Ivy's grey gaze. Would she look ashamed? Defiant? Mock him for being so foolish as to think she would ever have gone to a festival with someone like him?

But he found none of that in Ivy's eyes. It was so much worse. It was *nothing*. Just the curiosity and cool friendliness and shined-up manners you could find pinned to her coat any day of the week.

She'd forgotten. Or she'd never cared at all, and Osmo didn't know which was worse. He wasn't even important enough to make a fool of. In Ivy 's world, Osmo didn't even exist.

"Why are you looking at me like that?" she said. She didn't even have the decency to say it meanly. Osmo truly felt like nothing. Like steam on the river. Like the flat wooden fake Quidnunk with only sawdust and old paint inside it.

"Quit your gawping, Unknown, you bonk," laughed Barnaby. "Are turnips hard of hearing? Do you know how to beat the Nunk or don't you?"

"My game's fair as prayer, young man," Sloe said with a grin. "Just stand right there and lob it in, easy as getting up in the morning."

"Are you calling my daddy a cheat?" cried Ada.

Ivy's face went all cloudy for a moment, like she did remember, almost, that she was supposed to meet someone other than thick-headed, thick-mouthed, thick-hearted useless Barnaby Lud and eat big red honey-soaked beets with him under the stars.

"Who've you got those flowers for?" Ivy asked him quietly.

Osmo had forgotten he was still holding on to the lilies wrapped in Oona's black ribbon.

"Yeah," he choked out, his voice tight and wild. His nose was tingling again. "There's a trick to it."

Ivy pressed her lips together. She looked over her shoulder. Her friends milled about, poking their noses into the booths, chasing each other into the alleys like little kids.

"Win it for me, Bee," she cried out cheerfully over her shoulder. "You're *ever* so much stronger than I am." Barnaby blushed with pleasure and started pelting the board with clay balls and no strategy at all.

Ivy grabbed Osmo by the elbow, pushing him back between the throwing game booth and the pastry-seller's cart.

"They're for me, aren't they," she said flatly, and didn't wait for an answer. "I told you I couldn't possibly. I came with Barnaby. I was always going to come with Barnaby."

"You smiled," Osmo said miserably. This was really happening. Right now. He couldn't make it not happen. He wished he could pull up the ground over his head and never come out again. "I thought you wanted to come with me."

"It doesn't matter what I want," Ivy said wonderingly. "I smiled because I like you and you're nice and I didn't know what to say that wouldn't hurt your feelings. Why have you done this to yourself? Now I have to feel terrible for you. How could you think someone with a father like mine could ever go anywhere with someone with a mother like yours? That's just not how the world works, Osmo." Her eyes were so sad and full of torchlight.

"It could be," he whispered.

Ivy laughed. It was a strange, short, sharp, angry laugh that made him suddenly think that Ivy Aptrick's life might as well be a Quidnunk in the Forest for all he understood about it.

"No, it can't. We could live on the moon before the Heights and the Flats could meet. It's the motto of this town. We walk under it every day on the way to school. Did you just never look?"

Ivy Aptrick pointed up at the great seal of the city hanging over the Armory. A Quidnunk and a tall thin man, each touching the edge of a tower entwined with briars and flowers. And under it: NEMO NANCIT DESIDERIUM EORUM.

Osmo pushed his fists into his eyes. "Mottos don't mean anything, really," he sniffed. "It's just Latin. Latin can't make you hurt people like this." Osmo fought furiously not to cry. "Latin can't make you love Barnaby Lud when you know he's awful and it can't make you stuck-up and cruel like him. You're choosing to be, that's all. You're choosing. All you have to do is make a different choice, and suddenly *that's* the way the world works."

Ivy shook her head and sighed. She stared up at the city seal.

"Go home, Osmo Unknown, you turnip," she said, but she said it tenderly, as if maybe she really was sorry, and a turnip wasn't the worst thing in the world to be. *"Nemo Nancit Desiderium.* Nobody gets what they want."

And then the bells rang out in Dapplegrim Square, one after the other, each blue metal bell of Soothfaste Church bonging prettily against the cold night. With a rush of hot relief, Osmo bolted into the throngs just as Harigold Blust, the biggest voice in Littlebridge, bellowed out from a stage at the base of the skull-pillar:

"HEAR YE, HEAR YE! COME . . . ER . . . YE ONE AND YE ALL TO . . . AH . . . WHAT'S THAT? RIGHT. TO YE BEAUTIFULLY GARDENED BY YE CAMMAMYLD LADIES' CHARITY ASSOCIATION BONEFIRE PARK FOR THE CHOOSING OF THE FROSTFRAU! WHO WROTE THIS? TOO MANY YE'S, HELKA, YOU ONION. GO TO THE PARK, EVERYBODY! THE MAYOR'S GOT A DUNK TANK FULL OF HOT CIDER!"

Ivy and all the other girls clapped their hands and burst out from their circles of friends toward the square like flocks of magpies. The boys bolted after them. And then, halfway up the cobblestone alley, Ivy stopped. She froze, caught halfway between her friends and the motto of her city, as though, just for a moment, she might change her mind.

Ivy turned to call out to him, but he'd already gone.

*Chapter Four*

# GIRLS AND KNIGHTS AND NEEDLES

Every girl in Littlebridge dreamed of being crowned Frostfrau. For one thing, you got to wear a *very* pretty crown made of fir boughs and lingonberries and snowdrops and witch hazel and glass beads, all painted white and silver like perfect snow. For another, everyone had to bow to you when they passed by all year long until the next Frostfrau was crowned.

Osmo didn't blame them. Those things sounded fantastic. But boys couldn't be Frostfraus, so that was that.

The Frostfrau crown didn't go to the prettiest or the cleverest. There was no way to *earn* it at all, really, which made it all the more desirable. Fate had to *choose* you. Every year at First Frost, all the unmarried girls in the village gathered in Bonefire Park at the foot of the fountain. Their mothers blindfolded them with red handkerchiefs. Harigold Blust lit off a firecracker in a big iron pot and at the sound of the boom, the girls went running in all directions, laughing and screaming and tripping over everything they couldn't see. Meanwhile, the Mayor got all dolled up in a shaggy, matted, dank-smelling Quidnunk costume, climbed up onto a pair of terrifyingly unstable stilts, and chased the girls all over the park until he caught one. It's quite difficult to grab a sprinting child when you're up on stilts, so the whole thing took quite some time. One of the most important skills a politician in Littlebridge could have was being reasonably good at walking on stilts.

Mayor Lud was standing up on a makeshift stage in front of the Katja Kvass Memorial Fountain brandishing his fancy silver-tipped cane like a sword. Ice had formed a diamond crust around Katja's weeping eyes and wounded heart. Tanta Hopminder stood next to her boss, looking pained every time he awkwardly swung the cane round. As if Mayor Lud had ever held a sword in his life. Except maybe to cut himself another slice of pie. He had the Quidnunk pants on, complete with enormous papier-mâché feet to cover his shoes and curling thick toenails dipped in bloodred paint. He rested his rear on the giant headpiece, drinking with his free hand. Every once in a while he'd stick out a leg and poke at the growing crowd with the tip of his stilt and roar with laughter.

People poured into Bonefire Park from all sides. But Osmo hung back. He saw a couple of his sisters inching shyly toward the stage. All the older girls who knew this might be their last chance had already taken up strategic positions round the Mayor. And there stood Ada Sloe and Ivy Aptrick and the others his own age, pretending very pointedly not to care. He waved to Milja and Sanna as they arrived to join Klara and Lizbel. They waved back excitedly. But he didn't see his mother anywhere. He caught sight of Oona, finally, standing up on tiptoe to see from the back. She wore her other ribbon, the blue one, in her long hair. Their father hollered over the din to his six daughters, holding up a bunch of red handkerchiefs like a bouquet of roses. But Osmo didn't see his mother anywhere. He mouthed to Oona across the throng: *Where's Mama?* Oona just shrugged.

"Come on now!" Harigold bellowed. "We haven't got all night! Come on over here, girls, let's get a head count. Get a cup of cider, warm up, you've got ten minutes! No stragglers!"

Osmo wandered over to his favorite part of the park. Not far from the fountain, in a half circle of birch trees, someone had set up six little stone game tables with twelve inviting little stone seats. Any day of the week you could find the old folk of Littlebridge playing shockingly cutthroat rounds of doublechess and deep-checkers and backgammon. But nobody bothered at First Frost. Not when there were so many other things to do, some of which involved very fat, very drunk mayors on five-foot stilts.

Nevertheless, Osmo did not find the game grove empty. A lonely figure hunched over the doublechess table, paying absolutely no attention to the festivities, wrapped in a thick quilt to keep out the cold. Her back was broad and rounded with the years. She wore a big furry coat that bristled brown and white all over. Her hair hung down in tangled grey braids like moss.

"I always thought it was a bit of rubbish that the boys don't have anything to do while the girls smack into each other and fall on their faces," old Mrs. Brownbread chuckled when she saw him. "I tried to have a word with the bosses about it when I was Frostfrau, but it's a position with no real power, I'm afraid."

"*You* were Frostfrau?" Osmo Unknown said in disbelief.

He couldn't imagine Mrs. Brownbread ever having been young or quick, or even running at all without pain in her knees. She was the oldest person he'd ever known. She had more spots than a leopard and more wrinkles than a turtle. Osmo didn't know precisely *how* old. He'd never dared to ask. Mrs. Brownbread was just part of life in Littlebridge, like the bridge itself or the river. She still ran the old mill even though all her husbands had died long ago. She had all the money in the world for big fur coats and all the time in the universe to do as she pleased, which was mostly sitting in the game grove waiting for opponents.

Mrs. Brownbread snorted. "Believe it or not, young man, I was not hatched from an egg already old and frail." She gestured at the board. "Fancy a game while your father takes bets on how long the Mayor can go without falling on his rump roast?"

Mrs. Brownbread was old, yes. But she was also the best double-chess player in the history of Littlebridge. She hadn't just told him that. It was a fact. There was a big silver plaque in Bodeworde's Armory. Every summer the Armory sponsored a Tournament of Strategy and the champion got their name engraved on it. Kala Brownbread appeared there thirteen times.

The tournament had only been on for fourteen years.

But next year? Next year, Osmo felt very certain he'd be standing in the Armory watching them put his name on the silver. He hadn't told Mrs. Brownbread that he meant to beat her record. He didn't have to. She'd known him for a real player the day they'd met.

Not that he'd managed to beat her yet.

Brownbread racked up the pieces as the fiddles and drums picked up a melody a few yards away. Osmo Unknown could only be certain of a few things in this world: he loved his mother, anything you threw in the air came down again pretty quickly, Ivy Aptrick was the prettiest girl in the whole world, there was no such thing as monsters in the woods, and doublechess was the greatest game ever invented by mankind.

Littlebridge people were just such clever sorts, that was the trouble. After several hundred years, regular chess bored them. So a fellow by the name of Bello Draughts locked himself up in his attic until he came up with doublechess, all out of his own brilliant, bored head.

The basic rules were more or less the same as normal chess. Excepting an extra piece between the rook and the knight called the laundress. And . . . rather a lot of other differences, really. If chess meant to reflect war strategies, Bello Draughts reasoned that it was shamefully missing any representation of supply lines. The laundress had to remain behind all the other pieces at all times, only moving forward when they did. But if you lost her, all the other pieces could only move one square at a time.

But the laundress was a cinch to handle compared to the rest of the new rules. In doublechess, every piece had a little friend. A companion piece with special abilities. It was like playing two games at once. All the pawns had hedgehogs with tiny knight's helmets on them. If you attacked a pawn, it could sacrifice its hedgeknight to keep alive another turn. The rooks had whales with tiny feet and crowns on their heads. A whale could bring a captured piece back if it landed on one special unoccupied black space next to the queen, which didn't happen too often, because you always kept a royal guard round your queen if you knew what was good for her. The laundresses had salmon who could return them both to their starting position in one move from anywhere on the board. The bishops had wombats with saddles and plumes. A wombat could declare a "dig" and snatch the companion off another unsuspecting piece. That is, if you could get them into a Bishop's Burrow, which meant having both bishops in a kind of pincer formation around the target piece, three or less squares away on each side. There were heaps of little strategies like that. The knights had hippopotamuses which permanently killed any piece plus its companion on the attack, but if a hippopotamus had no offensive play, it immediately sacrificed itself. The queen had a pangolin, which let her armor up for a turn, but she couldn't move. The king, naturally, had a little Quidnunk on his shoulder. If you were silly enough to let a king get himself into position for a move called a Quidnunk's Roar, the game started over from the beginning. And if you lost, your opponent got to take a bride-piece. Just choose any one of your pieces they pleased and keep it *forever*.

Mrs. Brownbread's personal doublechess set was made entirely of bridepieces. Queens and knights and laundresses she'd won or stolen off the poor saps she beat, all different colors and sizes. Osmo adored it. Even though one of her pawns had belonged to him until pretty recently. The green one with the golden quartz flaw in its head. Her pieces were such a perfect, quiet show-off.

One look at that thing and you knew where you stood: well below Mrs. Brownbread.

Osmo sat down eagerly. He didn't even flinch when Harry Blust's firecracker went off and the blindfolded girls exploded out into the park, followed by Mayor Lud stumbling after them yelling his head off as he wavered dangerously on his stilts.

Osmo took Mrs. Brownbread's rookswhale right away. He felt the little victory flush through him, hotter than cider. He sent out his knight, a bit overconfident, but it worked. He took Brownbread's pieces left and right. Osmo started to frown. What was she playing at? Brownbread wasn't the type to let him win. So there had to be a strategy to her losing half her board like it didn't even matter.

A blindfolded girl burst through the trees, tripped over a back-gammon table, and landed facedown in a pile of half-frozen leaves. She peeked under her kerchief and aimed herself back in the right direction without missing a breath.

Osmo rolled his eyes. "What a lot of fuss for some old painted hat," he grumbled. Mrs. Brownbread's head creaked up.

"You know what all this is about, don't you, Osmo?" the old woman asked, peering out from under her fur coat.

"I know you have your queen unguarded. Are you feeling all right?"

"I meant all this." She gestured at the blind girls racing around the park and Mayor Lud stumbling after them, roaring.

"It's about having the right to be able to stab Aldred Mummer in the leg if he tries to kiss you and no one minding one bit for a whole year," Osmo said, and laughed.

Mrs. Brownbread didn't.

He shrugged, a little sad that she hadn't liked his joke. It was a good joke, he thought. He took his shadow turn, the special extra go you got after taking a companion piece without its master. Osmo hesitated, then slid his wombishop across seven squares at once. Very bold, but you had to be in doublechess. It did not reward timidity. He answered Mrs. Brownbread a little more seriously. "Everybody has some sort of party to mark the beginning of winter. I've read all about Christmas and Ramadan and Hanukkah and Saturnalia. We have this. I think I'd rather have Christmas."

Mrs. Brownbread's forehead gathered more wrinkles, if that was possible. "No, dear. It's about something far older and deeper than any kiss or candle. It's about what happened to Katja Kvass."

Mayor Lud careened by, barely keeping himself in the air, roaring and swooping down at the girls in the red blindfolds with his grotesque long hairy fake arms.

"Not you too," sighed Osmo. "You might as well tell me she used to spin straw into gold every Tuesday out on the Square."

Mrs. Brownbread shrugged. "Always so difficult, Mr. Unknown. Always so clever. I know what I know and I am what I am. You're awfully young to be such a cynic, little Unknown." She deftly brutalized his flank of pawns in a sudden flurry. "It was all our fault. That's what none of them will tell you."

"Oh, come *on*, Mrs. B! There's no such thing as—"

But Mrs. Brownbread wasn't listening. "But that all happened long before Katja. She was so terribly pretty. The fountain doesn't do right by that girl. Everyone loved her."

"How old *are* you?"

Mrs. Brownbread looked down at her pieces. She ignored his question. "Grief never really ends. It just changes." She looked out over the children of Littlebridge, banging into trees and laughing and grabbing for each other's hands. "Just like people, I expect. This is how a village grieves for the terrible things that happened when it was young. For a long time it is a wound. Then it becomes a memory. Then it is history. Then, when everyone has quite, *quite* forgotten, we turn it into a party." She took his vizier easily. "Everything has two natures, you see. The Frost Festival has the thing it is now, and the thing it imitates. The thing it used to be."

"Well, I don't know what that means. But I don't have two natures. I'm only Osmo," he said firmly.

"Aren't you just," Mrs. Brownbread chortled. Her laugh rumbled and thumped deep in her broad, ancient chest.

Mayor Lud yelped with triumph. He'd finally got a girl by the sash of her dress. She yanked off her handkerchief and jumped joyfully up and down, holding it up in her fist.

It was Ivy. Because of course it was Ivy.

Osmo watched the Mayor bend down to put the white crown on Ivy's head while the village cheered. He still wobbled ridiculously on his stilts like the clown he was. The old man nearly dropped the crown, but Ivy reached up quickly and grabbed it before it toppled out of his thick fingers. Osmo watched her, full of longing.

She looked so very much like a bride.

Just as the Mayor was opening his mouth to proclaim her

Frostfrau for the year, just as the bonfire light shone hot on the eel's old jeweled eyes, a shot rang out over the village, ever so much louder than Harigold Blust's firecracker.

A shot, and then a scream.

A scream no human throat could dream of. It sounded like the birth of the moon. It sounded like the death of the sun.

And it came from the direction of the Fourpenny Woods.

Osmo watched Ivy's face go pale and knew his had, too.

"Check your mate, little lovenunk," Mrs. Brownbread said, trapping his king. Then she took her shadow turn, sliding her queenolin smoothly into position. "And check your fate."

Osmo looked down. She had him. Again.

"Don't feel bad," she soothed him. "This game was a silver star in the dark, and our talk a golden one. For me, anyhow. Hope you enjoyed it, too."

The old champion looked over his pieces appraisingly and plucked his white stag-horn queen up with her thick brown fingers. Osmo felt a string in his heart go *twang* as it disappeared forever into her deep, spotted pockets. Mrs. Brownbread sat back on the stone chair with smug satisfaction, her fur coat closing her in like a bear's ruff.

It takes forty minutes to run from the edge of the Forest to the center of town. A little more if it's snowing, a little less if the sun is out and no one's crowding the streets.

Twenty minutes after the shot and the scream, Tilly Unknown

stumbled into Bonefire Park. Her breath came quick and ragged. Her eyes shone wild and huge. And her hands gleamed slick with blood in the night.

But the blood was not red, like the blood that pumps through your heart and mine.

It was gold.

## Chapter Five
# AN AWFUL WORD, AN IMPOSSIBLE HOUSE

Osmo Unknown said an awful word.

There are big swear words and little swear words in anybody's language. A little swearing is hardly swearing at all. A child could do it and everyone round the supper table would laugh, turn red, and stick a bun in that sour young mouth while secretly making a note to tell every one of their friends just what their beastly wee urchin had said last night on the subject of being served pea soup *again*.

This was not one of those. It was a big swearing. A beefy, grown-up swearing. The kind of swearing even a grown-up man would do when everything in his whole world has gone dreadful and ghastly and wrong. Only a moment ago Osmo's brain had been full up: the chill sticking to his bones and the game he'd lost just when he was sure he was about to win, the weird, probably rubbish story of poor, pretty Katja Kvass. Crammed in beside feeling quite sore still over Ivy, wondering what he'd say to her in the halls tomorrow.

But the moonlight and the golden blood took all that away. Cleaned his brain right out. Now there was nothing in Osmo

Unknown's head at all but the sight of his mother crouched on the grass, terrified, her hunting gun still smoking, her clothes covered in brilliant, wet, golden blood. It dripped off her fingers and soaked her hair. Wherever it touched the grass, the snow began to melt away.

Osmo said that awful word. Again.

So would you. So would I.

He ran to her. He could hear people yelling, footsteps behind him, frightened babies crying. He didn't care. All he saw was her. But she didn't seem to see him at all. It was too horrible to describe. No one who is only just thirteen can bear to see their own mother so afraid and alone. And she *was* alone. Even though his mother was surrounded by everyone she knew, Osmo had never seen anyone so alone.

"Mama, are you okay? Are you hurt?"

"No," his mother whispered. She closed her eyes, swallowed, then opened them again.

But it wasn't the sort of *no* to make anyone feel all right. And he didn't know which of his questions she meant to answer with that *no*. She carefully put her gun on the ground. Now that she'd let go of it, her hands began to shake. And she did seem to see him then. She saw him, and it filled her with such sick horror that she turned and threw up onto the neatly kept parkland.

Tilly Unknown wrapped her long arms around her knees, put her head down, and started to cry. Osmo didn't know what to do. His mother *never* cried. Neither did his father. So neither he nor his sisters had ever really learned how to do it. Their father always said: *Boys don't cry. Neither do girls. Crying is for kittens and birds.*

Osmo had no experience with this at all. So he did the only thing he could do: his best. He reached out and hugged his mother hard. He stroked her hair the way she stroked his when he was little and couldn't quite find his way out of his feelings.

Osmo looked at the color of the blood on his mother's hood and her boots. The color of a wedding ring or the sun coming up in the morning. It smelled like one of those oranges with cloves stuck all over them that Papa put in the winter punch. It had always looked strangely sinister to Osmo, like a spiky mace disappointed to find itself floating in sweet juice instead of sunk in some unsuspecting head.

He knew what had blood that color. He'd read about them in a hundred books. He'd taken exams on them at St. Whylom's. But it wasn't possible. It *couldn't* be. It was just a metaphor.

"What have you *done*, Matilda?" said Mayor Lud, staring down at her from his stilts. "What have you done?"

"Osmo," their mother said softly, with a terrible crushing sadness in her voice. "I'm so, so sorry, my love."

"Sorry for what?" Osmo said sharply.

His father and sisters finally pushed their way through the throng and surrounded Tilly. She staggered to her feet. A few slim, quiet figures followed them. They had bows and quivers and guns slung over their shoulders and long leather trousers thick enough to stop a tusk. The other hunters of Littlebridge, and their faces were as serious as starlight.

"Oh, Tilly," said one with a long red braid. Tears trickled down her weathered face. "It can't be."

"Hey," Tilly Unknown said gently, urgently. She pulled Osmo's chin back toward her and tucked his hair behind his ear with so much affection Osmo began to be really and truly frightened. Her fingers left hot smears of gold blood on his cheeks.

"Listen to me. Whatever happens now is my fault. Not yours. Mine and mine forever. I love you more than water and salt. I'm sorry, darling. My baby. My first baby. My only son."

Osmo's mouth felt so dry. "What are you talking about? What is *happening?*"

"Hush, boy," Mads Unknown said roughly. The girls clustered round them, trying to find a way to touch one or both of their parents, as if everything would go back to festivals and fun if they could only get one finger on the people who had made them. "Don't make a scene," Osmo's father whispered, embarrassed. "Come now, stand up straight, no blubbering, strong jaw, strong words, strong fists. Be a man."

But his mother held up her hand, soaked in golden, shimmering blood. It had begun to dry into a hard crust around her fingernails.

"I killed one," she whispered.

The hunters heard. Osmo heard. Mads and her daughters heard. Mayor Lud and Ivy Aptrick heard. They all recoiled like one being.

"Mama, *why?*" little Sanna gasped.

Their mother looked older than Osmo had ever seen her. "I only wanted a little meat. I hadn't caught anything in weeks. We'd almost stewed through the parsnips and onions and it's hardly winter yet."

"No we haven't, there's plenty left!" Oona protested.

Tilly shook her head. "I am a good mother. And a good mother never lets her babies know how bad things have gotten."

"But there's none left," the red-braided huntress said. "There hasn't been a sighting in fifty years. Seventy. How far into the Forest did you go?"

But that Tilly would not answer. She only turned her face in shame. "I saw deer's velvet on the trees. A deer could feed us for months. Feed our neighbors, too. I thought it was a deer." She locked eyes with the other hunters, pleading for understanding. "It *was* just a deer . . . I pulled the trigger . . . it screamed . . . it screamed like my own heart breaking."

"No you didn't," Osmo insisted, his voice high and panicked. "No you *didn't*, because that's just a *story*, they're not *real*, they're just *not*. You won't even say the word! That's how unreal they are. They're a joke, a stupid fake joke, like leprechauns or dragons . . . or . . . rich girls and poor boys." His eyes slid over to Ivy in her finery. He couldn't help it. But he yanked them back. Some things were more important just now. "It's just a *metaphor*," he finished lamely. Panic closed off his words. "You can't kill something that's a metaphor."

"I told you not to say that," snapped Ivy Aptrick. She stood behind him, beside the Mayor's stilts, her cheeks red and cold and proud below her beautiful crown. "I told you not to say it or they would come."

His mother tried to smile. "Maybe you're right. Maybe you've always been right. You're such a clever thing."

A light flashed on in the distance, far beyond the borders of Littlebridge.

Then another, and another, and another.

Hundreds. A thousand. All in a long, winding line down from the bluffs. Like candles in the nighttime, flickering and orangey blue and warm.

"Maybe it is just a story," Tilly said hopefully as the ribbon of strange lights popped and glittered into life behind her, one by one by one like a trail of periods at the end of a sentence that doesn't know how to end. "Maybe it's just a story and everything will be fine forever and ever." Osmo couldn't breathe. The lights were almost here. His mother kissed his forehead. He supposed it was the last time she ever would. His heart felt too tight and too small. "That would be awfully nice," his mother sighed.

The lights arrived.

One burst out of the ground at the edge of the park with a popping sound like Harigold's firecracker, if it went off inside a soft woolen sock. Then they came shooting up so fast all Osmo could see was an orangey-blue blur until one cracked the frozen earth right in front of him.

They were mushrooms.

But not any sort of mushroom you or I have seen sliced up nicely and browned in a pan. Each button cap was shaped like a perfect, tiny house. Their roofs glowed green. Their walls pulsed purple. Their doors blossomed blue. Yellow light poured out of the cozy round windows on each side of the stalk. Hundreds and hundreds of them had sprouted in an instant, racing toward the park with a terrible purpose—until they reached the feet of Osmo Unknown, and there they stopped. Not one person moved, even in the sudden cold wind. Not one soul in Littlebridge breathed. The small mushroom-houses glittered and glowed in the soft blue heart of the evening like fairy lanterns.

The one that pushed itself up out of the hardened ground an inch from Osmo's toes shivered.

Its walls wriggled.

Its door trembled.

It began to *grow*.

Bigger and bigger and bigger it bloomed. The Unknowns stumbled backward to make room for it. Everyone else stumbled backward to make room for them. Osmo tripped over a tree root and fell hard to the ground. He watched the impossible house rise and swell until it was as tall as a rich man's table.

The blue door opened. It was well made and well oiled. It did not creak. And a curious creature stepped out into the torchlight. It stared up at them without fear.

It stood comfortably on its hind legs, about three feet tall, sipping a large mug of steaming tea. It had a badger's fur and a wombat's shape, but it sported a larger, slender snout with a bright blue nose at the end and a long skunky tail that fanned out very beautifully on the grass behind it like a quill pen. A thick, lovely sleek white stripe ran down the middle of its black head. It wore a dark velvet robe with big pink flowers on it, as though it'd been roused out of bed without warning. Its eyes were large and moist and clever, but shrouded by so much silky fur that it gave it a permanently cross expression.

The creature glanced up calmly over its mug of tea. It took everything in: Ivy in her crown, the village girls with their red blindfolds shoved up on their foreheads, Tilly Unknown drenched in golden blood. But its gaze lingered on Mayor Lud, still up on his idiot stilts, wearing his fat furry matted Quidnunk pants. He clutched the giant papier-mâché head of the Quidnunk costume to one hip. The creature stared at its antlers, decorated with ugly red paint and smushed flowers, its fake teeth ripped off in the excitement, its dead empty eyes staring at nothing.

It took a long, pointed sip of its tea.

"That's offensive," it said matter-of-factly.

A male voice. Young, or at least he sounded young. An odd, old-fashioned accent Osmo couldn't place.

"Ah. Er. Well. Sorry?" Mayor Lud called down awkwardly.

"And you lot of broken doorbells." The creature nodded to the gathered population of Littlebridge, all gawking at him like he was the whole circus come to town. "You're humans, I suppose?"

"Yes," Osmo said firmly.

He could be sure of that, at least. Maybe it was the only thing he could be sure of right now. The only thing he could say with a strong voice that didn't shake or crack. Yes, he, Osmo Unknown, was a human being, and so was everyone he'd ever known.

"Rubbish," said the creature in that gruff, rough, unkempt voice. "Rubbish and lies. Humans don't exist."

*Chapter Six*

# SUBCLAUSE FOUR A

"I am," Osmo protested. "I *am* a human. We all are!"

"You're not," huffed the stout little figure. His voice sounded rich and plummy, like a librarian on his third brandy.

The moon rose a little higher above the tree line. It let out a bit more light, though still barely enough to even be called stingy. The little fellow seemed very vain of his tail. He swept it up over one arm to keep leaves and grass from getting tangled up in his fur.

"Are you . . . are you a Quidnunk?" whispered Osmo's little sister Milja.

The creature gave her a look that would wither stone. "On the day you were born, did you fall out of your mother *directly* onto your head? And then hit it again every day since?"

"Don't talk to her like that," Osmo snapped, even though he knew he ought to stay quiet.

"Look here, Mister Boy," the badger-wombat-skunk thing snapped. "Be glad I am not a Quidnunk! Which I am just . . . just *obviously* not. I am a skadgebat, thank you very much for knowing anything about anything. The *glorious* and *terrifyingly handsome* personage you see before you is none other than Bonk the Cross, most wise and noble and unyielding representative of the Fourpenny Woods and all who dwell within it. You hear the *MOST* in there? You'd better. And getting back to the point I was making, I say you are *not* humans. *If* humans existed, I of all people would have seen one before now. It's just a myth some old plum-headed geezer made up to keep us Forest folk out of the Valley. Every culture has them, don't you know. Little wicked monsters in the shadows. Better stay at home where it's safe, my cubs!" He waved a black-and-white paw in the air and took another slurpy gulp of tea. "But no one listens to Bonk the Cross on account of how I am rude and they don't like me. *But* I enjoy being rude more than I enjoy company, so they can stuff it. You, young sir, are *clearly* part monkey and part otter, and while, yes, 'motters' are rare, they're hardly anything to throw a party about. Believe me! I am really and truly never ever wrong, ask anybody. If I *am* wrong, it's only that I'm wrong just *now*. Wait a bit, and you'll see I'm right in the end. And if I'm *still* wrong, you just haven't waited long enough, so give it another few years. All right then, motters! Let's all go home and forget any of it happened over some cake."

"Splendid idea!" Mayor Lud shouted eagerly, sensing a path toward a jolly outcome he could take credit for at the next election. He began to finally climb down from the stilts. Tilly's and Mads's shoulders relaxed a little. Osmo's mother's face eased uncertainly. His sisters even smiled.

"It talks?" little Klara said shyly.

"So what?" snapped Bonk. "*You* talk, but I'm keeping thoroughly calm about it. Even though you sound like a mad parrot. *Blah blah murr murr scarumphy zumphy Polly want a punch in the mouth.*"

"I never met a talking animal, that's all," Osmo's sister huffed defensively.

The clutch of hunters exchanged nervous glances and stared pointedly anywhere but at the talking animal in question.

"Except all these motters, you mean," the creature replied craftily. "Seeing as how we're *all* animals here. Right?"

"Right!" the Mayor shouted hurriedly. Like all politicians, he was much quicker on the uptake than he seemed.

Bonk's striped snout curled up into a sly grin. "Terribly lucky for you, being motters. Because you know, if you *were* humans, there would be *no* cake. No cake at *all*. There would be a treaty broken, broken this very *night*. And a murder. A murder dark and ugly. Yes, yes, for motters, cake. For humans, a treaty and a murder and all these mushrooms and me. And a punishment agreed to before the moon knew her own name. *Take one of ours and we take one of yours.* So if you *were* humans, ipso facto and all the rest of the Latins, I'd have to take one of you." Bonk turned his head casually toward Osmo, whose blood had long ago forgotten that it was meant to run warm in his veins. "I'd have to take somebody to pay for all that blood. Blood spilt in the Forest. Blood more precious than every human drop all poured together. The blood of our queen, Melancholy the Grand, who will never stomp or shiver or sing again."

"Nope!" yelled Harigold Blust. "Motters! That's us! I'm Mr. Motter and this here is Mrs. Motter and all the little motterlings."

The almost-badger nodded sagely. "Just as I thought," he snorfled. "Humans are just a metaphor, after all."

"For what?" Tilly Unknown said softly.

Bonk snapped his head round. His eyeteeth glittered in the mushroom light and the moonlight. His eyes searched the hunter's broken, frightened face with an awful knowing stare.

"For *I know what you did, Matilda Unknown, and your son belongs to the Woods.*"

A murmur of horror moved through the crowd like a wave through the sea. "Please," Tilly said. "We're only motters, like you said. We don't know anything about any treaties."

"Oh, eat a sack of mud, woman." Bonk opened the door of the mushroom-house again and disappeared inside. They could all hear loud rummaging, banging, clanging noises, then the sort-of wombat calling out: "I was only having a bit of fun. Of *course* humans exist. All the worst things really do insist on existing. Ugh! If it's something nice you'd like to have round for dinner? *That's* when you know it's a myth. Nawp. I just wanted to see if you would lie about the deep-down, vital-est, most essential facts of your whole idiot existence just to avoid paying the bill after you've feasted where you oughtn't. I thought maybe humans had changed. That you wouldn't lie to my face covered in my mistress's *actual* blood. But you did! You really did! Because you *are* nasty, naughty, sneaky, greedy, cunning, mossfaced swindlers, that's why. And now I don't have to feel the least bit bad about anything that happens to any of you because you did it all to yourself."

Bonk backed out of the house rump-first, his gorgeous tail

poking out of a hole in his flowered bathrobe. He pulled and struggled for a moment. He grumbled and groaned. Then the creature popped free with a soft sucking sound, hauling a large, beaten-tin wheelbarrow out of the mushroom. Bits of soil and twigs clung to the bowl of the thing.

The badger-wombat thing pointed one stubby finger straight at Osmo Unknown.

"On you go, Mister Boy. Get in the wheelbarrow."

Osmo's mother tightened her arms around him.

"Why me?" he whispered.

"Because you're her son." Bonk rolled his eyes. "She did the crime, she's got to be the one punished."

"But that's not it," Osmo interrupted. "She's not being punished, I am!"

The little creature patted his hand. Osmo snatched it away. "You only think that 'cause you haven't got babies," Bonk tutted.

"It was an accident!" Tilly Unknown whispered.

"I didn't ask," the animal snorted. "You hurt us. So I'm going to hurt you back. Fair is fair. I don't know why you're all making such a *fuss*. We're well within our rights here. Nobody pulled faces and had a whinge about it last time."

"It's been hundreds of years since 'last time'!" the red-haired hunter protested. "We thought they were extinct."

Bonk's blue nostrils flared with rage. "*Extinct*? I have never been so insulted in all my days. *You're* extinct. Your *mother's* extinct. Why don't you go extinctify *yourself*? Do you think a couple of hundred years is a long time? How precious. They're only *almost* extinct, thank you very much. You're all so empty-headed the rain must fall right through your skulls to water your beds. I'll have him, I'll have him now, and I don't want any more arguments or *you-know-what*." He jabbed his mug at the hunters three times, for the *you* and the *know* and the *what*.

"Well, *I* don't know," Lizbel Unknown said.

"The Quidnunx will come," Bonk said simply. "And while I am only here for one skinny boy-shaped bag of bones, they will come for *all* of you, and then you will miss your old Bonk very much, I think. That's the mathematics of the thing, my fine upstanding motters. Him or you. Let's get on with it."

Osmo stared at the wheelbarrow. Littlebridge stared at Osmo. He wasn't going to be able to stop the tears this time. It was going to happen. He couldn't stop it happening. And right in front of everyone.

"This is brutality," grumbled someone behind him. It sounded like Headmaster Gudgeon, and Osmo, for once, loved that voice to the depths of his soul. "Shameful. We won't do it."

"You haven't got a choice, ya dumbers! It's the treaty. You agreed. We've kept up our end and haven't bothered you. All you had to do was not bother us! But nooooo. That was too hard for a bunch of grey-brains like you."

"*I* never signed any treaty," another voice piped up, and that one was definitely Adelard Sloe, of the Stupendous Throwing Game. "Nobody else here did neither so far as I know. To my mind, that makes the whole idea fit to stuff the roof with, but not much else."

"Go on then," yelled Barnaby Lud suddenly. "Shove off with

that turnip! I'll put a bow on him for you!" Gasps went up all round. "What? I'm *glad* it's him! I know *I* won't miss him babbling on about nothing or trying to tag along with his betters. Will you? I think not. Besides, him or us, you heard the skunk. I pick us. I pick me."

"Be *quiet*," snapped Ivy Aptrick. "For once in your life."

"I should have been informed of any outstanding treaties when I took office," complained Mayor Lud. "This is perfectly absurd! What's next, have we got a trade agreement with griffins I don't know about? Why wasn't I told?"

"It's *carved* into a *rock* in foot-high letters, you lump of cold gristle," Bonk said with disgust.

The Mayor blushed. "Oh. That. Well, I shall have to consult our lawyers. Evaluate our exact obligations *pro corpeus bono*, that sort of thing."

"It's five lines long," said Bonk. "Of course, that's just the main points. The rest was all hammered out proper-like with nice long words and subclauses and addendums. Why are you looking at me like that? You were given a copy fair and square!"

Mayor Lud's face crumpled up in confusion.

"There was a fire," Headmaster Gudgeon offered helpfully. "In the Armory. A hundred and fifty years ago or so. A lot of things didn't make it. Very understandable."

"*There was a fire,*" Bonk repeated mockingly. "It's not the fire's fault! I'll tell you what this is about. You all *forgot*. You *wanted* to forget. Nothing bad happened to you for ages and ages so you just decided it never could and you let yourselves forget about us.

I bet you forgot so hard you don't even know why there's hardly any meat on your tables anymore, do you? It was the best trick the Quidnunx ever played and you lot just sit there and mope over your dinner plates and wonder why you can't remember how a sausage tastes, don't you? Oh, they'll tell you they had nothing to do with it, but you can't believe anything a Quidnunk says. They are just ever so good at loopholes, see? NEVER EAT ANYTHING THAT TALKS. So a couple of hundred years ago or so *they taught us all to talk*. And as soon as we could tell each other what's what and who's garbage, we got well away from the border between the woods and the village. Except the rabbits, who are too quick for smarts to catch, and the deer, thought it was a fad and soon enough everyone would get back to keeping their thoughts to themselves. They fixed you good and didn't even sprain the treaty." The striped fellow shook his head in dumbfounded disbelief. "You *forgot*. Even your hunters! Just figured nothing spicier than a deer was coming out to play, did you? For five hundred years?" Tilly Unknown and the other hunters looked as though someone had hit them all on the head with invisible axes. "Well, history says *right back atcha* and don't let the fossil record hit you in the rump on your way out. You lot are thick as a brick of *butter*. You cut down our trees and shot our babies and pulled up our very stones. And then you *forgot* because it feels *good* to do whatever you want and it feels *bad* to be forced to think about anyone but yourselves. Well, now *we* get to feel good."

Bonk the Cross sighed and disappeared into his mushroom-house again. He rummaged again. He banged about again. He knocked something over that sounded very much bigger than a mushroom again. Then, he stomped out the blue round door with a piece of parchment in his paw. Bonk threw it overhand at Mayor Lud's chest. The great man fumbled in his waistcoat for his reading glasses. A judge and a brace of lawyers pushed their way up front. They tugged on their wigs and reading glasses and all four of them got down to their business.

"Please," Osmo whispered. "Please don't eat me."

"*Eat* you?" Bonk the Cross put one paw on his chest. "Five lines and that's too complicated for you broken monkeys." Bonk reached out and rapped his knuckles against Osmo's head. *Never Eat Anything That Talks*, remember? No, no, we've got something *much* worse than eating planned for you."

"Leave us alone," Mads Unknown growled. "He's just a boy."

*Thanks, Dad*, thought Osmo. *I'm sure the magic badger will listen to that. And anyway, I thought I was supposed to be a man?*

"No, no," the judge interrupted, holding up one gnarled finger. A patch of blond hair stuck out under his long white curly wig. "He's right. Nothing about eating in here."

Mayor Lud cleared his throat and read out loud from the treaty. "Subclause Four A, under *Take One of Us and We'll Take One of You*:

"*Hear Ye, Hear Ye, Human Beings of Littlebridge, You Gang of Nitwits. Now Listen As Well As You Can With Your Squiggly Crusty Snail Ears Because We Are Only Going to Say This Once. Since You Cannot Stop Killing Us and We Cannot Stop Killing You for Half a Second, Something Must Be Done and This Is What It Is Going to Be. Whenever One of You Kills One of Us from Now Until We Say So, You Will Pay a Price. Should a Human Murder One of Us, the Hunter Who Fells the Quidnunk Shall Provide Their Firstborn Child to Wed the Quidnunk Ghost and Go with Them to the Land of the Dead and Carry Their Ghost Bags and Other Useful Things Like That. And Also They Will Not Whine or Be a Brat About It. And Also We Will Expect NICE Wedding Gifts and Pretty Clothes and All That, Don't Cheap Out on Us. We Will Know Who Did It. You Cannot Lie to Us Because You Are Not Good at It But We Are Excellent at It. This Next Part Is Not a Lie, Though. We Promise It Will Be a Real Wedding. We Are Not Just Going to Throw Them Off a Cliff or Anything. If We Kill One of You, We Will Send a Quidnunk for Your Ghost, Too, Don't Worry. But That Probably Won't Happen Because We Don't Want to Go Anywhere Near Your Lot Ever Again. You Are Ugly and When You Laugh It Sounds Like Pigs Snorfling. Just Do What We Say or We Will Come Back and Eat You All Up and We Won't Be Sorry Because You Taste Good and You Will Deserve It, for Crying Out Loud. We Are Done Talking."*

A great silence descended over the First Frost Festival.

"It sounds more formal in Quidnunx," mumbled Bonk the Cross.

"All seems to be in order," sighed the judge, and the lawyers agreed. But they would not look Osmo in the eye.

"Congratulations, son." The Mayor stuck out his hand for Osmo to shake, as if it were an honor. As if he ought to be happy about it. "You're getting married!"

*Chapter Seven*

# THE MALE OF THE SPECIES

"In the sack, thanks much, don't be stingy, sir, this is a happy occasion."

Bonk, the badger-skunk-wombat with the lovely tail, waddled through the crowd with an open bag, collecting wedding gifts. No one quite knew what to do or what to give. In went earrings, pumpkin rinds, wooden dolls, water flasks, hats. The Mayor's wife put in her daughter's red blindfold. "Madam, you can do better than that. I may not be able to eat you by law, but I can bite you, by gum."

Mrs. Lud looked furious. She took off her ruby ring and tossed it in the bag.

"Clothes, too, folks!" Bonk hollered. "We are assembling a *trousseau* here. Don't want your lad to be embarrassed in front of the Forest! Coats, waistcoats, or petticoats, belts, bodices, or burlap sacks, I don't care, I don't follow fashion."

Bonk and his sack arrived in front of Ivy Aptrick, the newest Frostfrau. He glanced up at the glittering frost crown.

"No," whispered Ivy. "It's mine."

"Brat," Bonk whispered back.

He gave a little jump and yanked it off her head. Ivy tried to snatch it back before he could run off with her prize, but he didn't let go. They struggled back and forth, squashing the snowdrops and lingonberries in their fists. She grunted roughly. So did he, like two young deer cracking skulls for dominance. Finally, Bonk kicked her in the shin and snatched the crown away. "No wonder we needed a treaty just to survive humans living next door. You're all just the worst, even your kits."

"I don't want to get married, I'm *thirteen*," Osmo hissed at his mother.

"I'm sorry," she said, and it seemed she was entirely broken, because she wouldn't say anything else.

"Dad, please!" he pled. But his father turned his face away.

Bonk circled back around to Osmo Unknown and his family. He pulled a measuring tape out of his bathrobe pocket and sized Osmo up. Then, the little black-and-white beast got to work slicing up the satin and fur and silk and linen of Littlebridge into a bridegroom's suit. His paws moved unbelievably fast. He stitched and cut and hemmed and bit off the ends of threads in his neat sharp teeth.

Osmo watched as though it were happening to another boy. He couldn't seem to make himself move, even though he wanted to. He wanted to so badly. *Just stop*, he thought while a talking skunk-wombat sewed Helka Cutt's fur collar onto a wide swath sliced out of Freja Highberry's pale green skirt. Just *stop* and none of this had to happen. It was all so awful and stupid and miserable. It wasn't *fair*. He hadn't *done* anything. Just *stop* wrapping his mother's leather belt around his forearm. Just *stop* measuring his head. Just *stop* cutting Ada Sloe's festival dress into strips long and wide enough for a boy's suit of clothes. Just *stop* and everything could go back to the way it had always been. The way it had been only an hour ago.

But it didn't stop. Not for a minute.

"Maybe it'll be all right," Oona said hopefully. She tugged on the hem of his patchwork sleeve. "People get married every day."

"Not to a *ghost*," Osmo exploded. "Not to a dead monster!" He clenched his fists at his sides. "Wait, do I have to be dead to marry a ghost?"

Bonk grinned, his silky snout rising, his whiskers bristling. "Would that be a problem for you?" he said seriously.

"YES!" Osmo yelled. But the creature just shrugged and kept on with his work.

"All right, all right, if you're going to be so *picky*."

Osmo shook his head against it all, as if he could somehow make the world turn backward, make his mother come home dry and clean and happy, force tomorrow to be just another day. He could go to school. He could interrupt in class. He could play another game of doublechess with Mrs. Brownbread, and maybe even win this time. But he couldn't. Not ever again. He just wanted to be in his own bed, with his own candle to read by, and his own life ahead of him. Familiar, boring Littlebridge, where he knew every street and tree and bird and leaf. Dapplegrim Square and Bodeworde's Armory and Cammamyld Heights and St. Whylom's School for Excellent Young People. He took back everything he'd ever said about it. Littlebridge was beautiful. Littlebridge was perfect. If he could just go back and climb into his bed, he'd never complain again.

*But it won't be your bed anymore*, a little voice inside told him. *It won't be your life, either. Mama and Papa will give your room to Klara and Lizbel. They'll have another son as soon as they can. Before the harvest comes in everyone will have forgotten about you. And in two hundred years, kids will sit in that same classroom and read about how poor doomed Osmo Unknown married a monster and probably got eaten just like Katja Kvass.*

*I wonder where they'll put your fountain?*

But another voice spoke a deeper truth: *Isn't this what you wanted? Isn't this the Else you dreamed of?*

No. Not like this. Not this way.

It was his wedding day. Osmo Unknown had never been lonelier in his life.

Bonk the Cross stood up on his tiptoes and placed the Frostfrau's crown on Osmo's head. It was done. Osmo turned around numbly. It was the most astonishing suit of clothes he could imagine. He sparkled and shone like a wild thing. Each patch was a person he'd known, who had been kind or cruel, stingy or generous, miserable or content. Their waistcoats or sleeves or shoelaces or skirts. The tails of his bridegroom's coat flowed behind him like two patchwork veils. Osmo reached up hesitantly. His fingers brushed the white flowers and silver branches of the frost crown.

Osmo Unknown felt a bit proud, despite himself. The only boy to ever wear it. Ever, in all of history. *Him.*

He looked beautiful. He knew he did, even though he dreaded *why* he did.

"Is all that really necessary?" his father complained. "It's hardly fitting for a man. All those flowers and shiny bits."

"*That's* what you're worried about right now?" snorted a red-braided huntress, one of the Grumm girls, Osmo thought.

Bonk glared flatly at him. "I'm sure I don't know what you're talking about, you *massive* stale pie. The males of every species have the prettiest colors and the most attractive plumage." Bonk gestured at Mads Unknown's clothes, as plain and black and undecorated as those of most Littlebridge men. "It's not *my* fault you decided to defy nature."

"Now," Bonk went on as Osmo's family stood by helplessly. "Let's see that satchel. You really ought to only take what's absolutely necessary for survival." He peered into Osmo's bag. "Jug of something called Unknown's Goodest Stout . . . a doublechess board . . . whittling knife . . . a golden ball . . . perfect! You've even got a bouquet for your bride. How thoughtful of you."

At the bottom of his bag, the lilies Osmo had picked for Ivy lay squashed and sad, still bound by Oona's black ribbon.

"Ready then?"

"No," said Osmo loudly. "No, I'm not, and I don't want to be, and I never will be."

"Too bad." Bonk shrugged. "Say your goodbyes and then it's the wheelbarrow for you."

"You can't make me marry someone against my will," Osmo protested feebly.

"Well, I can," Bonk laughed. "The usual rules don't apply when it comes to the dead. And revenge. Besides, I suspect a lot of you ladies weren't too closely consulted on who you got hitched to, hm? Missus This? Missus That? Missus The Other Thing? That's what I thought. Always the way with your more savage predators. You won't mind if I don't take you too seriously, then, morally speaking?"

Tears slipped silently down Tilly's face. All she could say was *I'm sorry* over and over again.

"Stand up straight," Osmo's father said. His voice sounded so hollow, so defeated. But he was trying. He brushed some invisible dust from his son's spectacular coat. "Keep your knife sharp and your eyes sharper. Be a man. Come back to us if you can."

Osmo just stared at him. Was that really all his own father had to say to him? Even now?

"Yes, Dad," he whispered. "I'll try."

Numbly, Osmo kissed the top of his mother's head. What else could he do?

*Them or me. Them or me.*

*I pick me.*

*But they pick themselves. They want to live. Everyone wants to live.*

*I want to live, too.*

Osmo kissed his father and his sisters. He let the miller and the blacksmith and the dovekeeper hug him, as if that made it all better. As if that meant they weren't offering him up as a sacrifice to the Forest gods they hadn't even known were real a day ago. And he let Mrs. Brownbread press her wrinkled forehead to his and whisper:

"Remember your shadow turn."

That didn't make any kind of sense. But she was old, so Osmo didn't argue.

"You're my big brother," his sister Oona said quietly when all the hugging and apologizing was done. "You'll always be my big brother. You'll always get to go out further in the garden than me, and stay out longer into twilight, and venture deeper into the woods. So really, if you think about it, something like this was always bound to happen. It's what comes of being born first. Keep the ribbon." She squeezed him tight.

Osmo turned back to Bonk the Cross.

"Wheel. Barrow." Bonk said, and pointed with his stubby paw. "I don't know why you're dillydallying. This is a garbage place full of garbage people. I wouldn't want to stay a minute."

Osmo sucked in his last gulp of Littlebridge air and, just as he always had, quietly did as he was told. Then, a black-and-white beast in a bathrobe shoved him barrow-first into a mushroom, and the world he knew vanished all around him like it had never been.

All of Littlebridge watched without daring to breathe.

One by one, the little trail of glowing mushrooms blinked out and shriveled back into the earth, darkening back in the direction it had come, all the way to the Forest, and then further still.

## Chapter Eight

# AGATHA UNDERGROUND

"Don't touch that," Bonk the Cross scolded.

The skadgebat swatted at Osmo's hand.

Osmo Unknown couldn't budge. He didn't even know what he was touching that he wasn't meant to be touching. The little bright mushroom-house had shrunk all around him. But it hadn't shrunk him. His liver was squished up against his stomach. His heart was shoved back against his spine. His lungs felt like they were trying to wriggle up into his throat. The roof pressed down on his head as he curled over onto himself in the wheelbarrow, trying not to put his feet anywhere fragile. Some of the white twigs and flowers from the frost crown had already broken off and fallen all over the fungus-y floor.

But one thing was certain. They were moving. They were moving at incredible speed, positively hurtling through . . . something . . . toward . . . somewhere. The twigs on the floor vibrated as they barreled on.

"I said don't touch that!" Bonk yelped, and yanked his teapot out from under Osmo's left hand a moment before it decided to give up and let itself be crushed.

"Sorry!" Osmo yelped back. "It's not very roomy in here, you know."

Bonk puffed up his ruff under his bathrobe. "*You're* not very roomy," he retorted.

"That doesn't make sense," said Osmo. "I'm just telling you how it is for me."

"Your *FACE* isn't very roomy!" cried the deeply offended skadgebat. "How dare you say such a nasty, mean thing about Agatha! After all she's doing for you!"

"Who's Agatha?"

"The MUSHROOM, you *bucket!*" Bonk was nearly in tears.

"Calm down! I'm the one marrying a ghost, you know. If anyone should be yelling, it's me. And this isn't a mushroom, what do you take me for? Mushrooms don't have couches inside them!"

"Ooh, look who knows all the things about mushrooms when he's never been inside one before!"

"Well, I know what they are and what they're not!"

"And what are they for, pray tell, Little Lord Scholarly-Pants?"

"Food, obviously!"

Bonk the Cross gaped at him in sheer horror. "*Agatha* is my *friend* and *you* are a *potato*," he snarled. "And not a roasted one, either. You don't have any garlic or butter or sour cream on you *at all*. You are *dry*, Mister Boy. YOU ARE DRY AND UNSALTED."

"Turnip," Osmo mumbled miserably.

"What?"

"I'm not a potato, I'm a turnip. That's what the boys back home say. And the girls. Mostly everyone, unless they're related to me. So, yeah. Turnip." He sniffed. "Get it right at least."

Bonk the Cross finally, at long last, looked a little sorry for him. "Well," he grumbled. "I like a good turnip. Once in a while."

Osmo didn't know what to say then. Bonk studied his tea. There wasn't even anything to look at outside the windows. Because there weren't any windows. Agatha had markings on her walls that sort of looked like windows here and there, but it was all just fungus in the end. The warm golden light came from a lantern in the middle of the room. It was quite pretty: a misshapen ball made of twisted copper and glass. But inside, instead of a candle, there was only a chunk of wet, seedy pumpkin, glowing like a lump of iron on a blacksmith's bench. It was slowly melting waxily into its own orange puddle of lovely-smelling squash.

"Is this magic?" Osmo finally asked, desperate to break the silence.

"Huh?" Bonk hiccuped, then smoothed his fur like a tie. "No, this is a mushroom, where's your head?"

"No, I mean, the shrinking into the ground and the moving by itself and the melting pumpkin and . . . well, just everything."

"Is a horse and a cart magic?" The creature shrugged. "No, it's just how you get from place to place. Now, a butterfly would think it sorcery most foul! But that's just because a butterfly is *breathtakingly* stupid. Anyone who keeps their brain tidy knows what's what. The question is: Are you a tidybrain or a butterfly? I have *my* theory. Nawp. No such thing as magic. It's all just butterflies and carriages."

"I knew it!" Osmo coughed. He was far too squashed for triumphant yelling. "I knew there was no such thing as magic!"

"Well, except for the Thing," Bonk allowed.

"What thing?"

"That's the point. No one knows. When the Forest and the Valley fell in love—"

"The who?" Osmo shut his eyes. It couldn't *all* be true, it just couldn't.

"The Forest and the Valley. They fell in love. And made this world. Mostly using mushrooms. Which they didn't waste on mere *food*. You can train a mushroom to do nearly anything, so long as it likes you. They're better than dogs by half, since they don't piddle on the rug. This is how we get all the things that make life worth wasting. Humans have machines; we have mushrooms. My Agatha used to do public outreach, but the Forest rehabilitated her and now the old girl does public transportation."

"Transportation?" Osmo repeated. Agatha shuddered briefly, then soldiered on. Fine black soil sifted down through the ceiling. "Mr. Bonk, are we *underground*?"

A grinding, shuddering sound vibrated through the mushroom-house. Then a heavy thunk, a sliding and a scraping, and nearly a full stop. In another moment, they were zooming along again, as smoothly as you please. Bonk didn't even seem to notice.

"You really are determined to be the lump in my gravy, aren't you? Where else would we be? I thought you knew about mushrooms. The toadstool bit you can see in the sunshine is only the flower of the thing. Mushrooms go on for miles and miles underground. So Agatha just slings us along her root system and a bobcat's your emotionally distant uncle. Some people think the whole world is a mushroom. But I think they are idiots." Bonk the Cross scratched his chops. "Anyhow, Agatha's been around since the dawn of, well, dawns. I'm surprised you don't know all this, it's basic history. What do they teach you in school in Littlebridge? Strict lesson plan of murder and mayhem, I suppose? Wait, what was I talking about?"

"The Thing," Osmo said unhappily.

"RIGHT YOU ARE. So. After all the mushrooms, the Forest and the Valley got to squabbling, and their first argument was about magic. In those days, they were still in a mood to compromise occasionally, so they made one magical object and let it kick around, so long as it was hidden away very well and minded its business. And no making it glitter or glow or get up and do a dance, either, that would be cheating. So somewhere, there's the Thing, and it's magic. But it doesn't matter because it could be my toenail clippers for all anyone can tell, so we all just have to live life as though there's no such thing as magic. Which is basically the same as there not being any such thing. And now I need another cup of tea and my head hurts. Talking to you is hard work."

Bonk put the kettle on a stove with a lacy flowering mushroom hob blooming on top of it. The fungus pulsed blue as it heated up and shook back and forth as Agatha rattled on toward her destination. "By the way, it is not my toenail clippers. If you were wondering."

"I don't believe you," Osmo Unknown said quietly.

He was trying very hard to hold on to who he was just then, and who he was hadn't ever believed *The Ballad of the Forest and the Valley* for one moment that two landmasses could fall in love and make things together like people could, even though he'd had to take a quiz on it at St. Whylom's as though he did believe it. Fine, Quidnunx existed. He could accept that, barely. Lots of weird animals existed. But magic?

"So?" said Bonk, tapping his paw against the floor, impatient for tea. "Pretty soon I won't ever have to know you anymore. So you can not believe in gravity or grapes or my big beautiful tail for all the difference it makes to me."

"You're very rude."

"I told you I was! It's the best thing about me. Rude is polite for superior people."

"Okay," Osmo answered unhappily. "But I'm . . . I'm quite afraid at the moment. I don't know what's going to happen to me and it might be something horrible. There's really just an *excellent* chance it's something horrible. I miss my mother and my back hurts and I want to go home *a lot* but I can't, so could you *not* be rude? Just for a little while?"

The shuddering and the grinding and the scraping and the stopping battered the poor little mushroom again. Again, Bonk paid it no mind.

Bonk the Cross's black-and-white face softened ever so slightly. He patted Osmo's giant knee with his paw. "Aw," he said comfortingly. "Don't think so, ya great big whinge factory. I know it's hard to get through your head when you've got a kneecap and three nose hairs where your brain should be, but I hate you, and your people, and especially your mother. She killed our queen and if she hadn't I'd be at home in my burrow asleep, but instead I have to . . . er. Get you to the church on time. So to speak. We were all just fine before you humans insisted on up and *existing*, and we'd all be quite chuffed if you . . . you know . . . didn't do that anymore. So buck up, be a lot nicer to my mushroom, and shut it."

Osmo considered this for a moment. "If I'm to marry the ghost of your queen . . . does that mean I'm going to be your king?"

"SHUT. IT," Bonk roared. He aggressively shoved a mug of tea into Osmo's hands. "PUT TEA IN FACE-HOLE. CLOSE FACE-HOLE. REPEAT UNTIL YOU HAVE FULLY SHUTTED IT."

"All right, all right."

Agatha slammed into whatever it was for a third time. Osmo couldn't take it anymore. "What IS that?" he cried.

"What?" A sickly sound of rock dragging across soft mushroom flesh filled the room. "That? Oh, don't pay any attention to that. Just a big blue stone sticking itself where it don't belong. The Valley doesn't like us coming to visit its *pwecious viwwage*," the skunky badger whined mockingly. "Not with these grubby paws, thanks much! So it tries to get in the way sometimes. But it's a Valley, and it doesn't have a frontal lobe, so you shouldn't do what it wants. I'll tell you the great cosmic truth of the universe, the one constant through all of time and space: the Valley is a big meanie and it smells."

"What about the Forest?"

Bonk grunted. "Same."

Osmo sipped from the tiny mug. The tea was dark and way too sweet.

"Can you at least tell me if I'm going to die *tonight*? How long do I have before I have to . . . meet her?"

"Ugh, who *cares*?" Bonk whined.

"Well, *I* do!" Osmo gritted his teeth. This wasn't going very seriously at all. He didn't know what he'd expected after all those goodbyes, but he had certainly expected it to be serious. "Why are you doing this? Why are you acting like this is a joke? It's life and death to me! *My* life and death!"

Bonk the Cross raised his black eyes to the rafters, as if to beg heaven for mercy. "Because it *is* a joke, Mister Boy. Death is a joke. Life is the setup. It's the same punch line every time, but the world laughs all the same. I'm sorry you never learned that in your comfortable little village with your comfortable little people. Littlebridge for Little Minds. That's quite good, you know. You can have it for free. I insist. But cheer up! You're in the Forest now, and we have a *wicked* sense of humor." The skadgebat drained his tea with a long slurp and a short gasp. "Little motter, the truth is I don't know. This is beyond my burrow. It is a bargain forged in the time when the Forest walked and the Valley sang. My best advice is: shut it. My most sincere warning is: shut it. The greatest tool at your disposal is to immediately shut it. Your every meal must consist of the finest Shutitshire Cheese and nothing else. Drink only from the bottle marked: Ye Olde Shut It. The motto of your house should be: It Shall Most Verily Be Shut. Do you understand?"

"Yes," mumbled Osmo, barely able to breathe in the cramped

house. He was starting to panic. If he didn't move his legs soon, he wouldn't be able to stop himself. He'd kick a hole through the roof. He needed to get out. He needed to run away. He needed to move his legs and breathe a real lungful of real air.

"Do you?" Bonk wedged himself up onto the couch and wrapped his paws round the poles of the wheelbarrow. "Because we're here. So hold on to your very fetching hat and—"

"I know," groaned Osmo as the mushroom grew around him and he felt the unmistakable sensation of rising, rising out of the dirt and the earth and into the sky again. Blood rushed back where it was meant to be and air flowed in and out again, as it much preferred to do. "Shut it."

The little mushroom-house began to shrivel up and die away into dust all around them. Flakes of fungus flicked off and floated away into the evening breeze like ashes. The floor beneath them withered into the wet, dark, leafy ground.

The mushroom finished blowing away. It drifted far beyond this story and everyone in it, up over the tops of the red-leafed woods and the chimneys of Littlebridge and away beyond the last golden clouds you see before the dark settles in for supper.

And when it had gone, Osmo Unknown was left sitting in a wheelbarrow at the foot of a great grassy hill, staring out at all the hundreds of guests come to see his wedding.

None of them were human.

But they weren't any kinds of animals Osmo had ever seen before, either. It was as though someone had filled a cauldron with beasts, mixed them all together with a broken spoon, and tipped the whole thing out again. Like Bonk, who wasn't *exactly* a badger *or* a wombat *or* a skunk, these creatures weren't *exactly* deer or tigers or foxes or fish or bears or serpents, either.

They all stared back at him. Fury and grief burned in their eyes, on the tips of their fangs and their horns and their tufts, all down the blades of their claws and lengths of their tails and the slants of their eyes and the tenseness of their limbs. Fury and grief and hate, as bright and endless as the vast, sparkling city behind them.

And then the great grassy hill moved

*Chapter Nine*

# THIS CHAPTER IS SILVER

The great grassy hill moved.

It trembled.

It rocked from side to side.

It puffed its slopes like a bird's feathers. A great sound like drumbeats thumped from somewhere deep inside it.

Osmo scrambled backward in the wheelbarrow to get away from it. Whatever *it* was. Bonk the Cross watched with amused whiskers as the tin barrow wobbled, tilted, and tipped over. Osmo spilled out onto the ground in his splendid wedding coat. He stared up into the quaking hill and the heavy evening sky.

Another sound crept out from between the blades of dry October grass. A terrible sound, like rocks cracking open and guitar strings snapping.

The hill was crying.

Two huge catlike golden hot-green eyes opened in the soft brown moss near the summit.

All the assembled strange and wild and striped and scaled and spotted creatures of the Forest knelt at once. They fell to their knees, or whatever they had that was most *like* a knee, and bowed their heads.

The hill roared.

It shook itself all over like the biggest dog anyone could ever dream about. Wildflowers and grass seeds and twigs and red autumn leaves and pale pearly dandelion fluff exploded off its slopes and floated down to the Forest floor. The hill kept shaking from top to bottom. Chunks of earth and blue stone and cattails and nests and even little baby apple trees flew into the air. The wedding party valiantly allowed it all to tumble down on top of them without a word of complaint, although Osmo felt certain he heard several grunts, coughs, yelps, and mumbled swears. Roots cracked, birds and rabbits bolted. And where they had been roosting or burrowing or growing in peace, patches of glossy, long, thick fur in many beastly colors showed through the thirsty grass.

Finally, the great, grassy hill was gone. In its place was a much smaller (though still quite giant) rounded mound of fur with golden hot-green eyes and small nubby velvet antlers. Braids ran through the fur here and there, some thick as ship's rope, some thin as sewing thread. It stood about as tall as two big plough horses stacked up on top of each other. And even though its pelt still had quite a bit of cold dirt and rotten leaves and snails and such tangled up in it, the thing in front of him smelled rich and warm, like baking bread.

Osmo Unknown didn't know what was looming over him, exactly.

But it was, most certainly, without a doubt, something *Else*.

I suspect *you* will have guessed it by now, though. You've got just that sort of clever mind. You knew you'd come to something important because I took *such* a lot of time to tell you all about what it looked like and smelled like and sounded like.

That ten-foot-tall upside-down umbrella of fur and horn and beautiful feline eyes and at least one terrified squirrel still clinging to her head opened her mouth. She spoke to Osmo and Osmo alone.

"This sentence is silver," the Quidnunk rumbled.

Her voice bonged like a bell, scraped like a door across a gravelly street, and hummed like the wind through holes in old trees.

"O . . . okay," Osmo answered haltingly, because it was really always best to agree with people very much bigger than you are, even if—no, *especially* if what they say is pure crazy sleeptalking rubbish. Sentences couldn't be silver. But you couldn't argue with a hill.

Bonk the Cross jabbed him hard in the neck with his paw. Osmo spluttered and coughed. "Rude! Illiterate! It's part of their language, you sock. They aren't like us." Bonk looked dreamily up at the furry hill with eyes. "*Her* brain is a carnivorous crystal ocean, whereas *yours* is a day-old mincemeat pie. Their thoughts run too wild and fierce for verbs and nouns and rules about spelling. To them, words have colors. Music has a taste. Numbers have feelings. They try to help us poor idiots out by telling us what to think of when they talk, so we don't miss anything." The skadgebat grabbed Osmo by the shoulders and shook him excitedly. "A sentence without decoration can only mean what it actually *says*. Theirs mean . . . *more*. Like how a painting means more than just what it's a painting *of*, yeah? Show some respect, Mister Boy." Osmo blinked, confused. Bonk ground his teeth. "Come on, pie-brain, you can do it. A silver sentence is heavy, valuable, pure, royal. Try to feel it, all cold and pale and bright and gorgeous and not caring at all about you because it's a rare metal and you're a common squishy."

"Who's *they*?" Osmo whispered hoarsely, rubbing his throat.

"This *sentence* is *silver*," the gargantuan beast repeated pointedly. "I am Mumpsimus the Cloud-Eater, of the Vast, Hungry, and Undestructable Quidnunx."

Quidnunx.

The final weight and truth and reality of it all at last settled down right on top of Osmo Unknown, very like a sack of silver. He buried his face in his hands.

You mustn't blame Osmo for not recognizing the hill or think him stupid. He was doing his best. You and I have the advantage of only reading about the smell of the Quidnunx and the alien way their thoughts are shaped. We don't have to be scared out of our skulls of a really real and actual one showing us her teeth. And we can't shame him *too* much for being slow on the uptake. This beast looked no more like the thing painted on Adelard Sloe's Stupendous Throwing Game or Mayor Lud in his furry costume pants than a leather coat looks like a cow.

Now, at this point and at last, I shall have to stop and spend some time telling you just what a Quidnunk *is*, for I am almost certain you have never seen one. If you have, you can skip ahead of this bit to the part that begins *this sentence is hairy* . . . and I shan't be at all angry. But I must attend to readers less worldly and experienced than you.

Quidnunx are part tufted owl, part woolly mammoth, part kangaroo, part orangutan, part polar bear, part moose, and part coconut. They can be quieter than foxes and louder than marching bands. They make nests like magpies, nests of every shiny thing they can snatch. They see in the shadows better than any cat.

Quidnunx have fur like a patchwork quilt. Tufts and tails and puffs and pelts and fuzz and fleece! Every color fur comes in and a few it never has. Streaks of tabby cat, stripes of panther, squares of snow tiger, swirls of lion and rabbit and weasel and lynx, brushy hedgehog, velvet wolf, woolly ram, spotted deer. Brown, black, grey, rust, gold, sable, even a braid or two of green and blue, a great, round motley autumn scruff.

But though they are big they are *sneaky*. If you came upon one hunting in the wood, you might walk right by, especially if the sun was out and bold. A quiet Quidnunk is almost invisible. Perhaps a wild peony might even dare to grow out of its head. Quidnunx stay still for a long time when they are thinking, or hunting, which are much the same thing to them.

A Quidnunk's teeth are terrifically long and tusky and sharp, the sort you see on skeletons in museums. Quidnunx stand up only slowly. The one staring down Osmo Unknown began to do just that. She wasn't trying to be dramatic. She had a lot of body to unfold. First her arms opened up. Thick, shaggy bear-lion arms tipped with long midnight-blue claws. (In a pinch, you can always tell Quidnunx apart by their claws.) Then she stretched her neck up and peered out from her soft chest. She had a head stuck a third of the way between a battle-hardened lion, a wise owl, and an ancient huge sea tortoise.

Mumpsimus the Cloud-Eater blinked her enormous eyes in her jack-o'-lantern face. Tall, punky tufts of hair like a horned owl twitched in the wind, checking for snacks and spies. Some Quidnunx have stubby antlers and horns, some have bony nubbles like crowns of river rocks, some have wild stripes of electric blue or magenta. But *all* have tufts.

Then, the Quidnunk picked up her punch-bowl body in her arms, lifting her belly up so her feet could get free. Up she went on one furry-hippopotamus foot and then the other, stretching out her springy knees. She shook down her belly like a girl wiggling into a dress. She made the sound that Quidnunx make, which is called the Thumpus. This was the strange whipcrack of a drumbeat Osmo had heard when he thought the hill was a hill and everything still made sense.

*Whack-whong, whack-whong, whong-wack.*

Quidnunx can roar, too, and howl, and even carry a tune, but if you are within roaring range of a Quidnunk, you have other worries. And just then, Osmo had *all* the worries.

"This sentence is hairy," the Quidnunk growled.

Osmo tried to think of words having hair. He saw the shapes of the letters in his mind, bristling like a dog's ruff when he feels threatened. Spiky, musky, hostile.

*Oh.*

Mumpsimus towered over him. She was just so *big*.

"You are small and pasty like a turnip," the Quidnunk said.

"Ah," Bonk interrupted. "He don't like to be called that." A few of the still patiently kneeling Forest creatures glared at him from under their various brows. "What? I'm just *saying*. You gnashgobs always get on my tail for nothing but *telling the muddy truth*. Bonk the Cross and the truth are like THIS!" he yelled, twisting two stubby striped fingers together. "This little toenail-biter gets all sad round the edges if you make any kind of reference to root vegetables, it's very pathetic to watch."

"*I* do not like having my mother murdered," the Quidnunk hissed. "We all have our trials. My words have been red. Redder than red. The *reddest*."

Bonk shut his snout with a neat *snap* of his little teeth. "That's fair," he said, holding up both paws. "Very fair, very fair. Fair as frog soup."

"Lightning falls through my words!" Mumpsimus bellowed. "I will not accept you as my father! You're no bigger than an elephawn!" The Quidnunk grinned horribly. Her mouth was wide and her tongue was blue. "*This* sentence is the color of teeth. I am going to eat you instead."

Osmo Unknown knew it was his turn to speak. Speak for his people. Speak for his mother's sins. Speak for his life and his fate. His heart beat in his fingertips and his throat felt dry as pages and his stomach rumbled sick and sour and empty. Everyone expected him to speak. He could feel their expectation crackling in the air around him. He expected *himself* to speak.

But Osmo couldn't do it. He couldn't stand tall and brave and deliver noble words befitting the occasion. He just couldn't get his head around it. Some part of him had held out hope that just because Bonk and Agatha had . . . *happened* to him didn't mean Quidnunx, *Quidnunx* of all the things in his dumb, absurd, boring life, could actually *exist*.

Exist, but never once turn up to rescue him from the Little Minds of Littlebridge.

So when Osmo finally did open his mouth, all that came out was a mess.

"You're real," he blurted. "You're actually *real*. And *alive*. And enormous. And . . . wait, what's an elephawn?"

A murmur went through the crowd.

Osmo had honestly entirely forgotten about the audience kneeling behind him. Bonk started to answer, but Osmo's brain had already lapped itself. "Hold on, sorry. Go back. What's so fair about frog soup?"

"What?"

"Frog soup. You said 'fair as frog soup.' I don't understand. How is soup fair?"

The badger-wombat-skunkish creature fidgeted. "Well, if it's ladled out proportionally in everyone's bowl, you know . . ."

"Well, then you should say that. *Fair as frog soup equally ladled out to everyone in an equal-sized bowl.*"

"DON'T TELL ME HOW TO TALK," Bonk roared. "Is that *really* the most important thing you could possibly say right now, Mister Overboilt Squash, Esquire?"

"I thought he didn't like being called vegetables." A deep, rolling voice barreled up from the back of the crowd out of something shaped very like, but somehow not, a moose. It had mottled green-and-bluish frog's skin and bulging wet eyes.

Osmo thought Bonk might be in serious danger of actually exploding.

"*A SQUASH ISN'T A ROOT VEGETABLE, IS IT, WALTER? IT GROWS ON A MUDDY VINE ON THE MUDDY GROUND, DOESN'T IT?* Oh, it just goes to show nothing excites people here, there, and everywhere more than *contradicting* Bonk the Cross!"

"Don't talk to me like that, mammal. I am one hundred years ooooold," the froose began. He drew out every word as long as he could.

Bonk hissed at him like a cat. "Nobody cares how old you are, Walter!"

"Silence, worm-eater!" the Quidnunx commanded. She shook her great stomach from side to side, the drumbeat of the Thumpus pranging and bonging out through the woodland.

Bonk's snout snapped shut. His keen black eyes filled up with tears. He squeezed them up tight and vigorously shook his head. The ruff on the back of his neck bristled.

"I never. I *never*," he muttered. "You see, Mister Motter? You see how they all talk to me?"

Osmo whispered: "*Do* you eat worms?"

"Well, *yes*, but it's just so unnecessary!"

Bonk rubbed at his moist dark nose inconsolably. But Osmo's thoughts had already left the embarrassed skadgebat behind, racing to catch up with his surroundings.

"Wait, did she say I'm her *father?*"

"THIS SENTENCE IS—" Mumpsimus began to roar. But a sweet, gentle voice cut her off. The great beast instantly went silent, as though that tiny, velvety sound had cut her in half.

"Me," the voice said.

"You WHAT?" bellowed Bonk, squeezing his tail so tight in another moment he'd break it off.

"I'm an elephawn."

Osmo twisted his head round. One of the Forest creatures emerged hesitantly from the throng.

It was an elephant.

It *was* an elephant. It had short neat ivory tusks and a long trunk and huge ears and everything. But it stood almost a head shorter than him, with all the soft brown fur, white spots and huge, dark, trusting eyes of a fawn. It was positively adorable. It almost *begged* to be petted. Osmo started to reach out to it before he caught himself. He didn't think this was a petting kind of place.

"My name is Afterall," the elephawn said shyly. "I live in Puddleside Cross." She pointed her trunk back over her slender little shoulder down into the city below. "I have six sisters in my herd and three babies in my thicket. I eat tulips and I never forget."

"It's nice to meet you," Osmo said with quiet awe.

"It's terrible to meet you," Afterall trumpeted delicately. "Your mother killed Queen Melancholy. I hate you. Everyone does. Mumpsy is going to eat you up and I'm glad."

"We're going to watch," said a tall, handsome grey wolf with a long ivory horn in the center of his forehead. Now, that sounds very odd and a little silly, but somehow, it didn't look odd or silly at all. The horn twisted up out of his thick silvery fur, looking so natural and correct that it was as though all the other wolves in the world had always been missing something, all this time, and only now could Osmo see what it was. All the animals looked that way, no matter how bizarre their bodies. They seemed so entirely perfect, just the way they were.

Osmo glanced furtively under his brows at Bonk the Cross.

"Narwholf," Bonk whispered out of the corner of his mouth.

"Hopefully she'll leave a bit for the rest of us," cawed a huge, impossible bird, as black as a raven, but all its feathers were dark, round midnight petals and its chest shone pure purple.

A great lovely black cat yawned and waved his green-and-blue peacock's tail in the air. "Everything in the Fourpenny Woods has two natures, child of the Valley," he purred. "I am a panthock, my winged friend is a crowcus."

"Or three," Bonk snapped irritably.

"Or three," agreed the narwholf. "You understand?"

"My mother has hunted in the Fourpenny Woods all her life," Osmo said quietly. "And she has never told me about *anything* like you. *Any* of you. Where are the deer and the rabbits? Just . . . just the regular deer and the normal rabbits. She would have told me about elephawns. She would have. She told me everything." Osmo's eyes swam with tears. He would never see her again. He would never get to tell her that somewhere in the world lived a fawn with an elephant's nose.

"A forest is like an ocean," the crowcus crowed. "It has a beachhead—on top of the sheer blue cliffs where the meadow begins to turn into stones and maples."

"It has tide pools," purred the panthock, "the little clusters of elms and oaks and wild roses springing up in the long grass a ways out from the pine wall."

"It has shallows," howled the narwholf. "Where you first leave the world for the woods or the woods for the world, and the sun still shines bright. Where the firs and spruces are spaced far enough apart that yellow and purple wildflowers can grow underneath. Humans, even hunters, never get out of the shallows. But still you think the shallows are the whole of the sea."

An orcadile, a small, sleek black-and-white whale with four clawed feet and a wide mouth full of teeth, rumbled: "You're in the deeps now. Far past where you belong. The *real* Forest. Where strange creatures can grow, safe from fishermen, creatures whose names you could never guess. Creatures that glow in the dark. And"—the creature glanced up at the Quidnunk—"sharks, of course. Every ocean has sharks."

A girl his own age appeared on top of a large rock.

Osmo almost jumped out of his skin. He hadn't even known anyone was up there. There were so many mixed-up animals he could be forgiven for not seeing one out of the hundreds. But this one hadn't wanted to be seen. Until now. She really did *appear*. She somehow *unfurled* from a coppery ball into a person and settled down cross-legged on the boulder.

She couldn't really be said to be a girl at all. She had a girl's face—bright eyes and sharp cheekbones and thick eyebrows and a mouth that looked like it was hiding a laugh the way a child hides a biscuit she's stolen from the tin and already half eaten. She had a girl's arms and a girl's legs, more or less, even if her nails were *very* long and *very* green. But instead of hair she had a thick thatch of teardrop-shaped bronze scales, like a knight's armor. The scales ran from a sharp widow's peak all the way over her skull, down her back and the backs of her limbs, across her shoulders and down her legs almost to the leafy, loamy rock.

She was a pangirlin.

The pangirlin wore boys' clothes. A long shirt and leathery trousers and high boots, with an open waistcoat and a very practical belt. Osmo felt suddenly self-conscious about the wedding finery he was stuck in. She fished in her pocket and pulled out a pair of quite ordinary-looking spectacles. She put them on her nose and peered down at him through the glasses. She put her chin in her hands, watching Osmo carefully. She giggled suddenly, but not like Ivy and her friends giggled. Her giggle was more like a Quidnunk's sentence. Full of strange colors. When she spoke, he felt more self-conscious still.

"Come on, then," the pangirlin said with a grin. "What are *your* natures?"

"Motter," Bonk chirped with confidence. "Monkey and otter. Very rare."

"I'm just a boy," Osmo said quietly.

*A man,* his father's voice corrected him in his head, but he didn't feel much like a man at the moment, with all those wild eyes on him. He felt every inch a lost little boy.

Lost, finally. Just like he'd always wanted.

It didn't feel at all the way he'd hoped it would.

"Nah. You're just supper," said the narwholf.

Osmo stared miserably into the Quidnunk's waiting jaws. But they *were* waiting, weren't they? She could have swallowed him in one bite ages ago and saved everybody wasting time explaining the nature of forests to him. Mumpsimus the Cloud-Eater could grab him right now. But she didn't. Why? He couldn't stop her. He was small and pasty like a turnip.

In his mind, Osmo Unknown took a giant step to the left.

She was trying to cheat him, just like Adelard Sloe and his Stupendous Throwing Game. They all were. Trying to distract him with a lot of fancy talk. Trying to *scare* him.

"You *can't* eat me," Osmo said plainly. His stomach felt like that old clay ball sailing through the air. "There's a treaty. I'm only here because of the treaty, and the treaty says you can't eat me." Osmo's brain might have been a day-old mincemeat pie, but it was steaming now. "The elephawn said my mother killed your queen. And you said *she* was your mother. Then, you said you don't accept me as your father. But why would you say that? How could I ever be *your* dad? I'm just a kid. There's holes in the ground that'd make better father figures than me. But I know why. It's because I'm meant to marry the ghost of the queen." The Quidnunk's eyes narrowed in fury. "You just want to scare me off. If you can terrify me until I run away, you don't have to concern yourself one bit with this small, pasty turnip. If I run I'm breaking the treaty and you can chase me down and gobble me up like Katja Kvass and not feel any bit guilty. But if you can't . . . and I don't . . . then I'm going to be your king." The Fourpenny Woods stood in resentful silence.

"That's it, isn't it?" He faced their silence and lifted his chin. "I'm right. I *know* I'm right. Bonk wouldn't say it. But I'm right."

Mumpsimus the Cloud-Eater, of the Vast, Hungry, and Undestructable Quidnunx, put her head back and roared. Her voice boomed through the Forest, shattering stumps as it went, full of grief and fury and pain. Birds scattered up into the night. Apples fell from branches in fear.

Osmo didn't know where it came from. It certainly didn't belong to him. He'd never done such a thing in all his life.

He roared back at her. All his exhaustion and horror and confusion and sorrow and raw, wet fear burned away his shyness and stripped his throat sore as he yelled. And he kept on yelling until it was all out there in the Forest, flying away from him, leaving something not quite the same Osmo Unknown as he had always been standing in his boots.

No stumps burst into splinters. No apples tumbled to the ground. The birds overhead, to be honest, snickered. His roar was only a boy's roar. But he meant it very deeply, and no boy in Littlebridge could have put more fierceness into the thing.

"It's not like I *wanted* this to happen," he yelled. "I just want to go home! I just want to go back to a world where none of you exist and I have school in the morning. You hate me? Well, I hate you, too! *You made me want to go to school!*"

"This sentence is iron," Mumpsimus snarled. "You will *never* be my father. You will *never* be my king."

"I think you're wrong," the new Osmo blazed. "I think marrying your mother makes me just exactly what you fear." He took a deep breath. Was this going to work? If he'd ever been any good at confrontation, he'd have been able to ask Ivy to the festival properly. He'd have been able to tell her how badly she'd hurt him. He'd have been a lot of things. Osmo thought he might pass out. His face felt red and hot and huge. He dredged up his father's worst, most commanding, most unanswerable voice from the bottom of his memory. The voice Mads Unknown only used when he was horribly disappointed in his only son. That awful voice most children know by heart. "I'm your father, Mumpsimus, and you *will* listen to me under my own roof! YOU FETCH ME MY SLIPPERS AND YOU GO TO YOUR ROOM!"

The massive Quidnunk's mouth dropped open. Her eyes boiled with loathing. Her fangs glittered in the dark.

And then, Mumpsimus the Cloud-Eater, of the Vast, Hungry, and Undestructable Quidnunk, sighed. Her shoulders slumped. And she began to trudge resentfully down the hill toward the strange Forest city below the bluffs.

Osmo Unknown crumpled and hid his face in his hands. He shook all over as whatever bravery had landed on him let go and flew up and away. He *hated* that voice. He hated himself for having that voice anywhere in him. What was he doing? He was nobody's father, let alone anyone's king. He was cold and lonely and all he wanted in the world was one friendly human face.

But at least nobody had eaten him. For now.

"I don't want any of this," Osmo wept. "I just want to go home."

Bonk the Cross awkwardly patted his head with a stripey paw. "Aw," he said. "Poor dummy."

The Quidnunk paused on the long Forest grass. She turned back round to face him with those huge slitted eyes.

"It must occur at sunset. Not midnight, not morning, not noon. But no human can be trusted alone. The skadgebat will guard you."

Bonk the Cross protested. "I've already had a generous helping of doof-pie tonight. I'm sleepy. I did my part!"

Mumpsimus ignored him. "My words are plain stone. You will lodge with . . ." She looked over the gathered Forest folk. "The pangirlin. Bring him to Gudgeon Square at dusk tomorrow."

"*What?*" the pangirlin yelled. "*Me?* Why me?"

Bonk doubled over laughing at her. "Ha! HA! That's better!" He did a little dance in the leaves.

Osmo, and indeed, some of the other animals, frowned uncomfortably at the little creature's joyful prancing.

"What? Every day is a game, and as long as someone else is unhappier than me by close of business, Bonk the Cross wins! Don't look at me like that. I didn't make the rules. *You* lot made them by being so anti-Bonk all the time."

"I don't want him in my house! I don't want *anyone* in my house!" the pangirlin pled, almost in tears.

"Plain stone!" barked the Quidnunx, and stormed off down the bluffs.

Slowly, the wedding party followed, winding down back toward the city below, leaving only Osmo with an amused skadge-bat and a pangirlin in spectacles glaring angrily at him.

"Welp. Shake a leg, Your Majesty," Bonk chuckled, and kicked him square in the shin.

## Chapter Ten
# NEVERMORE

The Quidnunx city lay at the bottom of the bluffs like a brilliant blanket of many colors. It looked as though someone had stretched Littlebridge like summer taffy, left it to grow wild for a thousand years, and set it all on fire.

Everything glittered. Everything shone.

Osmo scrambled down the cliffside path after the pangirlin. He ran to catch up with her, tripped, caught himself, and ran again. He slowed up to walk alongside her, as steadily as he could manage on the rocky, uneven trail. She blinked several times and glanced cagily back and forth at him as if they'd never seen each other before.

The pangirlin sped up. Osmo did, too. He tried to say hello. The pangirlin slowed down and tried to let him go on ahead down the thin path. Osmo turned and jogged back to her. She sped up again. So did he. Slowed down again. So did he.

Bonk the Cross kept his own pace, not bothering with their games.

"Hello," Osmo tried again. He didn't know why he was trying

so hard, except that she was the only person he'd seen yet who was his own age and he was lonely and exhausted and she was . . . she was just . . . a *pangolin*. Right out of *St. Whylom's Book of Zoologicals Near and Far*. That just had to mean she was wonderful. Somehow, he didn't feel at all nervous, either. He'd used up all his nervousness on roaring and telling a monster to go to her room. He had nothing left for simply talking to a girl.

Even if she wasn't really a girl.

Maybe *because* she wasn't really a girl.

"My name is Osmo."

"Yes," she answered. "That certainly is a fact about you."

Osmo's quite limited supply of fearlessness began to dwindle. But he kept on. If he had to just walk and walk and walk with nothing but his own thoughts about what would happen when the walking *stopped*, he might just throw himself off the cliffside.

"What's your name?"

Nothing.

The city below crept closer and closer. The mist moved in the wind. The moon came out. Osmo could see, suddenly, that the flickering lights down among the buildings were not lanterns or lamps or torches, but *pumpkins*. Huge, vast pumpkins bigger than anything the farmers' guild had ever put up on the scale at the Harvest Carnival. They sprawled on the ground, pulsing with wet, vivid light. Their dark vines tangled out for miles through the streets. *Humans have machines; we have mushrooms.* Just the same, it seemed humans had candles and gas lamps; these creatures had pumpkins. They glowed in a hundred colors so rich and deep it would be insulting to call them red or green or purple or blue. No, you had to do better. Vermilion, emerald, magenta, ultramarine, indigo, tangerine, gold.

"Does *it* have a name?" he asked the pangirlin.

"I'm not an *it*," she answered. "My name is Never."

"I don't mean you."

"Quiddity," she said simply. She'd known what he meant.

Finally, the trail ended and the city engulfed them all.

Quiddity was just precisely the kind of place you think of when someone says the word *magical*. The castle-y turrets spiking up everywhere like a black pincushion. The houses hollowed out of whole trees with candles nestled in the forks and burls of the branches. The schoolhouse with chicken legs and the silver-and-violet river full of half-fish and half-eels and whole boats sewn together from blue leaves. The tavern carved out of a butternut squash as tall as a church, with a thousand delicate steps cut into the sides that wound up to a rooftop pavilion. The shops and mills and churches were all half again bigger, slantier, and finer than anything he'd yet known.

Built not at human scale, but Quidnunx.

Not one of the buildings stood straight up and down. They all leaned against each other at entirely unsafe angles, a city like a domino game about to be lost in spectacular fashion. The streets corkscrewed up high bluffs opposite the ones they'd just come down or spiraled lazily off into the mists, following the river further into the Forest.

Osmo tried to get his head around the idea that if he lived

through the night, he'd have to live here. Get to. Have to. Either way, it would be his home. Forever. If he was *lucky*. He'd be king of this place. And who knew how many others. He really had no notion of how far the Fourpenny Woods went or how many cities were in there.

In *here*.

The pangirlin turned sharply left down one of the side streets. Osmo had to jog to keep up again. Bonk strolled along behind as casually as ever. The tangle of shadowy alleys and passages opened up suddenly onto a wide lumpy green. Long grass grew over dozens of burrows. Rows and rows of round earthen humps rose up around neat half-moon-shaped doors and windows with boxes of greens and flowers growing in them. The moon turned it all black and silver, and the tremendous bronze pumpkin in the center of the park cast cinnamon shadows every which where. Never walked quickly across the lawn, keeping her head down, past all the rows of doors to a lump in the grass far off from all the others. This burrow was protected by a neat little hand-dug moat full of rainwater. And several long, sharp wooden spikes jammed into the ground. Osmo glanced down into the water. He *definitely* saw eyes down there. A hundred tiny lidless eyes, watching him and Bonk carefully cross Never's homey painted bridge.

Never put her hand on the door of her house. It was a rough black quartzy crystal hacked into shape. Ten huge locks, bolts, latches, and hooks ran down the side of it. She sighed very loudly, on purpose, so they could hear how much she didn't want to do this.

But she did. She unlocked the locks, unbolted the bolts, unlatched the latches, and unhooked the hooks. Her house was dark inside. Never whispered something Osmo couldn't quite catch. All round the little burrow, light whirled into existence. From the shelves, from the hearth, from the kitchen table, from the fireplace grate, from the windowsills, from the washbasin, from the bedside table. A little branch or log or tiny wedge of a stump nestled in each place, growing a thatch of delicate little pale green mushrooms with perfectly round heads like matchsticks. They glowed happily, cozily, leaning slightly toward the pangirlin the way flowers lean toward the sun.

They illuminated a lot of other things hanging, lying, or nearly falling off the shelves, the hearth, the kitchen table, the fireplace grate, the windowsills, the washbasin, the bedside table. Clothes, dishes, dog-eared half-read books, half-melted candles, projects half finished and half started.

"What?" Never snapped defensively. "I like a good mess. A good mess means you're home, where no one can tell you to pick up your socks."

"Are those *Frederick* mushrooms?" Bonk whistled. "They're devilishly stubborn. I've never seen someone convince them to be lamps. Pumpkins, now. Pumpies don't argue. Fredders, you scab. You'd never go lampy for *me*."

Never shrugged. "I just asked."

"Just asked? The last time someone asked a Frederick to do so much as be a mushroom it *ate itself* rather than obey anybody."

Never shrugged nervously. "Mushrooms like me. Dunno why.

I've never done anything for them. They turn up all the time. The moat out there is full of Bernadettes."

Bonk's little snout dropped open. "Those are *vicious*. My mum lost a foot to a Bernadette."

A fist pounded loudly at the door. They heard scuffling, then swearing, then: *Get 'em off me! Get off! Ow! It burns!*

"They'll stop if you leave," Never called out, smiling a little to herself.

"Don't want to leave! I wanna see him! I wanna see the tiny king!"

"Shove off, Mayhap!" bellowed Bonk. "You wait till tomorrow like everyone else!" The snub-nosed badger rolled his eyes. "Hap is a porcupinoceros. Very bossy. Not humble and kind like me."

"Don't wanna wait! *OW!* Oh, I hope you choke on those quills, muddy gnashers!" yelped Mayhap, muffled by the door.

"Go *home!*" the pangirlin growled. With much muttering and stomping and splashing, peace returned to the burrow.

"You have a very nice house," Osmo said politely.

And it was, despite the mess. Only one large room, but everything you could need for happiness stuffed into it. The rugs on the floor shone plush and thick in patterns like autumn leaves and spring flowers. The books on the shelves loomed thick and serious. Big downy blankets piled up high on the narrow round bed, a burrow within a burrow. The plates and mugs in her china cabinet were clean gleaming copper.

But there was nowhere much to sit. The table was set only for one, with one chair with a lot of books stacked up on it. The reading sofa in the corner with little clovers painted all over the upholstery was currently occupied by a tangle of knitting. Osmo and Bonk stood awkwardly in the center of the burrow. The bed was covered in tea trays and journals.

"Thank you," Never said stiffly. "I was orphaned here."

"Oh, I'm so sorry!" Osmo said.

Never shook her head and laughed a little, the very smallest possible unit of friendliness. "Pangolins are solitary animals," she said pointedly, with a meaningful glance them both. "Our parents abandon us as soon as possible. So when I say *I was orphaned*, that's just how a pangolin says *I was born*. I was orphaned in Quiddity, in this house. Someday I will die alone and friendless in Quiddity, in this house. For my kind, that's the same as a human saying *I hope to die rich and fat and happy surrounded by grandbabies*."

"But that's so sad," Osmo said, aghast.

"Why?" Never shrugged, pushing her glasses up her long, pretty nose. "I told you, we are *solitary* creatures. Did your parents . . . *not* abandon you as a baby?" She fixed him with a warm, sincere gaze. "I'm *so* sorry. That must have been very hard for you. I thought everyone loved their babies enough to leave them alone. How did you stand it, people telling you what to do all the time like they owned you?"

Osmo couldn't imagine life without his sisters and his mother and his father and Ivy and Ada and Barnaby and Adelard Sloe and Mrs. Brownbread and all of them . . . but then his heart caught up to his thoughts. Short or long, his life *would* go on without them, so he had better start imagining it.

Bonk fished a mug out of the cabinet and commenced rummaging around the hearth for a teakettle as though he owned the place.

"You know that's why Mumpsimus made you take in this weedy wee walloper, don't you? Because she's angry as *muck* and she knew you'd hate it the most. Quidnunx are wise and wonderful and ancient-er than stars, but they can be *very* petty. And smelly. Should be great fun to be married to one!"

Another pounding shook the black crystal door.

Bonk jerked up and hit his head on the mantel. He rubbed it with one black-and-white paw. "Toast it all black, haven't you got any muddy tea in this house, Pangy?"

"Let us in! You can't keep him all to yourself!" a voice hollered outside. It sounded quite birdlike, but also big and deep. Osmo peered carefully out the window and saw a mother and her baby, sparrows the size of horses with long shaggy legs. "Mind the moat, they'll have your hooves."

"I don't drink tea," Never said irritably.

"I knew you were a monster," Bonk harrumphed.

"I'm here on behalf of all spallions and we've every right!" the sparrow-horse insisted, and kicked the door with her foreleg.

"There's cider in the icebox," Never offered miserably.

"*Monster.*"

"Well, it's mine and you can't have it anyway! Get *out!*" she screamed at the door. "All of you! I hate this! I don't know how to do *guests!*"

"It's not hard!" Bonk bellowed. He ticked off his short furry fingers. "You feed them, you drink them, and you clean off a chair, for crying out loud. Then you say *my house is your house* and squirrel's your cousin, you've mastered the art!"

"But it ISN'T your house, that's the whole point!"

"IT'S JUST SOMETHING YOU SAY, YOU ORNERY WEE FORK!"

"Hey, it's all right," Osmo interrupted, trying to make peace. "I'm not hungry."

"No one cares!" Never and Bonk said together.

"We care! We want to see the human!" the spallions whinnied outside.

"TOO BAD SO SAD. TOOTLES!" Bonk snarled. After a moment's resentful silence, they heard hoofbeats cantering away across the moat.

"Feed them," Bonk repeated pointedly, "and drink them. That's the main part."

Never sighed and clenched her bronze fists. "I've got dragonfly pies and a silkworm scone in the leftmost cabinet. Dandelion-milk butter next to the cider. There might be a scrape of something left in the pot of buckthorn-and-fire-ant jam above the egg cups."

"You got an Archibald in this hoarder's palace?"

"Obviously. Under the pots and pans."

Bonk rummaged and banged for a moment before unearthing a wide, flat, black-and-yellow-dappled slab of mushroom glowing faintly beneath a pile of beaten cookery. He petted it nicely and murmured to it in a soft, kind tone he seemed to reserve exclusively for mushrooms. The glowing brightened and deepened into a serious, pulsing gleam. The skadgebat helped himself to the contents of Never's poor cabinet. He arranged the pastries on top of the mushroom, where they promptly began to toast up.

Osmo blinked. "That's . . . what you *eat*? Blegh. Buckthorn is nice, but fire ants?"

Never's cheeks had gone an anxious red. She squeezed up her iridescent eyes and tilted her head up to a heaven that would not save her from these intruders. *"They're spicy and crunchy and I like them, you absolute doorknob!"*

"Heh, heh, heh," chuckled Bonk, his mouth full of crumbs. "That's a good one. I'll have that off you, if you don't mind. He *is* a doorknob. One hundred percent doorknob, top to tail. Myself, I'd prefer an earthworm omelet or a big sticky cricket croquembouche."

The pangirlin took several deep breaths to calm down. "It's not *for* you, Mr. Unknown. Or you, Bonk. I eat what *I* like. I'm part pangolin. What a pangolin likes is bugs. But I'm also part girl. A girl prefers pies and stews and a nice scone in the morning. I do my best with what I've got! What do you eat?"

"Um . . . normal things. Meat and two vegetables."

"They eat mushrooms, Pangy," growled Bonk. "They *eat*. *Mushrooms.*"

The pangirlin gulped her breath in quick, distressed gasps. She soon gave herself the hiccups. She bent over and put her hands on her knees.

"So many," she panted. "So many people. Do you know," she said between *hics*, "pangolins don't even have any numbers other than one in our language! One is the *best* number. The only *correct* number. A pangolin does not count *one, two, three, four, five, six, a hundred*. A pangolin counts *one, awkward, unpleasant, disturbing, dreadful, suffocating, completely intolerable*. *Guest* is an extremely naughty word. *Company* is worse than that." Never straightened up, but her eyes were wild and wide with panic.

"What about *family?*" asked Osmo.

"Well, I wouldn't say it unless I was *very* upset," Never hiccuped. "But it's not as bad as, say"—she stood up straight and lowered her voice to a whisper—"*party.*"

"But how can you get through . . . through anything without a family? Without parents?" Osmo said stubbornly.

"Of course I *have* parents. I didn't come out of nowhere. One of my mothers was an architect and the other was a philosophess. But if they'd stayed around the burrow to raise me, they wouldn't have had time to do any of that, or have any hobbies like baking or knitting or building model pains. I've met them a few times. On holidays when the whole city . . . ugh." She looked as if she might be sick. "*Gathers.* Mama Oddest loves her model pains. I'd never want her to put away her paints and glue just to look after me. She can make a miniature heartbreak that looks just like the real thing, down to every detail! And Mother Notably carries her collected works on her back at all times, like a tortoiseshell of big fat heavy books. *I Think Therefore I'd Rather You Leave* is my favorite. Of course, *The Trolley Problem and Other Things That Aren't Really Problems* is wonderful, too."

"The Trolley Problem?" Osmo ventured.

"Yes, it's a famous thought experiment even more famously solved by my mother." She beamed with pride. "There's a runaway trolley barreling down the road. Ahead of it, five foolish people have got themselves tied up and unable to move out of the way. The trolley will certainly squish them. You stand a ways away, next to a lever. If you pull the lever, the trolley will switch to a different set of tracks. But! There is one equally foolish person tied up on that same side track. So, do you do nothing and let the trolley squish the five fools through no fault of your own except that you watched, or do you get involved and kill the one fool directly?"

Osmo gave it a bit of brain. "I suppose one is less than five, so I'd have to pull the lever," he said slowly.

"Wrong. You were never there in the first place, because you were minding your own business in your own burrow, and there is no reason at all to associate with trolleys or people ever (and all people are fools) unless you want this sort of thing to happen on the regular and keep on causing you a completely unreasonable amount of stress," Never said happily. Her eyes shone like coins when she was happy. "That is the Notably Solution. I'm surprised you didn't study it in school. You see, I *do* know my mothers. I'm awfully proud of my parents. They are *very* lonely people nowadays. And I'm having a perfectly desolate childhood."

Somehow, when Never said *lonely* and *desolate*, it did not sound bad at all, but grand and adventurous and enticing.

"Don't you have any brothers or sisters?"

Never looked horrified. "Ew, no!"

"Pangolins only ever have one child," Bonk butted in. "Not like us skadgebats. We have *heaps*. And we all ride along in our mother's pouches, having a constant all-day-all-night cuddle until we're big enough not to get *et*. It's a *noticeably* superior arrangement."

"Eurgh." Never shuddered. "Why, do you have . . . siblings?" She said it like she was asking whether he had fleas.

Osmo nodded, remembering all their little faces. "Six sisters."

Never's eyes widened. *"Gross,"* she breathed. But she seemed quite as fascinated by his alien ways as he was by hers. "And you . . . you just . . . live all in one burrow? And talk to each other every day? And . . . and . . . *play* together?"

Osmo nodded.

Never shuddered. "That's the most gruesome thing I've ever heard," she marveled. "Sometimes I go a whole year without talking to anyone but myself. I'm forsaken by all!" She beamed with pleasure at the idea.

"A year? But how do you go to school or get bread from the baker or greens from the grocer or books from the library? Or . . . do you not have libraries in Quiddity?"

"We have libraries. And grocers and bakers and parks and schools and all the rest of everything you have. Just mostly not made the same way or from the same stuff. I make my own lonesome bread and grow my own outcast greens and keep my own bashful books here in my burrow." She pointed to the many small shelves all over the walls. "Each book gets its own shelf, so they don't have to socialize." She suddenly found something quite interesting to pick at on her left thumb. "I wouldn't . . . I wouldn't talk much to anybody *anyhow*, even if pangolins loved parties and balls and sporting events and all sorts of . . . *gatherings.*" She looked nauseous at the word. "Quidditons don't care much for those of us with"—she lowered her voice shamefully— "human natures. It's all right to be a panthock or a snemu or a skadgebat like . . . him." She jabbed her armored thumb at Bonk. "But pangirlins or gladfish or hippopotamisters or wormaids . . . let's just say when I do talk to others, I'm usually disappointed."

Osmo wanted to pat her shoulder or hug her or something to show he knew a little of what it was like to feel forever apart. But he didn't think a solitary animal would feel comforted by that.

"I think that's hateful and cruel," he said instead.

"You're biased because *all* of your nature is a big human garbage mess," Bonk said.

"Is it?" Never said curiously.

"Yes!" Osmo replied testily. Why couldn't any of them believe he was just human, nothing more or less?

Never took off her glasses, which had got all frosted coming in from the night mist. She cleaned them on her shirttail and put them back on. The mushroom-lights played over the thick oil-slick scales that ran down Never's head and her shoulders and her back like hair—but then again, nothing like hair. Her scales were part of her, never cut or curled or tied with a ribbon. He saw now that her eyes were warm and green as the wood. She didn't seem scary to him at all anymore.

Never's face scrunched up with frustration. "You don't have to talk to me, you know. We can just sit here and wait. If you're going to be king, I'm not anybody to you. And if you're not, you're not anybody to me." She squeezed his shoulder gently and said in a quite soft and inviting voice: "Go away? Please? Just go away."

Osmo shrugged. "Why can't we talk? Everybody talks. Talking is *nice*. Talking is *normal*. And when you meet a kid your own age, sometimes you talk to them. Especially if they're lonely and scared and everything is going to change for them really soon. Sometimes they even turn into your friend. So I hear. I'm not very good at that part back home. Except with Mrs. Brownbread. But I think it's different with old people. Anyway, as long as we keep talking, I can distract my head and pretend it'll all turn out fine. Plus," he added quietly, "I really like pangolins. I only ever saw pictures of them before. I always thought it would be so fantastic to meet one. But you don't like me at all. And that's okay! Bonk doesn't either. But you don't have to like someone to talk at them. Believe me." Ivy's cold, pitying face flashed before him. And Barnaby's piggy, snide stare. He could almost hear Ada's and Gregory's cruel laughter, all the way out here in another world.

The pangirlin grimaced and disappeared.

No, not disappeared. Rolled up. A bronze ball sat by the hearth where Never had stood. It sat there for a long time. A *long* time. Really, far too long. Osmo began to feel painfully awkward and out of place. And when that feeling had taken him over completely, she was still curled up into a ball.

Eventually, Never peeked out from between her tail and her hip. "Are you okay?"

The pangirlin blinked and unfurled until she lay flat on the carpet. "N . . . no," she said, stuttering slightly. "You were sad. I

can't bear other people's sadness. If I have to be around other . . .
other people . . . then happiness is all right. Boredom is fine. I
can even handle anger. It comes easy and burns out fast, at least.
But sadness is just so *big* and *heavy* and *loud*. My own feelings are
hard enough to carry! Other people's sorrow is too much! So I roll
up and away from it until it goes away. My armor is very strong
against sadness. Not one tear gets in."

Osmo wiped his nose on the back of his sleeve. The sleeve that
until yesterday had been the butcher's cousin's necktie. "Well, I'm
sorry. I didn't mean to attack you with my feelings or whatever. I
promise not to . . . be sad at you again."

"Well, all right. If you promise. Promises are a very serious business. *If* you promise, you can keep talking to me if you want. If it
makes you feel less sad. But I'm still not going to be your friend.
I'm a lonely girl. Friendship is horrible. And it smells. It smells like
other people *all the time*." Her armored plates shuddered.

"Okay, fine," Osmo sighed.

"Good," Never said firmly.

"Good," he repeated.

"Never is an odd name." Osmo tried one last time to get out
of the hole of awkwardness he kept digging around himself. "So is
Afterall, come to think of it. And Mayhap and Bonk and all of them."

"I'll bonk *you*," the skadgebat snarled over his snacks. "Right
between the eyes."

Osmo ignored him. "Is Never short for something?"

She nodded. "Nevermore."

"That's just as odd!"

"It's not our fault humans took all the ordinary names in the world, and then the Quidnunx took all the extraordinary ones. We got left with nothing but the rest of the words," she sniffed, and nodded her head back over her shoulder. "Walter back there got the last proper name. And he's a hundred years old. Ask him, he'll tell you. He will tell you *a lot.*"

"That doesn't make any sense. More than one person can have a name. Nobody owns a name."

"Do you have anyone called Walter where you come from?"

"No, but that doesn't prove—"

"And we don't have anyone called Osmo here. *We* play fair. *We* don't take things that don't belong to us. A name is like a destiny. It should be yours and yours alone. You shouldn't have to share it with people you might not even *know.* It's not my fault the Valley-born do everything the wrong way and the Forest-born do everything the right way." She sniffed and rubbed at her nose. "You take everything, sooner or later. You do. Besides, Osmo Unknown is hardly the most usual name ever invented in the history of nameology."

"That's my whole name. How do you know my whole name?"

"We all know it, dingus," Bonk the Cross barked.

"Listen, if you're *so* superior and you know everything, what's going to happen tomorrow?" Osmo hated feeling this way. Like he was taking a test he hadn't studied for. That no one had *ever* studied for. "Can't you just tell me? Please. Anything."

Bonk and Nevermore exchanged glances. Even the Frederick mushrooms seemed a bit upset.

"Oh, fine, I'll tell you," Never sighed, and threw up her hands. She hopped up onto her bed and sat cross-legged.

"Never! You scab! Don't you dare."

"Well, maybe Mumpsimus shouldn't have saddled me with him if she wanted to play her games! I'll tell you the truth, Osmo: Nobody wants to say what's going to happen to you because nobody knows. But they don't want you to *know* they don't know. I don't care a bit, because when you're a solitary creature it doesn't matter what anyone else thinks and you can say whatever you're thinking all the time because no one is listening! Honestly, not always being worried about what everyone else thinks or knows or does is the best part of being solitary." She counted off on her coppery long fingers with their coppery long nails. "They don't know what's going to happen because one: anything can happen in a Forest. Awkward: no human has ever killed a royal before. So nobody knows what that's supposed to make you, and nobody likes thinking about it *at all*. Unpleasant: there are so few Quidnunx left in the Forest that we haven't had to have a dead wedding for hundreds of years and nobody really remembers how to do one, which is pretty embarrassing. Disturbing: no one has any idea what will happen if *we're* the ones to break the treaty and eat you because it's always been you people who have stomped all over it and wiped your feet on the pages. I guarantee you they're trying to work it all out while I'm stuck here with you. Weddings happen any old hour, it doesn't have to be dusk. They're stalling for time. Quidnunx don't tell the truth unless you have something to trade for it. And you've got nothing."

"What do you mean there's so few Quidnunx left?" Osmo asked. He'd only just discovered they existed!

Bonk the Cross gave Never the dirtiest, sourest, sulkiest look that ever was. "No one knows that either," he spat. "Give our thanks to your mum, chuckbucket."

The burrow boomed and shook as someone else banged at the door. Dust sifted down from the ceiling.

"*GO AWAY!*" all three of them shouted together.

## Chapter Eleven

# THE OCTOBERPOLE

Dusk arrived.

In the center of town where the crossroads met lay a wide, handsome square. The square was so very like Dapplegrim Square back home that Osmo looked automatically for the old Cruste and Cheddar Tavern on the eastward side. And there *was* a tavern here, too. A slanted black marble building with crescent windows and stained glass. Onlookers crowded the doors and shoved each other to get a good spot at the windows.

The sign out in front read: THE HAT & HUMAN.

But however packed the pub, the square itself spread out vast and empty under the stars. Osmo had thought it would be decorated for the wedding. Garlands and candles and tables for feasting. Maybe musicians playing lovely local folk songs. But there was nothing.

Except the Quidnunk, sitting hunched on the far side like a small hairy mountain. And the pillar.

The great black granite pillar stood in the middle of the market square, just like the red pillar in Littlebridge. It zoomed up toward the sky in the exact place the pillar in Littlebridge did. But from the tip-top of this stone pole hung long orange and gold and scarlet ribbons, black, twisted, shining soft ropes, chains of autumn leaves, vines of bittersweet and evening gloomys—just the same sort of flower as a morning glory, only black. In between each strand hung thick, luxurious, and quite alive arctic fox tails that fell almost to the street. Tall, pale torches ringed it round. And on the very tip-top of the pillar, a golden skull looked down on Osmo Unknown.

The skull was small.

The skull was ancient.

The skull was human.

Osmo cleared his throat. "It's . . . very beautiful."

"Of course it is," Never whispered back. "Why would we live anywhere that wasn't beautiful? What's the point of that?"

"It looks just like Dapplegrim Square back home . . . except . . ." Osmo nodded at the golden skull up there.

"*Dapplegrim?*" Bonk hissed. He drew back the furry skin over his snout, showing his teeth. "You called your town square *Dapplegrim?*"

"Yes? What's wrong with that?" Osmo hissed back. "It's just a silly old name. What do you call yours?"

Bonk and Never looked at each other and shrugged.

"Gareth," they said together.

"But that's a person's name," whispered Osmo.

Bonk glared defiantly at him. The pumpkin light made his eyes look red and piercing.

Osmo lifted his eyes up to the very, very, unmistakably human skull at the top of the garlanded pillar.

"I'm sorry," he said, a little too loudly. He pointed toward the hideous golden thing. "Is *that* Gareth, then?"

Before they could answer, Mumpsimus, the Quidnunk princess, stomped her feet on the ground for attention. The cobblestones trembled beneath her. Suddenly they were not alone. A parade of jumbled-up beasts piled in from all sides, shoving to get a good spot, filling up the square and the side roads and the tavern and everything else just to glimpse whatever was about to happen.

Mumpsimus put out one long, razor claw.

Bonk the Cross suddenly looked solemn and wistful. "I wonder if she's the last one left? Must be lonely as a leaf in January." Never's eyes sparkled. She gazed at the Quidnunk with new respect. "There used to be hundreds and hundreds. Before . . ." Bonk looked Osmo Unknown up and down with a bitterness that made him feel just *horrifically* human. "*Them*. And *that*. And *the other thing*. In the old days, Quidnunx used to have festivals that lasted for three years at a go and never ran out of songs to sing or games to play."

"Sounds *horrid*." Nevermore shuddered.

The wombat-shaped, skunk-tailed badger grinned at the pangirlin. "Don't you know your history? *Quiddity* is the collective noun for a group of Quidnunx. Like a pod of whales or a stench of skunks or a colony of badgers or a mob of wombats or a whatever of pangolins. Just as examples, you know, purely a random sampling."

"I don't care about collective nouns." Never shrugged. "So don't try to make me feel stupid. Pangolins don't have one. We don't *collect*."

Osmo's head pounded. He had only recently accepted that he was wrong about the existence of Quidnunx. His brain was not prepared to accept that he'd almost been *right* and they were nearly extinct.

"Wait, what happened to them? Are you saying *we* had something to do with it? I don't think that can possibly be right."

"My words are black and frozen!" hollered Mumpsimus to the people of Quiddity. "Stand there." She pointed at Osmo, and then to the horrifying, yet beautiful, yet horrifying pillar with the skull on top. "Shut up. Don't move. Don't touch anything."

Osmo moved obediently toward the ribbons and ropes and tails. He stood underneath, feeling very foolish.

"I don't understand," he whispered to Bonk, who hung back to watch. "I thought I was getting married tonight."

Bonk called over a jaguaranutan with wise, apelike eyes and spotted golden fur who was selling hot walnuts in little sacks. He shrugged at Osmo. "Dunno, but I'm pretty interested to find out!" He cracked a nut and munched on it happily. "Are you not?"

"This sentence is a slowly locking door," the Quidnunk said gravely. "Together as one Forest we witness this marriage between . . . *that* . . . and our mother's beautiful shade." The Quidnunk and the crowds and Gareth's empty golden eye sockets glared through to Osmo's heart and out the other side of his soul. His blood jellied in his veins and his stomach tried to find somewhere behind his spine to hide. "Fine. You are married. Go home." There was a long silence. "Bye-bye."

"What?" Osmo said finally.

"What?" Mumpsimus repeated.

"I thought . . . I was your father now. Remember?"

Mumpsimus sat down smugly. "Okay. Go home, Dad," her voice boomed. She seemed to have quite forgotten to decorate her sentences so others could experience the full sensation of the Quidnunk language. That, or she simply didn't care whether Osmo understood all the nuances and nooks and crannies and colors now. Why waste one big monstery breath on such a slice of nobody?

"Just go home? After all this?" Osmo's muscles didn't know if they were allowed to relax or not.

"Why are you complaining?" Mumpsimus thundered. Still not bothering with the colors of her words. He wasn't worth the effort.

The wind began to pick up over the tops of the tallest trees. Their trunks swayed back and forth, creaking, snapping branches against each other. The crowd held their breath, for once under-standing no more than Osmo did.

Osmo put his hands on his hips and breathed out his nose. He did know *some* things about the world. "Well, because that's not a wedding. I've been to loads of weddings. There's way more to them than *you're married, go home.*"

Mumpsimus scratched at the cobblestones idly with one long claw. "Like what?" she grumbled.

"Well, vows, for one thing! And dancing! And feasting and music!"

A deep, quiet groan echoed through the streets of Quiddity. Then a screech. Then a low, grinding moan.

"Do you promise to be a good husband?" the Quidnunk rumbled.

Osmo looked back over his shoulder. A nation of misfit beasts watched him expectantly. "Yes? I guess? I do?"

"Come on and sing something, Rarely," Bonk the Cross hissed at one of the crowcuses. She fluffed her violet petal-feathers and cawed a few notes while Bonk did another happy little badger dance. He finished with a little shaking of his paws. *Ta-da!* he mouthed silently. Nevermore called the jaguaranutan over. She grabbed a bag off his cart, dug her fingers in deep, and threw a hot walnut at Osmo. It bounced hard off the back of his head.

Mumpsimus glowered at him. "Okay. Vow. Music. Dance. Feast. Done. Now go home."

The earth beneath them quivered slightly. Just a little. Just enough that you might think it was nothing.

"What is *happening*?" Osmo yelled. "Go *home*? Katja Kvass didn't get to go home!"

"Who in the muddy well is Katja Kvass?" howled a narwholf from the direction of the pub.

"The last human that married one of you!" Osmo was so frustrated he could feel tears springing to his eyes. He told them to knock it right off, he had no time for that just now.

The pair of Quidnunx shrugged in unison. A loud shivery *crack* echoed down the side streets off the main square. Then another. And another. A *crack* and then a *thunk-pop* like deep stones wrenched out of sucking mud.

Osmo ignored it. Could it be this easy? Could it all be over, right here, right now? "What happens when I go home? What if I want to marry a human girl and have babies and all that? Will you all come and destroy my village?"

"No. Our mother is a very understanding ghost."

"You're *toying* with me, that's all. I've been so afraid all this time, of all of you, but you don't take anything seriously!"

"We take our toys very seriously," Mumpsimus said. Osmo thought the bubbling weedy river sound in her throat might have actually been a *giggle*.

"I'm not a toy," Osmo said in the biggest voice he could get out of his tight chest.

"You are, *kind* of," Bonk yelled.

"If I'm married to the queen, then I'm king. That's how politics work," the human boy insisted.

"King Toy!" laughed Bonk uproariously, his mouth full of walnuts. Never shushed him.

"My words have the weight of lead at the bottom of the sea," Mumpsimus said, finally caring enough to spiff up her sentences for him. "There is a long distance between a toy and a king, and you have yet to cross it. And even kings are the toys of the world. Keep your toy tongue in your toy mouth or we will have to take it out and play with it." She stamped both hippopotamus-like feet, left, then right, like punctuation. "It is done. We are done. Go. Home."

They turned their backs on him. Their huge, furry, many-colored backs.

They stood like that for an achingly long time.

And in that moment, perhaps *just* in that moment, Osmo Unknown didn't want to go home. How dare they bring him all this way and frighten the black out of his hair and all for nothing really at all? A joke? A game? He had never felt so much a pawn and not a player. And worst of all, somehow, he knew no more about Quidnunx than he had yesterday morning at school. Except now he knew they were real, and grumpy, and didn't like him very much, which certainly were three new facts, but hardly the good kinds of facts, the kind you could sink your heart into, the kind you could spend night after night examining, the kind you could hoard. Quidnunx, creatures too unreal to ever exist, only they did, they really did exist!

And they were kicking him out.

All his life, he'd longed for something *Else*. Now here it was, right in front of him. As *Else* as anything could possibly be. But this *Else* wasn't Paris or Rome or Helsinki, glittering with art and science and things to do and things to know. It wasn't a glorious new world of adventure eager to take him in and accept him as Littlebridge never had. It didn't recognize him and rejoice.

The *Else* was *mean*.

And Osmo Unknown might have said so. He might have said so right then, if Quiddity hadn't exploded.

Flagstones cracked and burst all around Gareth Square. Vermilion and lilac pumpkins blasted up into the air like cannonballs. Streetlamps creaked, groaned, and crashed to the ground. The doors of several slanty lovely black buildings sagged, ballooned sickly, and then banged open, shattering the dark bricks around them. Molten squash showered down like burning candy-colored rain, sizzling as it hit fur and skin alike. The people of Quiddity yelped, bleated, crowed, roared, and bolted for cover. But there was no cover to be found.

Huge, dark, gnarled roots like serpents from beyond time erupted out of the flagstones, under the pumpkin-lanterns, through the broken doors of the slanty buildings. Boulders rumbled down the alleyways and delicate little curly streets, bashing everything in their paths. Trees that had spent centuries growing at a stately, gracious pace on either side of the common suddenly shot up twenty feet, thirty, more. Their branches stretched out like terrible fingers toward each other, twisting and braiding and snatching into a black dome over everything. The boulders rolled to a rest in a protective ring like a regiment of soldiers. Great, titanic roots, as big around as a whale's belly, slammed down crosswise across Gareth Square, right in front of Mumpsimus.

It all happened so quickly. The windy rush of trees toppling, roots unrooting, and boulders barreling in put out every torch all at once and all together. Under the dome, darkness ruled.

The Quidnunk gawped. Her shoulders quaked. She clasped her paws behind her back and sniffled. Her big golden hot-green eyes filled up with big golden hot-green tears.

She was *ashamed*.

A line of mushrooms flared up all along the hulking length of the roots. Fiery red-orange ones with fluted, curling, slender caps and electric blue-white stalks. They glowed so fevery-bright that smoke wisped up from their bells into the sky. And, quick as you like, each and every one of them coiled and crimped into a rough crooked hand. A hundred accusing fingers pointed right at the mortified Quidnunk.

Not one brave lonely sound dared snap the silence.

"Sorry," Mumpsimus whispered. "My words are field mice. My words are the *feet* of field mice. My words are very small and submissive with unremarkable fur," she whined. The princess couldn't look the mushrooms in the eyes. Or, more precisely, the fingers. "Please don't be angry. We only wanted it to be over. To skip to the part where everything is all right, like jumping over two rocks in a river."

The furious fungus-fingers kept pointing knowingly.

Mumpsimus stamped her foot. "It is all so ancient and foolish! We do not live in caves anymore, either! Why must we do this? We do not know how. We do not remember. We cannot do what we cannot remember."

The flame-colored mushroom hands suddenly flushed brighter and hotter. They snapped their fingers together angrily and pointed again.

Mumpsimus moaned miserably. "Yes, you are right. Our words were chameleon-skinned. They were colored like the truthful branch they sat upon, but they were not the branch. We *do* know. We do remember. But we don't *want* to."

The mushrooms swiveled their terrible fierce thrusting fingers away from the Quidnunx. They pointed insistently, provoked, displeased, unforgiving.

They pointed at Osmo.

"What is *happening*?" Osmo looked around for his friends . . . well, not his *friends*, exactly, but at least faces he knew, faces that had once or twice held something other than contempt for him. But Bonk the Cross and Nevermore had disappeared into the gobsmacked crowd.

"The Forest has spoken," Mumpsimus said resentfully. "The words of the Forest are the fate of the world. We made the Forest angry. Usually, when we play tricks, the Forest is well pleased. But this time it is angry and it is taking our trick away." She pouted. It was very strange to see a mountain pout. "It was a good trick," she mumbled.

The flamey mushrooms waggled their fingers. Evidently, they did not agree.

"It is easier to tell our blood to stop moving in our bodies than to tell the Forest no. The Forest made us. The Forest made our every heart out of nothing and shadow. The Forest says we have to. So we have to. Go to the Octoberpole, human male, and know that my words are the sun and moon and stars who have no ears to hear arguments."

Octoberpole.

Osmo Unknown almost laughed. Of course. A maypole was all flowers and ribbons. This was leaves and vines and fur and black blossoms. You danced around a maypole for luck and joy and fertility. He didn't know what you danced around an Octoberpole for, but he reasoned it was . . . not that. He regretted arguing before when he could have made a run for it. What was he thinking? Of *course* he wanted to go home. Of *course* this was not where he belonged, not at all, not a little. This place was dangerous. The *Else* was dangerous. Just ask Gareth.

"Take up one of the white tails and name your witnesses."

"Witnesses?"

Mumpsimus narrowed her eyes in frustration.

"It is a wedding! It must have two witnesses! You said you knew about weddings!"

"But there's hundreds of witnesses!" Osmo protested, gesturing at the throngs of Quidditons.

A Quidnunk's smile is a curious thing. You cannot see it under all that fur. But when they smile, their eyes change from golden-green to violet, and that is just what happened. Osmo didn't understand it, as he did not know much at all about Quidnunx yet, but it shut him right up. He picked up the tufted white furry tip of the long fox tail hanging from the cap of the pillar. It was warm.

"This is not the wedding," Mumpsimus crooned. "*She* isn't even here. This sentence is a satisfied cat with three birds in its belly. It never was and could not be the wedding. Not here or now. You cannot marry the dead in the land of the living. You must go to the bride's house. You must go to the bride's house with your witnesses and *if* she accepts you, *if* you survive, and *if* she allows you to leave, you may return a husband and a king. One of those is a much nobler and more glorious thing than the other. If you don't come back, we get to eat the village after all, so please feel free not to come back."

"I have to go to . . . to hell? Or heaven?" Osmo asked. And then, more softly, he whispered: "But I just got here."

"To the Eightpenny Woods. Heaven and hell and other imaginary things are for humans. The dead of the Valley. Tiny children that require vast cosmic punishments and rewards just so that they don't stab each other *too* often. The Eightpenny Woods is ours. It belongs to the dead of the Forest. It is neither of those, and both, and also a riddle, and also a shadow, and also a knife, and also a crumpet with cold butter. Name your witnesses."

"What if I don't accept *her*? Does what I want matter at all?"

The Quidnunk just laughed.

"Fine. How do I get her to accept me?" Osmo asked, frantically digging for as much information as he could.

The daughter of the Quidnunk queen glared resentfully at the orange mushrooms. They glared back. Several formed themselves into hands again and snapped their fingers insistently. The Quidnunk would obviously much rather let him go in unprepared. She rolled her moony green-yellow eyes. "You must prove yourself both true and tricksy, clever and foolish, straightforward and sneaky, brave and vainglorious, wild and mild, kind and cruel. And able to make her a decent supper."

"Those are all opposites," Osmo protested.

"Name witnesses!" the Quidnunk bellowed.

There was no way out now. Not with all those mushrooms pointed at him like drawn arrows, and boulders standing guard in case he bolted, and the black branchy dome overhead to trap him here. He ran his thumb over the warm fox fur. If there was no way out, the only thing to do was press on, he reasoned. Be a man, like his father said. And what did men do?

Well, for one thing, they did sometimes get married.

"Bonk the Cross and Nevermore the pangirlin," he told the Quidnunk firmly, and also the mushrooms.

"No!" Never wailed. "I just want to be *left alone*. Why is that so hard to understand?"

"Not a chance, trashwit," Bonk laughed. "I've got better things to do than die with you."

"You are literally the only people here I know!" Osmo insisted. "Please!"

"What good am I to you? I'm only a kid! Take Walter!" Nevermore insisted. "He's a hundred years old!"

Walter the froose clattered forward on his iridescent green delicate legs. "I am one hundred years ooooold . . ."

"SHUT UP, WALTER!" Bonk roared. "You are the worst! You're not going anywhere, you'd throw up the first time the wind blew a little too hard."

"I have a sensitive stomach, it's not my fault," Walter mumbled.

"Once the witnesses are named, they cannot refuse the call." Mumpsimus shrugged.

"Says who?" Never protested.

The rows of red-and-white mushrooms uncurled out of their pointing and waved cheekily.

"If nature let anyone else have a say, we should still be floating in the air arguing over gravity," Mumpsimus said. She looked around for praise at her little joke. Finding none, she put a serious face back on. "My sentence was a happy little bluebird and you all are not," she grumped.

"Don't I have time to pack a bag?" Bonk asked. "I'm still in my bathrobe!"

"Please," the pangirlin begged. "I can't. I need to be alone. I don't know how to . . . to *people*."

"The dead," Walter mooed, "are not people. So you should be fine. I ought to know. I am one hundred years oooooooold."

"The dead do not mind your bathrobe," Rarely the crowcus sang smugly. "But have a care—wear nothing woven in the Land of the Dead. Eat, drink, do anything you wish, but do not let the cloth of that world touch your shoulders, and accept no gift of wool or linen from anyone beyond this life."

"Wait, what?" Osmo protested. "Why not?"

The crowcus pointed a wing at his patchwork suit. "It protects you. All those little scraps of your village and your people and your life. That is your armor! That alone will keep you safe! Do not give it up! Not for anything!"

"Aw," mumbled Mumpsimus. "What did you do that for? I wasn't gonna tell him."

"*What?*" Osmo cried.

But the throng shoved them forward, and Bonk, too. It had all gone on too long already, they wanted the wedding. They wanted the show. They wanted the angry roots and upset trees to play nicely with the city again. And no little skadgebat and pangirlin were going to hold it up any longer.

Nevermore took up one of the strands of evening gloomys bitterly. Bonk grabbed one of the garlands of leaves and scrunched it up between his fingers with a scowl.

"You said there must be music," Mumpsimus said softly. "Music and dancing. My sentences have been red and cold, but now they are purple and soft. *I* am purple and soft, mostly. If you knew me, you would know that. You will have your music and your dance. It is your wedding, after all."

And there was music, suddenly. A wild, mad music, birdsong and frogsong and whalesong, but also violins and pipes and drums. The mixed-up animals sang the songs of their species, and the half-human ones, like Never, played instruments with their scaled or furred or feathered or naked hands.

Osmo had never in all his life felt less like dancing. And he very rarely felt like dancing. But this was it. This was a moment when he could be his father and yell until he was red in the face and demand to see someone in charge of this seething pile of injustice and absurdity, or he could be someone else. And do something else. He didn't know what, exactly. But maybe if he did it, this place would stop being so baffling and cruel and become the Else he'd dreamed of for so long. It was too terrible a thought to bear: that magic and monsters and mysteries were as real as bricks and straw, but that he couldn't fit in with them any better than he did with the normal world.

So Osmo Unknown began to dance. It wasn't much of a dance. He wouldn't win a prize for it at any recital back home. Foot up, foot down, head back, head forward, a twist of the hips, a little jump. And he danced forward, like a maypole, dragging the foxtail with him.

Never and Bonk did not dance. But they moved. Gritting

their teeth, dragging their own long ribbons in the same direction, counterclockwise, the opposite direction of the bright, warm, generous sun. The leaves and flowers and tails wove together at the top of the black pillar. The music quickened, sweetened, thickened. And soon enough, they were dancing too, eyes shut, round and round and round, their footsteps echoing under the Forest dome.

Slowly, with a grinding sound like the opening of a deep and ancient grave, the pillar began to *turn*.

It screeched and wept and scraped against the flagstones of the village square. Faster and faster, until it was spinning, smoke peeling out from the base, the free ribbons and garlands flying wild into the air. And still Osmo, Bonk, and Never danced, counterclockwise, pulling it behind them, faster and faster—

—and faster

—and faster

until—

They were dancing in a white barren desert without a horizon under a blazing brilliant purple sky.

*Chapter Twelve*

# The Land of What Does It Matter Now

Osmo Unknown stood on white sand under an amethyst sky. The horizon went on until forever and then further still. In the living world, the place where the sky meets the land might be golden with sunlight or blue with evening. But here, it was a fuzzy emerald blur beneath the purple heavens. It made him feel a little ill to look at, almost like seasickness, but without a sea in sight. It was neither warm nor cold, neither day nor night, neither windy nor still. It simply *was*, wherever they were, however they'd got there, and it felt as though it always had been.

What it so clearly *wasn't* was Quiddity. Or Littlebridge. Or anywhere in the Fourpenny Woods or the Greengroat Valley or anyplace normal at all. They were Somewhere Else, emphasis on the *else*. Osmo would have called getting there magic, but he remembered what Bonk had said about butterflies and carriages and decided that he was, in this case, most definitely a butterfly, and examining the carriage too closely would probably lead to getting eaten by a horse.

Never turned around several times, her eyes enormous.

Bonk the Cross shoved his hands in his bathrobe and sniffed at the air with a moist nose.

"Are we dead?" Bonk the Cross whispered, though there was no one around to hear.

Nevermore grabbed the skadgebat's fuzzy, striped ear and yanked hard. Bonk howled in wounded fury, though his pride hurt much more than his ear.

"Heart beating fast?" she asked.

Bonk rubbed his head resentfully. "Yes, you trashcake! TRASH-CAKE SUPREME! Do I exist for the abuse of the entire universe? DO I? Don't answer! It's the truth. I know it."

"Then you still have a heart," the pangirlin said calmly. "Smear some logic on it, it'll feel better. A beating heart means we're not dead. At least, you're not."

"So," Osmo said, since no one else was going to, "what do we do now?"

"Well, *I* don't muddy well know," snapped Bonk. "I never been dead before!"

"You both must know more about this place than I do," Osmo said, quite sensibly. "I'd never heard of the Eightpenny Woods a day ago." He looked around again at the long empty pale plains. "Not much of a woods if you ask me."

"No one will ever ask you anything, ya dropped egg," Bonk mumbled. He scrabbled in his pocket for a biscuit, found one, called it his precious baby darling, and nibbled at the edges.

"Only what we learned in Monday school when we were little,"

Never answered reluctantly. "It's always twilight, there's a desert without thirst and a river without a bridge. There are countries and cities no less than the living build, and wild creatures, ghosts and coelacants and a million zillion birds, and in the center lies the beating Gnarlbind, the beating heart of the Forest." Never trailed off, as if she'd been reciting something and had forgotten how it went. "I don't know. I don't remember. I only liked the one hymn we had to sing about a lonely pier and a lonely boat and a tall black bird." She glared at him. "I never liked Monday school and honestly I'm still mad at you, Osmo. I could be home safe and comfy under my mess right now! I did *not* have the Land of the Dead on my calendar for today! It's just *so* inconsiderate."

"I don't know who you think you're fooling that you keep a calendar," Bonk laughed between nibbles of biscuit. "We saw your house. I'll give you a pound of gold and half a pie when we get back if you even *own* a calendar."

Never's bronze-scaled cheeks flushed dark. "I don't know who you think *you're* fooling that you've got a pound of gold," she snarled. "Or a pie."

Bonk reached deep into his bathrobe pocket, rummaged dramatically, and pulled out a rather squished, dried-out crust of a baked pie. He leaned in close to Never's sour bronze face, and popped it into his snout.

Osmo Unknown looked deep into the violet sky. He looked out into the blank dry fields, whiter than snow before anyone has mashed their feet into it. He felt surprisingly . . . fine. At least now he knew what to do. No one was going to eat his village. Unless he failed. But he wouldn't. *He couldn't.* No one was going to eat *him* in the next several minutes, at least. He'd gone when he was called and done as he was told. Fulfilled the terms of the treaty. Now, whatever lay ahead, it was all up to him and not an old piece of parchment. He could come out dead or married or something worse than both, but he didn't have to just *stand* there and hope for the best from creatures with claws bigger than his whole body. In a minute, that was probably going to scare the beating heart right out of him. But right now, it was ever so much better than waiting and knowing nothing. Not that he knew a lot. But it was no longer, technically, nothing.

Osmo tugged on the strap of his satchel and took a deep breath. He couldn't smell a thing. You can always smell *something*, even in the cleanest, emptiest place. You might be so used to the smells of your own world that you don't notice, but you're always smelling some little bit of ocean or dirt or perfume or cooking or laundry or flowers growing in the garden. But Osmo couldn't smell anything at all. It was the very strangest thing, even taking a purple sky into consideration.

He had no way to tell what was east or south or north or west. So Osmo just started walking where his toes were already pointed.

"Where are you going?" Never called after him.

"I don't know!" Osmo called back cheerfully. "But it stands to reason we're not meant to stay here in the great big nothing! Come on, my big furry bride is out there somewhere! It's called the Eightpenny *Woods*. So I'm gonna find us some trees."

The skadgebat and the pangirlin didn't move. Osmo turned around and held out his arms.

"It's the boldest plan since boiling water before you drink it," he laughed. His head felt light and giddy. "Come on!"

Bonk scratched the back of his striped head. "I thought you'd be more upset. You've been upset a lot. Since we met. You seem an upset kind of person. Generally."

Osmo jogged back to his companions. "I probably should be? It's the afterlife and all. But do you know, I've taken a million walks and I've always known exactly what I'd see on the way and who I would meet and how it would all end. But *this* walk"—he gestured in the direction he'd chosen out of all and none of them— "anything could happen. I could end up anywhere. Meet anyone. End any way. I guess it's easier to see the gleam on that without a Quidnunk breathing down your soul. I always wanted things to be different. And now they are. I just . . . didn't think *different* would be as scary as it is." He squinted in the gloaming. "I don't suppose time sticks its nose in here much, but I'd rather get going, wouldn't you?"

Bonk the Cross stuck the rest of his biscuit back in his pocket and gave Osmo a mocking salute. "I don't know about you, Pangy," he said, "but I am inspired as all get-out."

"All right, all right," Osmo sighed. "You don't have to make fun of me."

"I don't! But I *like* to. So I *will*. See, it works out for both of us!"

"Wait," Never said quickly. She looked around for something, but she had neither satchel nor bathrobe. "We have to be able to get back. There's no landmarks or anything, but we should remember where we came in."

She dragged the claws on her feet across the desert soil in the shape of a wide, sharp X. Beneath the white sands the deeper soil was livid turquoise. You could see Never's mark from the moon, Osmo thought. If there was a moon here. He didn't see one. But it might be hiding. He knew quite solidly now that you couldn't be sure of anything outside Littlebridge, even the moon.

And so they began to walk.

For a time, no one said a word, which was delightful for Never, unprecedented for Bonk, and agony for Osmo. At last, the horrifically human boy couldn't keep it in any longer.

"Are you going to explain what you said back there?" he blurted.

"What's that?" Bonk snorted back.

"About what happened to the Quidnunx. Why there are so few left. About *them*. And *that*. And *the other thing*. Did you mean us? Did you mean . . . me? It couldn't be me, though. I'm just a kid. If somebody did a bad thing ages and ages ago it can't be my fault now. That's not fair."

Bonk the Cross stopped in the white sand and spread his furry arms to take in the whole of the underworld. "Boy, look where we are! And why? Because your mum had a pinecone for a brain! Now, if you're not going to use *your* much smaller pinecone, kindly keep your muckymouth shut." He pushed a stubby finger hard into Osmo's chest. "If you don't know, it's not up to me to tell you. Not up to me to throw a strop about it, either. I would if I could! You know how much I like to throw strops about things. But me and mine aren't the ones it happened at. Though, not to put too fine a point on it, it's at *least* as bad that no one's mentioned it to you over breakfast in thirteen howling years that it happened at all! But do trust the Bonk, it *is* your fault. At least as much as it's your fault I'm stuck in the underbog of the cosmos with a motter and a bowling ball, so you should think long and hard about what you've done."

Osmo didn't try to talk again for several hours.

It was pleasant enough going, really. The air felt cool on their backs when they needed it and warm when they needed that. The color of the sky seemed quite normal and pretty after a while. And they never got thirsty or tired. But they never seemed to get anywhere, either. There weren't any hills or crags or valleys, just the same snowy warm sand, flat and regular and endless.

Until the sound.

The sound came for the first time when they'd been walking two or three hours, by Osmo's guess, which was no guess at all when the light never moved and the land never changed. It sounded like a cork coming out of a bottle, but also like an axe biting into a tree, and then again like butter sizzling across a black pan, and finally like a bird flying directly into a closed window. It startled them all so badly Bonk squealed and shoved Osmo in front of him to protect himself and Never instantly curled up into a big coppery ball. Osmo squealed too, but having been shoved in front, he had no choice but to be the one to find out first what was coming for them.

Twenty feet off, the air wobbled. The air *crisped*. The air flashed a color that didn't exist at all in the world of the living, neither orange nor blue but somehow everything both ever aspired to be.

And a turtle appeared.

Not *completely* a turtle. It had the size and savage lovely stripes and long teeth of a tiger. But a great hard shell, all the same, and leathery legs.

And it *glowed*. Faintly, all around its shell and its head and its legs and its toes. A writhing, wriggling, thin, sparkling gleam, like oily air over a hot fire. The glimmer was almost blue, and almost green, and almost violet, and almost white, and almost black and pink, too. If you looked at it dead-on, it disappeared. You could only see it out of the corner of your eye. When Osmo was very little, he'd gone scavenging on the edges of the Fourpenny Woods with his mother. They'd found a clutch of strange scalloped mushrooms clinging to a dead tree branch, glowing faintly phosphorescent in the night. That was the closest thing he could think of. But Osmo very quickly stopped thinking of it, because it made him think of his mother, too, and he could not bear that just now.

The beast glanced at them, unconcerned. It began walking in the same direction they were headed in.

Every time they heard the sound, someone else wobbled and crisped and flashed into being. Animals of every kind, and not just the wild mixtures of the deep woods. Plain old deer and cats and mice and dragonflies, too. No one spoke; everyone glimmered. And they all seemed to know by instinct where to go. Osmo felt a small puff of pride that he'd apparently chosen correctly, despite being alive and human and other unpleasant things.

Soon enough, Osmo, Bonk, and Never were no longer alone in the least, but part of a great caravan making its way across the white desert.

And soon after that, the caravan wasn't alone, either. Something so small it was almost invisible whizzed by at incredible speed. It zipped across the white flats, zigzagging, bouncing, loop-de-looping, then doubling back as if to look at them all and zooming off again. Little sparkling sprays and wakes of sand splashed up behind it into the lavender air.

And it brought friends.

Whatever they were, dozens of them danced and buzzed and darted alongside the traveling ghosts like dolphins diving alongside a ship at sea. Bonk scowled evilly at them every time they shot sand into his fur. Osmo tried to get an actual look at them whenever one streaked past, but it was impossible. They carved furrows into the desert, and the furrows hid them well.

One crashed into Osmo's shoe. The tiny lump of white sand tapped lightly against his heel twice in confusion. Nevermore glanced guiltily at the lumbering ghosts. Then, without warning, a long pink tongue, longer and pinker than any human girl's, shot out of her mouth and tried to snatch up the little intruder. Osmo laughed in delight. The lump bulleted back, shaking itself in reproachful surprise. Sand scattered; they saw just the smallest glimpse of something hard and shiny and brown—then it bolted off in another direction, burrowing into the earth again.

They all traveled together, ghosts, adventurers, and tiny desert zoomers, into the great purple horizon.

After ages and ages, finally, mercifully, something other than desert opened up in the distance.

A mist of hot green. A stripe of cold black.

An oasis, if this really was a desert. The flatland grew lumpier and bumpier. Stones appeared, then boulders, then mighty crags. But none of it was good old plain granite or sandstone. The rocks of this place shone rounded and polished, deep black and blue, with pale sparkles and speckles glittering all through them. Some kind of agate, Osmo guessed, agate stuffed full of the night sky itself.

Nestled between three sand dunes and a smattering of broken starry slabs lay a still black pool. Long, tall tangled green weeds grew thick around it. Some had pale tiny flowers. Some stood as high as trees. All sank their roots in the dark water and drank deep.

Many of the animals slowed and stopped at the oasis. Bonk veered off with purpose and plonked himself down on a heap of soft sand. The invisible zoomers burst off in all directions, rolling up the dunes, through the weeds, into the black pool, round the standing stones. They tucked themselves away out of sight so quickly it was as though they'd never been there. But Osmo could see little winkings of twilight catching behind every leaf and rock. He couldn't see them. But they could certainly see him.

"What *are* they?" Nevermore marveled.

"Jerks," grumphed Bonk.

"Let's press on," Osmo said. "It can't be so much further. I'm not a bit tired. Never? Do you need a rest?"

She shook her head. But Bonk was swiveling his rump back and forth in the sand to carve out a cozy seat.

"Never, *ever* pass up a nap-and-nosh when it comes to you, Mister Boy," the skadgebat announced with authority. "The absolute *right* of every creature to afternoon snacks"—he thrust his paw into the air and raised his voice like an old-fashioned politician, trilling his *r*'s and biting off his *t*'s with clean snaps—"whatsoever those snacks may consist of, transcends life, death, business hours, and moral law! It shall *not* be infringed!"

He fished in his pockets again, and this time came out with two fresh biscuits, a slice of green cake on a little plate with raspberries and ivy painted on it, and a teapot with a stopper in the spout. Bonk pulled the cork, tipped the pot back, and drank directly from the source.

"How much have you got in your pockets, Bonk?" Osmo asked in wonder.

"None of your business, raggabrash. I like a deep pocket, so what? It's the chief thing I look for in a good robe. Don't get snippy just because you didn't think to bring lunch and your clothes are stupid."

Bonk produced a dull butter knife and a new plate, this one with roses and oranges on it. The wombat-ish badger cut his cake in half and handed half to Never. She knelt beside him in the fine sand and ate delicately with her long nails.

"I'm not really hungry, though," she said between bites. "It's more like I remember I *should* be hungry."

"I'll have no excuses from a glorified billiard ball." Bonk waggled his paw at her. "Eat for tomorrow's hunger if you're full today."

"I'm a *bit* hungry," Osmo ventured.

Bonk shrugged and offered him a biscuit. "Now, you make

that last, that's a worm-and-tulip-bulb special out of my own oven. One hundred percent real worm."

Osmo looked down at the biscuit. It had Bonk's frowning face stamped into the crisp dough. He wanted to give it back. No. *No.* Insisting on chocolate or lemon drizzle biscuits was just what everyone he'd ever met would have done. He was in the Else now. He had to start acting like it.

Osmo shoved the whole biscuit in his mouth. It tasted exactly like what it was, no more, no less. Bonk passed the teapot to wash it down. Earthworm is quite dry. The tea, at least, was just tea, black leaf and hot water and that nice familiar *smack* of tannin at the back of the throat.

Osmo swallowed finally. He handed the pot back and wiped his mouth with the back of his sleeve.

Bonk patted his knee. "I know, I know, I forgot the sugar bowl. Well, I didn't know where I'd be today, did I? But then, wherever you are, you'll always want a sugar bowl." He sniffed in surprise. "Gosh! That's the only thing I've ever done wrong! What a refreshing experience!"

A slim, graceful, golden figure glided up beside Nevermore. She jumped a little, then grimaced.

"Company," she whispered with a shudder. "Bad enough to be *disturbing*"—she nearly spat out the pangolin word for *three*. "Now I have to deal with *dreadful* as well. *Apocalyptic* can't be far off at this rate."

Osmo didn't know what number *apocalyptic* was in pangolese. Probably ten or eleven, if he had to guess. Twelve, tops.

The golden figure belonged to a boy, a little older, perhaps, than Osmo and Never. Taller, certainly.

A boy, and also a goldfish.

Osmo had never seen any person as beautiful as this one. He didn't even know boys were *allowed* to be that beautiful. His father would certainly say they weren't. His skin glowed pale gold, his eyes gleamed black, and all up and down his body, long, thin, glassy orange fins like veils fluttered and floated. He wore a suit of pearly scales and his hair flowed down one side of his slender chest in a long red braid. The golden boy-fish held up one tropical yellow hand, full of the white sand they'd walked over for miles. A gladfish. It had to be. Never had mentioned them before, one of the other part-human creatures of the Fourpenny Woods.

"For your tea," he explained in a musical voice.

"Er. Don't take sand in my tea," Bonk said, shaking his head. How were they meant to talk to anyone here? Were there rules? Were there manners? Or had they traveled past all that, into the Land of What Does It Matter Now? "Thanks much and on your way."

"It is not sand," the gladfish answered, sifting it in through the spout of Bonk's precious teapot without asking permission.

Osmo picked up a few grains of the stuff and tasted it experimentally.

It was not sand. It was sugar.

The gladfish smiled. "For the sweetness of life," he said. He waved his beautiful hand toward the brilliant tufty green weeds. The translucent fins glittered in the twilight. "Chicory and wormwood and rye, for the bitterness of life. And the pool is filled with ink, for the story of our lives is ended. My name is Away." He bowed gorgeously. "I died at midnight on a Tuesday."

"Ah. Bonk the Cross, not even a little at your service. The *aggressively* introverted copper kettle over there is Never, this mess of boy parts is Osmo Unknown." Away waited expectantly. But for what? There were *some* kind of manners here, clearly. Bonk took a stab. "Died . . . hrm. Around three o'clock Saturday. Didn't think to check the old clocky. Fine day for it anyhow."

"How do you know all that?" Never asked. "I don't remember anything in church about sugar in the underworld."

"I just . . . *know*. I did not know it when I was alive, but now that I am here, I just . . . do. Do you not?"

"Uh, yes, of course we do," Osmo cut in. They were *not* dead. They were not like anyone else here. He doubted they were, strictly speaking, even allowed to be here in the first place. He didn't want to give up the truth unless they had to. He tried to communicate all of this to Never with his eyes. "Same as you, just popped into our heads the minute we turned up. Right? My friend . . . uh . . . died of a head wound. On Thursday. She's still a little groggy."

But communicating the urgent need to lie with a simple pointed stare is a thing only learned through many years of school or siblings or both. Never hadn't spent half enough time around other people to learn the knack.

"No, I didn't," she said quickly. "What are you talking about?"

"You poor creature." Away's voice swelled with sympathy. "This is the Meaningful Desert, which surrounds the Eightpenny

Woods. That is the reason for the sugar and the chicory weeds and the ink in the pond—everything here means something else. Look!" The beautiful orange boy reached out and ran his fingers along a crag of starry stone. A piece of it crumbled away like jeweled ash beneath his fingers. Tiny, soft shards drifted up and off into the sky. "Because life is fragile and precious," he explained. "Though it appears so solid and important. Soon we will reach the River After. There we will find a lonely boat and a lonely pier."

Nevermore brightened up. "I remember this part!"

"We will meet the ferryman Mustamakkara. She will question and judge us. If we convince her we have lived well, she will take us across the water into the Forest beyond life."

"Then what?" Bonk said between munches of biscuit.

"I do not understand."

"What happens in the Forest beyond life? Parties? Games? Treats? I bet there are treats. Maybe a shop or two? Every place needs a good shop or it's barely a place at all."

Away's graceful shoulders slumped. Osmo could not stop staring at him. The boy's chin was so delicate and sweet. He looked like a drawing. "I do not know that," the gladfish admitted. "Perhaps when I have crossed the river, I will, suddenly, like when the osprey got me and I woke up here."

The gladfish paused for a moment and turned his head in the direction they were all headed in. When he did, Osmo could see that same almost-blue, almost-green, almost-violet, almost-white, almost-black-and-pink glimmer that ringed the other poor traveling dead around them.

"Don't you feel it?" Away said softly. "The song of the river? The gravity of After? It wants me to come. It wants me not to wait. All my life I loved the water, even though half of me needed the land. I could never be happy. In each place I longed for the other. My lungs burned in the water. My gills choked in the grass. And in the end, a seabird caught me in a lake, like any other stupid, silly old fish who never dreamed of learning to bake bread in a real live oven in a real live house. The water betrayed me. But now the river will make it right. It's promising me, right now. No water has ever loved me as much as the River After does. It pulls me as surely as a friendly hand. Don't you feel it?"

But they didn't. None of them did. They heard nothing. They felt nothing. Because they did not belong, and they knew it.

Away glanced back at them without turning his head from the call of the river. And then he snapped his head round intently, searching the three of them with his deep black eyes.

"What's wrong with you?" he whispered so the other animals wouldn't hear. "You don't have it. It's not possible. But you don't."

"Don't have what?" Osmo said quickly. But he knew, he knew already, and he knew it would sink them if they had to be judged by any sort of ferryman.

Away's lovely apricot-colored face twisted strangely as he tried to find what they were most definitely missing.

"The gloss," the goldfish-boy said. He held up his braid and turned it back and forth so the glinting, shifting light they all had played brightly in the dusky air. And then, Away breathed deep. His elegant nostrils and gilded gills flared. "And you *smell*."

"I beg your actual pardon," Bonk huffed.

Away's face twisted up in feelings. Feelings like the gloss itself: neither anger nor fear nor longing nor love, neither blue nor green nor black nor pink, but all of them swirled into one and none. "You smell like *dirt* and *musk* and *breakfast*. Like *dangers* and *choices* and the *future*. You smell like *running around outside on a rainy day*."

Bonk shrugged casually, but his eyes were frantic. "Probably just my biscuits. Keep your nose to yourself or I've half a mind to put you in a bowl and forget to clean it for weeks on end."

Just then, a soft bonging bell sounded from somewhere both a thousand miles off and right next door. Big, heavy, white flakes tumbled slowly out of the lavender sky. The glittering blue gash Away's lemony-bright fingers left in the fragile and precious rock began to fill up with snow.

"The clock has struck winter!" one of the other dead beasts announced.

A narwholf, ancient and white of fur. She howled up into the sky. Others took up the call and soon the oasis was filled with the sound of ghosts singing and snow falling and wild tongues slowly drinking from the pool.

"I didn't know there could be winter in the afterworld," Osmo whispered, holding his hand out to catch the perfect, glittering snowflakes.

"There is every season," said the goldfish boy. "Why would this world obey the boring old rules of the last? Why would the Forest deprive us of the lovely bits of time and space now that we've outgrown all the ugly tricks it plays on the living? It is how we will tell the time now, since the moon is always up and the sun is always down. At six in the morning it is spring, at noon it is high summer, at suppertime it is a crisp and crackling autumn, and at midnight comes the winter. It is winter now. It is the middle of the night. Which means," Away said sternly, "it is the hour of telling the truth. You smell and do not shine and know nothing. What *are* you?"

Never shrugged and sighed. People had tried to explain manners to her many times and she'd shut her door in their faces. They were simply wrong. There wasn't any time or place at all where it was better to lie or keep a secret or even keep quiet. You never had to lie, when you lived alone, except to yourself.

"Alive," she said simply. "Sorry."

## Chapter Thirteen

# DOWN THE ROAD TO THE RIVER AFTER

"You don't belong here," Away hissed fearfully. "Go back. Get out. You're not allowed. I'll tell. I will. And if I tell, you'll be punished!"

"What kind of punishment?" Osmo asked. "Like a stern talking-to or . . . ? Because we're already *in* the afterlife, so what's the worst that could happen?"

"Nothing alive can enter the Land of the Dead. So I expect you'll have to be deadened. Or exorcised. At least kicked out."

The caravan of beasts began to move forward again. Without meaning to, Osmo, Bonk, and Never traveled with them, with Away trailing along behind.

Bonk barked laughter at Never, but nothing about it was merry. "Good job, mulchmouth. Head like a bag of laundry, you've got."

"I did do a good job. I told the truth," she fired back.

"Never, you can't just blurt things out!" Osmo cried.

"Why not? Why would you *ever* say anything but the truth? Pangirlins never lie."

"Can't lie?" Bonk asked, stunned. "But it's fun."

"I didn't say that. I *can*. But what's the point? When you live a good lonely life, there's no one to lie to but yourself, and *you'd* know it was a lie. You can't fool *yourself*. So why bother? Just say true things. It saves so much time."

The crowd seemed to almost carry them along with it. They found themselves walking without meaning to, flowing forward across the bone-white sand with all the others. "The living cannot enter the Woods." Big shimmering tears pooled in the goldfish-boy's dark eyes. "It's not *fair*. I can't go home. I can't *ever* go home. Why should you get to come here?"

But no one was listening to him anymore.

"Please, Never, we have to be careful!" Osmo pleaded.

"Oh, what do you know about what we have to do and what we don't? You didn't even know Quidnunx existed until about thirty-five seconds ago. I don't have to listen to you, you're not king yet!" Never's face burned. Her hands were shaking. She had never had to confront anything more serious than her mushrooms when they stubbornly refused to be a toaster. She hated it. She didn't know how to stop it. It just kept *happening*.

"I know we're in the underworld, looking for a ghost, and that's the kind of thing that happens in books, the kind of books I read *all the time*! And when you're in the Land of the Dead, being careful about what you say is pretty much step one!"

"Oh really? And what's step two, Your Majesty, Lord of All Geniuses?"

Osmo felt his own cheeks grow hot. He was tired of being treated like a fool. Tired of being called one repeatedly by an almost-skunk in a bathrobe. Tired of being the one at the center of everything but having no say at all in it. The boy Headmaster Gudgeon called a know-it-all at least five times a day *did* know *some* things. "I don't know, be careful what you eat!"

Nevermore knew she was yelling now, but she didn't know how to fix it. The yell was in control, not her. "This is so educational! Why did I ever go to Monday school at all? And step three?"

Osmo threw his hands in the air. "Pretty sure it's: don't look behind you! And before you ask, step four is *TRY TO BLEND IN!*"

Bonk the Cross shoved his biscuits back in his pockets, toddled over to stand between them, and puffed up his chest. "All right, all right, let's turn the kettle down juuuust a skosh, kits and cubs."

The stragglers behind gave them a wide berth, determined not to let these brawlers ruin their rites of passage into the next world. A few even jumped the queue in front of them, since their little group was clearly occupied with other business. *So sorry, excuse me, I'll just pop round, thank you, goodbye.*

They were losing their place in line.

"See?" Never yelled. "*See?* This is why the pangirlin way is best. No one argues with you when you're solitary. No one gets offended. There's nothing to upset you. You don't have to dance around the swamp of other people's feelings trying not to fall face-down in the mud! I hate it in the swamp of other people's feelings!" She stopped in her tracks. The scaled girl clenched her fists and threw her head back, squeezing her eyes shut beneath her glasses. "I'm sorry I'm yelling! I don't want to be yelling! It feels bad if I keep the yell in and it feels bad if I let it out! How do you stop yourself doing this once you've started?"

Osmo blinked. He had six sisters. Two parents. A schoolful of people who hardly ever saw things his way. He'd been arguing since before he could talk. It didn't bother him. Just because somebody yelled didn't mean it was the end of all things. Arguing was like the weather. It just *happened*. You got an umbrella and boots and sooner or later the sun would come out again.

So he did what he did when Oona got angry with him over the last potato or some other bit of brother-and-sister nonsense.

Osmo took three steps back across the sugary ground and hugged her.

He tried, anyway. She saw him coming and sidestepped it like a poison dart.

"What was that?" she said.

"Nothing. I'm sorry," said Osmo hurriedly. "A hug. To make you feel better."

"I don't get it. Why would it make me feel better?"

"I don't know, it just does. Usually."

Never wrinkled her nose. "No way. Got anything else?"

"The only other way I know to stop arguing is to say soft things in a soft voice and really mean it. I suppose it's like a hug with words. Like . . . um. Okay." He took a deep breath. "I yelled first. I don't really know you well enough to yell at you. I'm sorry I did that, it was wrong of me."

She nodded and sniffled a bit.

"You're supposed to say 'I'm sorry' back," he suggested gently. They were walking again, without even noticing.

"Why?" Never asked.

"Because you yelled, too, and you called me a name. So say you're sorry. You can hug me back that way."

"Do I have to? I don't want to. I think I shall feel much better if *you* say sorry and *I* don't."

Osmo laughed. "You don't *have* to, but if you don't, then other arguments later get worse and last longer."

"Why would we ever have another argument? We already had one. And it's over. Why would anyone ever do that twice? It's horrid."

Bonk peered up at her. "I don't believe it. I can't believe it. You absolute brand-new teeny baby fluffy *lamb*. Was that your *first* argument?"

Never crossed her arms defensively. "Yes. *Yes*. Of course. Why wouldn't it be? I've never annoyed *myself*." The green fire in the pangirlin's eyes went out and she crumpled a little. "You're all judging me. You haven't even got wigs and you're judging me. You think I'm stupid and small. I'm not. I'm lonesome. I *like* my lonesomeness. It's my best friend! So I don't know all these rules about arguing and apologizing and not always telling the truth. That's not my fault, it's their fault for being stupid. Ugh! There's more rules for getting along with people than rules about getting along through the underworld! I am sorry, Osmo. There. Rules obeyed. Everyone happy. Everyone"—she shuddered—"*hugged*. Let's get moving."

"You'll never make it across the river," the gladfish said flatly. They had completely forgotten him. But he trailed along beside them all the same. "You are not one of us. Mustamakkara will smell it on you. She'll see it. Only the dead go on."

Bonk the Cross whirled on the poor boy-fish. "Why are you still hanging back here with us? Go on, git! Keep your place in line! We'll be fine on our own! You don't like us? Don't think we belong? Don't let the desert hit you in the rump on your way to the great hereafter!"

Away trembled. His luminous fins drooped. "You smell like tomorrows," he whispered. "Like having so many tomorrows you could waste a whole day doing nothing at all and not even notice. I'm never going to smell that again. I'm never going to have that again. I was young. I didn't even know tomorrows *had* a smell. And now that's all I'll ever have of them. Soon we'll be on the banks of the River After, and the smell will be gone like spilled perfume. Because you're never getting past her. And I am. Just let me smell you a little longer."

"Ew!" Never yelped.

"I'm with you," Osmo said, shrinking away from the snuffling ghost. "Ew."

"Look," the skadgebat said, relenting. But only slightly. He kicked the sugar-sand gruffly, refusing to look the ghost of a gold-fish in the eye. "We sympathize."

"No you don't. You're alive. The living only care about each other."

"Well, we're trying! But quit it with the sniffy-sniffy. And you could at least help. Because we have to cross the river, one way or the other, so get off your pond, screw your head onto your neck, and tell us how to ride this boat without a ticket."

"How should I know?"

"You seem to know everything else," Never pointed out.

Away shrugged his glittering shoulders. "I am dead. I just plan to . . . get on the ferry."

"Fantastic," Bonk sighed. "Well, that's all I've got. You two figure it out. I tried! And that means no one can blame me for anything that happens after this."

Away's gentle brow creased and wrinkled. "Why must you cross the river?"

Nevermore jutted out her copper chin and determinedly said nothing. She wasn't going to stick her shell out again.

Osmo hesitated. He wished he really were a know-it-all, so he'd know what to do now.

"You might as well tell me, I already know you're alive. It can't be worse than that."

Osmo Unknown gave up and blurted it all out. "My mother killed the Quidnunk queen. Her ghost is somewhere out there in the Eightpenny Woods, and I've got to go and marry her so no one eats or otherwise explodes my village and the treaty will hold, which seems to be the only thing keeping Littlebridge and the Fourpenny Woods from doing something so dreadful to each other no one even wants to talk about it."

"Ah." The goldfish-boy nodded. "Like Katja Kvass."

Osmo's mouth fell open. "How do you know about Katja Kvass? Everyone just looks at me like I've taken off my head and used it for a chair when I say her name."

"I remember when she rounded the pole. I was only little, then. She was pretty. Hair like a sparrow's belly."

"I thought you said you were young," Never said. The bear in front of them moved forward, but they hung back, keeping their voices quiet.

Away smiled. His teeth shone so white they looked almost blue. "Just as a goldfish will grow as big as the bowl you put it in, a gladfish's life will grow as long as the land you give it. And the Forest is vast. Two hundred years old *is* young."

Osmo gripped the boy's arm. It was cool beneath his fingers. "Do you know what happened to her?"

But the goldfish shook his head. How could he? If she came through this way, no one living would know about it. Whether she found her beastly husband or not, who could have seen it? She hadn't come back to Littlebridge. But that left a thousand other paths for her.

And for Osmo.

Away frowned. "Do you *want* to marry a ghost, human boy? I don't know that we are the marrying kind."

"Not even a little. But no one cares what I want."

"Yes, that is what Katja said, too. Well. She said it better. Prettier. And I think it rhymed. But that was the gist of it."

"Right now, what matters most of all the things in all the worlds is what I *don't* want. I don't want anyone to get hurt, back home or in Quiddity. I don't want anyone else to have to suffer or be afraid because my mother made a mistake. And I don't want to go back. Not yet, anyway. Not before I've *seen* anything. All of this is wrong and ridiculous and mad, but it's what I've got. So I have to get on that boat."

Osmo looked out across the snowy dunes like a white sea. And there it was. No illusion, no mirage, no trick of the twilight. A river as wide as a bay. He couldn't even begin to glimpse the opposite shore. The water shone dully, the same deep black ink that had pooled between the starry rocks. At the end of the line rose a lonely dock, but it was too far off with too many creatures winding between to catch sight of the ferryman.

They were almost there, and they had no plan.

"All right," Osmo said quickly and quietly, slinging his satchel off his shoulder. "We're going to have to fake it. There's nothing else to be done."

"What, fake being dead?" said Never, pushing up her glasses on her slim coppery nose.

"I can punch you real hard if you want," snorted Bonk. "Out cold looks as good as dead if you're in a hurry."

"How would that help when all the dead here are up and walking around?" Osmo rolled his eyes—but then he saw Bonk grinning toothily, his eyes glittering.

"I know, but I haven't punched you even a *little* yet, and I think we can agree that's been hard on all of us. Thought I might sneak one in while you were thinking it over."

Osmo shook his head. "We don't need to be out cold. We don't need to be rotting or shambling or moldy or have any bones showing. We need the gloss. Somehow, we need to glow like they do."

The long line crawled forward, a dark curlicue down the white dunes.

"This is why you need a mess." Nevermore nodded sagely.

"When you travel all tidy and neat, you can only ever have what you could imagine needing the day you left. When you have a mess, a *really* good clutter, you don't need to bother with something as limited as your imagination. You always have something useful on hand even if you don't know it, because you've got just about everything. You only have to find it under the heaps." She sniffed the sugary desert air. "Well, come on, then," she said.

"Come on and do what?" Osmo answered, confused.

Never rolled her eyes. "Make a mess! Empty your bag. And your pockets, Bonk. Me, I didn't get a chance to pack a suitcase," the pangirlin said bitterly. "Who packs a suitcase for a wedding? All I've got are my spectacles and my lonely brain."

"You're right," Osmo agreed, unshouldering his satchel. "We've got to take stock." It was the best first step to any plan, his mother always said. Assess what you have and what you need. Or else, when it comes to it, you'll always need what you don't have and have what you don't need. It sounded a bit like what Never said, but much more straightforward and orderly, without any bits of old breakfast stuck to it.

"I will do no such thing, how very dare you," hissed Bonk. "My pockets are my own, you've no right."

"We're all in this together, Bonk. We have to pool our resources if we mean to get back whole," Osmo said quietly.

"No." Bonk turned on him, thrusting his little furry finger at the boy. "You're in this together with *yourself*. You're the one who's supposed to show how clever you are and how worthy to marry the big furry moppet and be our king. We're only witnesses. We don't have to do squishedy-squashedy. All we have to do is watch whatever you do. And it's very dull being your witness so far, I'll tell you what! Be more interesting, why don't you? But do it out of your own pockets!"

"Calm down, Bonk," Nevermore said softly. "What's gotten into you? What have you got in there, diamonds?"

Osmo thought Bonk might be in real danger of actually exploding. "I *won't*, it's none of your *busy bees*, and before you even *think* about asking me about my pockets again, you'd better pull your lip up over your head and swallow! He don't just get what's mine because he's got an empty hole in the ground he wants to fill with *my* resources!"

Osmo scratched the back of his head. "Well," he said with a bit of a smile, "that is rather what kings do top to bottom, isn't it?"

Bonk the Cross would have gone all over red if he hadn't had fur to hide it. He clutched his bathrobe around his chest and stamped his foot. Then he did it again, for good measure. "NO!" he barked. "You're not my king! You're not anybody's king and you never will be. You're the King of Being a Complete Idiot! King of Burps and Sneezes! King of . . . of Turnips!"

Osmo flinched and felt his heart deflate slowly inside him. "Fine," he said quietly. "Do whatever you want." He unbuckled his satchel and dumped its contents out onto the sugar-sand of the Meaningful Desert.

It wasn't much.

A folded doublechess board. The rest of his hard-won pieces, minus the white queen, which rested safely in the pockets of Mrs. Brownbread. Osmo hadn't had one solitary chance to think about something so little until now. His set was broken—a piece lost and no way to win it back. Would he ever meet anyone again who played? Osmo fought to keep every awful thing he felt about that safely off his face. You didn't show your feelings to someone who called you the King of Turnips when he knew how you felt about that word. You just didn't.

And the rest? A pair of hickory pencils. A pretty, flat stone he'd picked up by the river on the way home from school weeks ago. Two smallpennies and a littlecrown for treats at First Frost he'd never gotten to buy and never would. *The Ballad of the Forest and the Valley, Seventh Edition, Annotated*, PROPERTY OF ST. WHYLOM'S SCHOOL. DO NOT STEAL. The golden ball he'd won so many years ago off Adelard Sloe and the smallkeg of Unknown's Goodest Stout he'd given him only yesterday before the whole world changed. Six sad squashed red flowers with long limp stems. The flowers he'd picked for Ivy from the gentle familiar banks of the Catch-a-Crown River, still bound together with his sister Oona's sweet black velvet ribbon.

His whole old life, dumped out like morning rubbish. No, it wasn't much, and none of it useful.

"Plus my spectacles," Never offered helpfully.

"Plus your spectacles"—Osmo nodded—"that brings us to a grand total of I Have No Idea What to Do."

Away fidgeted fretfully. The golden gladfish glanced from human to skadgebat to pangirlin, down to the small useless mess and then back between them all. "I would like to be a helpful fish," he said softly.

"So be helpful, who's stopping you?" Bonk grumbled, still quite sore about his pockets.

Away pointed one long glittery finger down at Osmo's only earthly (or unearthly, as the case currently was) belongings. The line crept forward again. The ghosts behind them glared angrily at the backs of their heads, bent together in concentration and holding everyone else up. Osmo squinted, turned his head this way and that, stood on his tiptoes, then crouched down—and finally saw it.

A few drops of the gloss seeped from the bottom of those six long stems, broken where he'd snapped them off on the riverbank. Dead blossoms, dead hopes, and suddenly Osmo didn't feel half as confident and excited as he had before, staring at those stupid crushed flowers Ivy would never have cared about, even if he'd gotten a chance to give them to her.

"Your crown, too!" Never exclaimed. "Osmo, your crown!"

He took it off and turned it over in his hands. The Frostfrau's crown, somewhat worse for all the harassment it had gone through. The gloss flowed along the edges of the plucked flowers and picked berries like a slick of oil. It was almost invisible to the living. But Away shielded his eyes as though it outshone any sun that ever spun in the dark. Osmo rubbed a witch hazel sprig thoughtfully between his fingers.

A greasy slip of gloss came off and clung to his skin.

"Flowers die as surely as any fish," Away said in his kind, musical voice. "A berry off the vine is gone to the next world no less than a girl off her sickbed."

"Excellent, I'll have that then," Bonk said, helping himself to the flowers. Osmo watched in mild horror as the skadgebat crushed his love-gift up into a paste and set to work rubbing down his whole furry body.

Osmo slowly unwound the witch hazel whips and lingonberry vines and snowdrops and fir needles of the Frostfrau crown. He ran them down his arms and legs and round the back of his neck and down the strands of his hair like a washing cloth. He felt terribly guilty. It was the end of history. No one would ever wear this crown at the end of a festival again. The petals broke off and floated away on the wind as he pressed them against his skin to get as much gloss out of them as he could, like wine from the strangest of grapes.

He handed the last of the ruined crown to Nevermore, but she only got up to her knees before it was no more than snowy dust, crumbling to nothing in her coppery hands.

"Uh-oh," she said bluntly.

She pushed with one toe at the rest of the pile of items Osmo had poured out. He bent down and had begun stuffing them back into his bag before she kicked his chess set apart.

"How about a sandwich, Bonk?" Osmo suggested. "Bread's made of wheat, surely wheat that's got itself picked, threshed, ground, milled, and baked is extra dead, as plants go."

Bonk fished reluctantly in his flower-print bathrobe and came up with a crust. He held it up to the hazy sky, waved it about, then shoved it in his mouth and munched as if daring them to say something.

"Cooks off, I guess," he mumbled around his decidedly un-glossy snack.

"I would like to be a helpful fish," Away said again. A shy, lovely little smile pulled at the corners of his mouth.

"Have you got more flowers?" Never asked with a prickling of hope. "Oh! From your funeral! Of course. Your people would have laid water lilies for you."

"No," said Away. "They did, but no."

The pangirlin went stiff with suspicion. "How are you helpful then? What kind of help?"

Away held out his fin-fringed arms to her. He inched forward, and widened his arms.

"Oh *no*," Nevermore whispered. "You can't mean *that*. I won't. *I can't.*"

"It is the only way," the gladfish said solemnly. "I am sorry, pangirlin. Give us a hug."

She began to tremble. Her scales clattered. Her breaths came shallow and panicked and fast. "I'd rather *die*," she hissed. "Do you understand? I am one of only three living things in the underworld, infinity miles from everything I love, with at least a hundred good years ahead of me if I avoid high-risk behaviors other than the very dumb one I'm doing right now, and I would rather *actually* die and never leave this place than let you do that to me."

"What's she on about?" Bonk said, wrinkling his snout.

But Osmo understood.

"We'll find some other way," he said quickly. "It's not worth it, you don't have to."

"There is no other way," Away insisted. "You have nothing else. And no time. The line is moving on without you. And me."

"Please don't," Nevermore begged. And it really was begging. Just a desperate bid for escape. A very human sweat beaded on her green-tinged shimmery scales. "I won't survive."

"It's okay," Osmo said comfortingly. "Don't be afraid. We'll all be right here with you."

"*That's the problem!*" she squeaked miserably. "Fine. All right. You win. I lose. Just . . . don't watch. Either of you." Osmo and Bonk blinked uncertainly. "I mean it! Turn around! Look away!"

Osmo did as she asked, almost automatically. Six sisters in a small house meant he was physically incapable of not turning his back the moment he was asked. But Bonk the Cross lingered.

"I want to see," he insisted.

"Bonk, *please*," Nevermore hissed. Osmo grabbed the skadge-bat by the shoulders and spun him round by force.

Nevermore shut her eyes like someone about to get to the scariest part in their favorite book. The gladfish wrapped his long, fiery-finned arms around her and hugged her tight.

"Oh no," the pangirlin gasped in horror. "Make it stop."

"I am not so bad a fish," Away whispered apologetically. He squeezed tighter, nuzzling her cheek with his own. "I am giving you my gloss. I am helping."

Never shuddered. "It's nothing to do with you. Don't feel bad. You're nice enough, for a fish. But *this* is the worst thing that's ever happened," she wheezed, starting to panic. "To anyone. Ever. Is it over? What about now? I hate this. I'm lonely. I *want* to be lonely. Lonely girls do not *hug*. I would like this to be over. It *needs* to be over. That's enough!" She shoved the poor dead fish away, panting, hands on her knees, her scales flushed and hot. "Did it work?" she demanded. "Well?"

Osmo frowned. He turned his head this way and that. Finally, he saw a faint glimmer along her shoulder blades, misting away into the dusk like steam off a swamp.

"Ahem." Someone cleared their throat by way of interruption. *"Ahrm."*

The four of them turned to see a very elderly hedgedog with long floppy ears, standing on her hind legs. She tapped Bonk politely on the shoulder. "Ah. Yes. Would you mind terribly? It's just that . . . that is to say, would you be so kind as to . . . muddy well *shove on?* The rest of us would like to get on with our deaths if that's all right with you." Bonk blinked in the mist. "You're holding up the line, you walloping stripey stump," the hedgedog barked.

"Mind your business, rump roast!" Bonk shrugged her off. "We'll get to it when we get to it! Chase a ball! Lie down and roll over! Go . . . interfere with a hedge, I don't know!"

Osmo laughed despite himself, but stopped when the old hedgedog looked his way. She had a light in her eyes so much like any grandmother he'd ever met. He felt at once that he ought to go find a chore to do or a mint candy to bring her.

She growled, but held up her paws. "Right! I'll be off, just back there, you know, with the teeming thousands of recently deceased. Put a bit of cheetah in your step, lad. It's not like we've got all the time in the world."

"You do, actually!" Bonk yelled after her. "You really, *really* do!

So shut it! I'm not a stump, neither! I *am* stripey, though. Yes, I am," he said, patting his belly with satisfaction. "*Very* stripey."

The long, winding, ghostly line lurched ahead, gaining speed, and soon they were all tripping forward, running to keep up, down the sugar dunes toward the River After, and a lonely pier, a lonely boat, and a tall black bird.

## Chapter Fourteen
# WERE YOU KIND?

The lonely boat towered over them like a giant wedding cake.

Row after row of decks toppled upward into the wintery sky, drenched in swinging silk bunting and colored lamps. Fiery spindly torches dotted the balconies with licking flames of purple and pink and green. Light, light everywhere. And music, too. Tinkling pianos and seesawing fiddles and timp-tumping drums spilling out of hundreds of pretty windows.

A massive golden rope bound the ship to the pier, as big around as a horse's belly. But it could only be for show. That poor little ramp couldn't have held down a stray autumn leaf. Ancient grey planks and posts creaked and bowed underfoot. Nothing lashed them together but fond memories and crossed fingers. The river water seeped up through the cracks like dark soup.

A bird stood on the dock. The tallest bird Osmo had ever seen. At least as tall as his father, maybe even as tall as Headmaster Gudgeon.

Mustamakkara, the ferryman.

She stared down at them with huge, calculating, white-less eyes. Everything about her felt strange, as though she were somehow a person in a bird suit and not a bird at all. Her thick body, her wide, flat, grinning beak, her great folded wings, and her long stilted legs looked just exactly like the birds called shoebills in *St. Whylom's Book of Zoologicals Near and Far*, the same book that taught him what a pangolin was so long ago. But shoebills were bluish grey. And had yellow beaks. And lived in Africa. Every inch of Mustamakkara glowed dully like a raven, black as sleep.

*Ruebill*, Never mouthed silently.

Their turn came at last. Away stepped onto the boards first, trembling before the great bird. The very last scraps of paint peeled away from the wood and floated off on the quick wind like ash. Osmo watched them go.

Mustamakkara's odd, almost reptilian eyes searched the poor young gladfish up and down. She started with the fine hairs on his forehead and examined every cell of him until she reached the tiny fluttering fins at the heels of his feet. All three of them shifted uncomfortably on the last scrap of sweet, weedy land leading into the dock. It was as though the ferryman was looking *through* Away, through everything that made him Away and not some other beast. Searching through the drawers of his soul.

Finally, Mustamakkara spoke. Her voice was so much softer than Osmo had imagined it would be. He thought the ferryman in the Land of the Dead would speak commandingly, with a terrible boom. But the ruebill sounded, more than anything else, like someone's mother.

"Welcome, children of the Forest! Do not be afraid. I am Mustamakkara, the Great Last Bird. When the moon was new and lava ruled the land, I was. When the sky breaks wide, and only the wind still sings, I will remain. I know all, for I have become good friends with every cell in the universe over the eons. Nothing can be hidden from me, so don't even try it." Her onyx eyes sparkled mischievously. She lifted her gaze to include all of them, not just the poor trembling gladfish. "My goodness, it's so wonderful to meet all of you! I've waited such a long time for this moment!"

"For us?" Osmo ventured uncertainly. "Us . . . specifically?"

The huge black ruebill snapped her beak twice. "For every child of the Forest," she said.

"Ah." Osmo relaxed.

"But yes, Osmo Unknown, Matilda's only son, for you specifically."

Osmo's blood sizzled with sudden fear. This would never work. She knew. Of course she knew. Old as lava and the moon and all that. A little stale flower juice wouldn't fool the Great Last Bird.

But Mustamakkara said nothing more about the imposters in front of her. She focused completely on Away, who quivered head to toe, his glittering fins flickering as fast as wings.

In one graceful, horrible motion, Mustamakkara opened her jaw so wide it cracked something in that quite important space between Osmo's eyes *seeing* and Osmo's brain *understanding*, and swallowed Away whole.

Mustamakkara's body shifted beneath her feathers. Bulges pushed out from her neck, her breastbone, her belly, the pouch under her dark beak. Her shoulders ruffed out a little, as though all her plumage were really just a black overcoat hiding what was happening beneath the buttons.

All three of them waited, goggle-eyed, unable to breathe.

The ferryman stretched out her wings to either side, so wide that for a moment the whole world seemed the color of her feathers—and then she brought them close again and the sun shone. She opened her maw again and hurked the gladfish up like a mother bird chucking up breakfast for her babies. Away seemed more or less unharmed, though he trembled from head to foot and his eyes had gone as wide as ponds. She patted his cheek and handed him a large bundle wrapped in linen and tied up with old leather belts.

"This world is yours to build, my little darling," she said lovingly. Away took his bundle and bolted into the glittering boat and the music and the streamers and the throngs, anywhere that lay in the opposite direction to a bird's guts.

"Nope," Bonk blurted out. "Absolutely not."

"Shhhh," Never and Osmo hissed.

"Shhh me all you like, lick-twigs!" the little badger-faced creature hissed back. "Of all the things that will not be happening to me, *that* will not be happening the *most*."

It was nearly full morning. The snow had stopped. The air smelled different—greener, brighter, brand-new. Cherry blossoms and plum blossoms began to drift slowly through the weeds in place of snowflakes.

Spring o'clock had arrived.

"Oh, get over yourself," Never sighed.

The pangirlin stepped onto the pier. But she looked back nervously over one shoulder. Would this work? Would it hurt? The gloss still glimmered along her armored arms. But would that be enough?

Those same black eyes raked over her, searching silently.

"This is going to be ever so much worse than a hug, isn't it?" Nevermore whispered, and then the ruebill ate her.

Mustamakkara groaned and swelled and bulged and ruffed just as she'd done with Away. Was she taking longer than she had with the gladfish? Osmo thought so, but he couldn't be sure. Everything takes longer when you're scared.

Finally, the ferryman threw her head back and spat the pangirlin onto the pier. Never looked as though she'd seen several ghosts and they'd all told her they hated her. Mustamakkara handed over another large bundle, this one wrapped in sailcloth and tied up neatly with thick hemp rope.

"This world is yours to build, my little darling," the Great Last Bird said lovingly, and Never scrambled hurriedly off the dock onto the polished deck of the great ferry.

It worked. Somehow, it *had* worked. They were going to make it through.

"Don't you look at me like that, Little Lord Mudpuddle. Bonk the Cross is many things. Brave? Yes. Wise? Obviously. Handsome? Undebatable. But bird food I am *not*, never have been, never shall be! I will not, cannot, wontn't—"

Osmo put a hand flat on Bonk's furry back and shoved him forward. He tripped. He stumbled. He called Osmo *you utter carrot* under his breath. And he toppled face-first onto the feet of an unimpressed Mustamakkara. She gobbled him up fast as a sea gull snapping for fish in the sea before he could call her anything. The sash of his flowered bathrobe hung out of her beak awkwardly. She slurped it down like a cooked noodle.

The Great Last Bird did not look at all happy. Her feathers didn't puff out like they had with the others. Her belly didn't wriggle or bulge. She stood very still until she went slightly green in the plumage and burped wetly, entirely sick to her stomach. This was *definitely* taking longer than the others, Osmo thought. Panic began to pull at the laces of his heart. The other dead beasts in the line behind him knew it, too. They shifted uncomfortably on the suddenly warm spring sand and mumbled to one another.

Mustamakkara belched again and puked the skadgebat into the world once more. That really was the word for it this time. There'd been some grace and sense of ritual to it before, but this was just a bird being sick all over a pier. Bonk picked himself up and straightened his bathrobe. Slowly, he wrung a load of bile out of his fuzzy sash while maintaining resentful, defiant eye contact the entire time.

The Great Last Bird didn't spread her wings or call him darling. She shoved a small bundle wrapped in brown paper and tied up with parcel string into Bonk's paws.

"Bit small," he said quietly. "Compared to the others, eh?"

"Yes," the ferryman answered bluntly.

"Thanks a muddy lot then, you old hat rack. I hope you *molt*."

Bonk the Cross stepped onto the glittering ship with a dashing little prance, waving his fingers behind him. "Ta!" he called over his shoulder.

And then it was Osmo's turn. No avoiding it now.

Maybe it would be all right, he thought. The others got through. They were as alive as he was. So maybe this wouldn't be so bad. Sweat beaded up on his forehead, but he didn't dare wipe it away. Only the living sweat. He felt so terribly naked and alone suddenly. She'd see right through him, down to his bones and further, he knew it. And another thought slicked across his brain as cold and fast as sweat: What would happen if she did? Swallowing him whole was the *good* bit. What could this great ancient thing do to him if she found him out?

Could you die in the Land of the Dead?

He pulled his patchwork suit around him, his fingers finding a rough square of the butcher's cap and a soft triangle of Oona's rabbit-fur coat. The crowcus had said it would protect him. Did Osmo believe that? Not really. What magic could there be in a few old clothes? But he chose to *try* to believe it. Osmo Unknown stepped onto the little lonely pier.

Mustamakkara fixed him with her endless black gaze. Osmo braced himself. And then it was happening. Her mouth was opening brain-crackingly wide and coming straight for him full of darkness and he couldn't stop it. He was going to get eaten like a sausage for breakfast and that was that. He had time to wonder what Ivy would think of all this if she could see him now before the giant bird devoured him in one bite.

Everything changed.

The world blinked away.

The sounds of the River After and the impatient ghosts and the party ship and the spring wind blowing petals down the sugar dells.

Osmo stood somewhere . . . somehow . . . somewhen. A vast inky space. He'd no idea what he stood *on*, or *in*, if he was standing at all. Up and down and sideways were not on speaking terms here. He supposed he shouldn't be surprised. If you'd asked him last week what he thought the inside of a raven or a shoebill or both looked like, he would probably have said *just a lot of darkness* and gone on his way.

A tiny silver-violet star shot by his ear, out into the infinite shadows. Then another and another, pinging off nothing, changing direction in midair, zinging all around, in all directions, like lost fireflies. Had the others seen this too?

"You're broken," Mustamakkara said.

And as soon as she spoke, she was all around him, far bigger than she had been before she ate him. The size of the whole universe and a little extra on the side. The vast inky space wasn't space at all but a million black feathers, bigger and longer and wider than whalebones. Osmo could suddenly feel the rustle of them beneath him, beside him, closing him in. He looked up, at what he thought was up, and the shine of her sun-sized eyes slicked the dark.

There was nothing in the cosmos but bird and boy.

"You're broken," Mustamakkara said again. She didn't sound angry. Just puzzled. Curious.

"I'm not," Osmo insisted.

"Then I'm broken," she mused. "*Somebody* is broken and there's only two of us here. But if I am broken, you broke me, so really, it's all the same in the end."

"You don't seem broken to me."

Mustamakkara sighed. "Don't tell me my business, featherless chick. Right now, you should be seeing your very favorite place in all the world. The very specific and singular place where you felt safest and happiest and most *yourself* while you lived. But not only where you felt most comfortable, where you felt most ready-for-anything, most *interested* in life and lore and everything around you. Everyone has that special place! We should be there sharing whatever you like best to drink while I ask you three questions to determine whether or not you lived a good life. I *really* don't think your favorite place was in the lap of a bird the size of everything, so . . . one of us is broken."

Osmo Unknown tried to think. What place could that ever have been for him? His room? The library at St. Whylom's School? The edge of the Forest, with his mother, her strong stride beside him so certain and confident?

Mustamakkara's gargantuan eyes narrowed in frustration. "It's a very nice thing I do for everyone, though you wouldn't think so for all the appreciation I don't ever get," the Great Last Bird said, pouting. "It's all up to me, you know. The Forest doesn't care one bit about *hospitality*. I could terrify you with flames as tall as mountains or bore you with an efficient cleric's desk or just knock you about the head until you tell me the truth, but I don't, do I? I give you a last lovely memory of a place that made you feel your best. I thought of it myself, oh, sometime just after everyone had the bright idea of living under roofs instead of getting their nice things snowed on half the year. I'm terribly proud of it. I look forward to seeing each and every spirit's best place. And now you've spoilt it."

Osmo fidgeted in the infinite bird-void. He felt very distinctly like he was failing an exam. And he thought he knew why. He just couldn't tell her. You couldn't tell the giant African bird at the end of all things, who just wanted to paint a nice scene for you, that you'd never felt *yourself* anywhere in your life. Accepted or included or even overly wanted. That every single place you'd ever stood in just made you long to be somewhere *Else*.

"You could just ask me your questions anyway," he suggested delicately. "You don't have to worry about dressing the windows for me."

Mustamakkara's eyes and bony huge beak swooped down closer to him, peering closely. He stumbled backward, away from the ruebill's planet-sized head. "I can't even *see* your place," she crooned. "I can't see anything at all."

"Just ask me!" Osmo cried out.

The Great Last Bird cocked her head to the side like a parrot in a cage. "Is it because you're alive, do you think?"

Osmo froze. The sweat came back. He tried to will it away.

"I'm not!" he protested quickly, but even he didn't think it sounded convincing. And that wasn't the problem, anyhow. If he'd lived to be ninety in Littlebridge, he'd still end up floating in the dark without a favorite place in all the world, because his favorite place in all the world would always be wherever he *wasn't* at any given moment.

But the bird just laughed. "Not only are you alive, you are a hominid. A human being. A boy. The others were alive, but at least they were *mine*. You are so very far from where you should be, child of the Valley."

"I'm *not*," Osmo insisted with a fury that surprised even him. "I'm not any of those things. I'm wild and free and dead as dirt and my heart has belonged to the Forest since before I knew any one of those words. So ask me your questions."

"And what if I ask you how you died, little ghost?"

Osmo stalled for time. "Is that one of the three questions?"

What would she believe? Strangulation? Drowning? Fever? Diphtheria? Murder? Diphtheria was probably easier to sell than murder. Who would want to murder a thirteen-year-old boy? Besides a Quidnunk?

"No," admitted Mustamakkara. "But I'll know if you lie. I always know. I am the fifth thing the Forest made all by itself, without the Valley's help. That's how old I am. When I opened my eyes for the first time, lies hadn't been invented yet. When the first lie got itself told, the smell of the world changed, just a little. And every time a new one hits the air, it changes more. Only those who remember a world without lies can recognize their smell. But I'm one of them. Go on, then. Don't let the fact that I can smell the truth on your breath and snuff you out of existence with a sneeze slow you down. How did you die?"

No diphtheria, then. Osmo spoke very slowly and carefully.

"I . . . was doing something good. Something brave and stupid to help a lot of people who didn't even really like me all that much." He grimaced. "They really were so ready to toss me away, you know. It only took a minute. They hardly made any fuss at all. Barnaby Lud said he wouldn't miss me and nobody argued." Osmo sniffed and wiped his nose with his sleeve.

"Why didn't you let them get chomped, then? I would have. Think how much time and grief you'd have saved!" the bird clucked.

"Well, they didn't deserve to be eaten just because they're a bunch of snobs!"

Mustamakkara frowned.

"That's not why," she chirped.

Osmo winced. "It was at first. But then later . . . I did it . . . I *kept* doing it because I thought something interesting might happen. Something better than every day slipping by in the same place doing the same things until I had no more days left. So I ran into a pole and that's how I . . . passed out of the living world."

The Great Last Bird drew her head back into her feathers and brooded. For almost a full minute, Osmo Unknown thought the Great Last Bird accepted his not-technically-lies.

"Were you kind?" she said quietly, and the rumble of her voice did not sound pleased.

"Is this one of the questions? Did you ask Bonk and Never this? I don't blame you for looking so sick if you had to ask Bonk that and take his answer on the nose."

"Yes. They are always the same. I ask them a thousand times a day. No one may pass without my satisfaction. The answers are like pearls. Each one different from the others, but all of a family, round and shining and small. What is left over in the shell when everything else is finished and all the irritation of the earth has done. They are all I need to know to judge a life lived in the country of the quick and the loud. This is the most important one. That's why it comes first. Were you kind?"

"I tried," he said lamely. What did *kind* mean to a wild thing? "I'm the oldest of seven, it's not easy to always be kind. I'm sure I pulled *someone's* hair." But then he thought of Headmaster Gudgeon, too, and the others in his class glaring at him with annoyance while he went on and on about how there was no such thing as Quidnunx. He thought of his father's disappointment when he asked for the chess set. His stubborn refusal to take up hunting like his mother. Adelard Sloe's rage when he won the golden ball. Ivy's disgusted face when she realized he assumed she'd wanted to go to the festival with him. "I don't know," Osmo admitted. "I don't think it's up to me to say. I guess I wasn't always. I was a know-it-all and nobody likes a know-it-all."

"Were you tamed?" the ferryman asked.

*Tell the truth,* he told himself. *You have to tell the truth. It's bad enough you're a human being and not actually dead with no intention of staying in the Eightpenny Woods one minute longer than necessary. She wants the truth. She's testing you.*

"What does 'tamed' mean?" he said finally, throwing up his hands. "Does it mean I obeyed everyone who told me what to do? Or does it mean I never did anything even a little bit dangerous or fun? Are you asking whether I settled down and led a quiet life without any adventure in it? Or if I loved people and gave up what I wanted for what they wanted? I can think of a million meanings, but I don't know which one is *your* meaning. A tame cow gives milk. A tame dog fetches a ball or herds sheep. Tame cows and dogs are useful. Was *I* useful? Not to anyone ever. But I didn't get much of a chance, did I? I'm only little, still. I'm just a kid."

Mustamakkara said nothing.

Osmo Unknown thought of all those winding streets he knew so well. Those winding streets of Littlebridge that held no surprises at all and never would. The tamest place in the tamest world. "I guess the truth is, whatever you mean by the word, I was born tamed. But . . . I'm working on it."

Osmo waited for the next question. But it didn't come.

"*I* am a Know-It-All," the Great Last Bird mused instead.

"What?"

"You said before that you were a Know-It-All. And nobody likes a Know-It-All. But I am one. I Know It All." Mustamakkara grinned mischievously. "For example, I know why you are here, even though you do not want to tell me because you are silly and made of meat that cannot stop worrying what other meat thinks of it. Queen Melancholy passed through me on her way to the Eightpenny Woods. I have been expecting you."

"You *knew*? Then why all this talking round and round in circles? Why did poor Never have to get hugged for nothing? If you know who I am, why not just let me pass or don't?"

"I only knew once I ate you," the bird scoffed. "Once you eat something you know everything about it. But I wouldn't have eaten you in the first place if you didn't seem dead enough. I'm not a *monster*. And if you had told me the whole truth from the start, I would have used your soul to patch my nest. On the other hand, if you had told me an outlandish, gorgeous lie, full of color and high adventure, like a true wild creature trying to trick his way into my world would have done without thinking, I would have spat you up at the queen's feet and saved you so much time. Bonk told me he died saving the aurora borealis from being eaten by a great white shark. But you did neither, which is neither admirable nor wicked, though it is at least not very interesting. And now you have a long journey ahead of you. You are tamed as cut grass, my skinny hairless love. So you see, I *am* a Know-It-All. Do you like me?"

Silver-violet stars flitted by Osmo's face, winking out as they flew.

"I do, actually," he whispered, his throat dry. "You're awfully interesting to look at, and you tried to make us not feel afraid. You make those favorite places for all those people just to make them a little happier, even if they lived cruel lives. I suppose that's not so easy. To spend every day of forever trying to make people who've just died feel brave and hopeful and not alone."

The Great Last Bird's enormous glittering eyes narrowed to slits. She drew herself up to that terrifying height again and teetered perilously toward his face, her gaze swallowing everything around it.

"Are you trying to feel my feelings? You *dare*? That's quite dangerous stuff. Perilous, you might even say. Feeling your own feelings is brutal enough for most people. Feeling someone else's? Even the strongest kings forever fail that task. Why, it's the wildest, most untamed thing there is. Which is why it doesn't seem too wild at all. To trick you into thinking it's easy."

"I'm nobody's king!" Osmo yelped as she bore down on him, pressing her massive head to his tiny human one.

"Are you sure you're strong enough? My feelings were forged in the bellies of blue stars when gravity was a tiny squalling baby."

"I only meant—"

"But I am old and I am tired. No use putting another whiff of lie into the world about that. Feelings are so *heavy*. If someone else could carry mine for a while . . . I cannot imagine the relief."

"I . . . I will," he said shyly, with the whole weight of her gaze crushing him to nothing. "I don't mind. For a little while. While I'm here. While I can."

Osmo expected her to talk to him, or maybe sing to him, like a proper bird. To tell him her troubles, have a good cry. But instead Mustamakkara snapped back to her usual size, which hardly seemed unreasonable at all anymore. She worried her feathers with her beak, so very like a funny little nothing songbird you might see any day of the week that Osmo nearly laughed. He stopped himself just in time. When Mustamakkara lifted her head again, she held something small and black in her bill. She dropped it without ceremony into Osmo's hands.

It was a little carved stone box, locked up tight. The very color of the ferryman's feathers, deep and dark with bits of purple floating beneath.

"Thank you, Osmo." Mustamakkara took a deep breath. "Why, I feel almost young again! How odd that none of the Forest's children ever gave my feelings a first or second or seventieth thought. Naughty things. Now, don't you lose that. Something terrible might happen. Open it if you are lost. If you cannot see the path for the pebbles. And only in your wildest need. Not just if you need directions to the corner shop and nobody convenient is about, you understand? Only if you are well and truly stuck, and there is no other way free.

Now, the last question: Did you add your truth to the Great True Tale?"

Osmo blinked. "What's the Great True Tale?"

"The grand story of everything and everyone, once you've cut away all the things that don't matter, like clearing up the washing or brushing your hair or sleeping too late. Everything that lives learns and grows. There is a moment in every creature's life where they will arrive at some truth that no one else has ever thought of quite that way. It happens to everyone, even clams and dandelions. The trouble is remembering it, and recognizing it for what it is, when there is always so much washing and brushing and sleeping crowding in. What was yours?"

Osmo tried to think. He tried and tried. Of his family and school and Frost Festivals and carnival games and flowers picked by a river but never delivered. He tried to think of one special idea he'd had that no one else ever could, other than that Quidnunx didn't exist. But no matter how he searched, he couldn't find it.

"I didn't get a chance," he whispered helplessly.

"Everyone gets a chance," the Great Last Bird urged him.

Osmo shut his eyes. The years of his life rushed by like winds in his head. He couldn't think, he just couldn't. He'd never done anything special until the night his mother killed a mythical beast and everything changed. Until then, who had he even been? He groped desperately for something deep and important to say. But all he could think of was Adelard Sloe's stupid old throwing game and that perfect moment when he was four years old and knew something the grown-ups didn't.

"The game was fixed," he said miserably, knowing it was a

small thing that meant nothing, hardly a grand truth that summed up a whole life's experience. "No one else saw it, but I did. I did once. I saw that it was fixed. And not just the game . . . Littlebridge. All of it. Everything and everyone. If it weren't, I could grow up to be anything instead of a hunter or nothing. It's on the city seal. *Nemo Nanciunt Desiderium*. Nobody gets what they want. The fix is baked into the stones of the street and the wood of the houses." Osmo gritted his teeth. "The game *is* fixed. But one time, just one time . . . *I won anyway*."

Mustamakkara started to open up her beak, wider and wider—but Osmo called out to her before she could swallow him up again.

"Wait! Can I ask *you* a question?"

The ruebill paused, stunned. "No one ever has," she said slowly. "I don't see why not."

"Where is she? Where is Queen Melancholy? I have no idea where to find her, and it's so easy to get lost in the woods."

The ferryman snapped her beak a few times, considering the whole situation with much skepticism.

"You will find her where you would find any betrothed. She waits with her father, in the Gnarlbind, which lies deep within the beating heart of the Forest." The massive bird trilled a soft little song. "Poor baby hominid. You know so little. It's almost unfair. Do you know anything about her at all? Queen Melancholy is the most beautiful animal that ever lived."

"I thought she was old and frail," Osmo replied, puzzled.

"No one is old here, my child," laughed the vast black bird that dwelt between life and death. "And no one frail."

Mustamakkara opened her stony jaws as wide as the horizon and all the little silver-violet lights rushed into her throat and so did he and a moment later he was tumbling back out onto the pier head over tailbone, landing hard on his back. The tinkling sounds and glittering lights and spangled smells of the ferry of the dead came rushing in like a golden wave.

But there was no neatly wrapped bundle for Osmo. No promise that this world was his to build. Instead, the Great Last Bird merely left him where he lay, turning her wind-ruffled black back to him.

Only it wasn't black anymore. Something living had passed through her. All her feathers had turned a deep, bright, warm, glowing red.

And so had the shining stone feelings box in Osmo's hand.

"Best hurry," Mustamakkara warned as she opened her scarlet jaws to gobble up another ghost. "Brides don't like to be kept waiting."

*Chapter Fifteen*

# ON PROSERPINA AND THE DARK

Every single thing about the ferry on the River After looked like the opposite of death. Nothing dreary, nothing mournful, nothing drab or somber or bony or spiderwebby or even the littlest bit spooky. No one cried. No one sniffled. No one even frowned.

Tables wobbled under the weight of food all along the foredeck. Whatever each sort of animal liked best, neatly divided into sections for carnivores and herbivores, insectivores and nectarians. Towers of shimmering silver, pink, and blue fish for the fish-eaters and little festive fountains of blood for any combination of vampire bats, mosquitoes, leeches, or house cats. Music flowed out from every corner of the boat. Jigs from the upper decks, waltzes down below, ballads and foxtrots and polkas danced up and down the railings. Osmo could pick out pianos and accordions and fiddles and horns and drums and hurdy-gurdies and just about every other instrument he had ever heard of or seen in a book. But there were songbirds and twanging bullfrogs and howling wolves and whalesongs and thumping hooves and half-human voices singing, too. Somehow it all blended together perfectly, though everyone played a different song.

Osmo Unknown distinctly heard a familiar, marvelous sound echoing out from the heart of the ferry. Bells ringing. Balls rolling. Water splashing. Cards shuffling. Darts thunking. Cheers roaring— *actually* roaring, lions and bears and at least one walrus.

The sound of *games*.

"You made it!"

Osmo heard Never's bronzey voice call out to him. He couldn't think of any sound he'd been more grateful to hear in all his days.

The polished boards of the boat beneath him felt solid and thick and, most importantly, *not* a directionless void. He quickly shoved Mustamakkara's little red stone box into his satchel and ran toward his friends—if they were his friends. It was impossible to tell with those two.

"Took you long enough," groused Bonk, munching on what Osmo hoped was a turkey leg. "I bet Never you were bird food. Now I owe her a whole hour of 'keeping my mouth shut,' whatever that means. So thanks a lot."

Osmo pointed at the turkey leg. "I thought you ate earthworms and dragonflies."

The skadgebat shrugged. "You know the saying. When in Rome, eat whatever you want because nothing matters and there's no rules."

"I don't think that's a saying," Nevermore said doubtfully.

"I said it, didn't I? Thus, it is a saying! And if I make myself sick, that's my stomach's fault for not rolling with the punches. Maybe it'll learn its lesson for next time." He poked meaningfully at his belly.

"How do you know about Rome? Rome was a human thing," Osmo interrupted.

"Oh, look who's a classical scholar now," Bonk chortled between bites. "They got forests in Italy, you reckon?"

"I suppose. Of course. There's forests everywhere."

"Then it wasn't just a human thing, was it? Nothing is, when you've got a forest nearby. One of my ancient and aged ancestors on the badger side was Caesar's personal pet. Before the Forest decided to bash up more fabulous creatures than just the usual plain old furbags. Jules brought the old girl back from Gaul and fed her dates till she got so fat she exploded." Bonk tossed his turkey bone overboard and waddled away from the buffet toward the shimmering innards of the ferry. Never and Osmo trotted after him as he kept talking without missing a breath. "Then he had her made into a carpet. What a way to go. Wager she's in a museum now. You got any grammas good enough to hang in a museum?"

Osmo didn't know how to begin to answer that. He opened his mouth and shut it. They passed under a jeweled archway and into the merriest room Osmo had ever seen. Ghosts mingled joyfully, bundles strapped to their backs. They talked and sang and cheered and pointed at glittering knickknacks that covered the walls so thoroughly Osmo couldn't be sure there really was a wall under there at all.

The sound of games had definitely come from this place. Card tables and dice tables and ninepin lanes and ringtosses crammed every inch of free space. Ghosts crammed in round the tables so thick that Osmo, Never, and Bonk could hardly press any further on. Chess games and checkers games and doublechess and deep-checkers and mah-jongg and dominoes and jacks and every other sort of contest clattered on all around. The Quidnunx had told Osmo the Eightpenny Woods were neither heaven nor hell, but this . . . this looked very like heaven to him.

It looked like he'd always thought *proper* cities would.

Nevermore looked like she was going to throw up. She held her hands over her ears to keep out the din of voices. Osmo didn't think he'd ever seen so many people crushed together, so he felt certain she hadn't either. He felt sorry for her and wanted to put his arm around the pangirlin to comfort her. But that would only make it worse. How do you comfort someone who only needs comforting because you insist on being around her?

"There you go, then!" Bonk raised his voice to a yell and continued happily, as though he were not stuck between two dead leoparlings, their cat bodies and starling feathers crushing his shoulders on either side. "Everyone whose gramma's not good enough for people to pay to see her and say she's so pretty and soft should shoosh it about Rome, final word." He shoved one of the leoparlings hard and helped himself to a snack table piled high with chunks of slick, thick, pale yellow cheese surely meant for whatever half-mouse beasts had died that day.

But Osmo couldn't let that lie. Not even when a narwholf's horn was poking him painfully in the back. It was one thing to accept a whole other kingdom going on for years and years in the Forest right next door, but Rome was *his*. He'd read a hundred books about it if he'd read one. "Well, *maybe* you shouldn't eat so much in the underworld, if you're so keen on Rome," he yelled back, with a little more sneer than he'd meant to put on it.

Never froze, a ruby-colored grape halfway to her mouth.

"What's that supposed to mean, Mister Centurion?" Bonk barked.

"You know . . . Proserpina? Persephone in Greek, but I'm *sure* you knew that. They have forests in Greece, too, right? Pomegranates? Don't eat the food of the dead?"

The ghostly throng thinned a little as folk moved on to other tiers of the ship. Bonk wriggled in the newfound breathing room. He picked his tiny sharp teeth with a claw. "Why? My crowcus friend told you not to wear dead *clothes*, didn't you listen? Clothes bad. Food's fine. No animal would tell you to turn down food if you find it. Give up a meal? When winter could happen *whenever* and something's almost always hunting the pants off you? Such a human idea. Ew. No. Eat when you can, you may not get another chance. Anyway, all food is dead. Dead flowers, dead beasts, dead carrots, dead potatoes. Everything you've ever eaten was the food of the dead. Proserpina was a dingdong if you ask me. She *wanted* to stay. She just needed an excuse 'cause her mama wouldn't let her stay out late at night. Pomegranates, my stripedy *rump*. And that's the last I'll hear out of you about Rome, Mister Man, with your inferior gramma!" Bonk waggled a buttered roll in Osmo's face. Osmo flinched. "Ooooh look, he's scared of the spoooooky food! Watch out, motter, or the *hors d'oeuvres* will get you!"

"One of my pangolin ancestors was caught by human hunters in the jungle and made into a suit of armor. She's in a museum," Never remarked as she munched her grape. "Ming dynasty, I think.

Before . . . you know." She glanced at Osmo. "Them. And that. And the other thing."

"Ah! Congratulations on your excellent gramma then! You and I can discuss which emperors were best and which were secret shaved gorilla spies later. Only *he* has to butt out of it, since he's not in our Best Gramma Club." Bonk lowered his voice to a loud, entirely meant-to-be-overheard whisper. *"And he probably doesn't know about the spy thing."*

A long, loud horn blasted out of the smokestacks that crowned the ferry. The ship shuddered and began to glide smoothly through the water.

"What are they playing for, do you think?" Osmo changed the subject. A roar went up from the ninepin alley. Osmo stared longingly at the toppled pins. How nice and simple and not remotely Roman ninepins were! "I can play, you know," he mumbled. "Almost anything. I'm good at it, even. If it's worth playing."

His pride smarted, though he felt silly about it, because they were talking sheer *nonsense* so he shouldn't care. Anyway, he had a very nice gramma. Her name was Hanna. She could *so* be in a museum if she wanted. Besides, he knew *heaps* about Rome, and none of the emperors had been secret gorillas for heaven's sake. They were just making fun of him, no different than Ivy Aptrick and Barnaby Lud and Ada Sloe and the rest. Which was why it stung so. Osmo Unknown could travel to another world, and then another after that, all the way to the Land of the Dead, but he still couldn't escape everyone laughing at him.

He'd spent so much time wishing to be somewhere Else, he'd

just assumed he'd be someone Else when he got there. But he was still just Osmo.

"I've no idea," Never said, shrugging. "What could the dead possibly have to bet?" She squeezed her eyes shut behind her glasses. "I'm *trying*. I'm really trying, but it's horrid in here. Let's go to the next room. Maybe there's nobody in there. Wouldn't that be nice? I . . . I think it would be nice."

Osmo started to say something, to try to help. But Nevermore straightened her spine and shook her head all on her own and said: "No. No, I can do this. Just because there's a zillion people around doesn't mean I can't be lonely inside my own head." She cleared her throat. "Look around. Everyone's doing *something*, so there must be something important for the dead to do before we make landfall. We should try to do it too. That feels like logic to me."

Osmo nodded, reluctantly tearing himself away from the games. "We need help, as well. If not now, very soon."

"*I* don't," belched Bonk.

"Oh, go dunk your head in the blood fountain," Osmo snapped. He'd had *enough*. Bonk's furry eyebrow ridge shot up with delight.

"That's it, my wee motter! That's the good stuff! Tell me where to put my head! I've said a *lot* about your head. You've earned it." The skadgebat trilled happily.

"Yes, you do need help," Osmo pressed. "We all do. Once this ferry docks, we have no idea where to go. How are we supposed to find the queen? With whatever you two forgot from Monday school? If that's anything like how much I remember from Sunday school, we're sunk."

"Ew, why would you have school on a Sunday?" Never wrinkled her coppery nose.

"It doesn't matter! We have to tackle this logically. We need to know what's ahead of us. Maybe somebody here knows. Like Away knew about the Meaningful Desert. Unless there's a map in one of the bundles Mustamakkara gave you?"

Never made a funny sound, half exhausted giggle and half exasperated sigh.

"About that," she said, reaching for hers. She'd stashed it, apparently, under the buffet's roast hyena station.

"Hey, yeah, where's yours, Mister Sir?" Bonk asked.

"Didn't get one." Osmo shrugged. "I don't belong here." *Anywhere*, his mind added, even though he told it firmly to shove off. *Ever*.

"None of us belong here," Bonk argued. "You know, *alive* and all. But we got ours, fat lot of good they are."

Osmo shoved his hands in his pockets. "But you two *will* belong," he said quietly. "Eventually. I'm human. This place is not for me."

"Well, don't feel too bad," said Never. "You're not missing anything."

The pangirlin popped the knots on her bundle and unrolled the sailcloth onto the ferry deck.

Dried leaves and acorns tumbled out of it. Nothing else but a spray of dirt and a bit of petrified moss. No map, no compass, no neatly written set of instructions as to what to do next, nothing useful in the slightest.

"Come on," Never coaxed Bonk.

"Don't wanna."

"Don't care," Never said with a smug smirk. *You're* not alone either, so *you* don't get to do whatever you want. That's the rules."

Bonk the Cross held up his small brown paper package, ripped up as eagerly as a Christmas present. Osmo couldn't see anything but the wrapping. It seemed crueler to give Bonk a gift with nothing in it than to give Osmo nothing at all.

"She gave me a rock, all right?" the skadgebat blurted. "A *muddy* rock. And just the one, too. Not even another rock to bang against the first one to make fire. It's *prejudice*, I tell you what."

"Against what?" Never asked.

"Against *me!*" Bonk cried to the heavens.

"Maybe everyone got leaves and rocks," Osmo suggested. "It's not as though anything's made sense here yet."

"I doubt it," Bonk snuffled.

"STEP RIGHT UP!" someone yelled over the noise and hum. "Step right up and try your luck! Every winner gets a prize from the JUMBO shelf! A memory a play, just one itty-bitty memory gets you a mighty swing of my mighty hammer! Ring the bell and claim your treasure! Couldn't be simpler! Take your fate in your own two—or four—hands! Pardon me, my dear departed! I couldn't help but notice your kits are a bit . . . lacking. Care to play for a chance to improve your lot?"

They turned toward the voice. An orangutan gazed serenely at them from behind a pretty stall, upholstered, curtained, and wallpapered in plush burgundy spangled fabric. The orangutan sat up on the counter, long arms hanging low, balanced on short, powerful haunches. But it wasn't orange and it wasn't hairy and it hadn't eyes or a nose or anything. It was a silhouette, a shadow of a great ape. But not just a shadow. Stars shone inside it. *Real* stars, not just pinpricks of light. Distant burning balls of fire in space. Stars and green nebulae and rosy dust clouds and the wheeling silver Milky Way, moving and rising and falling inside a monkey shape cut out of the air in front of them.

"Hullo, preciouses," the space ape said in a friendlier voice than Osmo had heard directed at him since all this madness had begun.

"Well, boil my head and call me a pudding," breathed Bonk.

"What *are* you?" asked Never as bluntly as ever.

"You're *amazing!*" Osmo exclaimed. "What did they call you, when you were alive? Orangublack? Onyxutan?"

"Naw," the creature said. "I was never alive. Not dead, neither. I'm the Dark. I just work here."

## Chapter Sixteen
# NEW PUPPY DAY

"Dark's a funny name kind of name for a monkey," Bonk said doubtfully.

The slab of deep space sitting in the shape of an orangutan shook its starry head.

"You misunderstand, gentlesir," the creature said in a lilting showman's rhythm. "I am not *named* Dark, I *am* the Dark, trademarked, all rights reserved, accept no substitutes, the pleasure is mine, much obliged, your most sincere and humble servant, etcetera, etcetera, no autographs, please."

"*The* Dark," Osmo repeated.

"The very one."

"As in, the stuff that's not light?"

"A clever and perceptive lad if I ever met one!"

Osmo fidgeted. "Then why are you a monkey?"

The Dark glanced at its shadowy fingernails, irritated. "An orangutan is not, strictly speaking, a monkey, you know. It is a *great ape*, thank you very much. But then, I am not, strictly speaking, a great ape. I am the Dark! Native to the world beyond light and life!

Splendid and mysterious! Patron of spies and thieves and secrets! Terror of tiny children! Friend to owls and foxes and the undersides of beds everywhere! As to why I look the way I do, what can I say? I like apes. They're so *cute*. But I can be anything you prefer. The Dark can expand or contract to fill any space from the corner of a kitchen drawer to the whole of a cathedral. What would you have? A cat?" The glittering sky dribbled apart like candle wax. It dribbled up again into the shape of a huge house cat. The cat meowed. It rubbed a paw over the North Star that formed the tip of its nose. "A pony?" The cat melted into nothing. The nothing flowed back into the shape of a pretty little draft horse with wide furry space-colored hooves. It pranced up and down the boards of the spangled stall. "A *you?*" The Dark shivered out of its horse shape and into the silhouette of Osmo himself. The exact height, weight, disastrous hair, and tense posture. Osmo reached out his hand toward the boy made of night, but that shape wriggled away just as fast.

"That's enough showing off, Mister the Dark," Bonk growled. "You're giving me a headache."

The boy vanished and the galactic orangutan returned faster than the space between breaths. "Yes, I agree, chef's choice is always best. But I am not a mister. Nor a madam. Why, the Dark itself wears neither skirts nor trousers—what would be the point, I ask you? If you find yourself at a loss for a pronoun, you may simply use *dark/darkness* in place of *he/him* or *she/her*. Now! Let us start over again. STEP RIGHT UP AND TRY YOUR LUCK!"

"You said we could improve our kits?" Nevermore ventured.

A little star deep in the chest of the great ape went nova—then the night closed in around it again. "I daresay I've never seen any more pathetic than yours. You must have led *dreadful* lives. You won't be building much with dry leaves and *one* rock."

"Building?" Osmo asked. "Building what?"

The Dark patted his head with a cold, soft, smoky paw. "Your trip through the gullet of my friend Mustamakkara must have spit-roasted your head, little master. The kits contain everything you need to build your homestead in the Eightpenny Woods. Hammers, nails, wood, stone, iron, glass, the works! But what you get tends to roughly correspond to how you chose to live your life. What you thought was important. So if pleasure drove you, food and drink and feasting, you might find your kit packed with oven bricks and fine copper pans—but rather skimpy on the library supplies. If you loved the company of others best of all, your bundle of joy might contain everything you could want to lay out a parlor fit for six kings and a princess to entertain in. But if you never gave a thought to yourself, you could easily find no roof or bed included. If you were miserly and suspicious and hoarded more than you needed, perhaps you'd get the world's most marvelous and impregnable fence to protect your loot! But nothing else at all! You see?"

"Reward and punishment." Osmo frowned.

"Not at all, young . . . man?" The Dark furrowed its nebulae in confusion.

"Motter," Bonk piped up.

The Dark waved a paw. "Of course, of course. No, we do not reward and we do not punish. Let the humans have that old game.

We simply give you what you wanted. *Exactly* what you wanted. No judgment, no correction. If what you wanted isn't quite sufficient to make you happy forever . . . well. Perhaps that's something you should have thought about on the other side of the door, so to speak." A sparkling asteroid field curled up into the outline of a smile. "But then again . . . that's what the ferry is for! The SS *Last Chance*! How else do we fill the holes in our afterlives? Other people, naturally!"

Never crossed her arms resentfully. "Disagree," she mumbled. But the Dark was on a roll and paid her no attention.

"Barter, win, trade, only please don't steal. We've all got to get where we're going. Play nice with the other ghosties! Whatever you lack is around here somewhere. But you've got to pay for it. And you . . . need a lot. What did you *do* with your lives?"

"Complain." Bonk shrugged.

"Mind my own business," Never said pointedly.

"Waited for a different one to come along, I guess," Osmo admitted.

The Dark shimmered at him like shadows in the corner of a child's bedroom that might or might not be a monster. "Well, POOF! Wish granted! This is *well* different, isn't it? Now, put down your coin and we'll see what my bell thinks of you."

Osmo had been trying to size up the bell-and-hammer game while the Dark talked. It looked pretty standard: hit the mark with the hammer and see if you could drive the clapper up into the big silver bell at the top of a pillar. The pillar had levels marked off every foot or so:

HEADSTRONG, HEART STUPID
ALL INSPIRATION, NO EXECUTION
INSTINCTS BROKEN, TRY AGAIN LATER
GREEDY GUTS
TAME TO THE BONE
LIFE IN THE SAD LANE
KING OF THE BEASTS

But surely there was a trick. There was always a trick. Hadn't that been his truth for the Great True Tale?

"We haven't got any money," he sighed. "So it hardly matters, I suppose."

The Dark laughed. It sounded like thunderstorms blotting out the sun. "Sure you have! What did I say? A memory a play. That's the only currency around here. What do you think my prizes are, actual physical objects? Don't be silly, we're all ghosts here. Well, I'm not, but *you're* all ghosts here!" The Dark hooted, very like a real orangutan. "I can see by your faces you're in the dark on this one. Get it? HA! After all these eons I still amuse myself. Look, you've got no bodies anymore. Which means no brains. Which means your thoughts and memories have just exactly as much weight and substance as the rest of you, which is to say none. But which is also to say, maybe lots? There's equations about it. But it's impossible to write things down neatly in the dark, so roundabout and upside down, blah blah and a lot of awkward coughing, I can't *technically* read so I don't *know* those equations. I do know that in the Eightpenny Woods, a memory is as solid and functional as an elbow joint, and twice as useful for reaching things off the top shelf." The Dark swept a midnight arm overhead, taking in the shelves of prizes along the walls. "Everything you see is somebody's memory taken shape and form. Weird shapes, bizarre forms. Memory is like that. It never stays the way it happened. It always changes into something else over the years. Look, see that crystal goblet full of wine?"

Up in the corner of the stall, a cut-glass goblet glittered, full of pale, sparkling pink spring wine. It hardly seemed special. The Dark plucked it and held it out, turning it this way and that. But the wine stayed in the goblet, no matter how the Dark spun and juggled it.

"This was a chamelion's memory of the first time she saw her first newborn cub all blind and sweet and hers. How its fresh baby fur changed color to match, not a rock or a branch or a leaf, but herself. No matter how you twist and turn it, you can never spill that wine, because such love can never be emptied. See? Understand?"

"Yeah," Osmo said with a rueful laugh. "It's a metaphor."

The Dark replaced the glass on the prize shelf. "This is the economy of the underworld, my friends! Only what you bring with you! Vivid memories like my chamelion's are the most expensive: first kisses, last goodbyes, heights of triumph, lows of betrayal, hard choices, soft landings. Half-remembered song lyrics, disappointing birthday parties, facts from your final exams? Won't get you much. They're penny candy at best, but still warm and real in the hand. All you have to do is remember something you're willing to forget and STEP. RIGHT. UP."

"Willing to forget?" Osmo knew it. There was always a trick.

"Naturally. It's a wager. If you lose, I keep your bet. You don't get to take it with you, that's hardly fair to *me*. I've got to make a living, you know."

Bonk rolled his beady black eyes. "No you don't. You're the Dark." The skadgebat waggled his fingers mockingly. "*Wooooo*. You don't need anything."

The Dark grew very still. "No, I don't. I am beyond nature and time. I am beyond light and comprehension. I begin in the Land of the Dead like a great taproot, but I exist everywhere, even in the center of the sun. I need nothing and no one." The Dark relaxed a little. The sparkle returned to the stars. "But I never had a life of my own. The Dark doesn't love or lose or triumph or betray. I appear at dusk or when the candles burn out or when you pull a blanket over your head. That's all. So I like the memories. They're so full of people making *choices*. I can't get enough. They just insist on it. Choice after choice after choice. I don't make choices. I just exist. But the memories make me feel like I *could* make a choice. If I had to. I love them all. They are my pets. So you have to win them. I won't just give them away. And if you lose, I get a new puppy! Three hoorahs for New Puppy Day!"

Osmo raked his eyes over the prizes. They made no real sense to him, just a mishmash of *stuff*, like the back room of an antique shop.

"Would any of those help me find my way to Queen Melancholy? She lives in the Gnarlbind, in the beating heart of the Forest," he said. "Help *us*," he added quickly. "Us."

The Dark narrowed two blue dwarf stars at him. "Queen

Melancholy? What business have you with the strongest beast who ever lived? Why would you want to cross the whole of the Woods? Motters don't settle in the Gnarlbind. That place is for Quidnunx only and you're not half furry enough to pass."

Osmo didn't want to say. They couldn't just tell *everyone*. They needed to start playing their cards a little closer to the chest. Eventually, the little gloss they got from the flowers and the gladfish's hug would wear off. They had to do better. Osmo Unknown was a very excellent listener, even when he didn't seem to be paying attention at all. He remembered what the Dark had called . . . darkself.

*Patron of spies and thieves and secrets.*

"It's a secret," he said with a little smile.

"A secret!" crowed the Dark. "Then I am bound by my nature to keep it and hide it and provide cover of darkness to aid and abet all your schemes." The astral ape turned and ran thick, shadowy fingers over the objects on the wall. "I've got a compass that always points to joy and a spyglass that shows your heart's desire wherever you point the thing."

"I thought you said only one thing in the whole world was magic, Bonk," Osmo said accusingly. "Listen to that! *Everything* here is magic."

"Not magic." The Dark shooshed him before Bonk could give him a slice of his mind. "Everything has two natures. Even here. Especially here. The object and the feeling. The compass and the memory of joy. The spyglass and the remembrance of desire. The wineglass and the big mama cat's love."

Bonk the Cross stuck out his little pink tongue. "See? Told you so. Listen to Bonk."

But Osmo shook his head. It was no good. He'd know no joy at his wedding to Queen Melancholy, so the compass wouldn't help him. And his heart's desire just at this moment was to get out of here safe and sound, so the spyglass would only steer him back the way he came.

The Dark twinkled at him. "Perhaps this then." The Dark stretched up one long hairy arm and grabbed something from the very back of the deepest shelf. The ape-y hairs drifted in the air like pipe smoke tipped in starlight. "This was a sea captain's memory of sighting harbor after the worst storm of her life. A salty dog, she was! Well, half dog and half cat. Wolfhound pup and Norwegian Forest Cat, I believe. Name of Captain Badcat. It's a *terrible* cat who's half dog, you have to admit."

The Dark placed a gleaming sextant down on the counter. A perfect triangle of silver and red wood with neat little markings all along the curved lower edge. "Full name in the Books of Peerage: Captain Bad Cat Naughty Cat No No Stop Come Here Right This Second. The Second."

"Wait," Osmo interrupted. "Sextants are what sailors use to find their way when they can't see the shore. But there's no sea in the Forest. That's impossible. Once it's a sea . . . it's not a Forest anymore."

All three of them, the skadgebat, the pangirlin, and the Dark, frowned pityingly at Osmo.

"Anything's a sea if you're salty enough," the Dark scoffed.

"Captain Badcat sailed the Great Arctic Mud, far off in the cold-est north of the Fourpenny Woods. Nothing but black mud for miles around—but riches of fish in it, if you can catch them before the winter freezes every boat in the earth. And you don't mind them being moles. Oh yes, Badcat almost drowned twenty times over! But she never let go of the wheel. The line of pure greenery coming over the horizon felt so hot and good she never forgot it. And when she finally *did* drown and crossed the river, I got the memory of it off her fair and square."

Osmo scratched his head. It was getting loud in the gaming room again, more and more ghosts piling in behind them. "A sex-tant's no good without a chart," he protested.

"Good thing it's not a sextant. It's a *Nextant*." The Dark's shape ruffled itself in pleasure like real fur. "You know. Tells you where to go next."

"Puns are disgusting." Bonk rolled his eyes. "You ought to have to pay a fine."

"I like them," said Never quietly.

"Too bad," the Dark snapped. "It's not your stall, is it? What'll it be, young motter? Swing and a miss? Or the grand prize? Choices are so exciting! Life *is* choices, or so I'm told. This is the closest I'll ever get."

It wasn't much of a choice, though. The Nextant was the clos-est *he'd* get to guidance in the underworld. They had to have it. But what sort of memory could he afford to forget? Osmo was only thirteen, he didn't have so many memories to part with yet.

But there was one, wasn't there?

Osmo Unknown planted his feet on the boards of the ferry and thought as hard as he could of the night of the Frost Festival. That moment right before everyone ran off to Bonefire Park to see Mayor Lud run around like an idiot on stilts. That moment when Ivy Aptrick had looked at him with such pity and disgust and said, *How could you think someone with a father like mine could ever go anywhere with someone with a mother like yours?* That moment when he'd held out his flowers to her and she'd laughed. He remembered every detail as clearly as he could. The night, the stars, the smell of the roasting honeyed vegetables, the sounds of the festival, the beating of his own heart. The sad, cruel city seal above them both, hanging in the evening. Ivy's voice reading the words.

*Nemo Nancit Desiderium Eorum.* Nobody gets what they want.

*Go home, Osmo Unknown, you turnip.*

The Dark reached for Osmo's head like an old grandfather getting ready to do the tired old coin-behind-the-ear trick. But the celestial orangutan didn't pull a coin out of Osmo's ear.

He pulled out a turnip.

"Hope its other nature is something *really* swell," Bonk guffawed.

"Shut up, Bonk," Never snapped. "You know, I've been lonely all my life, so it makes sense I haven't got better manners. What's your excuse?"

Bonk did, for once, shut up.

The Dark set both the turnip and the Nextant down on the velvet counter and began to leap excitedly around the spangled stall like a real live monkey. Or ape.

"A bet has been entered and accepted! HEAR YE HEAR YE

FEATS OF STRENGTH ARE ABOUT TO BE PERFORMED FOR YOUR ENTERTAINMENT!"

The Dark handed Osmo a long, heavy hammer with a huge black block on one end. "Now, you haven't got any muscles anymore, remember," the Dark explained. "So your strength will come only from within. Your will. Your sense of self. Your essential wildness. The remnants of all your choices."

"Uh-oh, pistachios," Bonk giggled in singsong.

Without a word, Nevermore shot out one bronze hand and grabbed his snout in her fist. She held it there, not moving one scale while the skadgebat struggled.

Osmo Unknown looked at the pad and the bell. He suddenly understood. The game wasn't fixed, because it wasn't really a game. It was a test. To see who he was and what he lacked. The outcome was already locked in by everything he'd ever been in life. All that remained was to find out who he was.

The game wasn't fixed.

But Osmo was.

Because he *did* have muscles. And bones and skin and strength. Because Osmo was *alive*, where every other creature to swing this hammer and pound that bell had been nothing but a spirit and a shade. His secret. His advantage.

He was the cheat.

He was the fix.

He was the lie.

The same lie Adelard Sloe told with his rigged Quidnunk throwing game, the same lie that had filled him with such rage when he was small. Only now it was turned backward and upside down on him. Now it was his lie to tell. Would he tell it? Wouldn't that make him no better than any silly carnival man robbing coins from the eager and the unaware? No better than Littlebridge itself?

Osmo took a deep breath. He tensed his stomach muscles and the balls of his feet.

He swung the hammer.

As his swing swept through its highest arc, the ferry's horn blasted through the ship as they shuddered into the harbor on the other side of the River After. They had arrived.

The hammer came down.

The silver bell rang out like a siren.

KING OF THE BEASTS.

The Dark's mouth curled into a scream of thwarted rage.

*"What did you do?"* the Dark wailed. "They're my babies, my jewels, you can't take them, no one takes them, no one swings my hammer and doesn't miss! *What are you, you wicked little cheating devil?"*

"Run," whispered Nevermore.

"There's too many people!" shouted Osmo. "I can barely move as it is!"

"Don't you worry about that," Never assured him. "Just run."

The pangirlin coiled down into a great bronze ball and shot off across the deck like she'd got fired from a cannon, mowing down ghosts by the dozen. They scrambled to one side or the other, shouting angrily, fainting away, jumping to safety. Osmo didn't wait. He grabbed the Nextant. Bonk snatched the turnip-memory.

And they barreled down the path Never cleared for them while the Dark ranted and bellowed and shrieked.

"What are you doing? You can't escape the Dark, candy-brains! Where do you think you're going to go? I'll have you as soon as the sun goes down! I'll have you in the shade of every tree! I'll meet you in the dusk the first time a mushroom casts a shadow! *No one steals from the Dark!*" The Dark let loose an anguished sob. "Badcat, my puppy! Baby! Don't leave me!"

The Nextant stirred in Osmo's arms. Its telescope extended and retracted. Its triangular arc rocked back and forth like the rails on a rocking horse. A voice boomed out of the little silver telescope, which hardly seemed strong enough to contain it. A rough, salty sea voice, a voice hairy with barnacles and ice and whiskers, a voice that had seen everything there was to see and gotten bored with it all. A shaggy, sleek voice halfway between a cat and a dog.

"Pirates! Mutineers! *Children!* Oh this world is nothing but banditry, I tell you. *Banditryyyyy!* I love you, Darky! I'll never let 'em take me alive! I'll fight my way back to you if it's the last thing I do! By my cutlass and cummerbund, I'll have their tails on my belt before sunset! Let me go, you rotten powder monkey, I'll measure your face right off your skull, I will—"

Nevermore hit the ferry rail at full speed and rocketed into the air. Osmo was running too fast to stop himself. He half stumbled, half jumped after her, hitting the top of the polished bar and leaping, much less gracefully, off the side of the boat. The ball of the pangirlin's body turned end over end in the afternoon sunlight as it soared over the shallows of the River After. She landed wetly in the weeds of its far shore, half a second before Osmo Unknown tumbled down with a nauseating *crunch* in a heap of limbs beside her.

Bonk the Cross rewarded them both with a withering expression as he calmly jogged down the garlanded gangplank and disembarked like a proper gentleman.

## Chapter Seventeen

# WIDOWS' WEEDS

They landed in a reedy, weedy bank, sopping with green mud—and silence.

Osmo pulled himself half up onto his elbows and looked around for the boat. For the River After. For the Dark barreling down the planks behind them leaking stars left and right.

But there was no boat. There was no shore. There were no planks. There was no river. There had never been a river. There never would be one. Not here. A grand boggy marsh stretched from one edge of the sky to the other, where it disappeared into a watercolor smear of mountains. A low golden mist, lazy and lovely, steamed in the sunshine. The last of it clung to the stalks of tall black reeds crowned with nodding, heavy white flowers. Twisted saplings bowed over, dousing their branches in glittering puddles, streams, pools. Only a few trees here and there grew any taller than waist-high to a grown fellow. And those towered leafless, gnarled, forked like frozen lightning into the clouds.

Osmo rubbed his jangled head. Then his hip. Then his left elbow. Then too many parts of him hurt to rub them all at once and he gave up. His vision wobbled and swam. He could just make out the hulk of Nevermore next to him, still curled up into a ball, shivering.

"Where are we?" he croaked.

"Thumped if I know." Bonk shrugged. "Very short on signage around here. Rude, if you ask me, and *not* tourist-friendly. Ask the Nextant."

Osmo suddenly realized he was still clutching it tightly in one hand. The round edge of the Nextant's silver triangle cut a bright red mark into his palm. He held it up near his face.

"Um . . . hullo," he said to it, feeling completely ridiculous. "Hullo, Captain, I mean to say. Would you mind, er . . . I don't know how this works. Would you mind telling us where we are?"

The arc of the Nextant rocked back and forth through the slick wooden frame. The telescope stretched and pulled back.

It hissed at him. Hissed like a furious cat, then growled like a guard dog, then somehow both at once.

"Oh, come on, don't be like that," Osmo coaxed. He thought about bargaining. He thought about threatening. He thought about begging. But being humble and restrained like a hero on a quest ought to be never seemed to get him anywhere here. The only things that had won him any bit of progress so far were lying, cheating, and stealing. "All's fair on the high seas, right? Out of one berth and into another—that's the way the crow's nest crumbles." He was fast running out of nautical words. "But the voyage must go on."

The Nextant hissed again. But then it did speak. Resentfully.

"I'm a Nextant," the ghost of Captain Badcat grumbled. "I don't do where we are *now*. I only do where we go *next*. Figure it out among yourselves. I'll be in my cabin with a mug of brandy, a sword that needs polishing, and fur that needs licking. Good day, sir!"

"Well, that was about as useful as a hat on a horse," Bonk snorted. "I'm ever so glad we went through all that to get such a fantastically helpful item."

Nevermore slowly uncurled out of her tight bronze ball. She stretched her coppery arms as though she'd just woken up and looked quite a bit pleased with herself. The strange emerald-colored mud drenched her all down one side. She'd hit the marsh like a meteor and splattered the stuff everywhere. Osmo lifted up one hand, also caked in it—and realized that it really *was* emerald. Not moss or algae or frog slime. Glistening, metallic, glittering, gloppy emerald. A million billion gems all turned to a churning slop as thick and warm and greasy as butter left out of the icebox. Osmo stopped paying attention to his bashed-up flesh and bones and stared at it squooshing through his fingers. One cup of lousy mud and no one in his family would ever have to work again. They could live in Cammamyld Heights. They could own animals that didn't work land but just lazed around all day on pillows ignoring you.

"Hey!" Nevermore snapped her fingers to get his attention. Her glossy claws clicked together. "Isn't there something you want to say?"

Osmo squinted in the marshlight. "Hmm?"

"I rescued us!" Never said. Her face shone. "I did something for the *group*. I've never done anything for a group before! Don't tell my mothers. They'd be so mad." The pangirlin grinned cheekily.

"But it was good, wasn't it? *Pretty* brave and a *bit* spectacular, you have to admit." Osmo did indeed have to admit that. Even Bonk begrudgingly nodded. "So what happens now? Do I get a prize?"

"Why would you get a prize?"

"You got a prize for hitting that thing with a hammer. Two if you count the turnip. I hit *so many* ghosts. And a *boat*. That's got to be worth something."

"Thank you," Osmo said, and meant it all the way to his toes. "It's worth a thank-you. A big one."

"That's all? It's not even silver."

Osmo tried to remember that she wasn't trying to be rude or even strange to him. She was just . . . lonely.

"Uh . . . mostly the prize is just to keep doing things for the group until they're safe," he explained. But as he did, Osmo rather felt Never might be right. That wasn't half as good as a silver thing that talked like a cat and a dog at the same time.

"Ugh," Never sighed. "I don't see the logic in it. You'll never come out ahead, behaving like that." She picked at her scales and mumbled, "I turned into a whole cannonball for you." After a moment, she added, "You did good, too. With the hammer and whatnot. Fat lot of help you were, Bonk."

Bonk remained unconcerned. He picked his teeth with a claw.

Osmo smiled shakily. That was nice to hear, honestly, after everything. Even if she hadn't really wanted to say it. He grabbed onto one of the thicker, blacker saplings and hauled himself up out of the mud. The bark felt awfully soft and smooth, for bark. His head still felt fuzzy and muzzy and his sight still wouldn't sharpen up. Osmo rubbed his eye with the heel of his muddy hand and looked closer.

The reeds and trees weren't grass or wood at all, but patterned black cloth, braided and knotted into long strands growing straight out of the marsh. The nodding white flowers weren't even flowers—they were big ivory cameos like rich old ladies wore at their throats, with lacy metal frames.

"Wait," Never said. "I know this. I remember this! I know where we are!" She stopped and flushed a little. "I know where you two and me are. Not we. I'm not a *we*. Don't you go thinking there's a *we* here just because I helped out."

Bonk smirked at her. "Of course not. Wouldn't dream of it. Now spit it out. Where did that ugly barge dump us off?"

"The Widows' Weeds!" she exclaimed, clapping her hands, applauding herself. "We're in the Widows' Weeds! That's what those are, the plants and all. Widows' gowns. Black for mourning. And the rich ground is supposed to be inheritance. I think? You can only stay here as long as someone living still mourns you. Once no one cares or you're forgotten, the land just shoves you out. But it's only the edge of the Eightpenny Woods. Hardly anyone *does* stay here. There's loads more interesting places than a fussy old bog." She scrunched up her brassy eyebrows. "I don't remember what they *are* mostly, but not bogs."

Bonk piped up. "Ooh, the Ferals' Volcano, I remember that one. The pastor used to scare me bald with all that lava talk."

"And the Canyon of Singers," added Never. "For birds and wolves and bullfrogs and such. I know there's a glacier and some fjords, too . . . I just . . . I can't help it. I don't remember. I really was always rubbish at Monday school. So many other children around, I could never concentrate. It didn't seem important."

"But you did remember! Well done," Osmo congratulated her.

Nevermore wrinkled her nose and unwrinkled it. A shiver went over her scales. She didn't know what to say. No one had ever praised her before. You can't get praised when you're alone. Except by praising yourself, but it's not the same at all. The pangirlin kept trying to find her way out of it and back to lonely, but she couldn't. It was worse than the argument. And better. And worse.

"So somebody does miss me," Osmo said softly. Probably only his mother. But at least it was someone.

"Me too," Bonk said quickly. "Isn't that something? I wonder who the old roaster is?"

"And me," Never added. Her face moved oddly, trying to work it out. "Maybe my mothers. Maybe they're . . . maybe they're worried for me. Do you think it's possible?"

Osmo smiled. "I'm sure they are."

"But that's *awful*. I don't want them to be. I want them to stay lonesome and fierce and joyful! No, no." She wrung her long-fingered paws. "This is a nightmare. This is the danger of other people! They bring pain and worry and upset stomachs! You meet someone, and what's next? You just have to *worry* about them? *Forever?* That's no way to live!" Never started to snap into a protective ball. But she gave up halfway through her curl and plopped down among the twisted black silk brush. "I can't protect myself against my *own* sadness," she wailed. "What am I supposed to do now?"

Her answer was a fluttering of wings, a flickering of shadows on the still marsh, and a flashing of blue and rose and orange in all the tangled dark rushes.

Two creatures circled overhead, once, twice, then landed gracefully on a burly stump half sunk in sweet water.

They were called batterflies. It was obvious. No question. Osmo didn't have to ask. Big, well-fed bats, but not a bit of gloomy black on them. Their furry, squirrel-puppy bodies shone a bold, bright teal. Their wings were still leathery and clawed, but splattered with brilliant colors and spots and patterns of rose and orange and purple, like the best butterflies who ever lived.

"You're late," the first one said breathily.

"She won't be happy," the second one trilled.

"She's the oldest queen who ever ruled," the first one tut-tutted. "Both queens and old folk get grumpy very quickly. And old queens?"

"Look out," hooted the second batterfly.

"The queen sent you?" Osmo asked, leaping fully to his feet. "Queen Melancholy sent you?"

The one on the left stretched her wings and ruffled her fur. "Pardon us. We don't usually work in the daytime." She giggled. "Makes us all drunk on sunlight. Naughty old sunlight. Our names are Until and Unlike. We're her pets."

"We *were* her pets," the one called Unlike cut in. "When she was a young maid, wild and free and sneaky and sweet. We died before her. Batterflies' lives are longer than a thought but shorter than a dream." The batterfly lowered her voice confidentially. "A pet is like a daughter who sleeps on the floor. And gets walkies."

"*Sometimes* walkies," Until corrected her sister.

"Sometimes, yes," Unlike agreed mournfully. "But now we are together forever! She is the cleverest beast who ever lived. Every morning she tells us something new that we could never have imagined was true."

"And what did the old doorstop tell you this morning?" Bonk huffed.

"She said: *My sentence is a newborn pup in the nest.*"

"She said: *Today you will meet my husband.*"

Her bat eyes peered at Osmo through cerulean eyelashes. But the peering was all for show. Her eyes had a milky sheen to them—the girls were as blind as any bat. "Do you understand our names?" she crooned.

"Everyone here has the oddest names I've ever heard in my life," Osmo laughed. *At least she wants to meet me*, he thought. *That sounded like she does. Queens like newborn pups in nests, don't they?* He was beginning to see the trouble with the Quidnunx language.

"Yes, but do you understand them? Unlike and Until. Think hard. We had famous brothers, you know. Huginn and Muninn. *They* mean Thought and Memory."

Osmo did remember Huginn and Muninn from his school-books. A country not so far away worshipped a god named Odin, who traveled with two ravens by those names. But the batterflies' names were just words, plain as toast, in his own language.

"I don't think so," he confessed.

"Pity," chirruped Unlike.

"Pity," chimed Until.

"Will you take us to her?" Osmo asked. "To the Gnarlbind, in the thumping beating heart of the Forest."

Unlike and Until tittered. "No, of course not!" Until giggled.

"She'd pin us to a board!"

"You're not ready!"

"You have nothing for her!"

"Empty-handed, what a bad, bad boy."

"Then why are you here?" Nevermore snapped irritably. She rubbed her ears. The bats' high flutey voices throbbed in her head. "If you're not going to be any help, I mean."

"Oh, we help! We are an invitation!" Unlike and Until said in unison.

"Usually those come written down on pretty paper. With flowers pressed inside. And a ribbon," Osmo said.

"CAW," they spat. "Writing is a tool of the Valley. Don't worry, we memorized it."

The blue batterflies flapped up into the air and settled down again. Their voices trilled out like bells in a town square:

"You are cordially invited to the wedding of Queen Melancholy the Entirely Untamable and Osmo Unknown, Child of the Valley. The ceremony will take place at Autumn O'Clock sharp three days hence at the summit of the Gnarlbind. The Human Unknown will come accompanied by the Gown That Cannot Be Removed, the Ring That Fits No Finger, the Treasure That Cannot Be Taken, the Zither That No One Can Play, and the Rope That Cannot Be Untied." They went silent. Until fixed her milky blue eyes on Osmo. Ice slid through his limbs. He felt that somehow, somehow it was no longer a batterfly but the queen herself looking through him down to his soul.

"What's a zither?" Bonk the Cross whispered loudly.

"Shut up," Until cawed. "It's a harp, stupid. Only it lies on the ground and you play it sideways. We play *everything* sideways here. You'll see."

But Unlike went on, as grave as ever. "These are things that are necessary for a wedding. A ring, a dress, a feast, amusements. You will court me first as a bird, then as a deer, and finally as a fish. And only when you have placed these things in my paws and done this to my satisfaction will I grant the honor of standing by your side before the beating heart of the Forest. No negotiations, substitutions, or refunds. The End."

"How am I supposed to find all that?" Osmo protested. "It's impossible. I don't know anything about this place."

"That's the idea," thrummed Until apologetically. "Sorry."

The batterflies took to the warm noontime air and chittered at each other as they spiraled up and up toward the hazy sun.

Finally, after a long and awkward pause, Bonk blew a big breath out of his fuzzy cheeks.

"Yuck," he sighed. "I hate quests. Like getting water stuck in your ear. You jump and stamp about like a mad thing and what do you get? More annoyed. This is pure wormpoop and it's not going to be any fun at all, I promise you."

"I don't know," the pangirlin said slowly. "It sounds a *little* fun—"

"WELL, IT'S NOT!" yelled Bonk the Cross. He kicked green mud at her and gnashed his teeth. "Mostly," he admitted. "The treasure part sounded a bit all right. But *I* won't have fun, and you can't make me."

The screeching caw of the batterflies interrupted them as they wheeled round again.

"By the way," Unlike croaked. "In case you were feeling even faintly optimistic about the way your life is going, Osmo, someone is following you. Someone with an angry hungry heart."

"Someone with *very* big feet," Until added. "There's fish swimming in their footprints or my name's not . . . well. You'll see."

"Something with very big feet and a message," cawed Unlike.

Until circled wide above them. "It gave us the message and this is the message: IF YOU LOSE I GET TO TAKE A PIECE. GUESS WHAT PIECE I WANT?"

"Okay! Bye!" both batterflies trilled.

And then they were gone, two black blinks disappearing into the high, hot sun.

A soft, rich bell bonged invisibly through the clouds. Green leaves burst onto the bare, forked, twisted trees, and heavy black fruit, too, bending the branches down to the mud.

Summer o'clock had chimed.

*Chapter Eighteen*

# BUTTON, BUTTON

Osmo's limbs prickled with gooseflesh.

"What did they mean someone's following us?" he whispered, as though whoever it was could hear him, could be that close right this second, that careful. "Across the Meaningful Desert? Into Mustamakkara? Onto the ferry?"

"Maybe it's just the Dark come after the Nextant," fretted Nevermore.

"The Dark don't need feet, windybrains," Bonk grunted. "Big nor small."

The emerald mud steamed in the suddenly roasting summer sun. It cracked and dried around the Widows' Weeds, turning pale as the inside of a lime. Their own footprints slurped up the last of the spring melt and began to crumble at the edges. The ivory cameos blooming at the tips of the black silk reeds crisped at the edges, tottering, ready to fall or be plucked. Not a scrap of shadow lay anywhere. If the Dark hunted them, it would have to wait until autumn to pounce.

"Who, then?" Osmo asked. "That thing the batterflies said . . .

that's a doublechess thing. Do you play doublechess in the Fourpenny Woods?"

Never scoffed. "Who doesn't play doublechess?"

"I thought you didn't like company over."

The pangirlin shrugged and picked at emerald grime under her claws. "I play with my mothers. By post. We send sketches of the board and all our moves. And packets of tea. And pressed flowers. And jokes we've heard off the mushrooms and such. When one of us wins, we send over the bridepiece in a nice package with a ribbon. Been playing since I was teensy."

Osmo thought that sounded . . . honestly, as nice as anything he'd heard in days. A whole Forest of people who knew his favorite game. "Maybe . . . when this is all over . . . you and me could play that way," he ventured. Never said nothing. But her glasses fogged up a little. "But I'm not a *piece*. I'm not anybody's piece. And who are we meant to be playing against?"

His only answer was a quick, thin spray of green dust flying by on his left side. Then another on his right. He coughed as the dirt hit his face. The same zipping, darting, invisible *somethings* that had darted through the sugar desert alongside them. Back in force, now the land was dry and zoomable again.

"What *are* those little devils?" Bonk hissed. "They're tormenting me, and they're doing it on purpose, I tell you. *OW!*" The skadgebat hopped up on one foot, cursing. "Bashing me up now, are you? I bet you're nothing but nasty little bugs. Beetley ghostbugs having a laugh. Well, I *eat* bugs, you crawly crud-specks!" Bonk leapt about, trying to catch one in his paws or his snout. But his teeth came down on air and his claws came up with nothing but dust—dust that seemed to be laughing at him.

"*Eat!*" Bonk snarled. "Eat! Eat! Eat! Eat you up and never feel bad about it! Here, buggy, buggy, buggy . . ."

The pangirlin shrugged her bronze shoulders. "Don't look at me like that, I already tried to catch one. They're faster than the speed of tongue."

"You could ask the mushrooms to catch one for us," Osmo suggested. "Assuming mushrooms grow here, I suppose."

She stared. "Why?"

"I dunno," he answered uncomfortably. "Just to see. Just to know."

"Something is tracking us through the Land of the Dead, we have a grocery list of impossible items and no impossible item shop in sight, and you want to take a lunch break to catalogue some local fauna?" She rubbed at her glasses. They'd fogged up in the heat.

"*Ssst.*" Osmo sucked in his breath as one of the zipping zoomers bit at his heel again, in just the same spot as the one in the white sweet desert.

"Well, I won't, that's what," Nevermore answered herself. "Why do you think mushrooms like me in the first place?"

Osmo didn't have to think. He already had a theory. "Because they're like cats. They know you hate company so you're the only company they want. *Ahst!*" Another one nipped his toe. Or was it the same one?

"No, short-tongue, because I leave them *alone*. It's the nicest thing anyone could do for anyone else. Nobody else in the Fourpenny Woods leaves mushrooms alone for a minute. Do this, do that, do my laundry! I don't ask them to do anything very often. And even then, nothing they wouldn't already like to do and I don't bother them with silly tricks."

"You don't have to be angry with me, I was just curious."

Never softened. "All right," she said quietly. "They're a *little* like cats. Now get the Nextant out and let's go before whatever-it-is catches up to us and the worst happens."

"Do you really think someone wants to kill us?"

Osmo shuddered as he drew the silver instrument out of his satchel. Why? He'd only done *exactly* as he was told by a series of local authority figures. What quarrel could anyone have with him?

Never looked embarrassed. "No, I just meant there'd be four of us. Three is bad enough."

"*Owww!*" Osmo cried out.

The little zipper stubbed up against his other foot hard. He hopped around in real pain for a moment. Osmo had just enough time to wonder why Bonk wasn't laughing uproariously at him when the skadgebat dove into the dry summer dirt of the Widows' Weeds, knocking him over completely. A cloud of green dust puffed up after them.

"GOT IT!" crowed Bonk in triumph. "Ack, no, drown it all in a bucket, don't got it. Geddoff me, ya heap of guts."

"You landed on me!"

"Nope," Bonk said, leaping up, collecting himself quickly, and dusting off his robe. "I'd never do that, see. I don't roughhouse.

Bad for the fur. Whereas you are sprawled out all over the ground like a rug, so."

Osmo got his feet under him. He held on to the Nextant with one hand, brushed off his own patchwork trousers with the other—and noticed something trembling against him. It peeked out from behind his foot.

"Hey, little guy," Osmo said softly, sweetly, like he was talking to a donkey who'd broken out of its pen. "Hi, new friend! Don't be afraid. Come here, that's it." He bent down and offered his free hand to a clearly petrified tiny lump of green dirt. It glared furiously at Bonk for a moment, then shook itself off and rolled up Osmo's palm.

It was a button.

A round, hard, dark red button with two neat holes through its center. Its surface glimmered. It might have been cut out of a pearl or a shell or cut glass or some other shining, swirly stuff. Osmo couldn't tell. He didn't know much about buttons except to need them and to lose them.

The button spun around joyfully and nestled down against the pad of his thumb.

"I think it likes me!" Osmo laughed. It had been a while since someone had.

Bonk gawped. "It's trash," he said.

Never shook her head in disbelief. "And of *course* you like it back. You're the weirdest beast I've ever met."

"It's not weird to like people, Never."

"That's not a people, Osmo."

Osmo Unknown turned his hand left and right, looking at the button from all sides as it caught the light of the sun. It seemed to blush a bit under his gaze. "I don't know," he said thoughtfully. "Isn't it? You're a pangirlin. He's a badger, sort of. What's people? Hullo, Button. Are you people? Can you understand me?"

The button rocked side to side uncertainly.

"Osmo, we have to go," Never said, twisting her hands. "We can't stay here, it'll catch up to us. Whatever it is."

"All right, turn clockwise for yes and counterclockwise for no. Can you understand me?"

The button whirled clockwise in delight.

Osmo grinned, practically jumping on the dry marsh with excitement.

"Wow! Look at you! Aren't you something? Hullo, Button, indeed! Do you see this? Okay. Now. Button. This is very important. Were you following us all this way? All the way from the desert?"

Clockwise. Bashfully.

"Are all those zoomy things buttons like you?"

Clockwise. Proudly.

"See?" Osmo said with a sigh of relief. He turned his bright hazel eyes to Bonk and Never. "It was only Button. I doubt it meant any harm. There's so many of them, they probably made tracks that just *looked* like big footprints from the sky."

Button spun counterclockwise hurriedly. Osmo's stomach sank.

"It wasn't you?"

Counterclockwise.

"Someone else is back there?"

Clockwise.

"Someone with big feet?"

Clockwise, trembling with fear. The burgundy button stretched up and bent over in the middle as though it were made of taffy. It made a menacing lumpy shape with two pronged horns on top of it.

"Do you mean it's a Quidnunk, Button?"

It relaxed into its usual shape, spinning gravely clockwise.

"This is so . . . icky," Bonk marveled.

"He's so happy," Never said in disbelief.

"Well, maybe if you two stopped calling me names for five minutes, I wouldn't have to make friends with a button!" Osmo snapped. "Why would a Quidnunk come after us? We're doing what they wanted! I'm only here because they said I had to!"

"I can think of a reason," Bonk huffed. "Somebody doesn't want you to be king. Decided not to let fate take care of their business."

The pangirlin laughed sharply. "I don't want him to be king, either. Who ever heard of a human king? He'll muck it up before his first royal breakfast. Humans can't even make a good job of governing themselves. He only has one nature! What use is that?"

"I suppose a pangirlin could do better?" Osmo snapped back. Maybe he wouldn't be a great king at first, but he did think he could grow into it.

"I'd make a wonderful king." Nevermore shrugged. "It's a *very* lonely job. I don't tell lies or put on airs, I know how to find what's needed in a frightful mess—and kingdoms are always messes. Plus, I could never go mad with power. If I got too powerful, people would come and visit me all the time to influence me and curry favor. From miles and miles away. It's too disturbing to think about. So I'd behave myself always. I'd be the Lonely Little King and everyone would be happy because I'd leave them alone too, almost all the time unless they got very naughty or very needy. I can't see one single drawback."

"You're allergic to sadness," Osmo pointed out. "People get sad a lot. Even if you leave them alone. Sometimes *because* they're left alone."

"I'd invent an ointment." The pangirlin brushed it off.

"Look, Mr. and Mrs. King-a-ling. All one of those great big lunks has to do is catch you and put a horn through your brainpan and they'll have no more boy-king *or* Pangy-king to worry about and they'll get to gobble up Littlebridge in the bargain. Good day's work if you can get it. So let's shake a tail, eh?"

"Give me that," Never piped up. She snatched the Nextant out of his hands. "I don't want anything in my brainpan but my own good mess of thoughts, thank you very much. Let's go. You in there, Captain?"

The doggish-cattish voice growl-purred out of the silver device with a quickness. The Captain was clearly feeling much warmer toward them than she had when they spoke last. Or at least toward Never.

"At your service, My Lady Grubbylubber," Captain Badcat hummed. "What a beautiful sunset on the high seas! Care to join me in my cabin for a goblet of grog and a tale of my own bravery? I have a good stock of both, excellent vintage."

"It's lunch, and no seas in sight."

"Ah, the sea is in the heart, my dove! Mica glitters on the mud no less than foam on the wave! Sailing on water is for amateurs! The world is covered in the stuff! Too easy. Only the true mariner sails the *earth*."

"I see you're feeling better?" Bonk ventured.

"Silence! Scrub my decks until I can see my whiskers in them, both of you!" roared the ghost-memory of the pirate trapped in the Nextant. "I don't talk to *thieves*. But *you*, my walking treasure chest"—the cat-hound purred to Nevermore—"have done nothing to offend me or mine, and if you like I shall even let you wear my second-best feathered hat. It will make them jealous, and you will look *smashing*."

Nevermore tried not to smile and almost managed it. "No thank you. We need to . . . we need to leave."

"A voyage! A clarion call to adventure! Aha! You'll find I am a Bad Cat but a Good Dog, and I do love to do my little tricks. Cast off lines and rig the sails, boys! Thyme and tide wait for no pup! Heh, heh. *Thyme*. Get it? Where shall we point our prow, poppet?"

"You shouldn't talk to her like that," Osmo mumbled.

"Like what, villain?" Captain Badcat woofed cheerfully.

"Familiar. Calling her poppet and stuff like that. She doesn't like it. She doesn't like people."

"I can speak for myself," Never interrupted him.

"I know," Osmo protested, his cheeks warming. "I just—"

"She's hardly *people*, anyhow." Nevermore turned the Nextant over in her paws. "She's made of walnut wood and silver. She's got a telescope."

"Ah, we shall get along famously, my delightful little barrel of limes! *People* are nothing but bilge water and barnacles. Unless they are petting you correctly and constantly, which they hardly ever do. But that is exactly why *I* like *her*. She doesn't want me at all. A cat can always tell."

"Like the mushrooms." Osmo smirked. Oh, he'd missed that feeling of being right!

"So I can be certain that she will not use me ill or do naughty things to keep me under her thumb. Or pick me up when I don't want to be picked up. Or ever ever touch my belly. Whereas *you* already have grabbed me grabbingly with your grabby hands." The Nextant paused, as if considering. "Now, *poppet*, toward what isle doth our hull heave?"

"We were hoping you would know. We need to find . . ." Never scratched her scales, trying to remember the batterflies' list. "The Ring That Fits No Finger—is that right? Yes. And quickly. We can't stay."

"Enemies off the starboard bow, eh?" Captain Badcat gave a long wolfy howl of warning. "Well, isn't it lucky for you to join up with the finest, most courageous, wisest, most pettable captain ever to ply the earthen waves?" Badcat woofed, then meowed. "Kindly join hands with Bandit One and Bandit Two over there, I know it's distasteful, we will get through this together, my lady. Now, look into my lens."

Nevermore winced as they took her hands.

"Come on, Button," Osmo said, and clicked his teeth like he was calling a cat.

"Ugh, you're not bringing on strays, are you? Aren't there enough of us?" Never complained.

"Button likes me," Osmo said firmly. "Button is the only creature in this whole mad place who hasn't called me one name or insulted my mother or demanded I do something totally weird for it. And it's been very useful so far, you have to admit. So Button comes along. That's final."

"Maybe you're not a motter," Bonk chuckled. "Foolish, blather-brained, likes shiny objects . . . you're a cronkey! Crow and monkey, that's you in one. Or two."

Osmo ignored him. The burgundy button rolled up Osmo's wrist and tucked itself inside his sleeve. Never wriggled her glasses down her coppery nose and put the Nextant to one eye.

"I see an ocean!" she cried. "Only it's strange. It's all . . . black and white and scribbles and sketch marks. Like someone forgot to finish coloring it in."

"That's what we're after, mistress! The Unfinished Ocean. At the bottom of which you will find your ring. Now, if you would be so bold, line up my second mirror with my first . . . oh, and by the way, Bandit One! As I am the captain of this vessel and therefore obligated to advertise local points of interest, you should know that buttons are native to the Eightpenny Woods. They're a bit like squirrels. Always underfoot, always worrying about the future, usually idiots. They all come from here. That's why you never remember buying any but always have some on hand, and this is where they go when you lose them. Sometimes they do a spot of spying, but you shouldn't hold that against them, being such a naughty little thief yourself. They're the only things that go back and forth on a regular rotation. Buttons fasten one plane to another by passing through a lonely void. You know. Cuff to cuff through a button-hole. This is their natural environment. Now, man that rigging, badger!"

"I'm not a—"

But Bonk didn't get a chance to lay out his heritage for the talking navigational device. Nevermore gasped out loud. As the mirrors inside the Nextant slowly lined up, the image of that scribbly ocean grew bigger and bigger, and the cloudy sky on the other side grew wider and wider, until it swallowed them up with a grinding, clicking, final sound.

Where they'd stood, a puff of salt air floated out over the dry, emerald miles of the Widows' Weeds, suddenly terribly empty and still.

Only a few moments later, the summer trees groaned and quaked as footsteps like mountains falling came stomping, stomping, stomping.

## Chapter Nineteen
# AT THE BOTTOM OF THE UNFINISHED OCEAN

The three of them, plus the Nextant, plus a rather terrified burgundy button, tumbled out onto a beach the color of weak tea.

No sand crunched under their feet. No water pounded the rocks on the headlands. Even the sun in the sky was not *quite* a sun, nor the sky *quite* a sky. The beach was rough parchment, creased with a thousand ancient folds. Wherever a rock or a clam hole or a spattering of shells ought to have been, they were only sketched in broad, bold strokes. Lightly sketched guidelines bristled everywhere, to be erased later when the work was done. The sun was a child's drawing of a circle in a canvas sky. The clouds had no shading or depth yet, just outlines. And the great vast ocean rustled, tore, crumpled against itself. Paper waves covered in scribbles, rimmed in thick black ink, spewing chalk foam into the salty air.

But the ocean wasn't empty. Whale-y moans echoed from the deeps. Every now and then, unspeakable scribbled shapes humped up out of the water and crashed down again in a spray of eraser dust. Buttons whizzed here and there, popping off craggy rocks and diving into the water or rolling busily round the dunes.

"Bandit One, Bandit Two, and the most noble, blameless, and entirely peachy Not a Bandit At All, welcome to the Unfinished Ocean! Don't forget to bring me back a souvenir! Please leave your belongings stowed safely on board when you disembark and remember to keep your wits about you." Captain Badcat's voice went full cat, hissing pointedly: "Thieves. Are. *Everywhere*. Feel free to leave me in any convenient *shady* spot. Yes, anywhere is fine, under the pier, in the shadow of the lighthouse, anywhere cool and dry and . . . *dark*."

"I don't remember this from Monday school," Nevermore said.

She peered up the beachhead past rows of hastily drawn changing tents and cabanas. Each of them had a sign pummeled into the parchment sand. The letters were all outlined clearly, but only half filled in with rich black paint.

MY MOTHER DIED WHEN I WAS SMALL, read one.

I NEVER FOUND MY TRUE CALLING, read another.

I HURT SOMEONE AND I NEVER MADE IT RIGHT, read a third.

SOMEONE HURT ME AND NOTHING EVER SHONE AGAIN, spelled a fourth.

A fifth said: I WAS JUST SO WORRIED ALL THE TIME.

And so on and so forth up to a tissue-paper bluff and a huge lighthouse. The top half was beautifully painted with moody blue and grey and yellow watercolors. But the bottom was little more than chicken scratches and crosshatching.

"It's a dank, dull, embarrassing place, honestly," the Captain *aroo'd.* "Hasn't even got one tavern. It's for"—her voice dropped to a whisper—"people who can't let it go."

"Let what go?" Osmo asked.

"How should I know, burglar? Anything. Everything. Whatever stupid chum of living they can't pitch overboard and have done with. Unfinished business. They finish it here. If they want to. They could just waltz on to the Lake of Joy or the Party Archipelago or the Feasting Fjords! But some just can't find their way, even though the Party Archipelago sounds *much* better than this wretched place, it's not even an argument. A different sort of party on every tiny island? Hopping between Birthday Atoll, Halloween Reef, the Christmas Keys, Diwali Lagoon, New Year Bayou, where every hour is midnight? Then hop back in the dinghy and straight over to the Wedding Cliffs, the Islet of Eid, Big Fireworks Bay, First Frost Cove, the Easter Egg Volcano? Yes, please, sign me right up and don't dawdle!"

"Muddy well, me too," Bonk marveled. "Can't we go there instead?"

"You'd think everyone would feel that way, wouldn't you? But not this sorry lot. Please don't judge. It's not very common among our kind. When you're wild enough, sadness can't stick to you. You're too quick for the old villain! Trim your sails tight and outrun it, or steer clear of the shallows in the first place."

Osmo stared out to the unfinished sea. He could feel the button warm and snug against his skin. "Can you really outrun sadness? Is that true?"

Captain Badcat sighed. "No, my lad, it's not. But wouldn't it be something if it were?" The Nextant collapsed her mirrored scope. "You'd better hurry. The opening bell's about to ring. This place depresses me. My tail may never recover. This is why I sorted *my* cargo and dumped my ballast in the sunlit world like a proper pup! Put me away so I can open a cask of rum and stare at a mysterious painting from my past. Aye, this is no place for a Good Dog. Or a Bad Cat."

Osmo stuffed her into his satchel—but left the flap open so the Dark couldn't hook a thumb in there and grab her back. She was far too useful, and besides, he'd won her mostly fair and reasonably square, whatever she called him.

Osmo kicked at the beach sand with the tip of his toe.

It crumbled and curled back and Osmo thought it might actually have *whimpered*.

Then it caught on fire.

The little flame blew out quickly, but it left a black blast where Osmo's foot had disturbed the world. The ground around it shuddered.

"The land doesn't like us here," Never whispered. "We're alive. We're hurting it. We can't stay here long. We can't stay *anywhere* long. We'll be caught. Or it'll all burn."

A clear brass bell of the sort that hangs over a shop door clattered out a chime over the ocean wind. Folk of all sorts bustled out of their tents and cabanas to set up shop on the sand. They had registers and calculating instruments from every country and more besides: piles of contracts and stamps to seal them with, sacks of coin and leather checkbooks, deeds and letters of writ and nicely lettered stock certificates, and mountains upon mountains upon mountains of receipts.

"Come on, Button," Osmo whispered. "Out you come. You'll fall out that way."

The burgundy button rolled shyly out of his sleeve and looked around. It shuddered and tried to roll back in to safety. But Osmo tapped the cuff of his sleeve. "Just there," he coaxed. "Safe and sound."

Button flipped into the air and came down on the soft patch of Mrs. Brownbread's great grand fur coat that made up his cuff. It snuggled and wriggled and spun until the strands of silvery-brown-black fur crisscrossed tightly through its holes and held it fast.

Osmo jogged lightly over the beach, trying not to upset the earth too much. He headed toward a little polar bear cub with a long feathery tail like a white fox. She didn't look *too* frightening. She had tiny spectacles on her snout and a tidy stack of certificates of stock in something called Grief Unlimited on a little driftwood bench in front of her. She pawed through them, then moved a few beads on her abacus.

"Can I help you?" she said when she saw the human boy. Her voice sounded rough and tired; her eyes were red from crying. "What's your business, dear?"

"I'm not sure I know what you mean?"

The cub looked over her glasses at the three of them. "Your unfinished business. Can't leave until you've got your ledger in order. You can see mine here." She pointed at her certificates, made out in the name of Seldom the polx. "My mother rejected me when I was born. Too small, I s'pose. And then she went and got herself eaten by an orcadile anyhow, so I never could have had a mother no matter what."

Nevermore snapped up into a ball. Tiny whimpers of pain and relief came from inside it.

"Did you starve without her? Poor little biter. Hardly got to live at all, did you?" Bonk the Cross said. Osmo's eyes nearly popped out of his head. The skadgebat was being *kind*.

"Oh no, I lived to a ripe old age," Seldom the polx said, checking one long receipt against another. "Had many cubs of my own. Died on the ice with a full belly under the borealis. I had a good life." She looked up at them with the huge dark eyes of a frightened baby bear. "But this is how I felt inside all the time. I couldn't ever stop feeling so small, even when I was as big as an iceberg. I have to sort it out here. Understand why she didn't love me. Or at least how to not care about it. Then I'll feel big again, and I can be happy. What about you, little kit? You don't have to tell me everything! I respect your privacy. But I can direct you to the right tents if you give me a hint as to your business."

Bonk furrowed his striped brow. He shoved his paws in his bathrobe. He glanced furtively out from under his shaggy eyebrows at them. "Nothing," he grunted thickly. "I'm very healthy. Psychologically. And the other way too. Mentally and physically fit. Master Fit of Fit Manor, that's me. Punting on the Fitminster River. Not here for that, anyhow. Just want to get out to sea pickedy-bit, don't you know."

Never peeked out of her ball and slowly unfurled.

"You can't get out to sea with all your business on board, though," Seldom said sympathetically. "You'll keel right over and sink to the bottom. Across the sea is the Eightpenny Woods proper. If we could just hop over as soon as we arrive, none of us would be here counting out our frowns." She pointed to her pile of coins, very like crowns and half crowns, but with sorrowful faces on each one.

"I said I'm fine!" Bonk yelled. "I'll float away no problems! Leave it to me!" But he didn't move. He just stared down at his toes.

Osmo Unknown thought he might actually die under the weight of all the hugs he'd wanted to give but couldn't since he'd met these strange beasts.

"We can turn around, if you want," he said softly. "Like you and I did for Never. It's all right. I don't mind."

Never looked at him oddly, as though she had never met him before. She kept on looking at him even after they'd stepped away and turned their backs so Bonk could whisper his secret stripey heart to Seldom. Osmo wanted more than anything to hear. He strained and stretched his ears.

The skadgebat garrumphed and haroomed and ahemmed a great deal. Finally, he spat it out: "I guess when you carve it up and serve it for supper, it's just that nobody ever liked me. My mum had thirteen babies and I was the biggest and strongest and born first besides. But all the other twelve still stepped on my ears and ate up all the worms before I could get one and . . . and . . ." The skadgebat's black eyes filled up with awful tears. He whispered: "They wouldn't let me in the pouch. My own brothers and sisters, the horrid wee *pork pies*. All-day-all-night cuddle till you're big enough not to get *et*! That's how it's supposed to go with skadge-bats. Only on account of how I talk too much, too loud, about too many things no one else cares to hear, but all of which *I* feel exceedingly strongly about, they wouldn't let me in. Stopped up the entrance with their stupid feet. I . . . I *annoyed* everyone. From birth. But I can't help being myself, can I? I was the biggest at the starting gate, but I grew up smallest of all, because they never left any tea for me so I was hungry all the time. And I had to sleep between my mum's paws in the cold, 'cause we don't have fur when we're born, you know. That's why we need the pouch. How was I supposed to turn out nice and sweet and *thank you ever so kindly, sir* when the mean old harsh wind had its way with my bare skin since I first set teeth on the world? Makes you hard and tough and grouchy as a rotten chestnut, that does. Makes you *cross*. So's the wind can't ever do it to you again, and no one else, neither."

"But your mother did let you sleep between her paws. She liked you well enough for that," Seldom answered sullenly.

"Aye." Bonk the Cross nodded. "But she didn't like me *best*. Nobody did. Nobody does. Nobody never will. And I'm too big for anybody's pouch these days, so I'll never get well of that wound, will I? S'not *fair*. I'm big now! I could take a hurt like that and it'd be hardly a scratch. Oh no, you won't let me into your snickering little pouch party? I'll show you. I'll have my own party. I'll eat the whole cake in one bite, see if I don't. But when a beastie's so little, one lonely hurt slices up your whole self. You've only got a small naked self to begin with. Not enough real estate to lose a bit and keep the rest nice."

The polx cub nodded. "I understand completely, poor thing," she sighed. "I think you ought to stay right here with me." She waved a paw at her sign. It read: MY FAMILY COULDN'T FAMILY SO WELL.

Osmo couldn't speak for the lump in his throat. His family *familied* just fine . . . except for him. He always had to be difficult. He always had to be different. He couldn't just do what he was told. Couldn't fit in the pouch. Certainly not when his father was always there, staring stonily and saying a real man wouldn't need a pouch at all.

"What about you, love?" Seldom said when Bonk had done and was furiously wiping his nose on his sleeve.

"You didn't hear, did you?" Bonk asked roughly. "I'll put your face in a box and send it to the nearest volcano if you heard one *syllable*."

Osmo shook his head vigorously. Bonk narrowed his eyes.

"All innocence, eh? A little *too* innocent maybe?"

Never cut that line of questioning down before it could start. She waved her claws at the sad and helpful polx. "Not me, thank you. I saw the right sign for me on the way up the beach," she said quietly. She glanced toward it and pointed quickly, just to prove she didn't need help, but no more.

Bonk was deep in his feelings. He didn't even bother to check. But Osmo followed her claw to a cursive, half-illuminated sign spelling out, very clearly: I WAS LONELY ALL THE TIME.

And so it was Osmo's turn.

"Well. I . . . I loved someone and they didn't love me back," he confessed.

"Nope," said the polx.

"What do you mean 'nope'?"

"No, that's not it. That's not your unfinished business. I *know* business. And that's not it."

"Of course it is!" But he knew it wasn't. Not really. He already couldn't quite exactly remember Ivy's face. So many new things had crowded into his world in the last few days. He didn't even know her favorite color. Was that love? She certainly didn't know his. But Osmo Unknown didn't want to tell this strange animal the truth. Not here, not now, not just boldly out in the open. He wasn't a pangirlin. He had shame. He couldn't bring himself to say his life was *all* unfinished business. That there wasn't one single thing he could think of that his heart could call finished.

"Fine. If you want to stick with that story, you'll have to walk a fair bit down the way for it," Seldom the polx said, fluffing her silky white tail. "There's far too many of those to fit in a tent. That's what the lighthouse is for."

Osmo paled as he looked up the heights of the lighthouse, floor after floor, up to the cloud line, and the great bright lamp in the turret.

"Go all the way to the top. I'm sure there's still some room for you. You're just a wee thing. If they let you in. Which they won't."

Osmo swallowed hard. It was just *so* far. He had never imagined so many wild beasts had loved other beasts and gotten nothing but teeth and emptiness in return. Wasn't that a . . . specially human sort of misery? How horrifying to know that it was not!

Osmo shifted from one foot to another. The beach had begun

to curl back around his toes unhappily. It didn't want him there. It didn't want him anywhere. How much time before someone noticed? Or whatever was following them caught up?

"Bonk is right," Osmo protested. "We're not here for this. Not yet. I'm here to get the Ring That Fits No Finger from the bottom of the sea. Feeling right about Ivy can't help me with that. In fact, sinking to the bottom is probably the best we can hope for!"

"Who's Ivy?" Nevermore asked. "You've never mentioned her."

"Is she part girl and part plant?" Bonk said knowingly. "I've met a few greeners like that. Not the best conversationalists. Mostly want to go on about the weather for four to six hours."

"You've come for the ring?" Seldom interrupted. Her voice softened in awe. Her cub eyes widened even further. "*The* ring?"

"Yes, yes, you needn't be so precious about it." Bonk rolled his eyes. "One scrap of jewelry's much like another. It's not like it's *magic*."

"It might be, you said the Thing could be anything."

"It would never be something so obvious as a *ring*," Bonk scoffed. "The universe is just . . . better than that, Osmo."

Osmo noticed it.

Then Bonk noticed it.

Then Bonk turned away sharply so he could more easily pretend he *hadn't* noticed it. Bonk had called him by his name. Not *roaster* or *dummy* or *Mister Boy*. Osmo said nothing. It was enough to notice.

"It is the ring the Valley gave the Forest when they married," Seldom said dreamily. "That is why it is at the bottom of the Unfinished Ocean. The Forest wears it there, on its stony thumb."

A quiet, raspy sob broke the air.

"What's that?" Seldom the polx said, all dreaminess gone. "Who's hurt? I won't stand for a cub to be hurt on my beach, no I won't."

The sob rippled out again. Osmo, Never, and Bonk tried to step away and move toward fresh ground without being entirely obvious about it.

"Where are you going?" Seldom said sharply. "What's going on?"

The sand beneath their feet smoked and hissed and wept. It turned grey, then glassy, then black.

"I'm sorry," Osmo said. "It's not my fault."

"What have you done?" the polx gasped, seeing her beautiful sand blister and peel. "What's *wrong* with you?"

She stood up, scattering her stock certificates in Grief Unlimited. The sea wind began to pick them up and toss them into the air. The scarlet seals flashed as they turned over and over, rising into the sky. Seldom leapt up after them uselessly.

Never watched Seldom curiously.

"Hey," she said gently. But Seldom couldn't hear. She just kept trying to snatch her unfinished business back down to her. "Hey, Seldom. Seldom, stop," the pangirlin said.

Osmo stared out to sea. Then down to his feet where the papery parchment sand still desperately tried to escape him. A notion was happening in his head. A notion like the one he'd had on the ferry, and at Adelard Sloe's Stupendous Throwing Game so long ago. A cheat. Well, not exactly a cheat. A *slant*. Like the angle you had to throw a ball at to slip behind a false Quidnunk's mouth.

"I can't stop," the white bear-fox sobbed, and no one could tell anymore which sobs were hers and which belonged to the paper shore. "I need them!"

Nevermore took a deep breath, squeezed her eyes shut, and put her hand on the little cub's shoulder.

"My mother left me, too," she said. "But it's okay. She still loved me. Some beasts are like that. Sometimes. It wasn't because of you. It wasn't your fault. And being lonely made you strong. When you're lonely you can't lose anything, because you'll always have yourself. You are good and big and lonely, and that is enough. Just because someone isn't there doesn't mean they don't love you. That's all."

Seldom stared at the pangirlin. Her eyes filled up with big bear tears.

"Or not," Never said uncomfortably. "Never mind. Forget I said anything. This is what comes of trying things. Ugh. Why did I let Osmo convince me to try to hug people with words? Stupidest thing I've ever heard. That was *so hard* and it didn't even work. You won't catch me feeling anyone else's feelings again. I need a bath." She looked round for encouragement. Osmo always encouraged her. Never was already used to it.

But Osmo was gone. Already halfway to the pounding hand-drawn surf. Never and Bonk stumbled after him, turning the ground to ash and glass as they ran. So they didn't see it. It happened in a second, when their backs were turned. And they'd never know, either. By the time it was all over, they wouldn't recognize Seldom. They'd look for a cub, and look straight past the great tall pale polx, as big as an iceberg, grinning in the storm as her grief blew away like snow.

"If someone else comes looking for us," Osmo yelled back to the Unfinished Businessfolk, "tell them they don't have to hate me. They don't have to hunt me. I'm all right, I promise!"

Osmo Unknown turned around, gulped as much air down into his lungs as he could catch, and dove into the Unfinished Ocean, his hand stretched out, fingers curled into claws.

"Stop it!" Nevermore yelled after him. "Stop! You are not aquatic!"

Osmo heard nothing but the crashing surf. As soon as his fingertips touched the waves, they shrieked and burned away from him. The sea was much less strong than the earth. It hissed and whined and recoiled. Black spots came up, like they do when you hold a piece of paper in front of a candle. The pale brown paper ocean parted before him. He didn't need to swim. He just swung his arms wildly and it shrank away, making a path straight down to the ocean floor.

Osmo Unknown just walked right in.

And at the very moment Bonk reached Never at the tide line, the pages of the sea closed behind Osmo, swallowing him whole.

"Huh," grunted Bonk. "Didn't expect that."

The scrawled sun dipped behind a penciled cloud.

The wind guttered and died.

The watercolor lamp on the lighthouse spun round once, twice, three times.

And the Unfinished Ocean spat Osmo Unknown back up onto the beach. The boy lay there like driftwood. Little waves of tissue-paper seafoam washed up over him. He didn't move. He didn't speak. He didn't open his eyes.

But he clutched a small green ring in his right hand, tighter than death.

"Get him up," Bonk said, and his voice had no jokes in it, no mockery, no fun, not even a breath of grump to it. Only real, heavy worry. "Get under his arm. There, that side, that's it."

Never hoisted him up on one side and Bonk on the other. The ground beneath them seeped black. The stain spread and spread out from them. The Unfinished Businessfolk were all staring in horror.

And then they heard the sound. The stomp. The thump.

Not a thump, a *Thumpus*. Rhythmic, banging.

A Quidnunk. Coming for them. And it was so close. They couldn't see it, but they could feel every step it took deep down in the hollows of their bones. Nevermore fumbled in Osmo's satchel for the Nextant, but she couldn't get it out and hold the human up all at once.

"I got him," Bonk yipped. Never frowned doubtfully. A bit of his old bitter-happy grin came back. "I'm a fair way stronger than I look, ya fancy pinecone. Just 'cause I haven't got a tongue like a party favor. That blasted thing likes you best, anyhow."

The skadgebat grunted, wriggled, shoved, and hefted Osmo Unknown onto his back, just like every mother badger who's ever lived.

The pangirlin slid out the Nextant's scope.

"Darling!" Captain Badcat's rough growl-purr pealed out of the Nextant. "Come up to the crow's nest, the sunset looks like a million red candles all melting together! You'll love it." The old pirate hiccuped. "I've a coconut full of catnip tea just big enough for two."

"No time, we've got to get out of here! Take us to the . . . ugh, we should have written all this down when we had a chance. What comes next? The Zither That No One Can Play?"

The silver Nextant howled happily. "Man the rigging! The mud tide is rolling in, brown and thick! On to another port and another treasure! ZITHER AHOY! Put your pretty eye to the mirror—"

But it was too late for that now.

The rustling paper beach beneath them gave up. It sobbed horribly, as though it had lost everything it ever loved, and crumbled away into black ash.

The skadgebat, the pangirlin, the Nextant, the burgundy button, and the frighteningly still, cold human boy plunged down through the earth into nothingness.

## Chapter Twenty

# THE HINDERLANDS

A soft, low, melancholy bell bonged in the distance.

It didn't echo. It didn't chime. It sounded all wrapped up in thick velvet and terribly far away.

"Do you think he's dead?" Nevermore said, and her voice sounded just the same. She might have been a mile away or just nearby, it was impossible to tell.

"Mmmfsnnrumph," Bonk murmured, facedown on the ground under a very heavy boy. "Where is. Who go. How can?"

Facing up didn't help at all. Wherever they were, it was hot. And wet. And packed with dense, shimmering grey fog. So thick, in fact, it had broken their fall. Never had to concentrate to push her hand through it. She prodded at Osmo's body, lying sprawled across Bonk's.

"Geddoff," the skadgebat groaned, scrambling out from under the Quidnunk's currently very-much-not-moving betrothed. "I can't see a muddy *thing*. Am I blind? Am I mad? Ooh, hope so. Wouldn't have to look at anyone ever again if I was blind, or listen to them ever again if I went mad! Win-win for Bonk!" His blue nostrils widened. "Sorry. What is that *smell?*"

The pangirlin rubbed at her foggy glasses but it didn't help one bit. Nothing but silver drifting curling mist as far as forever in every direction. She groped blindly for the Nextant, but she'd dropped it. It could've fallen anywhere in this woolly mess. She sniffed the smoky air deeply. "I don't know. It's like . . . cinnamon and birch bark and lavender . . . and something else. Crusty bread, maybe. Nutshells. It's . . . really nice, though, isn't it?"

"Just about the best thing I've ever smelled, actually," Bonk admitted.

"He's breathing, at least," Never said, examining Osmo's limp body.

Bonk got to his feet. He peered into the haze. There were shapes out there, shapes and shadows and such, but the gloam hid them very well. It was like being inside a down pillow, or the whole held breath of the world. "What do you care?" He shrugged. "If he dies, that's one less person to trouble you. One step closer to being as lonely as you like."

Never turned Osmo over onto his back and sat on her heels. An odd, sweet feeling filled her chest. She felt . . . good. *Extremely* good. "He's less trouble than most," she said reluctantly. "He tries a lot. Do you know how many times he's wanted to pat my hand or help me up or hug me? Because it is a *lot*. But he didn't. People touch me all the time in Quiddity. They know what pangirlins are about, they just don't care. But he cares. And one time he praised me. He said 'well done.' Nobody's ever said anything so grand to anyone before in the history of the world, I expect. Maybe nobody ever will again."

Bonk pointed a claw at her. "You," he said, "are *weird*. Don't forget what he is, cheese-sweat. Don't forget what they do. There's never been a human born who wouldn't turn any of us into a shirt and a steak as soon as look at us. He's not different." Bonk glared at the boy he could barely make out in the mist, though he lay still as a fallen tree right beside them. "He's *not*. Just because he has pretty eyes and listens so nice when you talk and hardly ever interrupts you and doesn't punch you no matter how many times you call him a turnip doesn't make him any different than the rest. Stupid cronkey. Did I tell you what they were doing when I went to collect him? They were having a party with a fat man all dressed up like a Quidnunk grabbing girls and roaring. And they didn't even get the face right on the costume, I tell you what. They haven't changed. They can't. We beasts change our coats with the seasons. But a human is a human all year long."

"He does try, though," Never said. "I think he's a very lonely boy." She coughed. "But don't you dare tell him I said so."

"Dunno that we'll get to tell him anything again, if I'm honest." Bonk stood back like a fat little doctor pronouncing the worst. "I think he's done a runner on us. Bye-bye, turnip! Oh," the skadge-bat said. "Curse him straight into the lava, that dingbat's given me a sad. How very dare he?" He nudged Osmo's body with his foot. "Nobody gave you permission to make me *sad*, ya . . . ya . . . Osmo! Osmo, no one said you could make me feel my *own* feelings. Only *I* get to hurt *myself*, all right? Stop it right now, I mean it!"

But Osmo didn't move. Osmo didn't get up. Osmo's eyes stared straight ahead and didn't blink.

The sad, sweet bell rang again, even softer and more muffled this time. A little wind began to pick up through the dewy steam. Swirls of red maple leaves fluttered through the silver, leaving gaps in the mist behind them. It was autumn o'clock. They could smell woodsmoke now, too, little fires and charcoal. The heat still closed them in tight, but they could at least begin to see bits and pieces of the place they'd got to, or the place that had got them.

Row after row of even, slender birch trees broke through the curling clouds. The ground beneath their feet wasn't dirt or sand or paper or emerald mud but a polished floor of reddish, fragrant wood stretching out for ages on all sides. The red leaves blew and blew but never seemed to fall. Nothing cluttered up the freshly scrubbed floor, not moss or droppings or acorns or twigs. It didn't even turn black or curl away from their toes, either. The Forest floor seemed perfectly happy to have them. No more buttons zipping and clattering about, either. The whole place sat quiet and hot as the inside of a whole living heart. When they looked up, they saw not a sky, but rafters peeking out of the rising gorgeous fog. Impossibly high up, a mile perhaps, or more, but heavy wooden rafters all the same, disappearing into a peaked roof.

They stood in a stately, graceful, terribly clean wood. But they were also, somehow, *inside*.

They tried exploring and made it a few feet before stumbling skull over tailbone into a large, raised *something* hidden in the fog. For a moment, Never and Bonk both thought the object that came into view beside them was a campfire in a sturdy, waist-high iron fire pit. That would have been just terrifically convenient. But it wasn't. It was a pretty, wide stone bowl full of hot, flat, colorful stones. Two white clay pitchers with nice green patterns painted on them sat snuggled up against it, one full of black water, the other of fresh white cream. And there was the Nextant, lying between them. The stones gave out a loud hiss. More fog spiraled up off them and into the air.

"It's a sauna!" Bonk exclaimed. "The Sauna of Total Satisfaction! The Sauna at the End of the World! Well, of course life should end with a nice, relaxing sauna and a good, long soak. The dead've earned it. Some of them, anyway."

"It's lovely," Never agreed. She looked at the Nextant. She could pick it up right now and ask Captain Badcat where they were. But . . . why? It was safe here, she could feel it. No rotting land, no horrible footsteps. She stretched her tail. Who cared what the place was called when it was just so *nice*? "Think of the naps you could take here! But . . . we should help Osmo," Never said uncertainly. He wasn't getting up, and that wasn't nice at all. "We should. Shouldn't we? Or maybe we should just put a bit more water on the stones and see if there's a cold pond for dipping in nearby." She frowned. Then she giggled. Then she covered her mouth to stop herself. "We've got to wake him up."

"Do we?" Bonk yawned and stretched his shaggy, striped arms in the air. "I don't know. It's awfully nice here. If I could scratch up a comfy spot to lie down I could get *well* used to it. Maybe we're done. Maybe this is where we were headed! Superb spot for a wedding if you ask me. Plus he won't have to look at the bride."

Never smiled—a real, big smile, open and unguarded. She

didn't know why. What had come over her? "No, I know, you're right, it hardly matters but . . . he wouldn't want to miss how nice it is here. How nice it *smells*. Do you know how a boy works? How do you figure out what's gone wrong? Is there a lever or a hidden compartment or something?" She picked up Osmo's arm and dropped it; it flopped down again without resistance. "If we cut off the part that's broken, will he grow another one? Does he need to be pruned? Or returned to the river where he was born to spawn?" A look of horror crossed her copper face. "Do you think he has an egg stuck?" she whispered. "I saw that happen to a maidhen once. It was *grisly*. Or maybe he's just hibernating and we only have to wait till spring? Do they do that?"

"Don't look at me, this is the first one I ever handled. They need air, I know that. But water, too. You have to make sure his heart is doing heart things." Bonk squatted down and brushed Osmo's hair from his eyes. "What happened to you down there, you dumb little sausage? You can't have swallowed too much ocean, there wasn't any water to swallow. Are you faking? I bet you're faking. Just want to hear us say nice things about you while you lie there like a lazy lump of beef. Well, fat chance, fish-butt. You can wake up now, it's not happening."

Osmo's empty eyes stared up lifelessly into the misty rafters.

"Oh well." Bonk shrugged.

"You're acting strange," Never said.

"No, you are," Bonk snorted, backing away from Osmo.

He nearly tripped over a long, smooth ledge rising up out of the mist. It was made of the same polished reddish wood as the ground, formed up into a wide seat with little hollows and rises to nestle your knees and neck and rump into.

"Oooooh," Bonk crooned. "Don't mind if I do." He swung his legs up and laid himself out. The seat was shaped just perfectly for his little stout body.

"He might die if we leave him," Never said. She tried to fight the happiness. The *comfort*.

Bonk laughed. First he laughed a little, then it took him over and he couldn't stop.

"It's not funny," the pangirlin snapped. "Not at all funny, really."

"It's the funniest thing I've heard since *take a mushroom and go get that boy out of the village*. Look where we are, Little Miss Paperweight. So what if he dies? We're already here. Plus, this way, we can have his stuff. He's got a golden ball in that bag. I saw. It's very shiny. I'll have it off him. I deserve a prize for helping him get so far. He'd never have managed without Bonk the Cross. Uff, I feel funny, Never! Funny as a three-footed stoat."

Nevermore sat down. She hardly noticed the wooden seat rising up to catch her, shifting to fit her just as Bonk's did him. Her head felt warm and sweet and light. Thoughts just didn't want to stick anymore. "No . . . ," she murmured slowly. "Mostly the prize is just to keep doing things for the group until they're safe. That's what he said. And he's not safe. Not like that."

Bonk turned over on his side. "Yes, you're so right. We have to help him. Only . . . I'm just so *content*. So comfortable. So happy." The skadgebat sat bolt upright. "I've never been content from the day I climbed down off my mum's back. Why should I be now?

There's no reason. This is all wrong. Feels like wearing a robe made for another chap. Oh, but it's a *comfy* robe. Why shouldn't it be mine?"

The scented fog and the red leaves drifted softly between them like waves.

"I can do something," Never said. "I can call a mushroom."

"Are you sure there *are* mushrooms in the Eightpenny Woods? We're not exactly at home with our nice tame Fredericks making toast and Agathas chauffeuring us about."

Never crawled down off the warm seat. She could hardly make herself do it. She just felt so perfectly fine not moving or doing anything. Nothing was wrong in the world. Why insist on doing things? It was never worth it.

But Osmo's hollow eyes were *there*, right there beside her, with so little in them.

The pangirlin got her iridescent claws down under one of the floorboards. She pulled and groaned and pried it up. Underneath lay good moist comforting soil. The soil you could find anywhere, no matter how scarce everything else got, dark and rich, ready to make things grow.

And it was dark under the floorboards.

*Very* dark.

Never realized what she'd done only a moment before the huge, hairy, starry black hand of the Dark blossomed out from under the sauna floor. It groped around blindly, snatching at empty fog, scrabbling against birch trunks. Bonk scrambled to get out of its way.

Too slow.

The Dark snatched him up by the back of his robe, felt around his belly and his snout. But Bonk the Cross was not in the least Nextant-shaped. The starry hand tossed him casually aside.

Never tried to push the wooden plank back against the Dark's massive wrist. "Go *away*," she moaned. "We need it more than you!"

"I told you I'd find you with the first shadow." The voice of the Dark filled up the mist. "You can't run from the Dark, that's just ridiculous. I shall laugh about this later, you can be sure. You won't, but I will."

Never tried to stretch her tail out behind her to knock the Nextant out of the reach of the grasping paw. "You can't take her! I'm sorry Osmo stole her but without her we're lost!"

The hand shivered and became much slenderer and more deft, a human woman's hand, running its fingers over the wood, searching. The Dark called her by her full name. "Bad Cat Naughty Cat No No Stop Come Here Right This Second! The Second! I mean it!"

But for once the Captain decided to be good at being a cat. She did not come when her master called. The heavenly hand turned irritably to Nevermore.

"I am the Dark! What happens to you makes no difference to me. The Dark will go on forever. You and your whole adventure here, from start to stop, are just a minute's worth of light. You may have your fun in the Eightpenny Woods, but this is my *home*, you whining tourists! And you broke into my home and lied to me and *stole my puppy!*"

The graceful space-hand settled lightly against the steaming sauna grate. The Dark crowed triumph as it felt its fingers close around the Nextant.

"Poor darling, are you all right? What have they done to you? You're dented. Those beasts! Let's go home and I'll get you a nice bowl of grog and a fat skull and crossbones to munch on."

"She likes me," Never pleaded. "She likes me specially."

The hand paused. The Dark's voice gentled a bit. "She's not a person, little lampwick. She's just a memory. I told you that. The real Captain Badcat is somewhere in these woods whooping it up and sailing a ghostly sea of moss. It just means she *would've* liked you, if you'd ever met for real and true. And even then, only because she's a bad cat, and only likes those who don't want her. A lot of bad cats in this world, you'll find. This one's not special."

Never wanted to cry. They'd never find their way out of the Woods without the Captain. They really would be stuck here forever. She'd never see her mess again. Her mothers would never know why the next move in their doublechess game never arrived in the mail. Tears poured down her bronze cheeks. But she was smiling anyway. The biggest smile you ever saw. Somehow, she couldn't stop feeling completely happy and content, even while she sobbed in fear.

"But she *does* like me. She invited me up to the crow's nest." The tears dripped off her chin and onto the searing rocks. Steam hissed.

The Dark stroked Never's face with a black, glittering thumb. "Hush, kitten. You can't get so attached to things that don't belong to you. It happens when you're lonely, but it's no good for you. That crow's nest is long turned to dust. She died a hundred years ago and more. The Great Arctic Mud she sailed is covered in a glacier now. A real sea, frozen solid. That's the way of the world and time, I'm afraid. You do what you can, make your name out of nothing, conquer your powerful seas, and then everything changes anyway and your memory is all that's left. The sailor never gets to see what became of the ocean. But don't cry. Eventually, you'll all be my puppies. So you're not losing anything. You'll come to the ferry again one day. And I'll still be there with a shelf full of treasures. I *never* change. I might be the only thing that doesn't."

"Oi!" yelled Bonk, stomping across the birch Forest, shaking his fist. "Thief!"

"I beg your pardon?" the hand huffed in disbelief. "*You* stole from *me*."

"Did not, and I don't appreciate you besmirching my good character. I didn't see a sign that said MUST BE THIS DEAD TO PLAY THIS GAME. Did you, Never, my girl?"

"No!" Never replied cheerfully, though her face was still wet with weeping.

"Did you have one made up, Sir and/or Madam the Dark?"

"That's not the point," the hand said testily.

"Oh, ho, but I think it is precisely the point. My man Unknown there didn't cheat a blink. Ancient and Powerful Almighty Seen-It-All YOU got outwitted by a thirteen-year-old human with a couple of old flowers in his pocket and you're mad as a kangaroo on fire about it. He *got* you, Dark-utan. And he did it stressed out as a bunny in a trap, without a proper night's sleep or any good non-worm meals for days. So, in fact, *you* are stealing from *us*. If you're going to take our only way forward, back, or sideways, you better buy it with something just as good."

The Dark fumed.

"Fine," it hissed. "You may call on me, once, at great need. Great need, mind you! Not because it's too bright in your parlor! The deal is struck. Goodbye!"

"That's RUBBISH!" Bonk howled. "I meant a map! Or a guidebook! Something useful!"

But the long cosmic hand was already receding into the shadows where Never had pulled up the floorboards, chortling smugly as it went. The Dark pulled the Nextant down with it—but just as it disappeared, Captain Badcat's purr burst out of the mist.

"My love!" the old cat-dog called. "Listen! I *am* a good dog! I'm just a *wretched* cat! I never turn my tail and stride off as I should. I brought you as far as I could before we were so *rudely* interrupted by falling through space and time. You're in the Hinderlands! It's for the most exhausted souls who lived too hard and too long. It just wants to make you happy! But if you let it, the steam will make you *so* happy you'll build a house here and start planting tomatoes! No relaxing! Strong feelings beat back the steam! Get mad! Get sad! That's what I do! Find Beastly, she has the zither! We will meet again, precious pangirlin, where the horizon meets the tide! *Ow*, you're squeezing too tight, I missed you, too, Darko, you don't have to squish."

The plank clattered to the floor. The shadowy soil still showed through. But it was not alive and waiting to pounce any longer. The pair of them blinked in the sudden quiet.

"Where was I?" Never said sunnily. "Oh yes, mushrooms!"

"We're never going to find our way out of here," Bonk hooted with joy. "What a nightmare. I'll be happy *forever*."

Never wiped her eyes. "Maybe Osmo will know what to do." She grinned. Her cheeks hurt from grinning.

"Has he *ever* known what to do?"

The pangirlin shrugged. They were lost with no Nextant and Osmo was as good as dead. But she couldn't worry about it if she tried. The worry just wouldn't come. "Mushrooms are such odd little babies," she sighed happily as she poked in the dirt. "Do you ever think about them? *Really* think? They're not alive and they're not dead, they're not animals and they're not vegetables. Probably the whole world is connected by mushrooms underneath everything. Maybe the whole world *is* a mushroom, the fruit of a mushroom, and the part you can't see is the stars and the sky and dark space."

"You," Bonk said again, "are *weird*."

"Hullo," Never whispered to the soil. "It's me. Come out, Clarence. I know you're very busy, and I do respect your space and your time. You're very important and big and I'm just a pangirlin. But if you wouldn't mind awfully, if you have the time, and only if you want to, it would be wonderful if you could come out and fix that broken human boy."

Nothing happened.

"Aw, don't be like that, Clarence," Never said soothingly. "I'm sorry we haven't talked in so long. You know how I am."

A small ultramarine button mushroom emerged from the dirt. It nosed blindly toward her, pulling itself up. The Clarence mushroom had pretty pale green and lavender patterns on its bright blue-green body, spikes and tendrils and lacy cups, like a little sea dragon, all made of fungus.

"That's it?" Bonk yelped in disbelief. "*That's* what you do to get mushrooms to obey you?"

Never shrugged. "I said. I just ask. They started coming round when I was little. Just everywhere. I never wanted them. I never needed them. But they liked being near me. Like cats. Like Captain Badcat. But don't tell Osmo I said so. Can you imagine what he'd be like if he knew he was right about something around here? I don't even want to think about it."

The Clarence mushroom prickled up along a straight line toward Osmo. It writhed through the spaces between the floor boards. It pushed up new stalks and caps and hot-pink spores into the mist. When it reached Osmo Unknown, it crawled right into his mouth. And around his neck. And into his eyes. And all round his arms and his legs and his ears. Osmo lay there covered in brilliant bright fungus like a princess in a story, waiting for Clarence to kiss him back to life. You could hardly tell he was human at all under the tendrils and ultramarine lace and caps thick as lips.

Osmo coughed. He gagged. The glowing mushroom snaked back out of him as fast as a hiccup. He spluttered. His eyes bulged. He bolted up. His spine spasmed. He retched up a shower of tiny torn bits of burnt parchment. Then worse—more and more, crumpled-up balls of sketch paper, the kind you'd find at the bottom of a bin in someone's study. They shot out of him like little cannonballs, scattering across the wooden floor.

Finally, gasping, Osmo spat out a chunk of dark charcoal. Just the sort that whoever owned the study and the bin might draw with. He collapsed in a heap onto the sweet-smelling ground.

The skadgebat and the pangirlin leaned in. What would he say? Where had he been? Was he really all right?

"Never," he whispered.

"Yes?" she said hopefully. He was going to say *well done* to her again, she just knew it.

Osmo rolled over on his back and smiled at the rafters of the sky. "Wow, it's nice here," he sighed. "I'm so *hungry*. I don't think I've ever been this hungry in my whole life."

"Uh," said Bonk very seriously. "Um."

"What?"

Bonk pointed.

"Buddy. Pal. Mister. *Mate.*"

Never followed the line of the skadgebat's fat little paw. Her eyes widened behind her glasses.

"*What?*" Osmo asked. "Why do you sound upset? Why aren't you calling me names? Am I dead? Did I do something wrong? That fish had it coming, I swear."

The skadgebat knelt down and patted his shoulder. "Listen, friendo. I don't know about any fish. *What's wrong with your head?*"

## Chapter Twenty-One

# HEADS, BELLIES, AND HEARTS

Osmo Unknown's hands flew to his face. He tried to bat away the fog, but it only billowed in thicker.

"What do you mean?" he yelped. "There's nothing wrong with my head! See? Still on, all in one piece. What are you talking about? I'm fine!"

"*Big* disagree from me, ya drowned pony," Bonk barked. "You are Mayor Not Fine. You sit at the head of the Not Fine Council, charged with the maintenance of the whole of the Not-Fine-upon-Possibly-Very-Bad greater metropolitan zone."

Nevermore clacked her claws together awkwardly and pushed her glasses up on the ridge of her scaley bronze nose. "It's . . . ah . . . less the *one* piece . . . and more the *extra* pieces."

Osmo rolled his eyes. "Ha ha, very funny. Playing a joke on the recently unconscious. Well done, you're hilarious. Where are we? Is there anything to eat? Is Button okay?" He turned over his wrist to check on the little burgundy thing. It gleamed gratefully at him.

"*I'm* fine," Nevermore said, crossing her arms.

"Me too." Bonk did the same. "Never better. So kind of you to ask."

"Yes, but I can *see* that. I don't have to ask! Listen, I don't want to alarm you, but I might actually start biting one of you if I don't get something in my stomach. Or both of you. Let's get moving in a *foodward* direction."

Osmo got up and wiped his palms on his vest. He peered through the steam. He stuck out his arms and groped in front of him. But his hands came away only with dry red autumn leaves and wet air.

"Nope, nope, nope," Bonk insisted. "None of those logical, next-step, resolute-hero questions out of you, garbage-guts. We gotta deal with that melon and we gotta deal with it on the triple-fast." Bonk put on his crossest voice. "Sit *down*, ya big dumb joey."

Osmo sat. You didn't argue with a skadgebat once they pulled that voice on. You didn't argue with *anyone* once they pulled that voice on. He tried to see some hint of landscape through the mist, but all he got was Bonk's squat shape, Never's tall one, and a few other things that might have been trees or people or peppermint sticks for all he knew.

Osmo plopped down on the ground. He puffed up his cheeks and blew into the steam. It cleared for half a moment, enough for him to see that he'd done his plopping next to the basket of sauna coals. He let Bonk poke and prod him. His head *was* a bit sore, but he couldn't say whether it had been before the badgerish wombat started jabbing at it.

"Ow," Bonk hissed, and snatched his paw back. "Muddy *wells*."

He sucked on one furry finger. "What happened to you down there? Did you hit your head? Bash into something full-pelt?"

Osmo shuddered. "Fish," he whispered. "There were fish everywhere. I made a path down the middle of the ocean, but the fish were still in the . . . in the walls? I guess? In the miles and miles of Unfinished Ocean on either side of me. They weren't *drawings* of fish, either. They were real. They were finished. And I've never seen a fish like that. Black and blue and bumpy and the size of a nightmare you can't wake up from. And their eyes . . . looked dead. Just pale and dead and dull as a fossil. Their bodies swam in and out of the paper. Everywhere I looked: blue-black warty bellies flashing through a wave."

"And one of them bit you in the head, right?" Never said encouragingly. "That makes sense. That's all right, then."

"No, no, they didn't bite. Though they had teeth enough for it, if they'd wanted. They just . . . whispered to me." Osmo shuddered again. He didn't want to remember. He didn't want to tell them. But they were going to make him, he knew it. "It was worse than biting."

Bonk shrugged. "Whispering's not so bad. I can whisper. So can Never. Doesn't do . . . that." He pointed at Osmo's head. And now Osmo felt something warm trickling down from his temple. He touched his cheek. Blood. Only a little, but definitely blood.

"You don't understand. It was *what* they whispered. They knew . . . they knew *everything* about me. They hissed and laughed and whistled and whispered and it filled up the whole ocean. *You can't do this. You can't prove yourself true and tricksy, clever and foolish, straightforward and sneaky, brave and vainglorious, wild and mild, kind and cruel, because you're a nobody, and a nobody can't be any of those things. You can't beat Mrs. Brownbread at doublechess. You can't make top of your class. You can't make enough money to escape Littlebridge. You can't even make friends. We haven't seen anyone so pathetic since Katja Kvass, and that's saying something. Everyone hates you, did you know? They whisper about you behind your back when you can't hear. Everyone back home is glad you're gone. They threw a party to celebrate."*

Never and Bonk quickly found somewhere else to put their eyes and left them there.

*"You can't make your life interesting because* you're *not interesting and you never have been. You'll never be handsome or brave or clever or loved. That's for special people, and you can't ever be special because* you're *nothing."*

Osmo had to stop. His face was hot and hurting. His eyes throbbed with tears he would not let fall. *Be a man, you turnip*, he thought brutally to himself. *You muddy, stupid, unlovable turnip! Strong jaw! No blubbering!*

"That's . . . ahrm. That's a real punch in the ear, isn't it?" Bonk rumbled. For him, it was something.

Never reached out a long, slender hand and patted the empty air above Osmo's shoulder. For her, that was quite a lot.

"Coelacants," she said with a good dose of sympathy. "Remember? I did say. I said, back in the desert. I remember because I got *coelacants* wrong on a Monday school test. They're guardians. The Eightpenny Woods puts them anywhere it wants to hide something for itself and not just let any dead old thing use it. They're just . . . doubt, you know. Coelacants. They whisper all the things you're afraid you *can't* do or be or know. Doubt is almost as old as the Dark. They know everything you're afraid of and they say it all out loud. There's a hymn that says the soul at peace could meet one and it would have nothing to say."

Osmo rubbed his nose to make his eyes stop their nonsense. "I wanted to just lie down there on the ocean floor forever and never get up. But then everyone who couldn't ever love me and also my mother and my sisters and everyone else would get eaten. And this would all be for nothing. And I could see the ring hanging on this big blue stone in the distance." He opened his hand. A green woven-willow ring lay on his palm. It didn't look very impressive, as a wedding ring.

But it was just exactly the kind of ring a Forest would give to the Valley it loved. A Valley full of great big blue stones.

"They got louder and louder until the only thing in my head was *you're nothing, you're nothing, no one loves you and no one ever will.* I wasn't going to make it. I was just so tired. So tired and so sick of myself. They kept swimming in and out of the paper waves and I just thought . . . I had the idea that . . ." Osmo reached into his satchel with his other hand and pulled out a few torn-out pages from his notebook. One had a huge black hole hastily scribbled onto it with deep, thick strokes from a hickory pencil. "Everything was paper . . . so why couldn't paper be everything? I drew an unfinished hole to an unfinished place I needed to be. I stuck my hand through it and I felt it close on the ring—"

"And then something big and mad thumped you on the head, right?" Bonk added helpfully. "Twice?"

"No, then I passed out. I think my brain just wanted to get *away* from those voices more than it wanted to be a brain at that moment. And I woke up here. *Starving*," he finished emphatically, hoping they'd finally take the hint. This lovely little wood would be just perfect if he had a meal. Or seven. Or twenty. He opened his hand. He held up the green willow-whip ring.

"But I got it. I got the prize. They said I couldn't. But I *can*."

Bonk the Cross threw up his hands and grabbed the green clay pitcher full of cream. "I'm really not concerned with your stomach or your penny prize right this muddy minute, Osmo. You've got *horns*, mate."

Bonk slapped the back of his head. As Osmo rocked forward, he caught sight of his reflection in the shiny sauna pool.

Bonk was wrong.

He didn't have horns, not really. But he had something. Two lumps on the crown of his head where, yes, horns would sit, if he were some kind of devil out of an ancient book. The skin stretched thinly over whatever wanted to break free of his skull. The left one had already managed to pierce through. Osmo Unknown traced a thin trickle of blood, half dried on his cheekbone. He touched one horn gingerly. Hard and sharp and dark. But only the tiniest tip had . . . *sprouted*, for lack of a better word. It was *far* too early to say horns. Could be a wart. Or a coelacant bite. Or the plague. Osmo didn't feel too concerned about it, somehow. It was just so peaceful and pleasant here. He couldn't imagine being bothered about anything, really.

"I wouldn't worry about it," he sighed happily.

"That's the sauna talking, soapcrust," Bonk hiccuped. "You got horns. Possibly antlers. Maybe even antennae! Too early to tell."

"Probably for the best, whatever it is. I looked pretty plain before. Horns couldn't hurt! Can we ask the Nextant?" Osmo said, yawning. "She seems to know . . . a lot. She knew about Button." The burgundy button heard itself mentioned and spun happily on his sleeve.

"The . . . well. The Nextant is gone?" Never said in a way that sounded like a question she hoped would get answered in some way other than the truth.

Osmo blinked. Dread managed to pierce the blankets of steam cozying up his head. "How can it be *gone?*" he burst out. "It's the only thing keeping us one step ahead of whoever's trip-trip-trapping down the bridge after us! I'm out for a minute and you lost the best thing we've got?"

The steam rolled away from his dismay and anger. The sauna coals came into focus, and the pitchers and the polished floor and the smooth, branchless trees all around them.

Never's eyes got huge and very clear in her head. Her chin wobbled. "Don't you yell at me, Osmo Unknown!" she bellowed back. "How dare you? One more word and I'll re-deadify you. You were gone a lot longer than a minute! You didn't ask before you barged off into the ocean, you just left us! We're only here for you and you *left* us! And the last thing you talked about was some human girl you didn't bother to mention even when we were all introducing ourselves in my house, which is when you really *should* just tell everything there is to know about yourself so no one has to waste time asking later!"

Steam burned away from the pangirlin like she was the sun itself. Strong feelings beat back the mist, Badcat had said. Only, you could barely remember that when the mist rolled in. Or anything else.

"Who, Ivy?" Osmo asked, confused.

"Calm down, you beautiful brassy ball of love and kindness," Bonk the Cross giggled. He rolled backward onto the sauna bench where the fog still hung thick and fragrant. He waved his striped hindpaws around in the air. "She doesn't love him back, remember? It's all fiiiiine. Fine as feather-down."

The sweet mist crawled away unhappily through rows and rows of trees and coal baskets and clay pitchers. Enough for dozens of parties to go well into any night. "We did our best! It was hard and scary and you were *dead* and we couldn't see anything because of this stupid steam!" But the fog had grown very thin. Every time Never yelled into it, it shrank away. The rafters overhead floated into clear view. There were *stars* up there. And a thin green ribbon of aurora borealis. "Bonk didn't know what to do so I brought you back to life! I called a mushroom and I fixed you and you haven't even praised me, Osmo, you haven't, you ungrateful no-scales sack of defenseless *skin*! Don't *yell* at me! Why would you *yell* at me? I saved you! And for what? For nothing! Not one *well done*, not even one, and I should have gotten two, because I saved your dumb *satchel* and your dumb *you*. This is why you should never do anything or know anyone. It feels so amazing when they praise you and so unbearable when they yell at you! It's impossible! How can anyone stand it?"

"Well, I did carry his dumb body all the way here." Bonk stuck up for himself.

"Shut up, Bonk," Never sobbed.

He did.

Osmo felt his stomach, impossibly, punch itself. She'd lived alone all her life. Of course no one had ever blamed her for anything going wrong before. She'd only had herself. It felt so miserable to be blamed. The oldest of seven knew that better than most. And he'd done it to her. He'd made her feel that sour, hot guilt and injustice.

"I'm sorry, Never," he said as fast as he could make words. "I'm so sorry. Well done. Thank you. Well done. Okay? You can have as many *well dones* as you want."

"It was dark under the floorboards," the pangirlin said miserably. "I'm just me, I can't stop the Dark." She sniffled. "Could I have one more? I did what you said. I kept on doing things for the group until they were safe. Just a little one?"

"You did a really good job, Never. Thank you for saving me. You're the best," Osmo said, and he tried to fill up his voice with all the times he hadn't said that sort of thing to his sisters or anybody back home.

"The best?" Never, who had never had anyone to tell her anything about herself except that she couldn't draw coelacants, smiled with wonder. "Well, that's *something*. The *best*."

"Okay," Osmo said hesitantly, not wanting to spoil the moment, "but if I don't eat something *right now*, you're going to have to call another mushroom."

He had never felt anything like this hunger. It snaked through his whole body. His *ears* were hungry. His *toes* were hungry. His *eyelashes* were hungry. He felt certain that if someone cut him open right now, his blood would have lost all its red and dried up to dust in his veins. Osmo felt as though he had never eaten in his life, and maybe never would again, so food had to come now, and it had to be all the food, just to be safe.

"I guess we're not worried about spooky food anymore, hm?" Bonk groused. "I suppose there's got to be something here. It's just such a cozy place! And cozy means food and drink and snugness, so it's *got* to have those. Logically speaking."

Even Bonk the Cross could not be *too* cross in the face of the Hinderlands. Now that the yelling had stopped and the sauna was busy pumping out its sweet-smelling mist again.

The hunger boiled up so fiercely in Osmo that it came out as a roar. "I need to *EAT! PLEASE! NOW!*" said the roar.

Fog peeled back from his breath. Where it blew aside with a whirl of red leaves, a velvet bellpull hung down from a sudden tree standing, alarmingly, a few inches away. Well within flailing distance, if they'd only argued a little longer. Under the rope, a neat brass plaque read:

PULL FOR SERVICE.

*Chapter Twenty-Two*
# A BEASTLY FIGHT

"All right, Mister Greedy Trousers, hold on to your gums." Bonk tried to calm him down. "You don't have to blow out my eardrums, thanks for that. Quit your moaning. Just sit back and enjoy life, why not?"

"We're in the Land of the Dead, fuzzball," Never observed dryly.

Osmo yanked hard on the bellpull.

It came off in his hand. *Must have been weakened by the last fellows through here*, he thought, staring at the limp velvet rope he held. *I'm not half strong enough.*

A pleasant, businesslike bell tinkled up in the rafters of the sky. Not a moment later, they heard wheels clattering down the shining wooden planks toward them. Thin, hard, high wheels against the soft wood, and someone humming to themselves as they toddled along.

A powerfully built and fully armored sauna attendant burst through the steam of the Hinderlands. She pushed a splendid refreshments trolley in front of her, clamping the handlebar between her teeth. Osmo recognized her from *St. Whylom's Book of Zoologicals Near and Far:* a capybara. A big one, too—a female. Male capybaras were thinner and shorter, he remembered. Friendly, sleepy, contented eyes: yes. Soft reddish-brownish fur: absolutely. Barrel chest, long round muzzle, four stubby, strong legs: quite so. But they could only see that soft reddish-brownish fur on that friendly, sleepy, rounded face. The rest of her was covered in blue tropical crabshell like a burly knight's plated armor. Big, curved sky-blue pauldrons on her shoulders, teal greaves on her legs, a cobalt-blue barnacled chest plate. Most incredible of all, two huge turquoise crab claws crisscrossed over her back like swords. Their sawtooth blades deepened from blue to green to bright red at the tips.

"Good evening, *guten abend, dobry vecher, konbonwa, buonasera, naka ngon si, hyvää iltaa,*" said the crabbybara politely. Then she clicked like a dolphin, screeched like a koala, and roared directly in their faces like a tiger.

Her voice was just the *nicest* voice, Osmo thought. In the *nicest* place. At the *nicest* time of day. Rough at the edges, but soft and snuggly in the middle. Best voice. Almost nice enough to make him forget that trolley full of corked bottles, festive boxes, miniature wooden barrels, and crystal domes covering colorful plates, all steamed up by the hot dishes inside.

"Towels, anyone?" the crabbybara asked. "Loofas? Back scratchers? Shampoo? Nail-and-claw clippers? Flea bombs? Hoof picks? Udder scrubbers? Undercoat rake?" The sauna attendant ran her paw over a jar of implements and tools on the front of her trolley. She nodded to them each in turn. "Scale wax, miss? Fluffy robe, sir?" She glanced up at Osmo's head with concern, but yanked her eyes away quickly. "Er. Perhaps a shower cap for the young master? Or a . . . pretty bow for your hair? What can I supply to enhance, entertain, or otherwise enhappy-fy this eternal moment for you? My name is Beastly and I'll be your valet this lovely evening. Well, every evening is lovely here in the Sauna of Total Satisfaction, but that doesn't make any one less special."

Osmo declined the shower cap. And the bathrobe. And the slippers. He wasn't to wear the clothes of the dead. But the dead seemed to want him to *very* much.

Bonk the Cross helped himself to one of each.

"What do you need with an udder scrubber, Bonk?" Osmo laughed.

"NONE OF YOUR BUSY BEES, YOUNG DOOFUS," Bonk blustered back, and grabbed two. "I'll scrub your udder," he mumbled under his breath. "See if I don't."

The crabbybara eyed the swollen nubs on Osmo's forehead again. "Are you sure I can't interest you in a bow, sir? I've got every color. A bright focal point naturally draws attention away from . . . hrmurm . . . imperfections . . ."

But her words bounced right off his ears. "*Total* Satisfaction? Does that mean supper?" Osmo's mouth watered. He smelled his mother's rosemary-parsnip stew under one of those domes, he could swear it.

Beastly nodded heartily. "Yes! Of course! Take all you like, young—"

But she didn't get to guess at what sort of wild beast Osmo

might be. He attacked the tea trolley at once, pulling off crystal domes, slurping from serving spoons, cramming biscuits and cakes and tarts and bread rolls and anything his hands could catch into his mouth. And what do you know? It *was* his mother's rosemary-and-parsnip soup, or his name wasn't Unknown.

"Motter," Nevermore finished for the crabbybara.

"Cronkey," Bonk corrected.

"Sorry," Osmo said with his mouth full. His eyes had gone hollow; he saw nothing but the cart. Dragonfruit and coconut milk and magenta guava paste smeared his chin. Osmo was deeply embarrassed, but he couldn't help himself. The hunger was in charge. He had no say. "Oh god, I'm so sorry. Excuse me. I beg your pardon." He reached desperately for a skewer of roasted chestnuts and butternut squash and came away with four of them. And a slab of honeycomb. And several puff pastries. He'd no idea what they'd been puffed with, earthworms or beetles or cud, and he didn't care one bit. "So, *so* sorry."

Beastly laughed and patted her own big stomach. "Perfectly all right! Satisfy yourself, little master! That's your right! Life is a grueling thing, even if you have the knack for it. You all deserve to have your needs and wants and whims satisfied completely now that it's over and done with. We all do! I *myself* was eaten by a jaguar. Just minding my own business at the watering hole, having a spot of gossip with the camellama boys and a couple of pelikeets. One chomp and no more me! Exhausting! I needed a hundred-year snooze to recover after that bit of excitement. Liked it so much I stayed. Mind you, I met up with the jaguar later on when she got done by a crocodingo. I served her for a year before she even glanced at me! And even then it was only to get me to brush her fangs more thoroughly."

"Are the spirits really that rude to you?" Never asked wonderingly. "How do you stand it?"

"Oh, I pride myself on getting along with everyone, from quokka to quagga to quetzals and back! Even if they bite. And they do! It's the capybara in me, I suppose. Just want to snuggle with the whole animal kingdom. What's a year in the Eightpenny Woods, when you think about it? The jaguar and I are quite good friends now. That's the circle of death for you!"

Beastly paused delicately as Osmo powered through a loaf of milk bread and a banana flan. Nevermore stretched out a claw to pluck up a flan for herself. Osmo hissed at her like a cat. A look of horror swept over his face. He tried to give her the flan. But he couldn't make himself. He shoved it miserably into his mouth.

"Fine," Nevermore gasped, holding her hands up and backing away. "If that's how it is!"

"I'm sorry," he said again, helplessly. "Never, I'd never—really I am. I can't stop."

Beastly patted his skinny back. "At least you're polite about it. Most polish off the trolley and don't even talk to me. But that's all right, I don't mind! Everyone to their own happiness. Are you an omnivore, by chance? There's cold rabbit sandwiches in the icebox down the second shelf. Starling pies in the warmer. And please don't worry—no actual starlings or rabbits suffered to bring you this taste sensation. We're all dead here, after all! It's all organic, free-range, locally sourced dreams and memories of a million creatures' best meals. Go on, have a crumpet with a bit of bacon chutney on top, my pup, they're fresh."

"That's not what Captain Badcat called this place," Never said, stretching out her tail. Her pride was out of joint. She stared longingly at the trolley. Beastly tutted, then handed her a little vial of oil and a wrapped green mugwort cake snuck out of the side drawer. Never poured some out on her coppery scales. They shone in the mist, and the sweet, sharp smell of eucalyptus and oranges filled the fog. The hot stones hissed.

"Oh?" Beastly said casually.

Never nodded. "She called it the Hinderlands."

The crabbybara's face went pinchy and pursed. "Well, I don't think that's a very nice thing to call a place that only wants to make you happy and help you relax." Her small, dark eyes turned cold and hard. "I don't care for the implication, frankly." Beastly shrugged and shivered and put up her pleasant attitude again. "Then again, cats don't like water, so perhaps it's just a matter of taste and nothing to take personally. Have you tried the hot springs and the ice ponds? Each station has their own matched set!"

"Oh, but she's a very bad cat, you see," Osmo said between gulps of milk and cider. He'd eaten more in five minutes than he'd had in a week back home. He should be full. He should be loosening his belt and groaning and lying down for a long nap. But his belly screamed for more. "She loves the water." He ripped open a passion fruit with his fingers and slurped out the golden insides like an egg. Then he reached for the eggs.

"Perhaps a bit of entertainment for you three?" Beastly tried again. "I can tell you a tale, dance you a dance, paint your portrait, sing you a song, anything that would bring you deeper into relaxation and contentment."

"Didn't Badcat say to find a Beastly?" Bonk yawned. He scratched his back with the hoof pick and picked his toes with the back scratcher. "I thought she did. But I can hardly remember. Seemed important at the time. Probably wasn't. I'm going to break myself off a slice of that hot spring if you don't mind, and if you do, well, that's not important either." Bonk shook his head and wrinkled his muzzle. The fog clouded so thick around him, all any of them could see was his wet black nose. "Nothing is! Except my bath. What a relief. Caring about things was so much *work*."

"That's the spirit, if you'll pardon the pun!" Beastly laughed deep in her barrel chest. *What a sound*, thought Osmo as he moved on to the third shelf. He could listen to crabbybara laughs all day.

The third shelf offered slim pickings. Dry crackers, a couple of rinds of cheese, raw lemons, small pots of yellow, pink, and green jams. There wasn't much room left after the musical instruments and party supplies and books of adventurous tales stacked up down there.

And of course, the tree. That took up a great deal of space as well.

Just a little elm tree in a little clay pot. Osmo Unknown would not have known to call it a bonsai tree, for bonsai do not feature in *St. Whylom's Book of Zoologicals Near and Far*. But that's just what it was. Dark green leaves made elegant cloud shapes of the branches that looked somehow wistful and melancholy, though it was just a tree in a pot. But perhaps it was not *just* a tree. Two quite large branches, bare of needles, curved up on either side like elephants' trunks. Several of the other branches looked hollow, with little straight rows of holes down their lengths. The clay pot was only clay on top. The bottom was covered in goat fur and rather bouncy-looking. And the trunk was a beautiful golden plank of barkless wood with a wriggly delicate grain, a hollow in the middle, and several strings running across it.

Osmo's stomach had lost all reason. He grabbed the tree and gnawed on the top.

"Hey! Not food!" Beastly yelped.

But the tree was bitter and horrible. He tossed it back on the trolley, spat out a wad of elm leaves, then went for the fruit without a pause. Osmo bit into a lemon as cleanly and hungrily as a fresh apple, bitter peel and all.

"Oi!" Bonk hollered. He'd found the hot pool, only a few feet away in the endless mist. If all the fog cleared, the Hinderlands might be a hundred miles across or a bedroom's width, it was impossible to tell. The skadgebat soaked luxuriously in the dark water. "What's that then?"

"Ah! Just a moment, sir!" Beastly said, bending over to rummage in her trolley. Her blue crabshell armor glowed gorgeously in the twilight.

She came up with a glass pot in one hand and an odd little hand accordion in the other, with drum skins on either end instead of buttons on one side and a strap on the other. "Did you mean the royal jelly or the drummertina? We do get scads of insects through here, so I like to keep stocked with the good stuff. And everyone likes a song!" She set down the royal jelly and flexed the drummertina between her paws. A soothing, rhythmic beat and a lullaby waltz spooled out from the instrument all at once. Osmo had enough of himself left over still to notice that even the music had two natures in the woods. Or at least in *these* woods.

"Nawp, none of those," Bonk barked, climbing out of the hot pool. He dove into the cold pond just beside it, came up howling and shaking his bristles, then finally wrapped a thick black towel round his midsection and marched up to the rest of them. "That." He pointed at the third shelf. "That wee bush of all trades right there."

"Oh!" the crabbybara hooted. She shuffled from side to side like the crab half of her was. "That's not for patrons, I'm afraid."

"Then why've you got it on your trolley, hm?"

Beastly frowned. A capybara's face wasn't meant for frowning. It upset Never to see it, and it would have upset Osmo if he hadn't been working on his fifth lemon. "It's mine. I like to keep it with me and water it and pet it and call it Nikolas. Don't you think it looks like a Nikolas? Just 'cause I'm dead doesn't mean I don't have my little treasures still. You wouldn't be interested, anyway. Bit broken, poor Nikko. It doesn't play."

"OS. MO!" Bonk yelled sharply. "Kindly stop making a first-prize pig of yourself and pay attention! Did you hear what she said?"

"No," Osmo answered around a strip of fine rubber off the trolley tire. "Doanlookame," he choked as he swallowed. Tears rushed down his face. He had never felt so miserable. He'd demolished everything. But the hunger wasn't done with him. If anything, he was more ravenous than before. Blood trickled down the side of his head. The other thing had broken through the skin. And though he couldn't see it, everyone else could. One of his kind brown eyes had turned bright, hot, boiling green, with a knife-edge feline pupil.

"Ooookay." Bonk whistled through his nose. "Unsettling. At the least."

The skadgebat grimaced in embarrassment. Not for himself but for Osmo. Mortified for him. Distress sizzled all the way to the ends of his whiskers. The awful feeling coursed through Bonk, strong enough to clear a bit of steam away and pierce the cloud of sheer comfort that had settled over all of them.

"I don't understand," Beastly huffed. She squared her paws and stamped one sourly. "This is the Sauna of Total Satisfaction. Total! No one should cry here, or starve or thirst or anything unpleasant at all. Those hardships are for the living. No matter how rude my patrons are, they never *suffer*. What's wrong with him?"

"Isn't that a question and a half," Nevermore mumbled.

"Osmo," Bonk said again as the boy started on the other tire in anguish. He lowered his voice to an urgent hiss. "That's the Zither That No One Can Play! She's got it right there! Grab it! Go on, nick it!"

Osmo stuffed a stack of dry crackers into one cheek like a squirrel and snatched the tree of instruments. But Beastly was just so much bigger and stronger than he. She snatched it right back, cradling it in her arms like a baby.

"I remember now," Bonk said, tapping the side of his head. "Got the lid back on my noggin, and all because it just feels *that bad* to watch you snorfling your trough. Very heroic, Mister Boy. Really sacrificing for the team. Give it here, crabbybrains! Play nice and we'll get out of your fur."

"No," Beastly insisted. She rubbed her fuzzy cheek against the miniature elm leaves. "It's mine. It's special. What do you want it for?"

"Muddy well right it is, and we need it. You're supposed to give us what we need, yeah? Total satisfaction." He winked at the pangirlin lying half asleep beside the hot and hissing stones. Steam coiled around her drowsy face, pulling at her eyelids. "That's what we call a logical trap, sleepypuff. Betchoo thought I couldn't pull one of them off, eh?" He tapped his head again. "Mind like a crab trap! Heh, heh. So to speak. Now, listen here, ratty-boo. We need it to make a present for Queen Melancholy and we're willing to swap for it."

"Queen Melancholy? She's the wisest beast that ever lived," Beastly said uncertainly.

"Sure! I guess! Don't you want to make her happy, then? Osmo's got a whole pile of junk in his bag I don't mind bartering with. What's your pleasure?" Bonk rummaged in the satchel. "Ooh, pretty black ribbon? That's nice. Got us a notebook and some pencils, barely used. Practically new! Aha, this'll do it, a doublechess set, both sides AND the board. Uh, missing a queen but otherwise pristine. How's about it, Miss Clacky-Claws?"

Beastly shook her head. She crooned over the tree and stroked its pot. "Nikko played at the wedding of the Forest and the Valley.

Everyone danced. *Everyone.* The deer with the elephants. The crows with the crocuses. The narwhals with the wolves. The moose with the frogs. The lads with the goldfish. The . . . ah . . ." Her voice grew very soft and delicate. "The crabs with the capybaras. The girls with the pangolins. The monkeys with the otters. The badgers with the wombats and the skunks cut in. Even the sun and the moon danced together at the edge of the sea. That's how it all started. How we started. How the Forest first saw how wild the world could be. When Nikko plays, everything changes. He hasn't played since. He's no use to you. Nobody *can* play him. See?"

Beastly curled her paws so her claws stuck out like picks. She tried to strum the strings on the little bonsai's trunk. She almost got one whole note plucked before she yelped and squeaked and yanked back her paw in pain. Blood dripped from her footpad. The tree seemed to glare at her, though of course it had no eyes for glaring.

"Right, so you won't mind trading him for this shiny goldy ball, hm? Just as fine a toy as a mean nasty tree what bites you, I should think! Or this shiny new book for your trolley library?" He waved Osmo's copy of *The Ballad of the Forest and the Valley, Seventh Edition, Annotated* around. "*Do Not Steal.* That means it's valuable, in anyone's language. Or this keg of Unknown's Goodest Stout? Says Goodest. That's gotta be worth *something.* Or . . . what's this?" Bonk the Cross held up the little carved red box Mustamakkara had given Osmo.

"No!" Osmo cried. "Not that. Any of the rest of it. But not that." He added in a mumble: "And the ball isn't even real gold, you know. It's just painted clay over a wad of horsehair. It's worthless. Always has been." Osmo stuffed a handful of cake wrappers unhappily into his mouth. "Just like me."

Button spun firmly counterclockwise on his sleeve.

*No!*

"Shhht! Don't undersell the merch, blubbers!" Bonk hissed. "I don't know," the skadgebat said more loudly, his voice wobbling with temptation. He wiggled the ruebill's box enticingly in his paw. "Seems the gobbler over there holds this one dearest of all. Smells like a perfect bargain to me."

"Bonk, no," Osmo pleaded.

But it didn't matter. "I don't want any of that. I have what I want. You can only do commerce with unhappy people. I lack nothing, so I need nothing. I'm completely happy. Totally satisfied. Nikko and I have a jolly time together."

Bonk sighed heavily. He turned his head toward Nevermore, snoozing in the hot pool. Then toward Osmo, licking the trolley plates, utterly lost in whatever possessed him.

"Fine," the skadgebat said. He pitched the satchel behind him. Osmo scurried to the wreckage of his bag and shoved Mustamakkara's box into his pocket for safekeeping. Bonk the Cross drew himself up to his full, regal height of about three foot five and adjusted his fluffy towel. "Then I shall fight you for it."

Beastly stomped over to him, the tree of instruments in hand. She snorted through her nostrils. Hot breath blew back Bonk's cheek fur. Her armor bristled mightily. She towered over him. The crab claws crisscrossed like swords behind her back gave a decisive, echoing *clack-CRUNCH*.

"Will you now?" the crabbybara woofed deeply. "I have met some nasty, snobby patrons in this sauna, and the Gnarlbind knows they tried my patience, but none of them has tried to *fight* me."

"Well, I aim to, and I'll thank you to comport yourself like a civilized beast, you great walloping lug. Quiddity Rules, and not a one broken!"

"It's to be a duel, then? But you must know you have no chance."

"What's the worst that can happen? I'm already Ghostopher G. Ghost, Dead Boy of Ghostminster Academy." Bonk chuckled at his own joke, and felt even crosser that neither Never nor Osmo had heard it and Beastly didn't seem to appreciate it in the slightest. "Where else is there to go? The Sixteenpenny Woods?" He turned his striped snout back toward the others, trying to hold on to a big feeling so he could think clearly. He settled on indignation. His sense of indignance was very well developed. "Did you hear what I said to her? It was *very* good. I'm on top of my game and you're *missing it.*"

Beastly's hairy eyebrows rose and fell. "Don't you know? Everyone knows. If you hurt yourself very badly here, badly enough that you'd have died of it back in the sunlit world, you go . . ." A strange smile crossed her thick muzzle. Her teeth showed, and not in a friendly fashion. "Nowhere. Into nothing. Out like a matchstick. This is a peaceful place, there's no reason to hurt anyone or anything. If you break the peace, you don't get another chance." She sat back and scratched behind her blue crab pauldron with a hindpaw. "Still want to play by your Quiddity Rules?"

Bonk jabbed his black-and-white paw at her. "I *said* I'm on top of my game." He grinned cunningly. "And I *demand* satisfaction! Total Satisfaction!"

"Very well." Beastly rolled her eyes. "That is all I want for you, little creature."

Bonk the Cross ticked off the rules on his stubby fingers. "First! We count off ten paces. Better make it five in this fog. Then on three, we turn and fire. Two shots apiece, then reload. Repeat until disarmed, dismayed, or dead. No teeth, scent glands, burrowing to escape, poison sacs, or interfering with each other's eyeballs."

"Is that part of Quiddity Rules?"

"No, it's just icky." Bonk shuddered. "If I win, we get the tree. If you win . . . well, dunno. What do you want?"

"I told you, I don't want anything. This is your game."

"You must want something. Everyone wants something."

"Everyone living. But I am not. Oh, if you must. When I win, you stay here forever and ever and be my friend and run the trolley with me."

"Eurgh," Bonk said, curling up his whiskers. "Hideous. Imagine me, Bonk, serving tea for eternity. Being *nice* to the patrons. The worst. Fine. All agreed?"

The crabbybara inclined her head. "Agreed." She flexed her forepaws. "As challenger and guest, you may choose your weapons. I can summon a trolley from the storeroom with anything you like. What's it to be? Swords? Crossbows? Trebuchets? Nunchuks? How about a nice musket? Oooh, or blow darts!"

"Feelings," Bonk said simply. He put his paws behind his back and rocked up and down on his feet, powerfully proud of himself.

"Feelings? But that's not a weapon."

"Then you're not doing 'em right. My choice, no arguments. I can't call a mushroom to wipe my tail and I can't court a corpse, but I can do this."

The crabbybara paced nervously. "I hear the way you talk to them. And they're your friends. It's to be insults and cruelties and a lot of rot about my mother, I suppose. I might look gentle, but don't think I can't cut you to the quick."

"I'm sure you can. But you must admit my wit has a brilliant point on it at the moment. Good as a spear. Twice as direct."

Beastly hunkered down. Her ruff spiked up under her shells. She stalked in a circle around Bonk, prowling through the mist. "I was a scrapper when I was alive. That jaguar had it in for me since we were kittens. All because I said his brother got born with a litter box instead of a brain. The pelikeets thought it was funny. You haven't got the upper hand you think you do, you cube-dunged worm-guzzler. I lost my life over a *joke*. And I'm not even upset about it. I'll scoop out your heart like ice cream. I'll make your soul into a cozy for my teapot, and it won't be a pretty one, either. It'll be tacky, with fluffy pom-poms all over. I'll make you crawl back in to your mother's pouch."

"Well," Bonk snorted, "good luck with that—"

"Ever seen a pile of garbage cry?"

"Can't say I have."

"You're about to, stankbucket."

Bonk's pelt wriggled and flinched, like it was shooing off flies. "Warming up already, I see. Tsk, tsk. No cheating. Walk off your paces."

"I've been as nice as shortcake to everyone who's come through the Hinderlands for a thousand years, no matter how they snip and snipe at me. Do you have any idea how much snarl I've got stored up in my exoskeleton? You should pick poleaxes while you can. You'd have better chances."

"Thought it weren't called that."

"*Of course it's called that.* True happiness hinders everyone. If you're really and completely happy, you don't *strive.* You don't hope. You don't *crave.* You don't *progress.* This is where we keep the ghosts who are . . . problems. Who weren't anybody you'd want round for tea when they were alive. We satisfy them here so the problems don't bother anyone else. We keep them so satisfied they never even *want* to get out. And aren't you all just a big fat mangy pile of *problems.*" The crabbybara drew up close to Bonk's face, snout to snout. "You're *not* a ghost, are you, you overgrown bloodbin? I can smell your *heart.* The only reason the ground itself isn't burning itself black to get away from you is that the Hinderlands are cosmically incapable of being a bad host. You're *not* a ghost. You want to steal my tree-friend. Whatever you're doing is so wrong and bad that there's a Quidnunk the size of a mountain banging on the door of my sauna to get at you. It can't even be a good trick, it's just a bad deed, because a Quidnunk would *love* a good trick and call the family in to watch. It wouldn't break its claws on my roof. And I suppose you expected old Beastly to just turn a Quidnunk away? A Quidnunk, the wildest of us all? Never. Selfish reeking bonebuckets! You deserve *everything* that's coming for you."

Bonk growled softly. His small, sharp even teeth glinted in the half-light. His tail had bushed up thick as a hairbrush. "Good talking to you, chumtrail," he snarled through a clenched jaw. "You kiss wee Nikko with that mouth? No wonder he's got about as much use for your grimy paws as a lord's got for a horse fart. I was gonna go easy, but you're just such a wide target. Turn that low-tide seabug rump around and *count off.*"

One. They spun and put their backs to one another.

Two. Bonk and Beastly stepped off into the cinnamon-scented fog.

Three. Not one lonely sound broke the air of the sauna.

Four. The borealis wove greenly through the rafters and the garlands of stars hung low to watch the action.

Five. Nevermore snored in the hot pool and Osmo Unkown finally stopped eating, but only so he could scratch viciously at the underside of his wrist.

"Engage!" Bonk hollered, and both spun round to fire their shots.

Beastly roared: "A belch in the wind has a better soul than you! Boil your head in a pot of panda musk, you ugly, unlovable, bony-butted *human!*" Bonk staggered back. She'd gone deep, and right away. The crabbybara pressed her advantage. She loaded up her second shot. "You've got a face like a slapped yam and a hairless heart, you fat, puffed-up bully! Your father was so tame he had a satin bed and a water dish with his name on it and he went on walkies *every day!*"

Bonk's knees wobbled. His face burned. But he would not go down without taking his shot. She'd stung him, but at least the pain and shame cleared his mind brilliantly. The skadgebat blinked back hot tears and took the deepest breath of his short, wild life. He thought about sleeping in the cold before he'd grown fur and the tittering laughter of his brothers and sister. He thought about the villagers back in Quiddity, tittering too. He thought hard about how to knock this one down in one go.

Bonk the Cross locked eyes with Beastly the crabbybara through the steam and boomed with all his strength:

"All those surly jam-headed ghosts shouldn't have said any one tiny rude thing to you, Mrs. B! I see your worth and your wildness, you magnificent snuggly well-groomed always-on joyfaucet. *You deserve love and attention.* And I am genuinely sorry you got eaten by a jaguar!"

The keeper of the sauna gasped. Her eyes bulged. The claws on her back *clack-CRUNCH*ed. Her body trembled all over—and Beastly fell to the ground. Her powerful shoulders shook under all that armor.

"How could you?" she panted. *"How could you?* What a thing to say."

Bonk padded over to her and patted her shoulder. "I said feelings. Not hurt feelings. Up you get, there's a girl."

"But you're mean," Beastly said in confusion.

Bonk sniffed. "I am a complex beast with many facets and dimensions, thank you very much. Also I'm extremely smart."

The crabbybara knuckled her eyes dry. "I can't keep the Quidnunk out much longer," she said. "You have to go. Or you have to stay forever. I think if you stay it'll leave you alone. It's bashing away at the exit, not the entrance."

"What Quidnunk? I can't hear a thing."

"This is a peaceful place. I keep everything stressful outside. I'd never let you hear your doom knocking. It would spoil your soak. But it's making a *vicious* racket. Keeps hollering about its *piece*. By the sound of the fists I'd say it's a female, but don't hold me to it."

"All right then, how do we get out?"

Beastly smiled sidelong. "It's a bit of a tricksy," she confessed. "You're not trapped or anything. That's not peaceful at all!" She pointed to the pitchers filled with black water and white cream. "The way out has always been conveniently located for your use. Pour them out on the stones and the smoke will take you. The white one goes somewhere you shouldn't dare, and the black one goes somewhere you shouldn't know about. VERY exciting, don't you think? Designed to discourage departures."

"What's that mean?" Bonk raised his furry brow ridge.

"Dunno!" Beastly shrugged, then sniffled. "I never leave. But fair's fair. Please take care of Nikko. He's only a tree, he can't protect himself, and you know how dogs are about sticks . . ."

Bonk took Nikko carefully in his arms and wedged him into the satchel. The strings vibrated with emotion, though who could guess which one? The skadgebat jogged over and flicked Nevermore in the side of her scaley head.

"Hm?" she moaned, coming awake.

"It is I, your resentful yet handsome alarm clock. Bath time over. I've done all the work, as usual, let's shove off. Osmo? Where've you gone off to?"

"Right here," Osmo said from the depths of the hot, thick fog.

He stood next to the basket of hot stones. He'd already eaten three, but he tried his best to look as though he hadn't. He tucked his hand behind his back and cleared his throat. Button wiggled fretfully against his spine. "I'm fine now. Promise."

Bonk squinted in the mist. "You full?"

"Stuffed," Osmo assured him, even though he wasn't. Not by half.

Bonk sighed. "Whatever you say. You're welcome, by the way. If the pile of sleepy chain mail got a *well done* for a muddy mushroom, I should get . . . well, I don't know, but something better than that. I was spectacular. Just so you know." He handed over the satchel with the tree of instruments poking out of it. Osmo slung it over his shoulder without taking his hand from behind his back. The three huddled close together and held their breaths.

"Do we have to leave?" Never protested with another yawn. "It's so *nice* here . . ."

"Yeah . . . ," Osmo agreed. "Really just *wonderfully* nice . . ."

"Oh, shut up," Bonk growled.

The skadgebat hefted up the two clay pitchers, weighing them between his paws. Where you shouldn't dare and where you shouldn't know.

"Mrs. B! Anybody ever actually used these before?"

The crabbybara straightened up with pride. "Never. All my patrons are satisfied. And the wording sounds as scary as possible."

"Welp," Bonk said, "bottoms up."

He dumped them both on the sizzling stones at the same time.

Bonk grabbed Never's and Osmo's hands as white and black

smoke poured in. As soon as he touched Osmo's forearm, the badgerish skunky wombat whipped his head toward the human boy, already invisible in the billowing, hissing steam.

"What is *that?*" Bonk hissed.

All of them began to cough. Then the world was nothing but coughing and choking and hot, inescapable air. Through the fog they could finally hear the roar, the same roar they heard on the shores of the Unfinished Ocean. The Thumpus, slow, steady, inevitable, like a war drum, getting louder all the time.

"Osmo! I can't see! What *is* that?" Bonk yowled again between hacks and coughs as he clung to Osmo's arm. "Is that *fur?*"

And then the trees and the wooden floor and the basket of stones

and the pitchers and the bellpull

and the rafters full of stars and northern lights and all the Hinderlands and Beastly too were

gone—

Chapter Twenty-Three

# THE PARTY NEVER STOPS

Osmo Unknown swam up toward consciousness.

He could feel something soft and wet beneath him. He could hear quick, festive, dancing music, in a minor key, with a great many flourishes. He could see nothing at all. He could smell . . . oh, just about a million things.

But mostly popcorn. Hot, buttered, fresh, salty, a teensy bit sweet, popcorn.

And *apples*.

Something heavy thonked into the base of his skull. Then another one. A friendly walloping from Bonk, he figured.

"Well done," he said groggily. "I said well done, okay? Thank you for getting the zither, you did an amazing job. Happy?"

"Amazing!" Never's voice sang out. "Oh, that's fine. *You* get amazing. All you did was say *I love you* to a bathroom attendant. I defied death!"

"Yes, yes, we all defied death," Bonk's voice answered. "We're a very brave little band."

Another heavy thonk banged into the socket of Osmo's knee.

He pulled himself up on all fours. His head *throbbed*. It pounded. It pulsed. It thumped. He forced his eyes to open.

Stars spattered the sky overhead like a toppled bucket of silver coins. Sharp woodsmoke and old leaves and the faintest wisp of frost rode on the wind. Osmo turned to look behind him—a great black sea spread out sparkling into the horizon and past it. This ocean was very much not unfinished. Gentle cold waves foamed up the strand. Fresh ice clung to rocks and trees and sand. But unless the trip had taken a good long while, it shouldn't have been *near* winter o'clock.

Each new wave brought a flurry of hard, red apples *thonk*ing into his ankles.

Up the headlands a little Osmo could see colored lights spinning and glittering. The circus music came from there. Rickety black roofs rose up against the starry sky, the low din of voices drifted down curling white walkways that wound between moss-draped trees. The moon turned everything silver and crisp.

"OH MY GOD I HAVE HORNS," Osmo screamed suddenly.

He grabbed his head and felt for them. Little sharp needle-knives of bone, right there, right where they should never, ever be. The fog of the Hinderlands had left him. So had the strange, horrifying hunger that hollowed his bones. But . . . so had the gentle calm that allowed him to not worry about the *antlers* growing out of his *head* for so long. All the panic the hot sauna had soaked away came rushing in at once. Osmo couldn't breathe. His vision went woozy. The pangirlin and the skadgebat hurried back down the strand to catch him before he fell.

"What's happening?" he gasped. "What's happening to me?"

"Hey, don't go strange on us." Bonk the Cross clucked over him. "You haven't even considered that you're growing fur yet. Wait for that to sink in, then you can *really* lose it."

"*Fur?*"

Bonk patted his forearm. A patch of silvery-red, blackish-gold fur wavered in the wind. The sensation made Osmo shudder, like spilling candle wax on an unsuspecting finger.

"Yeah," Bonk said sympathetically. "Much fur. *Very* fur."

"Is it because I ate all that food? You said it was all right to eat the food here! I *knew* I shouldn't have! How many books have I read? Idiot!"

"You had the horns before the food, Osmo," Never reminded him.

"I feel sick," he moaned.

"I bet you do," laughed Bonk. "You ate rocks. And a tire! And *flan!*"

"Where are we? Why'd you pour those dumb pitchers out together, what kind of a plan was that?"

Bonk shrugged. "I couldn't decide! Who cares? Live in the present, please. And, look, I don't want to pat myself on the back too hard—"

"Yes, you do," Osmo and Never said at the same time.

"Fine, yes I do, and you should too, because I'm pretty firmly sure you and me and Pangy makes three are in the Party Archipelago." The skadgebat threw out his shaggy arms like a magician revealing his best trick. "Remember? The Nextant told us about it! How good is that? Of all the places we could have landed!"

The pangirlin pointed across the dark water. "I think that's

Birthday Atoll, just there. Remember all those places the Nextant talked about? You can see the giant cake and the candle-torches and the party hat mountains. And over there?"—she pointed across the little island in the other direction, across a thin, shallow channel—"I think that must be Diwali Lagoon."

There was no ice on the other island. Paper lanterns of maroon and deep green and indigo and ivory wafted up from the island. The two shores lay close enough for Osmo to hear sitars and drums and see the samosa trees bending down toward a tangle of sticky gulab jamun vines, all heavy with fruit.

Bonk preened. "You could have chosen *so* many people to be your witnesses back in Quiddity. You could have chosen Walter! How glad are you that you got Bonk the Cross in the mix? I have brought you to the party and brought the party to you!"

But which party, Osmo wondered? The ice all over everywhere said a winter party. So Christmas? New Year? St. Lucia's Day? This place felt familiar and strange all together at once. And how could they guess where the next gift for Queen Melancholy was hiding without the Nextant? Osmo didn't even want to think about how far they might have strayed from what little path they'd charted. How big *was* the Eightpenny Woods? He feared it was very big indeed.

"Nothing for it, I suppose," Osmo sighed.

He started inland, up the winding white path bordered by drooping mossy frozen trees. The others scrambled after him. The ice turned black once more where their feet landed. The angry land rejecting their aliveness again. But where Osmo walked, the ice stayed clear. He didn't like it. He didn't know what to make of it. But neither did Bonk or Never, so they all decided without a word that they would not be talking about that tonight.

The path emptied into a shadowy village square set for a feast to end all feasts.

But no one at all seemed to be at home.

The music they'd heard down on the beach still played, but it was a phantom sound, tinkling out of nowhere. The colored lights he'd glimpsed over the icy boulders flickered bravely. Strands of little square paper lanterns painted with pale winter scenes hung from weather vane to weather vane over the plaza. But half the strands had been pulled down, stomped on, their candles crushed to wax blast marks on the cobblestones. Stalls lined the alleyways, bashed in or slashed up or just standing dark. Big scarlet banners and garlands of golden flowers hung in tattered shreds from every streetlamp. The smell of root vegetables roasting in honey floated in the air, but the iron spits turning slowly over weak, guttering flames spun bare and empty. Violins and drums and pretty glass flutes lay broken on chairs that'd got all the stuffing yanked out of their seats and their legs kicked out from under them. Long banquet tables draped in lovely lace cloths stood in neatly planned rows. Heaps of dishes, goblets, silver trays, platters, tureens, punch bowls, jars and pitchers and roasting pans ran up and down their length. All of them empty, dented, tossed carelessly on the ground or against the silent stone walls of a tavern, an armory, a school, a laundry.

A great tall pillar rose up in the center of the square.

Osmo knew this party. Osmo knew this place.

He was home.

"This is the First Frost Festival," he said softly, afraid to break the spell. "First Frost Cove, then, I guess. This is Littlebridge. Sort of."

Only it was all turned upside down and broken down and all the lights shut off and maybe rats were living in it. Like a lovely sweater turned inside out to show the unwearable mess of yarn on the back of the pattern. And it all looked a bit . . . *cheap*. The stones seemed not so sturdy. The streetlamps didn't feel like iron so much as dry hay. Osmo glanced up at the great red granite pillar, expecting to see the great silver skull. But it stood quite empty. That troubled him most of all, somehow.

"I've been to Littlebridge, remember?" Bonk said, wriggling his black nose at the wreckage. "This isn't Littlebridge. This is *Rubbish* Littlebridge. And it's not like I think the original is anything special. The Captain made the archipelago seem a *little* more festive than this dreck. False advertising if you ask me."

"No, it is, see? That's the Cruste and Cheddar Tavern! That's my school! There's the Afyngred Agricultural Hall and that one's the Kalevala Opera House, I swear! This is Dapplegrim Square! Look! Bonk! That wobbly roof with the false owl to scare away real ones is Mittu Grumm's Toy and Shoe Shoppe."

Never pulled at his sleeve. Button protested, spinning resentfully at her.

"Osmo," she interrupted. But he didn't listen. He ran up and down the square, calling out landmarks like he'd lost his entire mind. "Behind the Ag Hall there? That's Hanna Gudgeon's

Laundry-for-Everyone, and all her yellow apple trees." He stopped for a moment and smiled wistfully. He knew every inch of stone and straw and window box. Even upside down and inside out, lights off and rats in the rafters. He knew it all. Was it even possible he *missed* it?

"Osmo, be *quiet*," Never hissed.

They weren't so alone after all. Near the granite pillar that no longer had a skull on it sat the big round table full of party bags. Little paper sacks of every color, full of candies and penny prizes to take home.

And there, hunched over the lot of them, meaty fists shoved into a green bag and a purple one, loomed Mayor Lud.

Still on his stilts and in his Quidnunk costume, the old fool. His back to them, wild with fur and sticky with leaves and lumpy with padding. Grunting and slobbering and scraping the bottoms of the bags for more. Washing it all down with a bucket from the well. Going back for seconds, thirds, hundredths. Osmo cringed in embarrassment. He knew he'd looked no different an hour ago. Gobbling up a tea trolley all to himself.

"M . . . Mayor Lud?" Osmo called. His voice sounded unpleasantly loud over the tinkling fairy music and the rustling fairy shadows. The Mayor ignored him. He snatched up an orange bag and ate it whole, paper and all. "Gregory?" Osmo tried his first name. "Greg?"

That worked.

Mayor Lud threw back his head, bellowed, and hurled an uneaten party bag at the wall of Soothfaste Church. It blew a hole in the bricks like a cannonball. He whirled around to face them, panting with fury and pain.

Bonk the Cross screamed. "Not Greg! Not Greg!" he squeaked.

And it wasn't. Not in the least Greg. Not one molecule of it had ever come near a molecule of Greg's and never would, if it could help it. It wasn't on stilts. It wasn't wearing a costume.

It was a *real* Quidnunk.

An impossibly old one, shaggy and matted and thin. His toenails glowered yellow and warped instead of pearly-pink and healthy. His tusks had grown far too long and his antlers too wide. His eyes hungered. His belly thumped.

They'd run all this way and somehow lapped it. They'd run straight into the thing that had been chasing them since the ferry and the desert and the soft emerald mud.

"Who are you? What do you want?" Osmo said, even though he didn't want to. Didn't want to do anything but run straight out of this ruined mirror of Dapplegrim Square, down the fake Catch-a-Crown River to the cheap copy of the Felefalden Flats and home. It didn't have to be real to be home enough. "What are you doing? Why are you here? Why can't you leave us alone?"

*Be a man*, he thought. *Stand up straight. Strong jaw, strong words, strong fists.*

As if monsters cared how straight he stood.

The Quidnunk roared at them. "This roar is a red flame!" he screamed. "My name is Dapplegrim!"

Osmo went pale at the sound of the name. A word he'd heard all his life and never thought about for one single second. A name he felt almost certain belonged to the great silver skull missing from the pillar in this Littlebridge, but very much not from the one he knew.

"My words are rows of snow-covered spears in defensive positions! Hear them and be slashed to bits! I am *here* because I was *there*. The Eightpenny Woods wants me to be happy. No different than the Great Danedeer jingling their bells over in the Christmas Keys or the bunhens gobbling chocolate lava in the Easter Egg Volcano. The Woods want me to be *full*. THIS IS MY HAPPY PLACE!" the Quidnunk thundered. "And I found the cove first, you can't have it. I earned every stone and branch. I was there in the beginning! At the First Frost! The *first* First Frost! I am the patron saint of this holiday. I am the reason for this season! Every festival has one. Santa, the Easter Rabbit, the New Year Baby . . . and me. I AM DARK CLAUS, FEEL THE WRATH OF MY JOLLY BELLY!" The ragged wild beast beckoned them. "Come closer, little bites. Celebrate with me. It is time for presents under the tree. Time for this. And That. And THE OTHER THING."

Dapplegrim bent down to get closer to their faces.

"I remember it like it's still happening. Centuries ago. The first First Frost. The Mayor crowned Cora Grumm the first Frostfrau at midnight that night. She slipped off the stage just as the crown touched her hair. Splashed snow and slush all over her blue sash and the Frostfrau crown. She laughed and laughed. She was still laughing when she heaved up the ceremonial sword to make the first cut in that huge Bonefire Pie, a pastry so big it took six men to get it out of the oven. And when she turned her head to laugh at the crowd and show how pretty her primate eyes could sparkle, I stepped out of the shadows and I *gobbled. Her. Up.* She didn't laugh ever again and she didn't touch *that* pie!"

Somehow, they could feel the weight of that scene, so long ago and far away. They could see it as a Quidnunk sees, all the senses at once.

Dapplegrim danced madly across the scale model of the square named for him. "More and more and more, more words like snow-flakes thick and fast and beautiful on the rooftops of time! I ate Cora Grumm over *there*, and Vallu Gudgeon over *there* and Annika Lud on the steps of the opera house and Jouko Aptrick inside the bell tower and the cheesemonger *here* and the tavern-master *here* and Tova Sloe *right where you're standing*! And there, there in the shade of all those apple trees I ate Jerome Unknown and I wasn't even sorry for half of a half of a second! I chased them down one by one, all the girls in pretty dresses and the boys in pretty capes! I didn't do it alone. My quiddity got their teeth out for vengeance and came marching up behind me, but I got here *first*. I got first bite. Ask the history books! I *am* the First Frost Festival. The first barren season to ever come to this cursed nest of humans. And what is the Party Archipelago for? Only to relive the best parts of your favorite holidays forever and ever!" Dapplegrim smelled the air. "You smell like sugar and memories. My words are sugar and memories. I've done the carnival games and the prizes and the banquet and the dancing already. Now it's time for presents." The Quidnunk leered, his huge mouth hungry, his lips chapped and dry. "Who's going to be my Frostfrau?"

Dapplegrim exploded toward them. Osmo couldn't believe anything so big and so old could move so fast. He grabbed Bonk's and Never's hands before they could get away—they'd get lost and Dapplegrim'd get them, just like he got all those great-great-great-grandparents whose names Osmo had only seen as a child on a school trip, in a census book under glass in Bodeworde's Armory's library.

But the boy with the hazel eyes had never gotten lost, not once, not in his whole life. He couldn't get lost in Littlebridge any more than you can get lost in your own body.

He dashed them toward Hanna's laundry and doubled back round the alleys to the Cruste and Cheddar keg entrance. But Dapplegrim ran like a desert cat, taking huge bites out of the air behind them. Osmo had a mind to make it to the old Brownbread Mill. They could hide there. It was like a fortress. Inside, small creatures like them had an advantage. Quidnunx were big and clumsy, built for outside, not little nooks in the threshing hall.

"This sentence is pure cold gold: you did it to yourselves," the Quidnunk howled. "You deserve it. Get in my mouth! That's where you belong! You know what you did!"

Osmo wheeled wide and careened down Cacherel Lane. He dragged the skadgebat and the pangirlin behind the stalls into a narrow corridor that the barkers used to get back and forth for supplies when the crowds on the main way got too thick. They stumbled together, practically rolling like the world's sloppiest pangolin ball. Bonk wheezed with the effort, his bathrobe flapping behind him. Never kept trying to turn into a ball, but Osmo wouldn't let her. A ball was faster, but a ball could get lost as easily as a girl. But Osmo wasn't tired at all. His muscles sang. His chest opened gorgeously to the frost-tipped night air.

Dapplegrim sniffed each stall as he passed. His gold-green eyes glowed hot in the shadows.

The trio burst out of the lane and onto the Old Unlordly Road. How well did the Archipelago copy places, Osmo wondered. They'd find out in a moment—yes. There it was. The Brownbread Mill, its towers and hunched dome and giant waterwheel promising safety. Or at least a chance at safety.

Dapplegrim punched a carnival stall out of the way and crushed the road beneath his hooves.

"Why are you running? Every night is First Frost in the Party Archipelago! This is what happened! You can't change it now! Come *on*, just let me eat you! You can't have First Frost without a *feast!*"

Osmo collided with the thick walnut double doors of the mill. The others skidded in after him, barely holding on to the tips of his fingers. Osmo pounded on the door with his fists.

No use. Locked.

Locked, on a party island in heaven.

Bonk's breath came in big gulping squeezes like a broken accordion. Nevermore balled up instantly, her bronze armor bristling. Osmo crouched down and considered his options. They really could never outrun a Quidnunk. Not without a Nextant or a couple of really weird pitchers and a sauna. They'd never make it to the mill. What an idea! A mile across open roads? No. This was . . . this was it. He had to accept that. Every road could end. He hadn't thought this one would hit a wall quite so soon or so messily. But it had. He wondered if Jerome Unknown had crouched in a corner, terrified, helpless, at that first festival.

*Huh*, he thought suddenly of his famous, nameless ancestor who had run away from a life he hated and never told anyone who he'd once been. *I guess his name was Jerome.*

"What a strange place you chose," observed Dapplegrim, taking in the mill with his mad, wild eyes.

Without another word, the Quidnunk dove for them.

*Bye, Mum*, Osmo thought as he winced and flattened himself against the wall. *I'm so sorry this happened to us.*

He looked up into Dapplegrim's strange, dark mouth. Nothing like the fake one in Adelard Sloe's Stupendous Throwing Game. A real mouth, and real teeth, and three very real balls about to disappear inside it forever.

Osmo felt Nevermore unfurl behind him. She was screaming. Louder than he'd ever heard her. The quiet girl could really make an unholy noise.

"DARK!" she shrieked. "Dark, Dark, Dark! Help! You promised! You promised! Captain! It's me! Please!"

Osmo didn't understand what was happening, but he did understand that Dapplegrim's mouth wasn't closing like it should have. Like it should have *ages* ago. He took his chance.

"Just LEAVE US ALONE!" Osmo roared back at the beast above them. "You've been following us all this way, through deserts and oceans and forests and every place just to EAT us?" Dapplegrim blinked, suddenly confused. Osmo kept going with that idea. It was all he had. "That's so boring! I'm disappointed in you. I thought you were *wild*. Magnificent! Untamed! *Magic*. Turns out you just skipped lunch."

The Quidnunk ran his paws over his huge face, such a strangely human gesture.

"My question is the color of a lost cat. What do you mean? I haven't been following you. This is where I live. This is the house I built with the stones the big black bird on the boat gave me. *You* came to *me*."

*"Dark, you can't break promises!"* Nevermore screamed into the mill's impenetrable doors.

A field of stars and bright blue nebulae and violet dust clouds light-years wide blossomed around them. And an endless expanse of pure black darkness came settling down like a blanket to tuck them in at the end of the night.

Before it covered the world completely, Osmo saw one single, terrible moment flash before his eyes. Something barreling down Cacherel Lane. Something with fur of a hundred colors and massive feet thundering on the earth. Something with teeth like moonlight.

Another Quidnunk rocketed down the Old Unlordly Road and slammed full-force into Dapplegrim. A much bigger, healthier, younger Quidnunk. The pair shot backward in a flying tangle of beast and bone. Both of them tumbled, roaring in agony, through the cheap back wall of what could only be St. Whylom's School for Excellent Young People.

And then that ugly scene vanished under a curtain of stars.

"Hush, baby," said a soothing deep orangutan voice. "I heard you the first time."

A familiar, jaunty growl-purr butted in. "Hold on to your tails, puppers—let an old sea-cat show you how the Stupendous Throwing Game is *really* played."

The door to the old Brownbread Mill melted into nothingness.

*Chapter Twenty-Four*

# THE WHISPERING PLACE

*Click, clack, smack-crack*

It was dark in the Dark.

It was *very* dark. And it smelled like fire.

It was very dark, and it smelled like fire, and someone was swearing.

*Click, clack, smack-CRACK*

"Stupid muddy son of an even stupider thing." Bonk the Cross's familiar voice bounced around, echoing. Wherever they were, it was *big*.

*Click, clack, smack-CRACK-fwwoosh*

"Took you long enough, cowards!" Bonk yawped.

A spray of sparks. Then a single slender wisp of fire blossomed out of the darkness. It sizzled over a small pyramid of grasses, gulping the black air as it grew. Bonk's furry, striped face came into view in the faint orange light. Then Nevermore's sweet, round scales reflecting the campfire and their exhausted expressions.

Bonk frowned deeply at a flint stone and steel in his paws.

"Do better next time," he warned the stones.

A soft, hollow bell rang clear and far away. Twice, thrice.

Osmo could hear another sound, too. So familiar, but he couldn't put his finger on it. He turned his head in every direction like an owl. The only light came from Bonk's flame—and a tall, wide, rounded window several feet away. Yet he could see well enough. The window showed a slightly lighter, bluer shade of black and the last of the fading stars as the Dark retreated and left them . . . here. Wherever here was.

Snowflakes began to drift and tumble down through the lightless air outside.

Winter o'clock.

"You could make fire all this time?" Never whispered. There really wasn't any reason to whisper, but Osmo understood. He felt it too. You *should* whisper here somehow. It was a whispering place.

What *was* that sound? He could almost place it, but it kept slipping away.

Bonk gave her a disappointed look. "I've got to make tea, haven't I? You ever heard of *cold* tea? Maybe that sort of thing flies where *he* chews his cud, but I won't have it. I will *not*. Up is up, down is down, life is a series of grand tragic jokes broken only by petty annoyances, and tea is hot. Cuppa?" He rummaged in his pockets and pulled out, improbably, a little silver grill with a tripod and an entirely different porcelain tea service than the one he'd shown them in the Meaningful Desert. This one had his own face painted expertly on the pot and every cup. He passed them out and they all waited for the water to boil over its sad little flame. "Not much of a fire, I'm afraid. There's nothing but shadows to burn round here. Take my word for it—I know you can't see in the dark any further than you can fart, poor cronkey."

"Bonk and me are crepuscular," Nevermore said quietly. "That means twilight's the best time of day for us."

"I know what crepuscular means." Osmo rolled his eyes.

"Plus one-third of me's stone-cold nocturnal." The skadgebat preened.

Osmo shrugged awkwardly. He didn't quite know how to say it. To admit it. "I can see fine," he said softly.

Suddenly, he knew the sound. That sweet, trickling, lulling, rushing sound down below the great window.

"My fabulous tail you can," Bonk snorted.

"It's not *that* dark in here."

Bonk pointed an accusing paw at him. "False! It's as black as panther poop at midnight in here! What are you playing at, no-snout?"

Nevermore got up and jogged ten or twelve paces away from the fire, deep into the shadows. "All right, how many fingers am I holding up?" she called back.

Osmo squinted. "Three. Also don't take any more steps back. You're standing in front of a threshing machine. There's a big mill-stone on the back wall and stalks of wheat and barley all over the floor. I guess that's what you found to burn? Smells like it. Scorched bread and all." Osmo couldn't help it. He was enjoying their dumbfounded expressions. The pangirlin carefully returned to their little camp. Osmo let himself linger in the moment just a little longer. He so rarely knew something they didn't. "I know where we are," he confessed. "This is the old Brownbread Mill. Second floor, I think. That sound is the wheel turning through the river outside."

The impressed looks on their faces vanished. "Don't think so, friendolyn," Bonk chortled, pleased to be on top of the knowledge game again.

"Good try, though," Never said encouragingly.

"No, it is," Osmo insisted, still whispering in that quiet space. But only barely. "I can *see* it. I've heard that sound every school day of my whole life."

Bonk sighed. He jabbed the boy in the chest with his stubby thumb. "You're *not* crepuscular and you *don't* know what you're talking about."

Nevermore rubbed at her broken glasses. "It can't be your mill, Osmo. I thought so, too, for a minute. But it can't. I don't know where we are, but I know that."

"It is!"

The pangirlin shook her head as Bonk poured their tea with a very unconcerned attitude. "Go touch the wall."

Osmo got up and made for the back wall where the huge, impossibly heavy millstone lay silently like a sleeping animal. The waterwheel turned outside. But the thing seemed not to *work* so much as *snore* or *dream*. Nothing like the industrial crush of the real thing in the real world. Osmo thought of that wild story from his schoolbooks, of all those strong men stealing the stone from winter itself and slowly dying to get it down the mountain.

The story did not seem so wild anymore. Maybe there *were* no untrue stories, only ones you didn't understand yet.

He put his hand on the wall of the mill (it *was* the mill, he knew it was) and spread out his fingers against the stone.

The stone *crinkled* under his palm.

Then it *rustled*. Then it *thumped*.

Osmo Unknown snatched his hand back as though the wall had cut him. His fingers came away sticky with golden sap.

The wall wasn't stone at all, but a dense, thick thatching of shining orange and golden and scarlet leaves. So dense and so thick and so shiny they seemed like solid stone from far away, hidden in shadows.

The wall *thump*ed again. And again, a moment later. Soft and rhythmic and steady. Like a heartbeat.

Or a Thumpus.

"Where are we?" Osmo shouted. "What did the Dark do to us?"

He took a step backward and looked up at the leafy walls. It was still the old mill . . . but it had a second nature now. Red and magic. His sight was getting better all the time. He could almost see totally clearly, as clearly as on a night with three full moons.

Each wall had a painting on it. Bold, dark strokes like cave paintings. A different scene on each wall. But Osmo couldn't really understand any of them, any more than he could understand what people meant to say with all those antelopes and handprints on ancient cave walls. *Good hunting? Antelopes are a bunch of jerks? Hands are nice, we all have hands?*

One painting showed something very like the Meaningful

Desert. Another showed a small Quidnunk, surely a baby, dancing happily with a crown of flowers on her head. The next showed a much larger Quidnunk, shaggy arms thrown into the air, crying out in pain, and where its heart should have been, a gush of red leaves poured out of the wall. After that came a grand city, full of towers and houses and enormous pumpkins, full of Quidnunx walking the streets, going to market, crowing at the moon. Then: familiar tall black weeds nodding under a blazing sun. An ocean full of strange, primitive sharks. A great foggy forest with stars for a ceiling. And the last, something very like the seal of Littlebridge, yet not like it at all: a tall, healthy Quidnunk with antlers like lightning, and a human, holding hands, their faces turned wonderingly toward one another.

"I don't understand," Osmo whispered miserably. He hated it. He hated not being able to put it together. He hated not knowing. Not knowing it all. "Am I supposed to understand? What am I supposed to do?"

Osmo felt Button wriggling against his sleeve. He turned over his wrist. He tried not to look at the fur that had spread up past the cuff of his coat. He couldn't think about that now. Or why he could see so well in the dark.

"Do you know where we are?" he asked the burgundy button urgently.

One spin clockwise against the rich fabric.

*Yes.*

"Tell me!"

A halfhearted turn counterclockwise.

*No.*

"Of course, you can only do yes or no. Ugh. Why is everything so hard all the time? Fine. Are we in the old Brownbread Mill?"

*No.*

"Are we still in the Archipelago?"

*No.*

"Okay! Progress. Are we still in the Eightpenny Woods?"

Half a turn clockwise. Then half a turn the other way.

*Yes, but no.*

That was worrisome. He needed to get better at this game, quickly. "I don't know what to ask! Give me some kind of hint." He ran his hand through his shaggy black hair, which felt somehow much shaggier than it should be. "Animal, vegetable, or mineral?" he blurted out in desperation.

*Yes.*

"Is that a joke? Do buttons make jokes?"

*No.*

Fear coiled in his heart. The red-leaf wall thumped softly beside him. It seemed to reach toward him gently, and then shrink back shyly.

"Button," he whispered. "Is this place alive?"

*No, but yes.*

Sweat stood out on his aching forehead. "Are we safe?"

One spin counterclockwise.

*No.*

"Is there a way out of here?"

*Yes.*

"Let's rephrase that, given the last . . . everything ever. An *easy* way?"

*No.*

"So we might be stuck here for a while." He breathed out through his teeth. "Is the Quidnunk still following us?"

*No.*

"So the danger is something else."

*Yes.*

"Something in here with us."

*Yes.*

"Not good. Are we at least anywhere near the Gown That Cannot Be Removed or the Treasure That Cannot Be Taken or the Rope That Cannot Be Untied? Or any others I'm forgetting?"

*Yes.*

"Really? Which one?"

*Yes.*

"What does that mean? All of them?"

*Yes.*

Osmo grinned. He concentrated fiercely on that small button. Whatever danger Button knew of fled his mind. A prize! Nearby! "That's something, then, isn't it? A pretty big something! Are any of them in here? In this . . . building?"

*Yes.*

"On this floor?"

*Yes.*

Excitement flooded Osmo's limbs. "Where?" he cried, leaping up, ignoring the awful cave paintings and the thumping, beating wall, dashing back and forth. He jackknifed back toward Bonk and Never, trying to cover a wide area.

"Here? Here? Over here? Hot and cold, Button, do hot and cold. Hot means close, cold means far. Clockwise for hot, counterclockwise for cold. Here?" He ran to the millstone.

*Cold.*

"Here?" He ran to the threshing machine.

*Cold.*

"Here?" Osmo scrambled halfway up the iron staircase leading to the foreman's office. He tripped and clung to the rail. His feet didn't seem to want to obey him.

Button spun hard and rocked back and forth. *Very cold.*

"All right, what about over there?" He went to the great tall rounded window.

A very small spin rightward.

*Warm.*

Osmo threw back his head and howled. Long and full, very like a wolf. Bonk and Never froze.

"Close! Okay, where then? Does *Bonk* have one?"

*No.*

Bonk settled his cup down. "Osmo, I think you should try to calm down."

"Never?"

*No.*

The pangirlin stepped back quickly from the fire. "Osmo, stop it," she hissed.

But he ignored them. They were *distracting* him. Osmo frowned, turning around in frustrated circles. "Where then? I can't see any-thing that could be any of the ridiculous rubbish we're looking for. None of them are exactly small. Bowls, treasures, gowns. There's just the fire and the tea and Bonk and Never and my satchel."

*Hot.*

"Button, don't play games. I know the zither and the ring are in my satchel, I meant the other ones."

*Yes.*

"They're in my satchel. Really. How many of them?"

*Yes.*

Osmo dropped to his knees and dumped his schoolbag out onto the floor of this alien place. He grabbed his belongings one by one. Notebook?

*Cold.*

Pencils?

*Cold.*

Oona's black ribbon?

*Cold.*

His doublechess board?

*Cold.*

"I can figure this out," Osmo insisted.

But Button hadn't given up. It rolled over and around Osmo's spilled-out satchel, as insistent as a mosquito. It rocked into his schoolbook, then away, then into his sister's sweet black velvet ribbon. Button knew something. It wanted to say what it knew so badly! But it had no mouth to tell its truth, or fingers to point the way, or anything at all but its sad, helpless spinning.

"I don't know!" Osmo yelled. His voice bounced all around the cavernous mill. "I don't understand! I keep trying to do what everyone tells me to. I keep trying to listen and learn and be good at things, no matter how weird they are, and by the way, they are VERY WEIRD right now. But I'm not! I always wanted to go Somewhere Else, but I was supposed to like it there! It was supposed to like me there! *I was supposed to be better Somewhere Else.* I was supposed to fit in and understand and know how to live. It was supposed to be the opposite of home! But the Else is just as hostile and rude and hard and bristly as anywhere and I don't belong here any more than I belonged in Littlebridge, which means I don't belong anywhere at all. *I'M SO STUCK AND I DON'T KNOW WHAT YOU WANT ME TO DO!*"

He gave a strangled sob and shoved the heels of his hands into his eyes in frustration.

Osmo gasped. He pulled his hands away from his eyes and and clapped them over his mouth.

His eyes.

His hands.

His mouth.

The first were very much bigger, the second had many more claws, and the third had many more teeth than any of them were allowed to have.

Bonk crossed his furry arms over his chest. "And there it is. I hope you're happy with yourself. I'm certainly not."

Osmo Unknown lowered his eyes to the shining golden bowl full of dark liquid as bright as a mirror. He knew what he would see. He didn't want to know. But he knew. That terrible hunger. Even children know what such hunger means.

It means you're about to grow.

"It's okay," Never said nervously. "It's okay. We'll fix it. There's lots of kinds of mushrooms . . ."

But then she couldn't bear it one second longer and somersaulted into an impenetrable ball against his horror.

Antlers. Fur of a thousand colors and patterns. Claws. Hot gold-green eyes that could see clear as the moon in the dark. A vast chest and a vast thumping belly. A mouth full of clean, moon-white tusky fangs. A mouth big enough to sing or eat the whole world or both at once.

And a very pretty peony growing out of his chest.

He was, head to hoof, a Quidnunk.

But Osmo hadn't a moment to scream about it.

Someone banged open a door on the west wall of the threshing room. Someone big and furious and marching straight toward them like everybody's mother when the chores aren't done.

Someone wearing an absolutely *huge* fur coat.

She grabbed his arm with a clawlike hand. Her hot gold-green eyes flashed like a cat's in the dark.

"Always so difficult, Mr. Unknown. Always so clever. You nearly *escaped* me there. And after I've come all this way to catch you."

"Mrs. *Brownbread?*"

*Chapter Twenty-Five*

# THE BLUE WHALE'S GAMBIT

Only it *wasn't* Mrs. Brownbread.

Not exactly.

Mrs. Brownbread was as old as the ocean and slow and kind and relaxed no matter what happened. Mrs. Brownbread's coat was threadbare and patchy and older than her, faded to no color in particular, with bits of lining torn out and the pockets ripped through and the hood hanging by a sad, lonely hair.

*This* girl was barely older than Osmo and Never, and she boiled with energy and might well not even know what the word *relaxed* meant. And this girl's coat bushed luxuriously around her pointed, lively face. Thick and sleek and colorful and new, still spangled with melting snowflakes.

They stood opposite one another, the human and the Quidnunk, right below the painting on the living red-leaf wall. Only Osmo the Quidnunk stood where the human figure did, and Mrs. Brownbread the human stood where the Quidnunk bowed its great shaggy head.

"Just *look* at yourself, Osmo," the girl clucked pityingly, and then he knew it really was Mrs. Brownbread, somehow, some way.

Nobody else's cluck could make him feel so chastened. But what had he done wrong? "Didn't listen to our elders, did we? Well, we played fair. Which is quite hard for us. Gives me hives, personally. But we did warn you. Now, we must have a very stern talk about not trespassing. You shouldn't be here. You shouldn't even know you *could* get here. This was not the plan."

"What plan?" Osmo rumbled. "We were desperate, Dapplegrim was about to eat us."

"Don't be stupid. He didn't, did he?"

"Well, no, another Quidnunk came along at the last minute."

Mrs. Brownbread grinned wolflishly. And sheepishly, too. "So you saw me. Naughty boy. No peeking."

"That was you?"

"Oh, you silly thing. It has always been me."

Osmo tossed his antlers in shock and frustration. It seemed such a natural movement, just as howling had seemed. As natural as a human rubbing their eyes when they're tired. "You. You're a *Quidnunk*? And you've been chasing us! All this way. All this time. Why? What have I done to deserve that?"

"You really have to stop thinking in such a limited way. It's nothing to do with *deserving*. It had to be done. So I did it. It was fun."

Osmo looked skeptical. "If you're a Quidnunk why aren't you talking funny? My sentences are full of rubbish and all that." He paused, realizing something. "Why aren't I? I was, just a moment ago?"

Mrs. Brownbread chuckled. "That's something we do for others. So they can experience our thoughts with all the bells and whistles we come by naturally. It's unnecessary between two Nunx. We are speaking pure Quidnunk right now and have been for a few good minutes. You have a bit of an accent, but it's perfectly charming, I promise."

Osmo flexed his claws in wonder. But his thoughts went cloudy. "Are you . . . are you going to hurt me? Was *that* the plan?"

The girl in the fur coat swept out her arm as though she owned the place. Osmo followed her gesture and saw a small table and two simple—but very large—chairs by the last of the fire. On the table, a doublechess set waited patiently to be played. Osmo began to guess the shape of what was to come. He was meant to play. But for what? And why?

"That's not enough chairs for my friends," he said simply.

"Friends? Is that what they are?"

Osmo narrowed his eyes at her. She was trying to get him to feel his own feelings, as Bonk would say. To feel uncertain that he had any friends, and therefore uncertain in himself, and therefore worse at the game and more likely to lose. He'd played Mrs. Brownbread plenty. The game started long before the first piece moved.

"I don't know," he said evenly. "Let's ask them. Where are they? What have you done?"

She saw his snow-leopard-furred chest start to rise and fall with panic. "No need to be so hostile. They're waiting for us. Don't worry. She let them out the back way. No one she wants to leave can stay. So you should feel very lucky you've still got two feet on this ground."

"No!" Osmo burst out. "I need them!"

Brownbread grumbled deep in her chest. "Doublechess requires only two players. We are all that matter here. They are a distraction. I promise, they're quite healthy and safe."

"I don't care. If we are to be married, what I want matters just as much as what Melancholy wants, and I want my friends back. They're not a distraction, they're . . . we're all in this together by now, can't you see?" He touched the tip of one of the doublechess pieces with his forefinger. "They're companions. If I get to move, they get to move. We all matter."

Mrs. Brownbread rolled her huge, feline eyes. In another moment, feet came thundering down the mill's stone staircase as Bonk and Never toppled back down into the great room.

"Rude!" snapped Bonk the Cross as he strode across the flagstones. "I have never in all my life so much as *sat upon* such rudeness."

"You can't leave a human alone like that," Never panted. "They're not built for it. Way too squishy."

"Happy now?" Brownbread said. "I doubt they'll improve your chances. Keep quiet, you two."

"Shan't," Bonk sniffed.

"Very doubtful," agreed Never.

Mrs. Brownbread glanced between the pair of them. She shrugged her great strong shoulders.

"Fine," she said, totally unconcerned. The girl cupped her hands around her mouth as though she meant to imitate a bird's song—and that's just what she did. A little trill, a bit of a chirp, and a long whistle.

But no birds came. Instead, the floor of the mill trembled, then sagged, then cracked open. A pair of gigantic lacy electric-blue mushrooms unfurled out of the ground like butterfly wings and snapped their great caps closed around Never and Bonk. They couldn't move, and though they could speak, no sound escaped the glassy walls of their mushroomy prisons. They stood as still in there as doublechess pieces.

"It's no bother to me whether anyone does as I ask when I ask it," Mrs. Brownbread sniffed. "I'm far too old not to get my way. Mushrooms are ever so much quicker than manners."

Osmo Unknown sank into one of the chairs, defeated. She would have her way. He might as well get on board before a mushroom came for him, too. His antlers cast shadows on all the painted walls. His enormous Quidnunk body curled up into the seat like a child. "I'm very confused," he said. "My skull feels like it's about to peel open like an orange. Where *are* we? Please tell me. Someplace both in and not in the Eightpenny Woods. Both alive and not alive. Someplace not safe."

"We are inside the heart of Queen Melancholy, Osmo," Mrs. Brownbread said simply, as though such a thing could be simply said, or simply understood. "That is her life painted on the walls. Her memories. This is what a Quidnunk's heart is made of. Red leaves and golden sap and shadows and memories. Only half different to yours and mine. Or yours, at least."

Osmo lifted his glowing Quidnunk eyes to the stone (but not stone) ceilings. He couldn't believe it. His mind hurt. He was living and breathing *inside* someone else's heart. "But it's *huge.*"

"Yes. It always was."

"But . . . Mrs. Brownbread. I don't mean to tell you your business. But those aren't Melancholy's memories. There's some kind of mistake. They're mine. That's the Widows' Weeds and that's the Unfinished Ocean and that's the Hinderlands. *I've* done these things. *I've* seen those places."

Mrs. Brownbread stretched her neck and cracked her knuckles. "Let me tell you what's going to happen, lovenunk. You're going to sit down. And I'm going to sit down. We will take the last of your friend's tea together. Then we will fight."

"I'm not going to fight you."

"Why? Because I'm a girl? In Quidnunk society, females are the bigger and the stronger. We will *fight*. In the traditional Nunkish fashion. After all, if you mean to be king, you'll have to know how to fight. If you win, you win it all: you can go on, and wed the queen, be king of all the mad creatures of the world, and do as you like till the end of your days. And *while* we fight, I will tell you two stories. When I have finished, if you still don't understand, there's no hope for you, and I shall tip you out that window and go about my day."

Osmo Unknown chewed on this. He didn't want to fight anyone. Why did so many things have to involve fights and hunts and arguments? His father never backed down from a fight. *Strong fists.* That was what that meant. But Osmo had never wanted his mother's gun and he'd never wanted his father's tavern fights, either. His new body felt so strong, but his old heart felt so tired. Finally, he settled on no choice at all. He simply changed the subject.

"If it's the queen's heart, why does it look like your mill?"

"Because Melancholy was my very best friend, and I told her all about it when we were both young," Mrs. Brownbread answered. "She loved all my stories." She lifted her chin and took the whole great room in. "It would seem she loved them more than I ever imagined. How marvelous. I never guessed. I'm actually terribly touched."

Osmo put his head in his paws. "You knew Queen Melancholy? As a child?"

Mrs. Brownbread sat herself grandly down in the other chair. "Osmo Unknown, what I know could keep your brain fed through to eternity."

When Osmo lifted his head out of his paws, he saw his double-chess board set up neatly on the table between them. The pieces glittered in the wheat-fire. All the unmatched, expensive knights and bishops and quidkings and queenolins and rookswhales Mrs. Brownbread had taken off her opponents over the years. Osmo's own stag-horn queen sat innocently in its proper square.

"I told you." Mrs. Brownbread smiled. "We will fight in the traditional Quidnunk fashion."

"But this is doublechess," he said, and even he knew he sounded stupid and slow.

"Who do you think invented such a game? Humans? Please. They got as far as chess, felt *very* chuffed about their superior intellect, and took the rest of the century off." She nodded smugly toward the board. "You're missing a piece."

"You're lying. Bello Draughts invented doublechess. Everyone knows that. I can prove it." He reached for his satchel and his old copy of *The Ballad of the Forest and the Valley, Seventh Edition, Annotated,* PROPERTY OF ST. WHYLOM'S SCHOOL. DO NOT STEAL.

"Osmo, look at the board. See with your new eyes. They are much better than human eyes. They can see through to the bones of things. This is a Quidnunk game! How could it ever be anything else? Every piece has two natures. You're rewarded for defeating an animal piece, not the usual ones. Ask yourself—what's the unoccupied black space beside the queen called? The one that brings the dead back into play?"

Osmo squeezed his eyes shut. He hadn't even thought about it. Hadn't made the connection. All this time, and his brain just hadn't done the job. He didn't even want to say it now. To admit a big giant bird had said the word to him, Osmo Unknown, who loved doublechess better than almost anyone, and he hadn't even blinked.

"The Gnarlbind," he mumbled.

To her very great credit, Mrs. Brownbread didn't humiliate him any further. She rested her case. She stretched out her wrinkle-less young hand toward his Quidnunk face. No fear at all touched her small, human face. "Does it hurt too badly?"

"No," Osmo said. He jumped at the sound of his own voice. Deep and gigantic and rumbly. "No, I . . . I feel amazing. I feel strong and big and . . . and . . . brand-new."

"Of course you do." She patted his left tusk affectionately. "It's the best feeling in the world. I remember."

"You *remember*?"

Mrs. Brownbread moved one of her pawns, then one of her hedgeknights after it. "Go on," she coaxed.

"I don't want to play! I don't want to fight! I don't want to fight *anyone.*"

"But you will."

"What do you mean you remember?"

"Play, and I'll tell you. Two stories. I promised. I do keep my promises, Osmo."

Osmo cringed. Cringing looked *very* odd on a fur-bound moss-clad mountain sitting in a perfectly normal armchair. "But I can't beat you," he admitted.

"Aw," crooned Mrs. Brownbread. "That's too bad, isn't it?"

"Anyway, I'm missing a piece, like you said. Can't play with no queen."

"You're a very clever sort, Osmo Unknown. I'm sure you can find an unusual solution."

In the end, Osmo wanted answers more than he wanted to be stubborn. He sat there foolishly for a moment, trying to think of what he could possibly use to replace his queen. He'd used up almost all his belongings just getting here.

And then he knew.

Osmo hadn't the foggiest whether he still had pockets. He rummaged in his fur, thick and soft and shockingly thrilling to pull back against the grain while looking for pockets. His hand closed over it. Osmo set Mustamakkara's warm red feelings box on the board where his queen should have stood. It was only a little bigger than a proper doublechess piece. Though *much* redder.

"What happens if I lose?" Osmo asked.

"I get to take a bridepiece," Brownbread answered him wolfishly.

"Same as always. If you lose, you and your friends will all stay here in the Eightpenny Woods until time gives up and the moon puts out her lanterns."

"So not at all the same as always," growled Osmo. "That's not fair. We've come so far."

"Then you'd better play your very best game, hadn't you? I would never let my dear friend marry someone who couldn't even man a decent doublechess side, what do you take me for?"

It seemed like a choice, but it wasn't one, not really. He couldn't leave Never and Bonk in this place, so long before their time. Not for his sake. That was even less fair.

So Osmo began. He used a more daring opening than he used to back in the game grove in Bonefire Park. The Blue Whale's Gambit. Mrs. Brownbread nodded approvingly. She countered with Grateful Sacrifice, took his rook's companion, and pulled off the Hippo's Crux on her shadow turn. Osmo's stomach curdled.

Mrs. Brownbread meant to play for keeps.

She knocked her bishop casually out of the way of his laundress. "First of all, I think we'd better have done with this Mrs. Brownbread business. Far too formal for beasts like us. You can call me Kalevala."

Osmo's mouth dropped open. His tusky teeth gleamed white. Heavy snow poured down in the blue darkness outside the heart-mill.

"Like the Opera House."

Kala Brownbread, now Kalevala, boxed in his queenolin early. "Precisely like. I know it's an odd name, but not much odder than any other Quidnunk. And much less odd than my father's, who gave it to me." She looked up at him sidelong. "I believe you met him. His name is—was—Dapplegrim."

"But . . . all that happened hundreds of years ago. The first First Frost! And you look so young! You look like me."

"No one is old in this place, my child," she said warmly, repeating the words of the Great Last Bird. "And no one frail."

She took her shadow turn.

"My name is Kalevala, just like the Opera House. And I am going to sing for you. Are you ready? Once upon a time, in the beginning of the world, a certain peculiar Forest fell in love with a deep, craggy Valley."

Osmo groaned so loudly the walls of Queen Melancholy's heart trembled. "I've heard this one."

Mrs. Brownbread flicked him in his big black moist nose. "Shoosh!"

## Chapter Twenty-Six
# TWO STORIES

This is the first story.

Once upon a time, in the beginning of the world, a certain peculiar Forest fell in love with a deep, craggy Valley.

Looking back, everything that happened after that was bound to happen one way or another. The history of every place is the history of the people inside it and the people outside it. The history of every person is the history of the love they've known and the hate they've grown.

My mother lost just the same game of chance as your mother. It happened so much more often in those days. We hunted humans. Humans hunted us. Back and forth and back and forth. Partly because the children of the Forest and the children of the Valley just never could understand one another. Why would anyone want to live in a house when you could live in the moonlight? Why would anyone want to live in the wilds and the wastes where you never ever knew what might happen, instead of a nice, cozy house?

Quidnunx are cunning, enormous, ferocious, rude, quick-tempered, and greedy. Humans are ferocious, cunning, quick-tempered, greedy, and somewhat smaller. The trouble is, neither are very wise.

It wasn't personal. Any more personal than cows or chickens.

*Dapplegrim told you about the First Frost. I tried to tell you when last we played, but you only listened to him. That's all right, almost getting eaten by a ghost tends to sharpen the ears. I'm not offended. All those girls running away from clumsy old Mayor Lud on his stilts! It's an echo of a memory of that terrible night.*

*But before that night?*

*Well, nobody in Littlebridge bothered to note down the name of the first hunter who killed a Quidnunk back in the beginnings of history. No one remembers the first butcher who turned that kill into steaks and roasts and cutlets and set the whole village to thirsting after more. Nor did they jot down the name of the fallen beast while they were making beast broth and beast soufflé and hanging monster mutton out to dry. But the Quidnunx did. They are very fond of jotting, as a rule. Her name was Cora Grumm. Dapplegrim told you about her. The first Frostfrau.*

*Dapplegrim and the others only took one human for each of the Quidnunx Cora and her friends took. The good folk of Littlebridge were not so careful with the numbers when they rode out to slay back the monsters in the wood. That's how they got my father. And all the others who came to town on First Frost. Soothfaste and Whylom and Bonefire and Afyngred. Bodeworde and Yclept and Cacherel. Cammamyld and Felefalden. They buried them all over Littlebridge, and gave their names to what they built on top. And they dipped my father's bones in silver and put it up in the square forever after.*

*Humans hurt us first. Never forget that. They were the strangers. The Valley didn't make them. They weren't family.*

*But, well. We hurt you, too. You don't want to know what happened to Gareth. Poor chap.*

*And so it went, horribly, for so long, until the treaty. The treaty was our solution to an argument the Forest and the Valley started and left us to finish. Dreadfully rude of them. We thought it would help. To understand completely the life that was taken. To walk their path through the country beyond life. To take a child, and raise them in a stranger's world so that nothing after would seem strange at all. And then, when they went home again at long, long last, they would be like a beautiful sneeze: all they learned and knew would spread to anyone who came near. We thought the treaty would keep us connected, like sisters and brothers, and one day the connections would grow so thick and thorny we would all wake up and be one world again, laughing at the very idea that we were ever cross with one another.*

*But it never worked right. The children understood. They grew wild or mild and their half-and-half hearts were precious as jade. But the lessons they learned were just for them. No one else. Humans kept hunting us, even after the treaty. The Quidnunx cheated, too, of course. But not like people. Quidnunx taught all the animals to talk and convinced the moon to come to tea on Tuesdays and paid off Bello Draughts to smuggle doublechess in to keep the primates distracted. But humans just kept on building roads into the Forest and eating Quidnunx croissants for breakfast.*

*There's ever so many more Quidnunk cities than Quiddity, you know. There is always someplace more Else, deeper, wilder, darker, brighter. You could spend your whole life sprinting from one to the next, and never run out. Fourpenny, Eightpenny. Sixteenpenny. Thirty-two.*

*And yet through all that huge wide world of places, one way or two ways, we just couldn't keep away from each other. Forest and Valley,* round and round. What hope did we ever have, with them as our parents? But make no mistake, my mother meant to go on the forbidden hunt that day. So did a lot of mothers back then. I begged her not to. It wasn't worth it. But she was angry and hungry and there was more and more Valley and less and less Forest all the time. The Valley was winning the argument.

And so it came my turn to pay for my mother's sin and wed a ghost. And I was just like you. I didn't listen, either.

I was very young. Only a slip of a beast. I took every step you have taken—but backward, and on sharp hooves. An Agatha mushroom packed me up cozytight. I went into Littlebridge. I was so afraid of the humans, the terrible, slavering, monstrous humans who knew nothing of poetry or love or real feeling.

But they mostly fed me soup and brushed my fur. I traveled to the human underworld—they still knew how to get there in those days. I made friends there. Daring battles. Near escapes. A wedding. A peculiar wedding, but a wedding just the same. Do you know what a wedding is? It's a change. Two natures meet and make something new. That the real magic, you know. Change. That's all magic has ever been. Nothing so frightening as I thought when the mushroom came for me. Hades really isn't a bit like the storybooks say. Wears a lot of black scarves and he's rather grouchy, but no more than your Bonk.

And I was careless. I didn't listen. I ate something I shouldn't have. Never did I imagine six little seeds would cause such a fuss! But then, I didn't know the plan. I didn't know the trick. So I changed. Just like you.

Osmo interrupted. "Stop! Just stop. You keep saying I didn't listen. But I did! I've listened to everything everyone has told me, even when it's made no sense at all. Somebody made a mistake. I shouldn't have changed. You ate something that didn't agree with you—fine. But I did what I was told."

"You haven't, though. Mumpsimus told you back in Quiddity. Don't wear the clothes of the dead."

"But I haven't!" Osmo yelped like a cat. He stopped his flurry of strategy and stared at her, wounded. "I swear! I turned down all kinds of fluffy robes and shower caps. I followed instructions. To the letter!"

"If you hadn't, you'd still look like a boy and not a mountain of fur and flowers." Kalevala lifted her arm and tapped the cuff of her sleeve knowingly.

Right where Button clung to Osmo's new pelt. Button hid away cheekily.

"Did you *know*?" he yelled.

Half a mischievous turn clockwise.

*Maybe.*

"That's not *fair*. That's not fair! Buttons aren't clothes!"

"Aren't they? Where else do you find them? Are laces not clothes? Belts? Don't take it too hard, son. Quidnunx always cheat a *little*. And anyway, it had to be done. Shoosh. I'm not finished. And it's your turn. Your laundress is in trouble."

Osmo moved his laundress and her salmon backward quickly. Kalevala began again.

I went back to Littlebridge. That's the bargain. They lost one, so they gained one. It had to stay balanced, or one side would sooner or later win on numbers alone. The living cannot stay with the dead forever. Hades is a very understanding sort. My hair was just brown. Not striped or spotted. My forehead was just skin. No antlers or horns. I was short and small and my voice only did one thing at a time. But time does what it will do. A family adopted me. They'd never had children of their own. They were so happy. They hugged me every day. I liked that a great deal. Quidnunx are famous for our affection, if you earn it.

I got less short. I walked by my father's silver bones in the square that bore his name every day. And after a few years, I stopped looking up. People forgot where I came from. I had just . . . always been there. I met Mr. Brownbread. I had children and I made flour from wheat and bread from flour and gold from bread. But you see, I was still a Quidnunk. I grew up, but once I was grown, I never got any older. Quidnunx live so long. You can barely see the moss grow. Someone would notice, sooner or later. Mr. Brownbread, if no one else.

So one day, when my children were grown, I went home. The wonderful thing about a fur coat is that you can take it off and put it back on. I took it out of its drawer and disappeared into it and I became myself again. I practically flew to Quiddity. Only for fifty years or so, until people forgot again. Humans are so good at forgetting. Well, the truth of it is I let myself get too tame. It's always there, the temptation. Just as you are tempted to be wild. I couldn't leave them. My family. So I went back . . . much later. Ever so much later. When I had a bit of silver in my hair and a rounder belly.

Everything had changed, but nothing had. I bought my husband's mill, for the Forest hills are full of gold and gems if you care to look. I ran it well. I looked after my grandbabies and my great-grandbabies. I even had another child of my own. And maybe they were strange and shaggy and did the Thumpus all night, or we had to keep them in knit caps to hide their little half-horns. But what child doesn't have challenges?

Every once in a while I would disappear again for a century or two, then pop back in and see how everyone was getting along. Marry again. Buy the mill again. Kept it all tidy as roses. I lived in both worlds. I was both worlds. Two natures. Humans have them too, you know. It's only that they don't show on the outside. Trapped inside their humanity lives a crow's cleverness or an otter's curiosity or a peacock's beauty or a panther's cunning or a crocodile's cold heart or a pangolin's joy in loneliness.

And it's more of them than you'd think.

And so do Quidnunx. I didn't understand that. Not until I lived both ways so long I could see the bigger story. The Quidnunx seem to have many natures, more than anyone, but in truth they have only two: the wild and the mild. And they need both to thrive. Everybody does, kitten.

I saw many young people uphold the treaty, marry ghosts, and go off into the borderlands they feared. I saw the grand plan trip and smack its face into the mud. It's just so hard to keep what you've won, even if it took everything to do the winning. Everyday life takes up so much strength, so much time, so much heart. I watched folk who had fought their way through another world get so wrapped up in making the butter and the bread and buying the knife to slice them that they forgot what color a sentence can be. I saw everyone else so quickly forget that the new humans and new Quidnunx had ever been new. Most of them had eaten well more than six seeds and couldn't go back and forth like I did. Their minds and their bodies just sank back into agreement again.

But my mind stayed the size of a Quidnunk mind. I took note of all the human children whose parents had once been new in town. I watched them. And their hearts were red leaves and golden sap and they saw down into the bones of things and they made wonders out of nothing at all. They were wild, like us.

But the Quidnunk became fewer and fewer all the time. Hardly anyone crossed. Sometimes you keep fighting the same fight over again. Retreating over and over until there's nothing left of you. And sometimes you just give up. The Quidnunx are giving up. Retreating deeper and deeper into the Forest. Into safety. Into legend, which is the safest place of all. There are other places than Littlebridge. Some of them grow faster yet. And few of them have treaties at all.

Except one big, dumb, brave, sentimental, brilliant, silly Nunk whose heart got so tame she just had to go home one last time to peep at the First Frost Festival and all new children running in circles around a fountain with her own face carved on it.

Osmo was so transfixed he didn't notice Kalevala closing in. She swept his laundress off the board and closed a Quidnunk's Roar around his poor pieces with a yawp of triumph. Osmo howled in frustration.

The game began all over again.

And so did the story.

It was much, much shorter. Or much longer, depending on how you counted the words.

Once upon a time, oh, so long ago, a girl named Katja Kvass was born in Littlebridge and nothing interesting had ever happened to her there. The very last treaty child. Until you.

She was born, quite poor indeed, in a little green one-room hut on the south side of the Catch-a-Crown River, outside the furthest edge of town. She thought she would most likely die an old lady with a white shawl, quite poor indeed, in a little one-room hut on the south side of the Catch-a-Crown River.

She was quite, quite wrong about that.

You already know her story. It is written on the walls of her heart.

The sweet sugar world of her childhood, a gentle place where everything had meaning and nothing hurt.

A festival full of games in the dark, when she was crowned Frostfrau.

Her grief when her mother killed a Quidnunk on a grand hunt and she was chosen. The Widows' Weeds her mother wore when she had gone.

The journey under the world, through frightening waters and knowing creatures, toward a story she could not know how to finish.

The long and happy time she spent in Quiddity as sweet as steam. Her new name. Her endless reign. Her children and her family, her great deeds and small, everything she could want at hand, wild and dancing and untroubled and totally satisfied.

And the last—a fight with an outsider she could not imagine losing until she did. Your mother. Poor Tilly. Who had no idea that she'd stumbled upon little lost Katja Kvass peeking at the festival hundreds of years after she'd left her home.

*You have walked in her life. She hoped it would make it easier on you. She knows more than anyone how frightening and confusing it all feels. She thought if you knew her, by the time you found her, you would understand the riddle of the courtship. Bird, deer, fish. And you could be happy.*

*Melancholy does want you to be happy.*

Pieces zoomed up and down the board. Osmo's mind leapt and bounded, hunting his moves, hunting her pieces, faster and more complicated than he'd ever been able to play before.

"Queen Melancholy. Is. Katja Kvass," he said as he closed in on a difficult move called Double Defrocking that could take down both bishops at once. He'd *never* been able to pull one off against Mrs. Brownbread. "I don't believe it."

"Quidnunx are tricksy, but we rarely tell flat-out lies. Stories are strange beasts. They love company. They tend to connect, one to another. And that's called history."

"If she wants me to be happy, why have you chased me all the way through two worlds? Scared me half to death? Made me think I was done for?"

Kalevala looked up at him under heavy eyelids. Her eyebrows seemed hairier than they had been a moment before. But then, he'd had his shadow bishop a moment before. "I did that, yes," she said carefully. "So that you'd know what it was like to be hunted. So *we* could know that you weren't like the other humans. That you wouldn't hurt us. That you wouldn't just take from us and leave us with nothing. So that you could choose."

Osmo laughed bitterly. The laugh of a much older person. "What choice have I ever had in any of this?"

"Lovenunk, it was always your choice. You can always choose. Choosing is the second-wildest thing there is. You could always have just . . . stopped. Stop playing the game. Stop moving from place to place. Stop that terrible human habit of doing things all the time. But you never did, not for a second."

But he did stop. Right then. Osmo Unknown froze. He looked down at the board.

He'd won.

Somehow, he'd won. Her quidking was trapped.

"Check your mate," he rumbled deep in his inhuman, Quidnunk chest. "And check your fate."

Osmo was staring so intensely at the winning board that Brownbread just laughed. An easy, untroubled laugh like stones rolling down a great hill.

"Check yours," she boomed. She didn't even glance at the pieces. "I've got you."

She'd trapped his quidking, too. You could never do it in regular chess. But doublechess is a Quidnunk game. Neither could attack without making themselves vulnerable. Neither could win without losing. What did that mean? He'd technically both lost and won. Would he and Bonk and Never be trapped here forever? He couldn't let that happen. Not because of the treaty. Not because of what might happen to Littlebridge if he failed. Or that he'd never be king of anybody. Not even because he could be trapped too. Osmo couldn't let anything happen to *them.* Because they were his pod. His stench. His mob. His collective noun.

His family.

"I still have my shadow turn," whispered Osmo Unknown. "You smashed my quidrook on your go. But mine is still in play."

A cool blue light began to tint the sky outside the window of the heart-mill. Osmo reached out for his queen's companion piece. Mustamakkara's red box.

*Open it if you are lost. If you cannot see the path for the pebbles. Only in your wildest need. If you are well and truly stuck and cannot get free.*

He had no idea what would happen. Best to just do it. He would never be more lost in all his life than this. He, Osmo, who a week ago had never been lost once.

He ran a claw down the seam of the box and popped it open.

Inside was a flat, polished oval stone. It had long black and white stripes like a zebra's skin, but quite faded with time. For it was ancient, worn smooth by countless centuries, almost as thin as the last scrap of a bar of soap the whole family has used all the summer long.

Osmo Unknown lifted it out. He moved his fingers like he was dreaming. He knew what he was going to do. He'd carried Mustamakkara's feelings all this way. She wouldn't have told him he *could* open it if she didn't mean him *to* open it, would she? That wasn't sensical. And anyway, it was the only companion piece he had left. The only man left standing after the battle, and it was his most special piece. That had to mean something. If it had been the laundress's salmon or the hedgeknight or the rookswhale, Osmo would have been forced to make a normal move. And almost certainly get nabbed on the next turn. The piece was too far from the action for much beyond stalling. But it wasn't any hedgeknight.

It was something new.

What did you do with an opponent you just couldn't beat? Perhaps you broke bread with them. Perhaps you tried something new.

Osmo could hardly breathe, but it felt right, and it seemed right, and he was definitely going to do it anyway, no matter what the logical side of his brain said. That side spoke with his father's voice, and he didn't care what it thought anymore.

He saw the false back in the throat of the throwing game. He saw the fix. He saw the whole sorry rigged world. And he took a step to the left.

Osmo snapped the stone in half.

And the world exploded.

Don't say I didn't warn you.

# THE EXPLOSION AT
# THE END OF THIS BOOK

This chapter does not have a number.

It is not even really a chapter.

It took less than a second to happen. Less than a quarter of a second. But that less-than-a-quarter took place outside of time and space and life and death and up and down and right and wrong and most certainly outside of the rules and boundaries of books.

I promised you that there was an explosion at the end of this book, and here it is.

It erupted out of the stone that Osmo Unknown broke in half, as hot and fast and terrifying as fire. But it was quite invisible. It blazed away from Osmo's trembling hands in a vast, irresistible circle. Everyone felt it. Everyone stopped dead in their tracks or their strides or midflight or midswim, unable to move or even think until the explosion blew through them and moved on. But no one could see what had burned them down to their deepest hearts.

And I do mean everyone.

Everyone in the shadow mill. Everyone in the Party Archipelago. Everyone in the Eightpenny Woods.

Everyone in Quiddity also felt it. Everyone in their burrows and their nests and their caves and their tall rickety houses. Everyone on the Great Arctic Mud. Everyone in all the Fourpenny Woods.

Everyone in Littlebridge, too. Everyone in all the Forest and the Valley, down to the last mayor and the last mushroom.

For less than a quarter of a second, everyone felt what Osmo felt, and this is what it was.

Osmo Unknown felt as though a pair of black wings took him in and hugged him forever.

He felt *everything*.

Everything Mustamakkara, the Great Last Bird, had ever felt. He saw centuries of people crossing the River After, dancing across, laughing, crying, raging, pleading. He felt everything a being could feel at the end of their time and the beginning of a new world. He felt the love the enormous ancient bird had felt for all of them, and the sorrow when the Quidnunx began to come more and more and others less and less. All the secrets and passions and mercy of a million lives. A million natures. Ever so much more than two.

But that was only the beginning of it. The broad strokes that hinted at the shape of what was happening. It was a stone, after all, and stones are impossibly ancient, even the littlest pebbles. Stones were made in fire when the world began. They only look dull and boring so no one will ask them to tattle on history. They've rolled under glaciers and over mountains, from one end of the planet to the other, and touched everything in between. Mustamakkara had known the hearts of the dead, but the stone had known the living since the dawn of dawns.

A wave of memory came crashing through his whole being.

Osmo Unknown felt Mrs. Brownbread's whole life. Her fierceness and her fear. Her joy and absolute love at the birth of her children and the founding of the mill and her bone-shattering sorrow when she had to leave them. He felt it down to the prickling of the hairs on her arms at the coming of winter.

*He felt it as though it were happening to him.* All at once, all right now, as though he were living her life. As though he *were* Mrs. Brownbread.

But not only Mrs. Brownbread.

He felt Never's pride and solitude. He felt what it was like to be completely happy alone, to need nothing and no one else. And he felt the terror of slowly becoming attached to others, and how easily they could be lost, leaving a loneliness that would give no warmth or comfort, only cold loss. He felt what it was like to be praised for the first time, and to do something brave you never thought you could.

Osmo felt the essential crossness of Bonk the Cross. He felt the freeze of being left outside his mother's pouch. The rejection of his siblings. The burning desire to avoid that freeze coming back to take him forever. He knew suddenly that all those insults were really just dares, daring Osmo to not like him, to reject him too, to get it over with and refuse him like everyone else. He felt how much Bonk did like him after all, and always had, so much that it was far better to push Osmo away than risk it all happening to Bonk as it had when he was a baby, leaving him shivering with no one.

And he felt Mumpsimus, her grief and rage. He felt Walter the froose's great age and wisdom and silliness. He felt the trees of the Fourpenny Woods. Osmo felt everyone. Living and dead. He felt their every feeling, good and bad.

He felt his mother, how much she longed for more in her life, just as her son did. Yet she never got it, and Osmo had never known.

He felt his father, struggling, longing, always angry. He felt his father's childhood, his grandfather telling him to be a man and punishing poor Mads every time he let himself be soft or small or curious, until he forgot how to be those things at all. He felt his sister Oona, too, all his sisters, but especially Oona, stroking the velvet of her remaining blue ribbon, praying every night that Osmo was somewhere safe but never knowing.

And Osmo felt Ivy Aptrick's satin soul, stuck in her father's rich house, with no choices at all in front of her. He was a stranger, only wanting something of her for himself, like everyone else. She hadn't ever meant to be cruel. Everyone had decided her life before she started school, and no one once asked what she wanted. Her parents had practically married her already to the Mayor's son, who she hated with all her heart. She had nothing at all to look forward to except more choices she wouldn't be allowed to make. He understood her, completely, in a flash. She hadn't said yes to him, he was just a stranger. She was just being polite, as everyone had always forced her to be. Ivy's life was full of its own hard, sharp edges. She deserved love she didn't get, freedom she couldn't find, and her favorite color was yellow.

Osmo felt Mayor Lud's father screaming about how stupid he was until he cried. He felt the Mayor doing that to Barnaby, too, when his time came to have a little boy. And he felt Adelard Sloe's excitement as he designed the Stupendous Throwing Game and painted the false mouth on the Quidnunk board himself.

He even felt old Jerome Unknown, longing for Somewhere *Else*, leaving his life for a distant valley without a name, a place where he could find some wilder life than the one he had. A legacy for Osmo, after all.

And under and through and beneath and over and around it all, Osmo felt Quidnunx hearts beating in the world. He felt the Quidnunx in their cities and villages when life was better, their love of the moon, of squirrels, of tricks and games. He felt their big, thundering feelings and their long, secret lives. He understood what they were. It was so obvious. It had been in front of him all this time. What the Forest had done when it was young and in love.

Everything had two natures in the Fourpenny Woods. Two at *least*. And not just the Quidnunx. Osmo could see so clearly now. So clearly it made him ache. Two natures everywhere. The wild and the mild. Littlebridge and the Fourpenny Woods.

The Forest and the Valley.

No, that wasn't it. That wasn't quite right. They were more like Bonk the Cross now. Three natures. The Forest and the Valley and the fight between them. He could feel them both as though he *were* a Forest with a beast for a soul. As though he were a sweet, rich Valley with a village for a heart. Osmo Unknown could feel the love they'd once shared like a picnic. He could feel the acid wince of their betrayal. That the Forest made monsters. That the Valley brought strangers. That the Valley could have forgiven the monsters if they were not quite so monstrous. That the Forest could have forgiven the strangers if they were not quite so strange. He felt them harden against each other like the first frost of the year. And he felt the hardening turn to frozen fury. Oh, but it was so much worse than fury, really! Fury burns bright and burns out. This just went on and on and on. Forests and valleys live millions of years. They don't ever have to let go of a grudge if they don't want to.

Osmo stretched further, trying to understand. It was much harder than understanding Ivy or Mayor Lud. It was like trying to understand what mud is saying about the rain.

Osmo gasped. There it was. Crushing his heart like a planet. The truth. It almost buckled his knees. The Forest and the Valley, whispering the same little prayer down deep in the core of them.

*If I can only make the Quidnunx leave, everything will go back to the way it was when we were happy.*

*If I can only make the humans leave, everything will go back to the way it was when we were new.*

Osmo felt it all happen, the whole sad history of everything. The Forest pushed its favorite babies toward the borders, to hunt and stalk and feast. To frighten and fight. The Valley pushed its beloved children to the edge of the woods, to hunt and stalk and feast. To take and use and give nothing back. Both hoping every hunt would be the last, and the intruders would finally just give up and abandon this place, and everything could go back, everything could be as it was when a certain peculiar Forest fell in love with a deep, craggy Valley in the beginning of the world.

And through it all, Katja and Mrs. Brownbread and Osmo and others like them, bridging the worlds, holding it all together with a terrible, frightful treaty they had because the Forest and the Valley couldn't stop fighting, and their children just wanted a little scrap of peace. Children, all of them, just trying to live in the house their parents built.

Osmo tried to cry. Nothing came but sap and hay. He felt his arms turning to trees and his head turning to a great blue stone. The Forest and the Valley were so *BIG*. Ever so much bigger than him. He was very suddenly afraid he could never get out of the country of their feelings, that he'd be overwhelmed and never be Osmo again. It was too much for one small human only just thirteen.

Osmo Unknown felt it all. Everything. Everyone. It was all one great storm of feeling, pouring through his heart like rain.

And everyone else in the Forest and the Valley felt it too.

So did the Forest and the Valley themselves.

For less than a quarter of a second, every single person and creature knew what it was like to live in this world as every other person and creature. Osmo snapped that stone in half and blew down the doors that separate every mind from every other, and that whole little kingdom burst into heavy, warm tears, falling to their knees with the weight of it.

And the very last thing they all saw, and felt, and knew, and heard and touched and smelled, was a tall black bird, half a shoebill stork and half a raven, walking down a lonely grey beach long before civilization and history had ever got the bright idea of starting. The bird looked down at the pebbly shore and saw a small, black-and-white-striped stone shaped like an oval. She thought it seemed as good a stone as any other to help with her digestion, for birds have no teeth, and gobble up rocks from time to time to crush everything they eat into pieces small enough to manage.

The Forest and the Valley and all their children felt the stone slip down their feathery throats as though they were all the Great Last Bird. They felt the Thing settle in their stomachs, a plain beach rock that was, all unknown to anybody, the only magical thing in the universe.

Then, as quickly as the explosion had done its work, it was over. Everyone was only themselves again. And no different than any bomb that has ever gone off anywhere, when it seemed to be safe, they all blinked in the sun and looked around at the rubble with no idea how to clean it up or what to do now.

When Osmo Unknown opened his eyes again, all he saw was darkness. He couldn't hear anything, either. He hadn't the first idea where he was.

"It's okay," said a familiar voice. "Don't be afraid. I just . . .

I couldn't bear it. All the sadness. So much sadness. Like a wave. Like a mountain. But it's okay. I protected us. I'm keeping us safe. I understand why people want to do that for each other now."

Osmo looked around for Nevermore. It was her voice, but he couldn't see her. He could smell her. Pine and copper and earthworm cake and worry. So familiar and dear.

"Oof," Bonk grunted. "Not a lot of kicking room in here. Scoot over."

They were inside Never's ball. She'd grabbed them and scooped them into the curve of her belly and her spine as she rolled into her armored shell and brought them safe within a shield of her whole self.

"You were trapped in Kala's mushroom!" Osmo exclaimed. "You couldn't even move! I was rescuing you!"

"Oh, don't be such a human. I was talking to the mushroom the whole time. It's a very nice girl. Her name is Cristine. She let us out as soon as she realized I was Clarence and Frederick's friend. Well. *They* said friend. I don't care for that word. It's not nice."

"You still got your bones on the inside, motter?" Bonk asked with a little shiver in his voice. "Not sure I do. Not sure at all."

"Do you think it'll fade?" Never whispered. "Do you think we'll forget? It was the greatest mess I've ever known. I don't want to leave it. But I don't want to stay."

"I'm not going to stop calling you names, is that clear?" Bonk said hurriedly. "Magic, schmagic." The furry little fellow fell quiet. After a moment, he added: "I don't want to forget. I don't want it to fade." His voice sounded quite strangled. "You're a nice boy, Osmo," Bonk squeaked. "You too, Never."

"I'm a—"

"Shhh," whispered the skadgebat lovingly. "You all look the same to me."

What could Osmo say? Would this change anything? Would it outlast the sunrise? He didn't know. He didn't even know what would happen when the armor fell away and he had to deal with the world again. It seemed too much to imagine. He only wanted to sleep.

"It's nice in here," Bonk mumbled in the shadows of the pangirlin. "Not so different than a pouch. Only . . . er. This time I'm kicked *in*, not *out*."

Osmo squeezed his friend's paw.

Never squeezed his hand.

And when she unfurled her coppery scales to let them all out into the story again, they found they were not alone. They were not in the mill. They were not in darkness. They stood in a green orchard surrounded by a great many people drenched in sunshine.

# A Brief and Late Intermission

**G**oodness, it *has* been a moment since we spoke!

Of course, technically, I have been speaking to you this whole time. But telling a story is not quite the same as talking face to face, and I shouldn't like you to forget about me and get a nasty shock at the end of the story.

And we *are* almost at the end, now. Everything will make sense soon.

Some people would very much like to tell you that in real life, endings are nothing like this. Nothing makes sense and foreshadowing never pays off, loose threads aren't woven back in, the rifle on the mantel just stays on the mantel with a silly look on its trigger, and nothing is ever as elegant or tidy as it is in a story.

But I am here to tell you, since we have come to trust and rely upon each other, since we have quite specifically and actually been to the end of the world and (almost) back together: that's a load of rubbish.

How dare they speak so unkindly of stories?

Stories never did anything to them! Stories are only here to love you and look after you and show you a good time. (They certainly never do anything so rash and ill-considered as *mean* anything significant that you might remember for a long time after, and notice the ways in which they explain bits and pieces of your own life and the world around you. Heavens no!) Stories don't even ask anything in return but not to have grape juice spilled on them, and, every once in a while, to be thought of fondly, years and years after you shut their covers.

Those people who think life doesn't have endings like story-books are telling you *fibs*, my darlings, and I won't stand for it.

No.

In real life, there are no endings at all.

# THE WILDEST THING THERE IS

Nevermore's vast tail uncurled uncertainly around them. Everything had changed. The stone doublechess table and comfortable chairs pressed down into wet, warm Forest dirt. Clouds cast shadows over the defeated pieces. Above towered a great tangled ball of roots, wedged into the crook of a narrow little ravine crammed full of big blue stones. So great and so tangled, so big and so crammed, you could hardly see the beginning or end of it.

The Gnarlbind.

"Hi," said Katja Kvass.

An awkward cough echoed far too loudly through the rocks and trees.

Osmo finally shook his shaggy head. He blinked in the sudden light.

Bonk the Cross and Nevermore the pangirlin stood before the Gnarlbind. They looked quite spiffed up since the last time he'd seen them. Never's scales glowed with spit and polish. Bonk's fur was brushed clean, even curled a bit. Between them rose the grand mountain that was the late, great queen of the Quidnunx.

OSMO UNKNOWN AND

Melancholy winked at Osmo with one yellow-green eye. She had gorgeous glossy fur and shining antlers wrapped in roses.

Queen Melancholy wasn't just waiting for Osmo by herself. They were all there. Beastly and Away and Seldom the polx and Mrs. Brownbread stood as her wedding party. Everyone they'd met. Even hangdog Dapplegrim stood up like a best man. His eyes looked so different now. No longer feral with pain and mud and memory. The Gnarlbind loomed over all of them.

It was just so horribly *awkward*, having lived everybody else's life in half a heartbeat. No one knew what to say next.

Through the cracks and crevices between the roots of the Gnarlbind, they could see all the way back to Quiddity. Osmo stretched out his mossy paw toward the lattice of wood that separated life and death.

Finally, Mrs. Brownbread broke the tense silence. "Are you ready?"

"Ready for what?" Osmo said nervously. "Did I do it? Did I win? Are we . . . okay?"

"For the wedding, dingus." Bonk rolled his eyes. "Muddy *well*, you are slow sometimes."

"I can look more human, if you want," Queen Melancholy offered. "If it makes it easier."

"No, that's all right," Osmo said sheepishly. "I . . . I forgot about the wedding. In the . . . in the everything. It seems so small and silly now."

"Less silly than ever. Maybe," Mrs. Brownbread murmured. She tottered a bit on her feet. They all looked as though a puff of dandelion seeds could knock them down. All those lives, still bubbling through them and sloshing over the edges of their eyeballs.

They could all have done with a nap and a good lunch spread. But it wasn't likely to happen for them.

"Okay. Well. If that's how this ends, that's how it ends. I suppose? I'm not sure. But I am sure that I'm sorry," Osmo said, scrambling to get his mind solidly back in charge of his mouth.

"Sorry for what, sweatervest?" Bonk the Cross asked in his rough, half-friendly voice. Osmo saw him wringing his lovely tail brutally in both paws. Everyone was so upset, but no one wanted to be the first to show it! It was like they were all up on the stage at St. Whylom's School doing the summer play, and had all clearly heard a terrible crash and a scream from the Headmaster backstage, but had to go on with their lines like nothing had gone toes-up.

"Well, um. I'm here. It's over, I guess. And I didn't get all your gifts," Osmo said ruefully. "The Rope That Cannot Be Untied, the Gown That Cannot Be Removed, the Treasure That Cannot Be Taken. I failed."

"We are very sneaky, we Quidnunx." The Quidnunk queen smiled toothily at him. It was more than a bit terrifying. "We never ask for anything that is not also somehow a trick. Honestly, that would have been *some* trick." She waved her claws in the air. "They were never my gifts. No true beast would send you on a quest to win a lady like a prize at Adelard Sloe's game. They were always my gifts to you. Your ring. Your music to walk you down the aisle. Your gown."

"My gown? But I . . . I didn't get it."

Melancholy laughed, a big boulder-rolling boom of a laugh. "You're wearing it, my dear. Your antlers, your pelt, your tusks, your hooves! The Gown That Cannot Be Removed. And you, Osmo, you are the Treasure That Cannot Be Taken. Only given. You will have to learn to think in these sorts of riddles, if you mean to make a go of it back in Quiddity. I am ready for the last courtship, Mr. Unknown."

Osmo furrowed his furry brow. "What last courtship?"

Melancholy held out her shaggy arm. Two batterflies alighted on it, cawing like mad.

"We told you," Unlike bawked.

"First as a bird, then as a deer," Until crowed.

Melancholy sat down in the meadowy grass. "And last as a fish. A bird courts by making himself beautiful and collecting shiny objects. You've done that. A deer courts by battle, bashing heads together with a strong opponent. You did that in my heart, just now, with Mrs. Brownbread. Only you cracked wits instead of skulls."

"How does a fish court?" Osmo asked.

Queen Melancholy's face grew warm and wide and loving. She rose and put both paws on his shoulders. "A fish goes *home*. To the place where they were born."

"What? What do you mean? I choose. It's all right. I understand now. I lived it, after all. All of it. No one to push me or trick me anymore. I'll stay. I'll marry you and save everybody and keep the balance. One of us for one of you. I won't forget like the others.

I'll remember. I'll do what the treaty was supposed to do all along. I played and I won and I made it through everything and I can finish this. I choose."

The Quidnunk queen shook her mane and a hundred birds flew out, then settled again anywhere they could. "Do you know what a marriage is? I will tell you. It is a change of world. It is a Forest and a Valley making a new universe between them. You had to come all this way to wed—but not you to me. The village to the wood. As it was meant to be. Marriage is a gown that cannot be removed. It is a rope that cannot be untied. It is a treasure that cannot be taken. It is a zither that cannot be played—because it must be played by two. And it is a ring that fits no hand. Because it fits only the heart. And the paw."

Osmo looked down. The Forest's green willow-whip ring circled his wrist like a bracelet.

"You may stay as long as you like, Osmo. But not here. Not in the Eightpenny Woods. It is not a place for the living. You can court me by leaving. And living. Live in Quiddity, or anywhere else in the Fourpenny Woods. Live a life. Raise wonders and children. Know it all. Be happy. Keep the Forest and the Valley connected a little while longer, balance the wild and the mild. And then, when the time is right, go home." She reached down to the cuff of his sleeve. "After all, it's only a button. It barely counts. Like Kalevala's silly seeds. You may come and go, as Mrs. Brownbread does. Two natures. Two worlds. As we all have. Look how much it has taken just to show yours on the outside!"

"Do you understand our names, now, Osmo?" Until croaked.

"We gave you a lot of time to think," Unlike cawed.

But Osmo didn't. He wanted to, but he didn't.

"Their names are Time and Change," Melancholy said. "That's what they mean. You are *Unlike* what you were before. And *Until* the Forest ends, you may take tea with the moon and the Quidnunx, as wild as any of us."

The queen tried to keep up her warm, comforting, inviting smile. But she faltered. Her face fell. She shook her head like a bull trying to shoo a fly off her horns. Something was wrong.

"Wait," the ghost of the Quidnunk whispered. "Wait."

"Wait for what?" Unlike hissed. "We practiced all this. Just get on with it."

"You're doing fine, Melly," Until crowed. "Your speech was perfect."

"Yes," the queen mumbled, her hot golden eyes faraway. "It was just the speech the old Quidnunk gave to me when I came all this way to marry him so long ago. I was careful to memorize it exactly. It sounded nice. It sounded right. It sounded the way it always does."

"Then what's the problem?" Beastly grumbled, clacking her crabby claws.

Osmo and Melancholy stood very still in the beating heart of the Forest, watching one another. The memory of the stone and the magic still crackled around them like fireflies. Osmo wasn't smiling, either. He looked from the queen to the doublechess pieces, in the usual end game disarray. Lying on their sides, tossed this way and that as they'd fallen or lined up outside the field of play waiting to return.

"The problem is us," Melancholy growled. "Everything's different now. How can *this* stay the same? How can we just . . . have another wedding and another journey home and another . . ." Her feline eyes wriggled with tears. "Another sweet face on a memorial fountain?"

No one answered her. No one could. It was different now. They all felt it. Would it stay different? Was it different enough?

"Well, say something," Bonk gruffed. "I'm not built for awkwardness this thick."

Never picked at her claws delicately. "Osmo," she whispered. He looked up at her, confused and exhausted. "Osmo, you're in your ball. Just like mine. Only mine is scaley and hard and unpierceable. It's all too much, so you went into a ball. It's okay. It's okay to come out. Loneliness is for pangolins, not people."

She was right. Osmo tried to unfurl himself in his head the way Never did in real life. He lifted one paw shakily and ran it along his shiny new antlers. "Sorry," he said. "It's just . . . the queen . . . my wife, I suppose. She's talking about the whole world changing. We all know that, don't we?"

Beastly and Seldom and Away and Bonk and Never and all the others nodded slowly. "What if nothing was ever the same again? It's so scary. It's the scariest thing I've ever even *thought* about, I kind of panicked. And then Never said I was a ball like her, and it made me think of *my* ball. My golden ball."

"What?" Unlike cawed.

"Come again?" Mrs. Brownbread rumbled.

"What about your ball, Osmo?" Queen Melancholy coaxed.

"It's not real gold, see," Osmo said, rubbing his nose with the back of his furry knuckles. "I always knew that. Old Sloe might've run a tight game, but there was always a chance someone would beat him. And he's far too cheap to risk a real treasure. If you cracked it open, it'd only be a wad of horsehair or goat hair in a clay container." Osmo laughed hoarsely. "Two natures, right? Wild animal hair painted to look so pretty folks would play his game a million times to get it. A game they *know* is rigged. A game they're certain was designed not to be won. I've loved it all my life, but it's a fake prize. A cheat. And so is this."

"But it wasn't us cheating," protested Away the gladfish, his golden-orange veils fluttering. "We did everything we were supposed to! We all followed the treaty!"

"The best tricks are the ones where no one ever knows they got swindled," came a deep ape-y voice from the shadows of the big blue stones crowding in the Gnarlbind. The Dark, who is never far.

"All that, everything that's happened, all the death and tears and running and riddles and darkness and fear, just terrible, sour fear, all for what?" Never asked, wringing her hands. "So everything can go on as it always has?"

"Only now I'm stuck between Littlebridge and Quiddity instead of between where I wanted to be and where I was? Stuck is stuck!" Osmo added. "Mrs. Brownbread said I could choose, but that was a trick, too. Every choice only ever looked like one on the outside. Inside it was just fur and lies."

"It's not us," Bonk the Cross said angrily. "It's *Them*." He jerked his thumb over his shoulder at the blue stones and the Gnarlbind.

"Mum and Dad. Or Mum and Mum. Or Dad and Dad. Or whatever they are, I get confused. The Forest and the Valley. We all know what they've been on about so long now. Pair of *rumps*, if you ask me. They needed us to get here, to this place and this time. They need Osmo to accept this fate, to finish the story like he's supposed to, like we're supposed to, so the Forest and the Valley can keep playing this *rubbish* game with each other."

Nevermore's eyes grew wide. "And what happens years and years from now? The treaty still holds and another poor creature gets killed? Another child has to go through all of this again? Has to be so afraid, has to hurt so badly, has to face the dark and the sharks and the truth about everything? Has to feel so"—tears toppled over her cheeks—"so *alone?*"

"Never." Osmo stopped dead in the tracks of his thoughts. A pangirlin weeping over someone else's loneliness cut straight through every single other thing in his head. "Are you all right?"

"Sorry!" she yelped, wiping her eyes under her fogged-up spectacles. "Sorry. I didn't mean it. Some of the . . . I don't know. The magic. The stone. The . . . the feeling. It's still all over me. Like jam after lunch. I can't help it. Shut up."

"This world is not in love with letting folk choose their lots," Melancholy said quietly. "I thought it was all to a purpose before. But now . . . this is all wrong. It's all wrong, Osmo. It's *Their* story. Their fight. Not ours."

"Yes, a purpose. So I would understand. That's what Mrs. Brownbread said. What Kala said." It felt wrong to call her Mrs. when he'd lived her whole life in a heartbeat. "Well, I do understand, and I hate it! Why can't everyone choose to just not be so *terrible* to each other all the time? Why did we have to go through all that just to really understand somebody else? Because that part is true, I never would've cared as much about Quidnunx as about people who are like me otherwise. But why should it be like that? The seal of Littlebridge says *Nemo Nanciunt Desiderium*. No one gets what they want. But why should it be so? Why is the world such a huge pot of garbage? Why are we stuck like this, teeth bared, furious, trying to come out on top?" He picked up a carved rookswhale and chucked it on the ground in frustration. "I didn't win *anything*. Everyone on both sides is still sad and afraid *all the time* and us being married won't change it. I thought, just for one stupid, boneheaded second, that I was actually *playing*. A player. In control. I said it just a moment ago, like the fool Bonk always calls me. But I was just a piece."

"We all are," Mrs. Brownbread sighed unhappily. They all felt very much like someone who has spent all day swimming hard, and can still feel the water sloshing against them long after they're dry. The stone still sloshed, but it was already getting softer. "We've just been moving along in the pattern set out for us hundreds of years ago by people we never met. Playing out a story about hurting and getting hurt because *They* can't get over it. Think about it: the Forest and the Valley didn't make that treaty. That was all us. Doing the same thing *They* do to each other because that's who taught us how to play with others. But not *us* us. Ancestors. Ghosts. Ghosts we're still married to even though we can't see so much as their shadows on the ground. We're no better than pieces on squares, in a game the past plays with the future."

Osmo stood up and bellowed at the board. "The Forest and the Valley have got us all stuck on hurt like a thorn and we can't get loose of it. Each trying to get rid of the stepchildren like the worst fairy tale ever." Osmo looked deep into the twists and spirals of the Gnarlbind. "I thought this was an adventure. But it was just as rigged as Littlebridge ever was. At the end, nothing's really changed. And we're just supposed to accept it, recite some speeches, and keep on hurting and getting hurt."

"I don't accept nothing," Bonk barked. "I bite. I don't accept."

"Me neither," said Nevermore.

"Not anymore," trilled Queen Melancholy.

"Yeah." Osmo nodded. "Yeah. If we accepted that, we truly would be tame."

"Tame?" said the great white polx called Seldom, finally grown bigger than her own hurt. "Ew."

Osmo Unknown laughed. He didn't know where this came from, except that wherever it was, it was certainly on his Quidnunk side. He remembered Bonk's battle, how he'd followed the rules more exactly than the crabbybara, and won by surprise. Osmo felt giddy, light-headed. He was going to do something absolutely incredible or absolutely stupid. It could go either way. But he could see it, slantwise, like the false back of an old wooden Quidnunk's mouth. "What if we just . . . didn't?"

"Er," Queen Melancholy interrupted. "But we already have. We're already married. You're wearing the Valley's ring. We said some pretty words in a pretty place. It's done."

"Fine." Nevermore lifted her chin determinedly. "Then Osmo

is the last. Nothing like this has ever happened before. All that feeling! It has to mean something. It has to change something. It just *has* to. *They* must have felt it all, too. They must know what we know. Maybe nobody else will ever have this chance again."

"Your first act as king." The Dark rippled from the shadows. "A new treaty."

Osmo spread his claws and clacked them together. "Strong jaw, strong spine, strong fists. No blubbering. That's what my father always said. Be a man. I don't know that I've done a spectacular job of it. A man, that kind of man, would be happy to be king and lord it over everyone. But I can't. I can't. You can only lord over people you don't *know*. Not your friends. Not your family. Not anybody you *love*. And now . . . now I know everybody. Just *everybody*. But . . . but the thing of it is, I'm *not* a man." He thumped his chest with his paw. From within it, an answering Thumpus began, deep and echoing. "I'm a crow. I'm a bear. I'm a motter and a pangolin and a badger and a wombat and a hunter and a sad girl who loves yellow and a great black bird at the end of everything. I'm a Quidnunk. And so are you. All of you. All of us. We all matter. Just like I told Kala in the mill." He rubbed tears off his fur. "Ah, it's so confusing and I don't care! I can cry if I want to cry. Crows do. I can laugh if I want to laugh. Hyenas don't care. Every animal makes its great sound. Its Great True Tale. Barking, chirping, howling, meowing, hooting. Weeping is the human song, I think. Mrs. Brownbread told me choosing is the second-wildest thing there is—but feeling is the first! Feeling everything as hard and strong as you can is the wildest thing you can do! It's terrifying! But it's so bright!"

"And feeling someone else's feelings . . . ," Never said softly. "It's still lonely, but it's so much bigger than lonely. It's not hitting five people or one with the trolley but flying it off the tracks into the stars and sparing them all."

Osmo nodded. He understood her. They all did. "Only the very wildest can do it. Only the very wildest can stop playing the rigged game long enough to smash it to bits."

"I wonder if the stone got them, too," Bonk rumbled. "Right between the eyes, like it got us. I wonder if everybody there felt us like we felt them. What if they did? Wouldn't that be . . . well, very sloppy and a lot to clean up . . . but wouldn't it be *wild*? The only magical thing that's ever happened. You gotta stand up on your hind legs and pay attention to that. You just gotta."

Osmo Unknown felt the inside of him swell up as big as the outside. And he did cry. And laugh. And bellow. And purr. And roar. And sing. All of it, as hard and strong as he could.

Queen Melancholy nodded sagely. "And there is the Rope That Cannot Be Untied. Love, and mercy. Tying you to our world and us to you. That's the only true collective noun: *us*."

"I could be an us, I think," Never mumbled with a blush on her scales. "So long as I got weekends off."

"Not just us," said Osmo. "We are the Else. The Else I was always looking for. And that's why I can't be king. I don't want to be *anyone's* king, Especially now. How could I order anyone to do anything when I know their whole and actual heart? Not any one of us deserves to be king over one lousy pebble. At least any more than any other of us."

"This part is up to you, my love," the queen said warmly. "I am dead. All the magic in the world won't change that. The living must sort it out among themselves. But it has been something extraordinary to meet you. And marry you. Kind of."

"Maybe . . . maybe we could take turns," Osmo said. "I could be king on Thursdays—" And then they were all talking together, because a moment ago they'd all been together, one person, one heart, and they all knew what the other was thinking—though it was already fading, already dimmer.

"I could be King Never on Mondays!"

"King Bonk the First! I'd take Fridays, best day, everyone knows it."

"And Mumpsimus Wednesdays and me Saturdays," Mrs. Brownbread added. Bonk the Cross snorted. "Walter could have every third Tuesday but only for the lunch hour!"

"And maybe," Osmo said quietly. "Maybe on a few days, it could be people. Headmaster Gudgeon could take a Sunday every other March. And Oona could have Leap Days, that's only every four years. Not often, not always. Just once in a while. On the first full moon in autumn, my mum could be too."

"And so on and so forth and that way nobody could cause too much sadness or bear too much fault," Queen Melancholy said shyly, though she knew she was not really allowed to weigh in on the business of the living. "And if there is to be a new treaty, everyone will have their paws on it."

"We could all visit each other in the palace for the morning coronation, and again in the evening for abdication," Osmo finished with a hopeful look that seemed almost human.

"Sounds like a *mess*," Nevermore said with an enormous smile.

Mrs. Brownbread seemed suddenly very small and uncertain.

"What happens now?" she asked nervously. "Will the Quidnunx come back? Will everything just go back to the way it was, fighting and vengeance and misunderstandings all over again?"

"Wait," Never piped up. "Just wait. I'm going to do something. Gah, should I? Yes. I should. I'm going to do it. Nobody watch. Okay, well, I guess you can. I can't stop you. But don't."

The pangirlin hopped nimbly up the big blue stones, finding footholds where they touched the loops and snarls of the Gnarlbind's root ball. She got down on her knees on a particularly enormous boulder, covered in thick moss and dirt and leaves. She bent her coppery scaled head down until her nose touched the moss and whispered something none of the others could hear. She whispered for a long time. Whatever she was saying didn't seem to be sinking in.

At last, she sat back on her heels and just said: "Please. Please, Agatha."

A snap and a crack and a screech and the big blue stone split down the side as one solitary Agatha mushroom crowned at Never's feet. Its little golden house and green roof and round windows and purple door waited expectantly. Never brushed her hands off on her trousers. She stuck her fingers in her mouth and whistled. "Button!" the pangirlin yelled.

The burgundy button unspooled thread from its eyes, leapt off Osmo's shaggy arm, and rolled across the green and up the boulder until it got to the Agatha mushroom.

"Do you know what I want?"

*Clockwise.*

"Will you do it?"

Hesitation. Then a slow clockwise turn.

"Do you think it'll work?"

*Counterclockwise.*

"Just try. Agatha will take you back and forth. Carry their messages. From the Forest to the Valley. And the Valley to the Forest. Maybe if they can only say *yes* or *no*, they won't be able to argue for centuries on end. They'll just have to speak plainly. Tell them we're all here together now, so they have to figure out how to love us. All of us." Never sniffled a little in the cool air. "Buttons keep things together, after all."

"The wee thing can't go alone," Beastly piped up. "It'll get eaten by the first owl that sees it sparkling along. I'll go too. I'll help. I'll keep the little fellow safe. After all, total satisfaction is guaranteed."

Never clambered back down the rocks, her cheeks bright. Osmo hugged her, as Away had done all the way back in the Meaningful Desert, as he'd wanted to do but hadn't, because she so clearly hated it.

Nevermore hugged him back with both arms.

But only for a moment. Half a moment. At best.

"I'm still me," she grumbled. "Don't get any ideas."

"I got ideas." Bonk the Cross puffed out his stripey chest. "I've got heaps of ideas. Number one: you should hug me, too, equality is very important in the new order." He wriggled his snout. "But whenever. Take your time. Years, if you need 'em." He cleared his throat. "Nerd."

Osmo shivered. He could hardly see Queen Melancholy now. The Forest shadows seemed to be eating away at the edges of her. Whatever this was, it was almost over. "Will the humans remember? Will everything be good now, at least for a little while?" Osmo dropped his voice to a whisper. "Did we do the right thing?"

"Of course we did," said Nevermore. She pushed her spectacles up on the bridge of her nose. "We won."

Osmo made a frustrated noise in his throat. "We just went over that, it's not about—"

"The prize is just to keep doing things for the group until they're safe," she said tenderly. "Just like you told me. I said you could never get ahead like that. But look at us now. We turned into a cannonball, about to blow through everything."

Osmo blinked with surprise. It had never really occurred to him that anybody was *listening* when he talked. At least, before the stone.

"Well done, Never," he said now.

"Well done, Osmo Unknown," she replied, beaming with pride.

"Well done BONK, you mean!" the skadgebat barked. "You do, don't you?"

Osmo bent down and hugged the stripey creature hard.

The queen reached out for her mate. Osmo took her claws in his. She squeezed his paw. "For the first time in forever, what happens next is a mystery. We shall all have to find out together. Just remember there are always more worlds than the one you know. You could never have guessed what lay just beyond the woods! And then once you did know, you couldn't imagine that even more waited so near! Who knows what places we shall find yet."

Osmo kissed Queen Melancholy's claw in a very courtly fashion.

"I'm ready to go home, Osmo," Never said.

"All right then, turnip?" Bonk growled gruffly.

"I *am* a turnip," said Osmo, and the word didn't bother him at all. "I'll last the whole winter. I hope a lot of winters. And if I am king today, I decree that we should *feast*."

From somewhere far off they could all hear the howls and purrs of a terrible cat, but a very, very good dog.

"Never fear!" Captain Badcat howled up through the starry fingers of the Dark. "I defeated my nap! I am here! Just in time! Haven't missed anything important, have I?"

Button leapt off Osmo's sleeve. It bounced around the Gnarlbind until it found the little instrument tree leaning against a hump in the root knot. Pausing only a moment, the little burgundy button leapt up and plucked the strings with the edge of its rim. Beastly put her lips to one of the long hollow branches and began to blow.

The thumping, beating, singing, loving heart of the Forest filled with music.

And everyone, just everyone, began to dance.

## Chapter Twenty-Eight
# A Fish Goes Home

In the deep winter when cold was king, a knock came at the door of a little white four-room cottage on the north side of the Catch-a-Crown River, almost at the furthest edge of a town called Littlebridge, where hardly anything interesting ever happened.

Tilly Unknown wiped her hands on her trousers and went to the door. She was baking bread, a hot and floury sort of work. Lines of worry and sadness had sprung up at the corners of her eyes over these last weeks, like sneaky little mushrooms after a rain. Her hair had gone white as January that terrible night, the night of the festival, when she lost her only son. Her husband had gone away to the new markets miles away from Littlebridge to sell the famous Unknown's Goodest Stout, promising to return in time for the new year. All her other children had gone out on errands or play or both. Tilly had the house to herself.

She closed her brown hand on the brass doorknob and swung it open.

A young man stood there in the crisp fall air. A few red leaves stuck to his patchwork coat. He was tall and thin, with long clever fingers and bright hazel eyes, the color of old pages and old leaves. He pushed his black shaggy hair out of his eyes.

The young man held out his hand on one side. A girl's fingers slid into his, tipped with long, greenish copper claws. He held out his other hand. A furry black-and-white paw grabbed it. And behind the three guests, a great, huge, long, but very uncertain shadow grew greater and huger and longer and even more uncertain. The shadow had a grand crown of antlers. And gorgeous thick pointy tufts. And it made the richest, warmest *thumping* noise, deep in its belly.

An evening wind picked up across the Forest and the Valley, full of fireflies and the scent of mushrooms and the sound of a very brave Button rolling through the snow and the wonderful strange red-gold light of the unknown.

"Hiya, Mum," Osmo said shyly. "I missed you so."

# Last Things Last

I f you went looking for the village of Littlebridge or the Fourpenny Woods nowadays, I am not at all sure what you would find. They are not and never were in England. They are not in Finland. They are not in America or France or Australia or Russia or India or Germany or Argentina.

They were somewhere between all those places, between and beside and beneath and beyond. And it is always in the between and beside and beneath and beyond that the most wonderful and awful things happen, where no one is looking but the stars.

The explosion did fade, as all memories do. You can never hold on to anything forever. But for a while, people in Littlebridge were kinder. They were sweeter. They were softer. A little button went back and forth and back and forth inside a mushroom and tried harder than you or I can imagine trying anything for all the lengths of our lives. And when a Quidnunk or two came to look at the festival lights in midsummer, they were greeted with cups of cherry punch and shy little waves from shy little children.

They even changed the city motto. And if you could find the ruins of the old town now, and dug up the seal and the sign, you wouldn't find the name of Littlebridge and those sad, hard words *Nemo Nanciunt Desiderium*. The great plaque would read:

WELCOME TO LITTLEPENNY

REMEMBER THE STONE

And no fussy Latin at all.

But some things cannot be undone with magic. As the years went on, people were born who had never experienced what a little black-and-white-striped stone can do, and those people came to strength and power. And there were no more shy waves and cherry punch then, but suspicion and fear and old legends and old lies. At long last, the Quidnunx began their retreat once more, further and further into the woods and the wild. The humans continued to advance, over the woods and into the world.

And history became more and more like the one you and I have heard of.

But if you know the Quidnunx, and by now I think you do, you know that there is always one more trick to be played.

Osmo stayed in Littlebridge for a long while before he went back into the woods again. And he went back and forth several times, just like Mrs. Brownbread.

He was the last one that ever did.

He lived a good life, I can promise you that. He got to be king some days, but most days he was just Osmo.

And if some of his children were born with stripes in their hair or a belly that thumped like a wild drum or the ability to talk to animals or little knobbly horns that had to be covered up with knit caps, well, what child does not have challenges?

Time passed, and *their* children had smaller horns and fewer stripes and softer Thumpuses.

And *those* children's children had even smaller and fewer and softer.

And those children's children had none at all.

Until, down the centuries and ages, you came along.

Yes, you.

I told you I knew you as soon as I saw you in the bookshop. I told you I was ever so glad we found each other. I knew you were a special sort of person. My sort of person.

A wild sort of person.

And I knew you would keep the secret. Because your heart is made of red leaves and golden sap and wonders, even if you didn't know it until right now. In some ways, the Forest and the Valley have never got on worse, and the Quidnunx have all hidden or gone.

But in some ways, they are right here. Right *there*, actually.

Right where you're sitting.

You will find others, as you go through life. As you move between worlds. Worlds called New York and Paris and Rome and Helsinki and Melbourne and Small Town and Sleepy Village and

Important Job and Cozy Family and Exciting Opportunity. You'll recognize each other. You'll almost be able to see the antlers, but not quite. Sometimes you'll think it's a trick of the light. But sometimes you'll get coffee and spend the afternoon as though nothing else matters, talking about mushrooms and moonlight and poems and buttons and feelings big and small and how extraordinary animals are and books you read when you were young.

You mustn't tell, not until you're very certain the secret is safe. What is wild and wonderful is also delicate, and hunters still roam this world. But when the sun gets low in the sky and your coffee has run out and the nice folk behind the counter say you've got to be moving on, it's time to close up, you can tell each other how silver your words are. And a new story, ever so much wilder and brighter than Osmo's, will begin.

# *Acknowledgments*

One cold, rainy Monday morning when I was in fifth grade, my teacher, Mr. Danielson (Mr. D to all of us) stood up in front of the class with no lesson on the board. In fact, there would not be any lessons that week at all.

Instead, he was going to tell us a story.

For six days. Seven hours a day.

But before he started, Clark Danielson made us all swear that we would never, ever discuss that story with anyone who hadn't been a student in his class at some point and heard it themselves. Not even our parents. It was a secret, our secret, and we were to take it absolutely seriously.

We did. Of course we did! And because we did, and I still do, I'm not going to tell you about Mr. D's epic story. I have, to this day, only ever talked about it with my brother, who was in his class six years later.

Thirty ten-year-olds sat transfixed by a story told out loud without a soundtrack or a tie-in game for seven hours a day.

But I think, for my entire career, I have been trying to share with other people the extraordinary, tense, tingling, magical feeling I had sitting in that hard, uncomfortable public school chair that morning, swearing never to tell anyone the story of magic and space and time I was about to hear from a wise old man. As if stories were something that important. As if they were that powerful. As if they could change you.

Of course, the real secret, the most terrible and wonderful and frightening secret is: they are. They can.

And as for wise old men, well. As I am sitting at my desk (with a slightly more comfortable chair) writing this on a cold rainy Monday morning in November on the opposite end of the country, a little quick googling and quicker math tells me Mr. Danielson was all of forty-five. Three years older than I am now.

And I laugh at the leaves and the moss and the damp and the gray outside my window because my god, he was so young, and he seemed like Gandalf to us.

I don't think many teachers would be allowed to stop teaching for a whole week to tell a story nowadays. Epic quests and love and tragedy and impregnable cities aren't on standardized tests. And keeping a secret from our parents? Not a chance.

But it changed my life then. Mr. Danielson was just about the only person in that school who was nice to me, the awkward loud geeky girl with a haircut that ought to have been punishable by law who couldn't even fit in with the geeks. I already loved stories and storytelling, but what he taught me was that stories could bind you to other people, forever, could be full of all kinds of whimsical things and still be desperately important. Could make strangers a family.

What a wild freewheeling magic to bring into a classroom with drop ceilings in a far suburb of Seattle just as the '90s were dawning. What a legend.

I'll tell you another secret, since you've made it this far in a part of novels that most people skip completely. A much smaller secret, but still important, because everything is.

All acknowledgments are stories about love.

Even the very shortest ones, the ones that are just a list of names readers don't recognize.

Still about love.

The people we loved and who loved us while we were writing a book, and that span includes all the years leading up to the first word and a good while after the last one. An accounting of the gifts given to a book at its fairy christening. Those who said or did things sometime between our birth and the whirr of the printing presses that made this particular tale at this particular time what it had to be, that made it the tale we particularly had to tell. Those who gave us their faith and their time and their labor; those to whom we gave our faith and our time and our labor. Those who took care of us or helped us while we went out into the wilderness where stories live to try to catch and keep one and bring it home to hang on the wall over the hearth.

Those we lost while we were hunting.

As with many books that come out in 2022, simple math will tell you I wrote the bulk of *Osmo Unknown* during the very worst of the COVID-19 pandemic. I do not recommend this. I also recognize that by using those words, I fix this work so specifically in a time and a place, a time and a place that will mark everyone who experienced it for the rest of our lives, however short or long that may be. Just in case you're reading this in 2050 or something and we managed to escape the price that dinosaur magic demanded for its service: one of the little-discussed symptoms of the pandemic is we all lost our filters and got way too real at the drop of a mask. So strap in, it's full of feelings in here and no one knows how to lock the door anymore.

Over the course of the writing and editing of this book, I lost seven family members, and an eighth became very, very sick.

Another thing I do not recommend is writing a fairy tale that primarily takes place among ghosts in the afterlife while your loved ones die around you and the world shuts down.

It is . . . less than ideal. I am no pangirlin, I did not thrive so alone.

I don't have anywhere else to put their names so that they last. At least as long as trade paperbacks last.

Goodbye, Albert Valenty, my great-uncle on the East Coast. I'm sorry you didn't like my red book. I'll do better next time.

Goodbye, George Henry, my great-uncle on the West Coast. Thank you for being so good to my aunt when so many in her life were not.

Goodbye, John Barris and Vadim Zagidulin. You were both storytellers; you just never got paid for it. I am sorry I wasn't better when I ought to have been. I tried. I always tried.

Goodbye, Margaret Meagher, my grandmother-in-law. I will always remember and treasure that day with the Golden Wattle Cookbook in your kitchen, and that little stolen overheard moment of pride in your family at the Christmas barbecue that year.

Goodbye, Jack Thomas. My grandfather. I'm sorry I wasn't there. You've always been there, for all of us, and I'm so glad you got to see so much of our lives. You are, and always were, why September is from Omaha. Please hug Grammy Carolyne for me. I will miss you both forever.

Goodbye, Michael Miller. My father-in-law. Who told me to call him Dad eight days after meeting me. Whose birthday, by one of those magics so little, people just call them coincidences, is today. The Great Last Bird. I'm so sorry the world ended and we couldn't be by your side. I'm so sorry you only got to see your grandson once—but at least there was the once. I should have taken you to Worldcon. Nobody gets what they want, as the sign says. To me, you are always driving me to that reading through the Western Australian sunshine and telling me that even then, even that very day, you never in your life felt older than fifteen.

You never were, not by one hour. None of us are.

And Cynthia Thomas, my aunt Cyndi, who is still with us as I type, and I hope somehow stays that way, you are one of the least tame humans I ever met, and I love you, and it isn't fair.

None of it's fair. I don't know what happens when we die, whether it's clouds or circles or nothing or a forest and a river and a desert of sweetness or if we all come back and do this dance again, but I know it's not fair. What a terribly designed system! I should like to speak to the engineers.

I don't know what matters most in the end either, not really, though I have my suspicions. But I know what Mr. Danielson did for me. I know how long that's lasted, with no signs of letting up.

And I know I've at least wasted a great deal of paper trying to make all the love I've got a thing that can be read out loud and shipped through the mail and resold for a dollar to a secondhand shop and reviewed poorly on Goodreads. This book you're holding, and every book you hold, is a moment, a time and a place and a moment, made solid and manifest so that it could find you, across so much distance and so many years, and allow me to, very quietly, hold your hand. You and I were born to be strangers and have defied the laws of everything to connect through a mushed-up tree and some flax and soybeans, and a whole lot of wild brilliant astonishing dead dinosaurs.

Did you know that? Industrial ink is made from flax, like the fairy tale about the girl who spun flax with her bare hands to save her brothers, and soybean oil, like the fairy tale about the boy who climbed to the sky on a beanstalk, and petroleum, which comes from the extremely weird process by which fossilized corpses of giant lizards turn into oil that make our cars go and our lights glow and our words fly.

And they say there's no such thing as magic.

I have tried to bring Mr. Danielson's magic to this book about understanding other people and loving the world for what it is, not only for what it could be if only everyone agreed with us all the time. By telling you about that day in fifth grade, I hope I'm making him a little famous, because he should be. I hope I'm spreading that spell much further than the boundaries of King County, Washington. And I hope I am making clear the grave and awesome power of what one single teacher can do for a child.

I doubt Mr. D remembers me out of the hundreds of children he taught over the decades. (And that's ok!) But I remember him, and, well, as the old commercials used to say, this Bud, and this book, is for you.

But not only him. For my family who is gone, and my family who remains. As for those who looked after me, thank you to my wonderful agent Howard Morhaim, my patient editor Kate Proswimmer and all four editors that came before her in the circuitous progress of this book: Kristin Ostby, Annie Nybo, Karen Wojtyla, and Ruta Rimas, as well as Justin Chanda at McElderry Books; the wonderful artist Lauren Myers, who brought Osmo's world to life with her illustrations and the gorgeous cover; my turtles and first readers, Cylia Amendolara, Kris McDermott, and Sarah Schmeer; my dear Rebecca Frankel; Laura Fitton and her two children, Sue and Z; my online community in general but very specifically, my Patreon subscribers, especially Sean Elliott; my assistant, Chanie Beckman; the staff at the Peaks Island Children's Workshop, Katie, Sallie, Sharoan, and Arria; my husband, Heath Miller; his mother, Donna Meagher; and my son, Sebastian (who falls more securely into the category of those I cared for, but true care never goes only one way). You were so small when I wrote this, but never think I was so busy that the fact that your first word was technically a roar didn't make an impression.

As for those who shaped this particular tale, thank you, Seanan McGuire, for once making me write a story about autumn for very little money, and thank you to the attendees of Åcon 2011 in Finland, who shared so much Finnish folklore with me in exchange for a really huge bag of candy.

The pandemic is not thanked. For anything. Ever.

And thank you, too. For reading. For caring. For being.

I suppose what I want to say to the very specific (and excellent) kind of person who reads all the way to the end of the acknowledgments, is that things always get hard, even if you do everything right—and no one does everything right. Some books, and some times, and some people, and some problems, are harder than others. Ever so much harder than a lonely ten-year-old girl in a classroom that was still pretty hopped up on the amazing technology of *Oregon Trail* could ever imagine.

And when things get hard—which, remember, they always will—you have to find the magic. It sounds like a shallow thing to say, but it's not; that's what you figure out when you get really old, like, I don't know, forty-fiveish. Magic isn't very easy to see and harder to feel and people don't take it very seriously. Just like it's so difficult to really see the story of love in a million terse acknowledgments in the front or back of novels. The mushed-up tree and the flax and the dinosaurs. Taking care of people, and being taken care of. Inspiring, and being inspired. Buying a book and letting it change you. All your children's children living long enough for you to see their adulthoods. Babies that roar like lions. Stealing a bust of Lenin that was actually Lunacharsky with your best friend and both your girlfriends, never guessing all four of you would be Americans long before the century changed. An old broken car made so new and beautiful it saved people. An old Australian cookbook that tells you how to tan hides and cook brains and preserve flowers. A hat you bought when you were so young and on the make in Chicago becoming your granddaughter's treasured talisman. *Oregon Trail.* Cold Novembers. Former punk musicians making tamales with their kids in the Colorado light. Looking in the mirror and seeing fifteen. Finding someone who loves you the way you need to be loved. Loving someone the way they need to be loved. And maybe, sometimes, when you've had a really nice day, loving everyone like that. The forty-five-year-old Gandalf saying, "Guess what? Screw the curriculum this week," and somehow being allowed to do it.

The secret of a story.

I don't really see things getting less hard for the world anytime soon. I'm sorry about that. We all meant to do better for you. By you. By ourselves, too. There isn't anything I wouldn't give to have a real stone that would let us all feel, really feel, what it's like to live, really live, as each other for a moment.

But the only thing I know like that in the real world is a book.

I wrote this because I love you, whoever you are. I really do. I love you and I love this dumb, silly, poorly designed, locked-up world, and I wish nobody ever had to leave before the lights go up at the end of the show and everyone claps and smiles and throws flowers and leans their heads on the shoulders of the folks they came with and gathers their coats while talking about how good it all was, and all their favorite parts. Because that's what I want it to be like, on the other side. Just intermission.

And hey, maybe it is. I've seen stranger magic.

Remember the Stone. Keep the secret and share the story. Say what's inside you, say it loud, don't wait.

And if things get especially hard, come and find me and tell me you're one of Mr. D's kids. Because if you read all this, you are. One step removed is barely removed at all. And I will buy you something warm to drink and sit with you by a big window and together we will be wild and wise and canny Quidnunx whose every thought has a color while time streams by on the other side of the glass.

After all, we're family now.